"I always enjoy a story of personal struggles and eventual triumphs. But *Ours for a Season* takes it up a notch. Kim sensitively weaves in a contemporary social issue that we all need to care more about. Both Marty and Brooke set an inspiring example of true Christian love. Well done, Kim!"

—Melody Carlson, award-winning author of *We'll Meet Again*

"Kim Vogel Sawyer has a unique ability to connect readers to their own foibles and needs by exploring the hearts of her characters with great insight. I highly recommend this amazing novelist."

—Hannah Alexander, author of the Hallowed Halls series

OURS
for a
SEASON

OURS
for a
SEASON

Kim Vogel
A NOVEL
Sawyer

WATERBROOK

OURS FOR A SEASON

Scripture quotations and paraphrases are taken from the following versions: The King James Version. The Holy Bible, New International Version®, NIV®. Copyright © 1973, 1978, 1984, 2011 by Biblica Inc.® Used by permission. All rights reserved worldwide.

The characters and events in this book are fictional, and any resemblance to actual persons or events is coincidental.

Trade Paperback ISBN 978-0-7352-9008-2
eBook ISBN 978-0-7352-9011-2

Published in the United States by WaterBrook, an imprint of the Crown Publishing Group, a division of Penguin Random House LLC, New York.

WATERBROOK® and its deer colophon are registered trademarks of Penguin Random House LLC.

Library of Congress Cataloging-in-Publication Data
Names: Sawyer, Kim Vogel, author.
Title: Ours for a season : a novel / Kim Vogel Sawyer.
Description: First edition. | Colorado Springs : WaterBrook, 2018.
Identifiers: LCCN 2017057643 | ISBN 9780735290082 (paperback) | ISBN 9780735290112 (electronic)
Subjects: LCSH: Spouses—Fiction. | Childlessness—Fiction. | Friendship—Fiction. | Resilience (Personality trait)—Fiction. | God—Love—Fiction. | Mennonites—Fiction. | Psychological fiction. | BISAC: FICTION / Christian / Romance. | FICTION / Romance / Contemporary. | GSAFD: Christian fiction.
Classification: LCC PS3619.A97 O97 2018 | DDC 813/.6—dc23
LC record available at https://lccn.loc.gov/2017057643

Printed in the United States of America
2018—First Edition

10 9 8 7 6 5 4 3 2 1

In memory of Diann Hunt, who fought with beauty and grace and finished strong.

My plans are shattered.
   Yet the desires of my heart
turn night into day;
   in the face of the darkness light is near.

—Job 17:11–12, NIV

Pine Hill, Indiana
Marty Krieger Hirschler

*M*arty followed her husband to the front door, keeping enough distance between them to prevent bumping her knee against the bulky suitcase that hung from his hand. Anthony gripped the battered case's handle hard. Angrily hard. So hard the tendons stood out on the back of his hand. She stared at the discernible ridges and wished his angst were for the same reason as hers.

The carved front door—one of Anthony's woodshop projects—stood open, but the screen door sat firmly in its frame, the little hook latch secured to prevent the seemingly endless Indiana wind from bouncing the door against the casing. When Marty was a child and let the screen door smack into place, Mother always scolded, and Marty had determined early she wouldn't yell at her children for letting the screen door smack. Not that she'd had the chance to honor the vow.

Anthony unlatched the hook with a flick of his finger and put his palm against the door's frame, but then he stood frozen, gazing outward. A question hovered on her lips—*Have you changed your mind about going?* She tried to swallow the knot in her throat, but it refused to budge. No words could work their way past such a mighty lump, but her heart beat with hope.

Still facing the mesh screen, he spoke through gritted teeth. "I hate arguing with you."

"I won't argue anymore if you'll stay." The words rasped out, as if sliding over sandpaper. She worried her apron skirt in her hands, waiting, hoping he'd take his broad hand from the door's wood frame and carry his suitcase back to their bedroom.

A sigh heaved from his chest. Hand still braced, he angled an unsmiling look at her. "You know, it'd be a lot easier on me if you'd try to understand."

Easier on him? What about him making things easier on her? The hope swept away on a gust of frustration. She released the wad of fabric and raised her chin. "I do understand. That's the problem. You'd rather spend time away from me than with me."

He released the door and ran his hand over his face. Slowly. Drawing his tanned skin downward. Even after he lowered his hand, his lips remained downturned. "That's not true. I go because I have to make a living."

"You could use your business telephone and computer to do the subcontracting. Your team of workers is dependable. They'd perform just as well without you there acting as supervisor. You don't have to travel to every jobsite and oversee every project, but you choose to." Her voice quavered with her attempt to control her emotions. She wanted to rail at the top of her lungs, but good Mennonite wives did not raise their voices to their husbands. She'd failed in so many other things—at the very least she could refrain from yelling.

She clasped her hands at her waist and pressed hard against her aching stomach. "If you have to go, then take me along."

He groaned. "We've been over this. And over it and over it. A construction site is no place for—"

"I wouldn't go to work with you. I'd stay in the hotel. Or do some sightseeing. At least we'd have the evenings together." How she hated the long, lonely days when he was away. But then, sometimes it was lonely with him home.

Anthony drew in a breath that strained the buttons on his chambray work shirt. Thirty-six years old and more broad shouldered and muscular than he'd been at twenty. But she hadn't changed, still as slender as she'd been the day they exchanged vows. How she envied the women with broadened hips, pooching bellies, and sagging breasts.

His shoulders seemed to wilt as his lungs emptied of air. He set the suitcase on the floor with a light thud and cupped his wide hands over her shoulders. "Martha . . ." He called her Martha only when his patience was spent. He'd called her Martha more times than she could count over the past two years. "Noblesville is lots bigger than Pine Hill, that's true, but there aren't enough sights to see to keep you busy for a full week."

"Then I'll—"

"And before you say you'll stay in the hotel room and read, I already told you no." His blue eyes, usually the color of a cloudless summer sky, darkened, as if a storm brewed within. "I need to focus on the job, on the materials, on the workers. Sure, my men can be trusted, but some of the subcontractors aren't honest. If I'm not there to inspect things, they might bring me warped boards or watered-down paint, thinking they can put one over on a simpleminded Mennonite man. That's why I go to the sites. So my reputation doesn't get banged up because somebody else didn't do their best."

"Knowing why you go doesn't make me any less lonely."

He rubbed his palms up and down her short sleeves, the firm touch sending shivers across her frame. "Then don't stay here by yourself. Invite some of your friends to the house for cake and coffee. Drive to Lafayette and browse the mall."

She shrugged. "I don't know . . ."

"Well, then visit Dawna. You've hardly gone out to the farm since she had her last baby. She'd probably appreciate help with the other kids, especially now that school's out and all four of 'em are underfoot."

He couldn't have hurt her more if he'd skewered her with a sword. For him to suggest such a thing meant he didn't know her. Not at her core, where she desperately needed his understanding. She hugged herself and battled tears. "I . . . can't."

His expression hardened, and his hands stilled on her upper arms. "Then stay here by yourself and be lonely. I don't know what else to tell you. But I've gotta go." He dipped his head, his lips puckering. She shifted her face slightly, and the kiss landed next to instead of on her mouth. He released a soft snort as he let go of her and picked up the suitcase. "I'll call when I get settled in the hotel. Bye, Marty."

At least he'd called her Marty.

She trailed him as far as the edge of the porch, then remained rooted in place, bare toes curled over the gray-painted planks, arms loosely wrapped around a post. He tossed his suitcase into the bed of his pickup truck in one smooth motion and opened the driver's door. He paused, his head low, as if he was contemplating something important, and a tiny flicker of hope came to life in the center of her heart. Was he rethinking his decision to leave her behind? Would he let her come?

Without glancing in her direction, he jolted, climbed behind the wheel, and pulled the door shut with a firm yank. Moments later the engine roared to life. The tiny flicker was extinguished as effectively as a birthday candle from a puff of breath. As he pulled out of their gravel driveway and onto the dirt street, the neighbor's children darted across their grassy yard and chased after him, kicking at the billows of dust stirred up by the truck's rubber tires. Their laughter rubbed salt into the ever-festering wounds on Marty's heart, and she scuttled inside.

Even in the house she could hear the childish voices that carried through the screen, so she closed the solid inner door. Silence fell. A silence so big it threatened to consume her. Although the room was uncomfortably warm, chill bumps rose on her arms. She sent a slow glance across the neat living room, and her gaze stilled on the wide band of morning sunlight flowing through the plate-glass window. The beam glittered with hundreds of dust motes—a shower of diamonds—and made the pink roses on the area rug glow like rubies. So bright. So beautiful. A smile tugged at the corners of her lips.

While she watched, transfixed, the beam began to shrink. First shorter and then thinner. Thinner and thinner, until it disappeared. She hurried to the window and peered out. A large bank of clouds had drifted across the sun. The sun still glowed behind the clouds, but its beams had been erased. A sense of loss gripped Marty, and she blinked rapidly against the sting of tears.

"There'll be days in life when the S-U-N-shine hides behind a cloud, but there ain't any cloud so big it can hide the S-O-N-shine. So you always walk in the Sonshine, Martha Grace, you hear?"

Great-Grandma Lois's gentle voice whispered from the past, and in Marty's memory she heard her own childish reply.

"I'll walk in the Sonshine always. I promise."

Marty turned from the window with a sigh and trudged to the kitchen sink. How she'd relished her week every summer at Granddad and Grandma Krieger's farm in Pennsylvania, where Granddad's mother, Lois, also lived. As much as she loved her grandparents, she'd spent most of the time with her kind-faced, warbly voiced great-grandmother, who was no taller than the wire tomato cages Granddad fashioned for the garden. She taught Marty to knit scarves, embroider flowers on pillowcases, and stitch squares into little quilts and talked from morning to night about the One she loved most, the God she faithfully served.

Guilt pressed hard. Marty hadn't honored her promise to Great-Grandma Lois. But it wasn't entirely her fault. The Sonshine had stopped shining on her a long time ago. Or so it seemed.

She drained the now-cool water and ran a fresh basin. Lowering the few breakfast dishes into the steamy, sudsy water, she glanced out the small window above the sink into the backyard. Anthony's garage and attached workshop took up more than half the yard, leaving a narrow grassy patch with a garden at the far end. A century-old oak tree stood sentinel in the middle of the remaining yard, its branches casting shade over all but the corners of the rectangular patch of grass.

Anthony had wanted to cut down the oak and build his shop in the middle of the yard, but she'd asked him to leave it, pointing out the sturdy limb that begged for a swing. Of course, back then she'd envisioned a child's tire swing, but she had come to enjoy the double-sized cedar swing Anthony crafted for her thirty-fourth birthday almost two years ago. She'd thanked him with manufactured enthusiasm for the gift, realizing he had meant well, but underneath she still mourned the silent message it sent. He didn't expect to ever hang a tire swing.

She gave herself a mental shake and returned her attention to the dishes. Her daily chores still needed to be checked off her list. By noon, they'd be complete. Then she'd go to her basement sewing room and work on the little quilt she should have finished weeks ago for her newest niece. The basement was cooler, and the hum of the machine would mask the otherwise deathly silence of her too-empty house.

Kansas City, Kansas
Brooke Spalding

Brooke signed her name to the bottom of the check with a flourish. She set the gold-inlaid pen aside, pulled the check from the pad with a satisfying *scriiiitch,* and pinched it up by opposite corners. Holding the business check at arm's length, she ignored the burn of acid in the back of her throat and lifted her attention to the six men seated along the sides of the long table in the bank's meeting room. "Done."

Ronald Blackburn—the gray-haired, big-bellied, sagging-jowled banker at her right—inched his hand toward the check. His smooth pink palm and short, pudgy fingers absent of calluses spoke of years behind a desk. He licked his lips, a fox ready to devour a hen. But Brooke was no hen.

With a casual sweep of her arm, she presented the check to the man on her left, an unpretentious older gentleman lacking the gleam of greed that showed in every other pair of eyes around the table. She knew the gleam well. She'd glimpsed it in her own reflection. "Here you are, Mr. Miller. As they say, it's been a pleasure doing business with you."

The man held the check gingerly, as if fearful it would shatter. His gaze seemed locked on the amount written in black ink in her meticulous handwriting. She stifled a chortle. She'd seen dozens of businessmen gawk at her handwritten business checks. Why use computer-generated checks if a person wrote legibly? Every one of her purchases culminated in a personally inscribed check—what those in the corporate real estate business world called her trademark. That and her fuchsia suits, always with skirts instead of trousers. In all likelihood, however, the dollar amount on the check held Harvey Miller's attention.

She leaned slightly in his direction. "Is it correct?"

He zipped his gaze to her. His mouth opened and closed several times, like a goldfish releasing air bubbles, and he nodded. "Yes, Miss Spalding. It sure is." His thick eyebrows rose, and he let out a throaty chuckle. "I sure never thought that chunk of land my father left me would amount to this."

Mr. Blackburn cleared his throat. "Of course, you must remember there are fees and agent commissions, as well as escrow costs, title insurance costs, surveyor—"

Brooke put up her hand, and to her satisfaction the man abruptly ceased talking. "Mr. Blackburn, does Harvey Miller seem like the type of person who would cheat these gentlemen"—she swept her arm to indicate the other men in Armani suits—"out of their agreed-upon payments for their assistance in this transaction?"

The banker settled back in his chair and harrumphed. "I never intended to intimate—"

"All fees, commissions, and costs are outlined in the contract Mr. Miller signed." She maintained a firm tone, but tiredness tugged at her. Usually finalizing a business deal left her too buzzed to sit still. Leapin' lizards, from where was this weariness coming? And when would the heartburn abate? She'd popped two antacids before the meeting started.

She folded her hands on the polished tabletop and forced herself to continue. "Everyone will receive their piece of the pie. Allow the man a few minutes to enjoy the fruits of his deal making."

Blackburn pursed his lips, irritation sparking in his grayish-green eyes, but he ceased his blather.

Brooke pushed back her executive chair and rose. Every man around the table rose, too, Blackburn finding his feet last. She slid the thick folder containing Mr. Miller's copy of the multipage contract to the center of the table, then reached for her briefcase, which she'd left resting against a table leg. Holding her leather case, she made her way around the table and shook each man's hand, offering a few congratulatory words for his role in the most monumental exchange of her career. She ended with Mr. Miller, and she held the mild-mannered gentleman's hand rather than offering a brief handshake.

"Mr. Miller, it truly has been a pleasure to meet you. I don't believe this 'windfall,' as you've repeatedly called it, could have come to a nicer individual."

The man ducked his head for a moment, chuckling. "Thank you, Miss Spalding."

"Now, may I make one suggestion before you begin setting up college funds for your quiverful"—she'd loved the quaint turn of phrase he'd used—"of grandchildren?"

"What's that?"

She gave his hand a squeeze. "Take your wife on a cruise. After forty-five years of marriage, she's earned it, yes?"

He chuckled again. "Oh, that she has."

Brooke smiled and gently withdrew her hand. "I suggest the Rhine River in Germany."

His eyebrows shot up.

"You can afford it."

His gaze drifted to the check. A slow smile curved his lips. Tears winked in his eyes. He turned to look her full in the face. "Thank you, Miss Spalding. We'll look into it."

"Good." Brooke shifted to send one last glance around the circle of faces. "Gentlemen, I leave you to complete your business."

She aimed herself for the door, and Blackburn commandeered her chair at the head of the table. "Yes, let's finish this up. Harvey, I—" She closed the door on the banker's voice. She dug in the little pocket on the outside of her briefcase and withdrew the crumpled foil wrapper holding one last antacid. She stuck the white tablet in her mouth, jammed the string of foil into her case, and turned in the direction of the lobby. For a few seconds her shoulders wilted, a dull ache in her lower spine holding her captive. Chewing the chalky tablet, she ground her fist against the achy spot and forced her feet to carry her across the marble tiles leading to the bank's front doors. Eagerness to bring the day to a close pressed at her. If she didn't know better, she'd think old age was creeping up on her. She'd certainly felt closer to eighty-six than thirty-six the past few weeks.

She pushed the revolving door and stepped from cool air-conditioning to cloying humidity and heat. She unbuttoned her jacket with one hand while moving toward her waiting Lexus. Her steps lagged, unlike her usual heel-clicking progress. She huffed, irritated with herself. How tiresome to always be so tired. Maybe she should schedule a checkup. She rolled her eyes. As if she had time.

Brooke punched the code into the number pad on the car's door, and the lock released. She slid into the driver's seat, grimacing as her body connected with the sun-heated cream-colored leather, and swung her legs beneath the steering wheel. Pain shot through her lower back. She sat for a moment, hissing through her teeth until the sharp stab eased into the too-familiar dull throb. Sighing in relief, she tossed her briefcase into the passenger's seat and started the engine.

She turned the AC level to high, fastened her seat belt, and twisted to look over her shoulder. Another pain gripped her. She slapped the steering wheel. That was it. Limited time or not, she would schedule a visit to a chiropractor. Her hours hunched over a desk had probably pulled something out of whack. But the appointment would have to wait a day or two. She still had work to do. Now that the land officially belonged to her, she needed to give the go-ahead to reestablish utilities in the abandoned buildings, have a sturdy fence erected to keep out vandals, and secure a reputable construction manager. She knew who she wanted to oversee the rebuilding. If she dangled a plump enough carrot, she could likely coax him from Indiana to northeast Kansas.

She'd already written a sizable check. When she got home, she'd put her writing hand to crafting a letter.

2

Noblesville, Indiana
Anthony Hirschler

*A*nthony plopped his suitcase on the rickety stand at the foot of the bed and unfastened the tarnished latches. He lifted the lid, but instead of removing his clothes from the suitcase, he stood staring at the stacks of folded shirts, trousers, socks, and underwear. Marty might not like it when he left for a job, but she always packed his clothes neatly. So neatly he'd never had to make use of a motel's iron and ironing board. She took good care of him. She really did.

He transferred his clothes to the long three-drawer chest centered on the wall across from the bed—socks and underwear in the top drawer, shirts second, trousers at the bottom, the same way Marty organized his clothes at home. He gave the bottom drawer a push with his foot, but it jammed. He crouched and took a closer look. One runner had come loose from the guide. He wriggled it into place and gave the drawer another push. It slid like a child's feet on ice.

Standing, he brushed his palms together. "That was easy." His words seemed to bounce from the walls and smack him on the return. Too bad the things of life couldn't be fixed with such a simple adjustment. He couldn't remember the last time something in life had been easy. Not a construction job, because somebody else didn't honor their part of the deal. Not balancing his bank book, because the money never seemed to stretch as far as he needed it to. Not pleasing Marty, because—

"You'd rather spend time away from me than with me."

He hung his head. The accusation stung as much in remembrance as it had in reality. His conscience pricked. He'd denied it, but he'd lied. Heaven forgive him, sometimes he did want to be away from her. Away from her melancholy sighs, her flat stomach, her looks of betrayal. As hard and wearying as completing the jobs might be, the most stressful ones were still easier than trying to please Marty.

His cell phone weighted his shirt pocket. He tapped his fingers on the hard casing. He should call her, let her know he'd arrived safely and had already perused the building site. Frustration tightened his chest. Why hadn't the local concrete mason followed his specifications? Was it because they'd been given by a Plain man? Some folks saw the members of the Old Order sects as less intelligent. Less worthy. The mind-set aggravated him, but he couldn't change it.

Whatever the reason, the foundation was an inch too narrow to support the two-level, thirty-two-by-forty-eight-foot carriage house he'd been hired to build. The mason had done his best to convince Anthony to build on it anyway. "Who would know?" he'd asked while nudging Anthony with his elbow. Then he'd outright laughed when Anthony said they would know and, more importantly, God would know. Only when Anthony warned that the owners of the building would know in time, because the foundation would crack beneath the weight of the structure and both of them would be held accountable, did the man agree to redo it.

Having to wait for the mason's team to break up the concrete, haul it off, and pour a new foundation would add at least another week to his time in Noblesville. He'd sent his team home to paint the Brunstetters' barn— the next project on his list of arranged jobs—but he intended to supervise the replacement so he'd know it was done right. He wasn't happy about the delay. Marty would be less happy.

Back in '06 when he'd started his business, she'd been supportive. Had asked to see his drawings, sympathized with the challenges he faced. She'd pressed her lips to his in celebration when he finished a job, was hired for a job, when the job went well. And when he lost out on a bid or the job didn't go well, she comforted him and encouraged him and took his mind off the disappointment in ways only a wife could. When had it changed?

He sank onto the edge of the bed and covered his face with his hands. He knew when. He could name the day. Marty used to tease him about his penchant for forgetting anniversaries and birthdays and other important dates, but this one was embedded in his memory. The day his world collapsed and took her with it. He'd reconciled himself, had learned to be content in his circumstances, the way the apostle Paul was even in a dank prison cell. But Marty would never be content.

"You'd rather spend time away from me than with me."

With a stifled groan, he pushed himself upright, making the bedspring *whang* in protest. He stalked to the suitcase and yanked out his bag of toiletries. He'd take a shower, go find something to eat, and then call. Or maybe he'd call her tomorrow instead. Yes, tomorrow would be better. Let her spend a night missing him. Then she might be more understanding than resentful about the extra week or so he'd have to stay in Noblesville.

Pine Hill

Marty

"You'll still come home on the weekend, though, won't you?" Marty gripped the receiver and waited for Anthony's reply.

"Prob'ly will—"

She closed her eyes, relief flooding her.

"—unless the mason's team ends up working Saturday and Sunday. I wanna watch the whole process. Make sure it's all done the right way this time."

Her eyes popped open. "You'll go to the site . . . on Sunday?" None of the men in their sect labored on Sunday. The women performed only necessary duties, such as cooking and dish washing. The Lord commanded them to keep the Sabbath day holy. Surely Anthony wouldn't work on a Sunday even if he was in a community away from home.

"What choice do I have?" She heard both guilt and defensiveness in his tone. "If the mason puts his men to work Sunday, I'll need to be there, too. But I won't labor. I'll only watch."

She wasn't sure that justified things, but she kept her lips tight against a protest. A good Mennonite wife did not argue with her husband. Even when she thought he was wrong.

"Once my men come back and we start putting up the structure, though, we'll have to stay and work through to make up for lost time."

Her jaw ached from clenching her teeth so hard. Noblesville was only a little over an hour away. He could come home Saturday after working, spend Sunday with her, and drive back Sunday evening or Monday morning without losing work time. If he wanted to.

"I'm sorry, Marty. If the team here had done the job right, we'd be ready to build, but they didn't. I don't have any control over what other people do."

There was no mistaking the anger in his final statement. Anger at the mason or at her? She countered it with calmness, as the Bible advised. "I know. I'm sorry, too." Sorry about the situation, sorry for Anthony's frustration, or sorry for her reaction to it? She couldn't be sure.

A pause followed, and then a tired sigh came through the line. "Listen, I'm gonna be putting in some long days, so I prob'ly won't call again unless I end up staying for the weekend. Let me give you the number for the hotel here in case you need to get in touch with me and you can't get through on the cell—in case there's an emergency or something."

She grabbed the pencil hanging by a string next to the notepad they kept tacked to the bulletin board and recorded the name of the hotel, the phone number, and Anthony's room number. She dropped the pencil and watched it swing gently back and forth on its dirty string. "I've got it."

"Once my guys are here, we'll work sunup to sundown Monday through Saturday, finish as quick as we can. Okay?"

What else could she do but agree? "All right. Thank you for letting me know about the delay." She cringed at the way she spoke to him. So formal. So impersonal. So . . . wrong.

They said their goodbyes, not bothering with the obligatory I-love-yous, and then she placed the handset on the base as gently as her sister-in-law, Dawna, laid her babies in the Anthony-built cradle. Marty commended herself for her restraint. She really wanted to slam the receiver hard enough to crack the telephone. She rested her hips against a kitchen cabinet and folded her arms over her chest, battling the urge to cry. Or scream. Or throw something. Now instead of only a week looming in front of her, it would be two weeks, maybe more, depending on how quickly the mason's team worked. Even with the quick-setting concrete, the foundation needed to cure at least three days before Anthony's men could start framing the building.

The delay wasn't his fault, so she shouldn't be angry at him. Deep down, she wasn't angry. She was weary. Weary of spending so much time alone. Weary of missing the always smiling, always whistling, always teasing man she'd married sixteen years ago.

If only she had someone to confide in. Well, besides Brooke. How many letters had she sent to her childhood friend, pouring her loneliness and heartache onto the page? Writing it all down helped, but it didn't change anything. Brooke didn't understand Marty's underlying sadness any better than the women in her community did, but at least she listened. Commiserated. Didn't quote Scripture meant to stifle the feelings she couldn't control any more than Anthony could control the Noblesville mason's choices.

During Anthony's last lengthy time away, she'd complained to her sister-in-law, hoping for sympathy. Dawna had chided her that absence should make the heart grow fonder and Marty should use these times of separation to prepare elaborate welcome-home dinners or find some other means of letting Anthony know how much she missed him instead of using the time to mope. Stung by Dawna's criticism, she'd blurted, *"If I had children, I wouldn't be so lonely when he's gone."*

Dawna's shocked face remained etched in Marty's memory, and she could still hear her sister-in-law's aghast response. *"You don't blame Anthony, do you?"*

Of course she didn't blame him. Of course he couldn't have prevented contracting mumps when it spread through the community the second year of their marriage. Of course he couldn't have kept her from losing the baby who had just begun to grow in her womb shortly before that time. None of it was Anthony's fault. She didn't blame Anthony. She blamed—

She slammed the door on her thoughts and hurried to the kitchen to wash her few breakfast dishes. Only a bowl, spoon, and coffee mug. Shouldn't take more than a few minutes. Then she'd move on to her regular chores. Or would she? Who would notice if the shelves didn't get dusted, the floors swept, the bathroom cleaned? Maybe instead she'd do something for herself. Something frivolous. Such as packing a lunch, tucking in a book, and driving to Wildcat Creek. She loved the gentle song of the creek, and the trees offered shade. She might even dip her feet in the water if she found a secluded spot, away from kayakers or other picnickers.

Her heart tripped in eagerness, but a sudden worry stilled her excitement. Would Anthony disapprove of her going to the creek alone? Maybe she should wait until he returned. Then they could go together. She shook her head and twisted the hot and cold knobs. She needed the excursion now, not two weeks from now. Even then, there was no guarantee he would agree to spend a few idle hours at the creek, anyway. Building his company consumed his attention. He had no time to fritter away an afternoon. If she wanted to go, she'd have to go alone.

Kansas City

Brooke

Brooke stretched herself awake, relishing the way her muscles went from taut to liquidy. She yawned, rolled over, and squinted at her cell phone, which she'd propped up against her bedside lamp before falling asleep last night. The numbers seemed to waver. She rubbed her eyes and looked again. Nine forty-two? With a squawk, she threw back the covers and leaped out of bed.

Immediately a sharp pain stabbed her lower back. She gasped and flopped sideways onto the mattress, clutching her back with both hands. She gritted her teeth and rocked gently, waiting for the pain to subside. It took a while—at least three minutes—during which time she cursed under her breath and considered herself fortunate that she'd never been forced to endure childbirth. According to her mother, labor pains hurt worse than anything else, ever. When the pain faded to a barely discernible throb, she gingerly pushed herself upright and hobbled to the bathroom, her nerves on edge, waiting for the next stab.

She finished her morning routine and then stared at herself in the bathroom mirror. Under the harsh light, her skin held an almost gray pallor, the circles under her eyes a deep purple. She snorted. "Aren't you the pretty one today, Ms. Spalding? Good thing you planned to work at home the rest of the week. You'd scare people if you went out in public."

Yawning again, she ran her hands through her short bleached hair. She grimaced. Lately the strands had thinned and were as dry as straw. Maybe she'd treat herself to one of those deep-conditioning treatments her salon advertised. If she was going to take time to see a chiropractor—and after this morning's rude awakening, she'd be making a call ASAP—she might as well schedule a salon visit, too. Then she could dive into this newest project looking and feeling more like herself.

Despite her tiredness and the persistent dull throb in her back, she smiled at her wan reflection. Retired by forty—that was the goal she'd set for herself when she graduated from college. If this latest acquisition turned out to be as profitable as she hoped, she might beat her goal by a year or two. Then she could sell her town house, book a flight to Belize or Tahiti or some other island paradise, and spend the rest of her life lazing on a beach. No encumbrances. No demands. No responsibilities. She'd be as carefree as a child . . . the way she'd never been.

"Bliss . . ." She sighed the word.

Before she could capture the bliss, though, she had to capture the builder. Her half-finished letter waited on the desk in her office. She'd been too tired to finish it last night, but after she'd dressed, patted on a little makeup so she wouldn't startle herself when she caught glimpses of her reflection in the half-dozen mirrors decorating the walls of her town house, and downed a cup or two—she yawned—or three of coffee, she'd finish the letter and get it sent.

3

Pine Hill
Marty

*B*y treating herself to a little something extra each day, Marty made it through the first week on her own. She enjoyed Tuesday's excursion to Wildcat Creek the most, but Wednesday's trip to the mall in Lafayette was a close second. She browsed the shoe and specialty stores, sniffed nearly every candle in a home decor store, and read half the cards in the rack at the big card and gift shop before choosing one to send to Brooke.

Thursday morning she wrote a letter to Brooke and tucked it inside the card with the intention of mailing it that day, but Dawna called mid-morning and invited Marty to lunch. She couldn't refuse without seeming ungrateful, so she wrapped the little pastel pinwheel quilt she'd finished for baby Audrey in tissue paper and drove to the farm east of town where Anthony's brother and sister-in-law lived. She stayed for nearly two hours—long enough to eat chicken salad sandwiches, help Dawna wash dishes, read a story to eight-year-old Levi and six-year-old Jaxton, help three-year-old Ava put clothes on her half-dozen dolls, and hold the baby while Dawna put Ava down for a nap.

Seeing the baby and spending time with the children should have been the highlight of her week, especially since they were all so happy to see her—with the exception of the baby, who only wanted her mama. But jealousy hung like a millstone around her neck, and she battled tears the entire drive back to town. Safe in her house, she sat at the kitchen table and added another page to Brooke's letter. Without the worry of Anthony peeking over her shoulder, she had the freedom to share openly. Unashamedly. Unrestrainedly. But when she was finished, she realized that writing out the unfairness didn't purge her envy. And what a poor example of Christian benevolence now glared up at her from the paper. Brooke often referred to Marty as her "moral compass." Marty couldn't lead her friend astray, even if her own faith was mostly fabricated these days.

Instead of putting the page into the card, she wadded it up, threw it away, and took a book to the swing in the backyard. She read until dusk fell, then went to bed without bothering to eat supper. Stomach cramps awakened her early on Friday, and for the first time since Anthony left for Noblesville, she ate something more substantial than a bowl of cereal or a piece of toast for breakfast. The bacon, scrambled eggs, and hash browns tasted better than usual, given her hunger, but when she'd finished, she felt sluggish and overfull. She knew what would cure the feeling—a walk.

Pine Hill's tiny post office was in the middle of the business district, between Kroeker's Sewing Notions and Rieger & Sons Hardware, ten blocks from her house, which sat at the far west edge of town. She'd made the roughly half-mile walk to the post office many times, and she'd dreamed of pushing a stroller or pulling a little wagon over the uneven sidewalks or at the edge of the dirt streets. She often pulled a wagon, but she left the house with it empty and returned with the bed filled with groceries from Vogt's Food Store. Not as satisfying as taking a child for a ride.

The morning was already warm and sticky, and only a mild breeze tousled flower petals and tree leaves. Marty kicked off the sandals she'd chosen for the day and donned a pair of anklet socks and her tennis shoes, experiencing a pang of self-consciousness as she tied the laces. She'd never felt as though sneakers went well with her cape dresses and linen cap, but comfort had to override appearance. With Brooke's card tucked in her little shoulder purse, she set out.

In nearly every yard of her neighborhood, barefoot children roughhoused, chased each other, or sat in shady patches beneath the limbs of trees. Laughter and chatter rang—the sounds of summer. Nearly all the children waved and called hello to Marty as she passed by, and she returned their waves but didn't pause to chat. Not even with the pleading pigtailed pair selling lemonade from a cardboard stand on the corner. Guilt pricked, as it often did when she scurried past the fellowship's children, but her emotions were still raw, although the intense heat of envy that had risen within her during yesterday's visit with Anthony's nieces and nephews now only smoldered. If she stopped to chat, though, and allowed herself to become enchanted by the little lemonade sellers, the fire would once again rage.

One of the verses she'd memorized before she joined the church taunted her, the words reverberating through her mind in beat with her footfalls on the sidewalk. *"A sound heart is the life of the flesh: but envy the rottenness of the bones."* She knew the truth of the proverb. The perpetual ache in the center of her soul was most likely caused by her refusal to accept her childless state. How long had she prayed for the envy to flee, for her heart to heal, for the Lord to restore joy within her? For two years and two months, beginning the very evening the fertility specialist in Lafayette delivered the devastating news that Anthony could not father children and, by default, she would never bear any. Two years and two months of daily pleading for acceptance after a dozen years of pleading for a child. And then she'd stopped. If He hadn't answered by then, He wasn't going to, and she wouldn't waste any more time on her knees, sobbing her pain to Someone who didn't listen.

She reached the cinder-block post office and stepped up onto the square concrete slab that served as its front porch. The screen door stood open, propped in place with a rock the size of a homemade loaf of bread. Tiny bits of graphite glistened on the rock's surface, seeming to dance as she moved past and entered the post office.

The town's postmaster, Frank Chupp, was busy with one of the town's few non-Mennonite residents, so Marty went to the far end of the counter to wait her turn. Non-Mennonites stuck out in Pine Hill as much as Mennonites stuck out in secular cities, and for the same reason—their attire set them apart. Marty's gaze was drawn to the woman's snug-fitting, sleeveless shirt that followed the shape of her expanded belly. A knot formed in her throat. How old was this woman? Judging by her smooth skin and rumpled ponytail, not much past her teens. Marty swallowed, but the knot of agony remained.

The woman turned with a sheet of stamps in one hand and her free hand cupping the underside of her belly. She came to a stop. A soft chuckle left her throat.

Marty lifted her gaze and discovered that the woman was smiling at her. She tried once more to swallow the lump of emotion filling her throat, but again she failed.

Caressing her stomach in circular motions, the young woman nodded, as if answering some internal question. "I know. It's hard not to stare. I'm as big as a barn. And not due until August! I hope I last that long. The doctor says I should, but after last time . . ." She shrugged, and her hand drifted to the top of her stomach and rested there. "I guess most everyone worries when they're expecting a rainbow baby."

The girl had completely misinterpreted Marty's reason for staring. Marty cleared her throat with a rough *ahem!* She planned to apologize for staring, but she surprised herself when a question emerged instead. "What does that mean, a rainbow baby?"

Sadness flickered in the younger woman's blue eyes. "It's what you call a baby born after you've lost one. My husband and me lost our first baby, a little girl, two years ago. Her heart just . , . stopped beating when I was a little more than five months along." She blinked back tears.

Marty hugged her purse tight against her ribs. The pain in this worldly girl's face too closely reflected the expression Marty viewed frequently in the mirror. What should she say? "I'm sorry." How paltry. How trite. How useless.

The girl idly rubbed her hand back and forth across the top of her bulging belly. "Yeah. Thanks. It was hard. But I'm at seven months now with a boy, and everything's looking really good, so . . ." She shrugged again, grinning. "We've changed all the nursery bedding from pink to blue. We're ready for him when he gets here."

Marty nodded, but she lost her ability to speak. Nursery bedding . . . How many little quilts had she made for other people's babies? She should offer to make one for this baby. In rainbow colors. She licked her dry lips, gathering courage.

"I better go." The woman waved her stamps. "I need to put these on the shower invitations and get 'em sent. Bye now—nice talking to you." She headed out the door, her steps amazingly light considering the bulk she carried out front.

Marty stared after her, heart aching. How would it feel to send shower invitations for a coming child?

"Mrs. Hirschler?"

She gave a start and shifted to face the postal clerk.

He held up a handful of mail, including a large manila envelope. "Is this all you need, or did you want some stamps, too?"

She took the stack and glanced through it. The electric bill, an invitation for a business credit card, and an advertising postcard for wheel alignment by an automotive shop in Lafayette. To her surprise, the large envelope was addressed to Mr. and Mrs. Anthony Hirschler from Brooke. Since when did Brooke send letters to Anthony? And never had such a large envelope arrived from her longtime friend.

Marty had intended to stamp the card and send it, but after holding the unexpected arrival from Brooke, she decided to wait. "No, thank you, this is all I need. Goodbye, Mr. Chupp."

She left the post office and headed for home, her steps quick and eager. The sun had climbed a bit higher, and the morning's dew had all burned away. Perspiration formed on her forehead and made her prickly under her lightweight cotton dress, but she didn't slow her pace. She passed the little lemonade sellers, the playing children, and a neighbor hanging towels on a line without acknowledging any of them—a breach in her small community. Curiosity propelled her forward. What had Brooke sent to her and Anthony?

At her kitchen table, Marty set the other mail aside and peeled back the flap on the large envelope. She peeked inside it and found two handwritten sheets of paper—Brooke's standard letter, although she usually folded it inside a regular envelope—and a second, plump manila envelope just a little smaller than the big one. Marty pulled the envelope out first. On its face was a message written in all caps.

OPEN WITH ANTHONY PRESENT

She frowned. What was Brooke up to? In all their years of corresponding—which dated back to when they were fourteen, the year Marty finished her education and had no more face-to-face contact with her friend—Brooke had never even included a short message for Anthony. To send a full envelope set Marty's curiosity buzzing. She tapped the thick packet on the table, temptation tugging hard to open it and read its contents. Anthony might not be home for weeks, and Brooke might need a response to something before then. Besides, how would Brooke know if Marty looked at it all by herself?

After several tense minutes of inward debate, Marty slapped the sealed envelope aside and removed the handwritten pages. She settled into a chair and flattened the letter on the table. Brooke's penmanship was so beautifully flowing, Marty paused for a moment to admire the entire page before reading the words.

Hey, Marty, thanks for your latest letter. Always great to hear from you. Congrats on the new baby in the family. Funny how

your pen cut deeper in the paper when you shared about Audrey
Eileen. Still battling it, aren't you? Well, I hope you'll get over
yourself enough to pour a little love on the new arrival. I don't
say that without sympathy, as you know (LYLAS), but I think
you'll do yourself a disservice if you don't let some of that ma-
ternal loving come out somewhere. Enough on that.

Marty blinked back tears—part fond remembrance, part pain.
Brooke had always been frank. Sometimes blunt. But whatever she said
came from a genuine concern for Marty. The abbreviation for Love Ya
Like a Sis reminded her how much she meant to Brooke. Neither of them
had been blessed with a sister, so they filled that role for each other. Funny,
too, considering their vast differences.

She sniffed and leaned over the letter again.

I've been busier than three people the last couple of weeks. Big
doings for Dreams Realized. Remember how we used to talk
about what we wanted to be when we grew up? You'd never say
anything more than "a wife and mother," which made me mad
because those were the very things I didn't want to be. I always
said I wanted to own my own business and be rich enough to be
able to pay somebody else to clean my house. Dreams Realized
let me do it. It really is an amazing feeling to accomplish your
goals.

Marty blew out a breath. She couldn't begin to imagine living alone
in a big city, operating her own business, meeting with bankers and land
developers and other important people. Although Brooke had told her
about countless acquisitions of run-down businesses she restored and sold
at a profit, Marty had never really understood any of it. Truth be told, the
whole idea intimidated her.

Brooke had always been braver, wiser, bolder—so much so that Marty's parents had discouraged their friendship, worried that Brooke would be a bad influence. Brooke's mother had worried, too, fearful Marty would pull Brooke into organized religion, something she abhorred. Well, Marty hadn't become brash, and Brooke hadn't declared her need for Jesus as her Savior. So all the worry from their parents was for naught.

Marty used her finger to trace the last line about accomplishing goals. The familiar ache of envy built in her chest. She was already envious of Dawna, of every other mother in the fellowship, and even of the young woman from the post office. She didn't want the ugly emotion attached to Brooke, too. She pushed the feeling aside and focused on the letter.

I have to admit, though, this last deal stressed me out. Leapin' lizards—

A blast of laughter left Marty's throat. Brooke's form of cursing always made Marty laugh, no matter how hard she tried to rein in her amusement. After all, cursing wasn't supposed to be funny. But that phrase . . . Brooke had adopted it from lines in the junior high musical *Annie.* Brooke played a tough character named Pepper, and even though Marty hadn't been allowed to try out for the musical, her parents had taken her to see her friend perform. After that, whenever Brooke was startled or upset, she blurted out "leapin' lizards," just like Annie.

With an abrupt *ahem* that cleared her chortles, Marty started the paragraph again.

I have to admit, though, this last deal stressed me out. Leapin' lizards, I've never been so tired, and I pretty much kept the antacid companies in business by eating a roll of pills a day— ugh, heartburn! I must have pulled something in my back, too, because it's bothered me quite a bit. Yes, yes, I know you're

*probably worrying. Well, don't. I've already decided to schedule
an appointment with a chiropractor to get my back fixed, and
now that the dust is settling on the latest deal, I won't be
worrying so much, so I can quit with the antacids and regain my
energy. I haven't been to the gym in more than two weeks, so
that's on the agenda, too. That'll do me the most good, I'm sure.*

Despite Brooke's glib instruction not to worry, Marty couldn't squelch
a rush of concern. Brooke never complained. Not as a child when she fell
off her bike and skinned her knees so badly she could barely walk for several days, and not as a young teen when her mother's most recent boyfriend
beat her up for sassing him. Never had she hinted at any kind of illness.
The symptoms must be severe for her to even mention them. Marty wished
she still believed that God listened when she spoke to Him. If she did,
she'd send up a huge prayer for her friend.

*I'm sure I caught your attention with the packet you're supposed
to show to Anthony.*

Marty's gaze zipped to the sealed envelope and then back to the
letter.

*I'm trusting you not to break into it unless he's sitting right there
next to you. I want you two to read it together.*

Marty sighed. Her conscience would never allow her to open the envelope now. Not when Brooke trusted her to wait.

*I know life threw you a curveball when you found out you
wouldn't get to be a mom like you wanted, but you're still a wife.
And up until that curveball you were a happy wife. I've got the*

letters to prove it. Unless you were fibbing in all those letters, and
I can't imagine my friend Marty fibbing to me. I want you to find
your way to happiness again, and I think I've discovered the
pathway. BUT DON'T PEEK. Wait until Anthony's home and
look at it together. It's time you did something together again.

How odd for Brooke to want to force Marty and Anthony into col-
laboration, given her opinion of marriage in general—*"Who needs a man,*
anyway?"—and Old Order Mennonite marriages specifically. Brooke had
been aghast—*"Sight unseen? Are you crazy?"*—when Marty told her she
was going to Indiana at her parents' instruction to meet the man they believed would be a good husband for her. Brooke hadn't understood Marty's excitement at the prospect of establishing her own household, raising
her own family.

Tears stung again. So much heartache. So many regrets. So much
happiness swallowed up by a monster of sorrow. Not even someone as
smart and business minded and spunky as Brooke could restore everything that was broken between Marty and Anthony.

Well, my longtime (and, for the most part, only) friend, I will sign
off here and get this in the mail. Sure miss your face and wish we
weren't so many miles apart. Ah, wishes . . . They're not worth more
than the pennies we toss in a fountain, seeking them. Good thing
there's such a thing as Dreams Realized.
    Love ya,
    Brooke

An unsettled feeling whispered through Marty's chest. Should she call
Anthony, open the letter, and read it to him over the telephone even though
Brooke wanted him to be present when she looked at it? She wanted to
know what her friend had put inside that envelope.

4

Noblesville
Anthony

*A*nthony shook hands with the mason. His stomach growled, and he spoke a little louder than usual to cover the sound. "Thank you for your good work, Mr. Johnson." The man had grumbled quite a bit about redoing the foundation, but Anthony couldn't fault the finished product. He only wished it had been done correctly the first time. Even though the mason's crew had worked overtime to pour the new foundation so it would be firm enough to begin construction of the garage on Monday, his summer schedule was a week behind.

"I'm glad it's finally to your specifications." Only a tinge of sarcasm colored his tone. "I guess my foreman will read the blueprints more carefully from now on."

Anthony suspected it wasn't a foreman's incorrect reading but a boss's deliberate attempt to cut corners that created the discrepancy. Romans 12:18—*"If it be possible, as much as lieth in you, live peaceably with all men"*—whispered through the back of his mind. Expressing his thoughts would only incite anger, so he forced a smile and took a sideways step toward his pickup. Suppertime had come and gone, and his stomach was getting impatient. "Enjoy the rest of your weekend."

The mason strode in the opposite direction, and Anthony trotted the final distance to his pickup. He climbed into the cab and glanced at the cell phone lying on the dash. It showed one missed call. He hadn't talked to Marty all week. Had she gotten lonely enough to call him? He flipped open the phone, hoping to see his own home phone number on the little screen. Disappointment sagged his shoulders. Instead of Marty, his longest-term employee, Steve Kanagy, had called. Concern replaced the disappointment. Had something gone wrong at the Brunstetters'? He pushed aside his hunger and punched the button to return the call.

Steve answered on the second ring. "Hello, Anthony. How are things in Noblesville?"

"Good." Anthony fiddled with the key in the ignition. "What about there?"

"Good here, too. Thought you should know we finished the barn early. A couple of Pat's nephews helped. As a service. They didn't expect pay."

Anthony nodded. Many Old Order parents sent their children to perform work projects for others without expectation of pay, teaching them to possess a servant's heart. Some projects gave the young people the opportunity to learn new skills. "That was kind of them. I hope you thanked them for me."

"I did. Since we finished ahead of schedule, I took the men over to Dan Wengerdt's, and we rebuilt the burned-out summer kitchen, like his wife wanted. The old rock foundation was still sound, so the building went up quick. We finished it this afternoon."

"That's good news." So they weren't as far behind as he feared. Anthony filled his lungs with air and then let it ease out, tension easing with it. "Everything here is ready for us to start framing on Monday. I was gonna call you later and ask you to tell the team to come on Sunday night so we can get going early Monday morning. I hope we can finish quick and get over to Kokomo close to the date I gave Mr. Packer. He was pretty antsy about getting that second garage built." Anthony couldn't imagine having four vehicles. And all for pleasure, none for work.

"Well . . ."

At once Anthony's tension returned. "What?"

"I drove over to Kokomo on Wednesday, like you wanted me to, to see if the excavator had leveled the ground."

Anthony stifled a groan. Had another subcontractor not done his job correctly?

"The excavation was done."

"Phew. That's good."

"So was the foundation. And the framework."

"Framework?" Anthony's chest went tight. He sat straight up and gripped the steering wheel. "Who—"

"A new outfit from Marion. They undercut us by almost two thousand dollars. Mr. Packer said he couldn't pass it up, not with them being able to start right away."

"Me and him had an agreement." They hadn't put anything on paper, but Anthony had never needed a formal contract. A handshake and a man's word had always been enough. "Why didn't he call me? I could've worked with him on the price."

"He said he'd planned to tell you but hadn't got around to it yet."

Anthony's hunger fled, and a dull headache built in the back of his skull. He'd been counting on the proceeds from the Packer garage—one of those rare projects where he put his brick-laying skills to work, which fetched a higher price than a simple wood structure—to cover the money he'd pulled out of savings to pay his quarterly taxes. Now how would he replace it?

He searched for a silver lining in the storm cloud. "At least we found out before I took the whole team over there."

"Yeah, that's what I thought, too."

Still reeling from the unexpected news, Anthony fell silent for several seconds. Then Steve's voice came again.

"I'll talk to the team at worship tomorrow, tell them to be ready to leave after supper. I doubt any of them will be surprised—we all figured we'd be heading down there pretty soon."

"Thanks, Steve. I appreciate your help."

"You're welcome. I'll see you tomorrow evening."

Anthony snapped the phone closed and dropped it into his shirt pocket. He leaned forward and rested his forehead on the steering wheel. He'd lost out on bids before. It was part of his business. But this loss was different. He'd trusted Mr. Packer. More than that, he'd let himself count the chickens before they hatched. Something he knew wasn't a wise practice.

He needed to call Marty. He'd never gone so long without talking to her. But if he called her now, she'd hear the frustration in his voice and want to know what was wrong. If he told her, he'd only upset her and make her worry. Why should both of them be upset? As much as he wished he could share his concerns with her, he knew he couldn't. Not the way he had before. He was on his own. Well, not completely on his own. He hadn't given up on God the way Marty had. His heart twisted in his chest, creating a stabbing pain. Would Marty return to faith? Real faith, not the pretend faith she modeled for the community? He'd told her there was a purpose in everything, even in them losing the chance to be parents, but—

He gave a little jolt. Was there a purpose in losing the job in Kokomo? He hung his head. Instead of worrying, he should trust, the way his parents had taught him. The way he preached to Marty. The way he tried to live, even though he failed more than he cared to admit.

He sucked in a big breath. "All right, God. I'm gonna give this to You. That quarterly payment took a big chunk of our savings, savings we need to live on. You're Jehovah Jireh, the Provider. So provide for us, Lord. Amen." He couldn't remember the last time he'd prayed such a selfish prayer, empty of praise or adoration. But God understood everything, so He'd understand the weariness behind this self-serving prayer.

Anthony started the engine and backed onto the street. He'd get something from a fast-food restaurant and take it to his hotel room. After he ate—after he'd had a chance to recover from this latest blow—he'd call his wife.

Pine Hill

Marty

Marty picked up her white linen cap from the bureau and slipped it into place over her thick coiled braid. She secured it with bobby pins, then turned her head this way and that to be certain no wisps of hair escaped. Brown hair, like mud. When she and Anthony were first married, he'd loved running his hands through her long hair. He claimed it was the color of roasted chestnuts and was as soft as a newborn lamb's ears. She teased him about comparing her hair to nuts and a sheep, and he reminded her King Solomon compared his love's hair to a flock of goats, and they'd laughed. Now he didn't even want to spend time with her.

She took a backward step, her gaze locked on the square mirror. The cap's black ribbons—black to show her married status—looked stark against the dress's bodice. Her only solid-color dress. Powder blue. Anthony's favorite, because he said it matched her eyes. And she'd chosen to wear it on a Sunday when he chose to remain an hour away from her at a jobsite. She'd come close to begging last night when he said he was too tired to drive home after his long week. The weariness in his voice squashed her plan to open the envelope and read the contents to him. If he was too tired to talk, he'd be too tired to listen. Sometimes she thought he worked as hard as he did to make himself too tired to listen or talk.

With a sigh, she retrieved her Bible from the nightstand and trudged up the dim hallway, through the kitchen, and to the small mudroom at the back of the house. Car keys hung from a little wire holder nailed to the beadboard paneling. She fingered the keys. Should she walk or drive? When Anthony was home and it wasn't raining, snowing, or blowing a gale, he and Marty walked to church. Earlier that morning she'd stepped outside to water her potted petunias, and she'd encountered a dry, warm, breezy, beautiful summer morn. Temptation pulled . . .

She didn't want to walk alone. She unhooked the key ring. Anthony had left the heavy door open on the half of the garage that housed her older-model Chevy. She started the engine, backed out of the stall, and pulled onto the street. As she drove to the plain, white-painted chapel near the business area, she passed several of her neighbors, who were taking advantage of the nice day and walking. Some parents held their children's hands, and others allowed their children to scamper ahead. She drove slowly to avoid creating clouds of dust that would choke her neighbors or coat their Sunday clothes with fine powder, even though it meant being forced to acknowledge every person with a wave and a smile her heart didn't feel.

At the church she parked in the gravel patch next to the chapel and hurried across the grass to the women's door at the left side of the building's front. At least inside she could pretend she wasn't alone, since she never sat with Anthony. Families divided as they entered the place of worship, men filling the rows of pews on the right, and women sitting on the left. She hesitated next to the empty cloak pegs and scanned the pews, seeking an open spot.

Her sister-in-law was in one of the back pews. Baby Audrey drowsed on her shoulder, and Ava wriggled beside her. Dawna beckoned to Marty with her finger. Marty sidestepped through the narrow space between pews and stopped next to Ava. She couldn't resist toying with one of the little girl's skinny blond braids. "Good morning."

"G' mo'ning," Ava parroted, offering Marty a nose-crinkling smile.

Dawna repeated the greeting, too, then patted the seat. "Would you sit with us today?"

Ordinarily only mothers with small children took the rear seats.

Dawna's expression pleaded. "Audrey woke extra early this morning, so she'll want to nurse again well before the service is over. I can't leave Ava by herself. It would help me a lot if you sat with us."

Marty chewed the inside of her lip. Sitting where she couldn't ignore the babies' whimpers or coos or sleepy murmurs would be torment. Yet she couldn't refuse to help. She'd been taught to put others' needs ahead of her own. But why did so many of those needs have to center around the loss that pained her above all others? "Well, I—"

Ava wrapped her pudgy fingers around Marty's hand and swung it gently to and fro.

Marty couldn't deny the child. She sank onto the pew. Ava snuggled close, draping her arm over Marty's leg and resting her head on Marty's breast. Marty slipped her arm around the little girl as the four song leaders moved up the aisle and positioned themselves at the edge of the dais. Eli Stutzman, the music director, invited everyone to join in singing "Praise to the Lord, the Almighty."

The congregation rose, and Marty settled Ava's feet on the floor as she stood. Dawna and two other mothers with small babies remained seated. Mr. Stutzman blew an F-sharp with his pitch pipe, each of the men at the front hummed a note to harmonize with the pipe's note, and Mr. Stutzman raised his hand. "One, two, three—" At his down thrust on the next count of one, everyone broke into the opening lines of the hymn in four-part harmony.

Marty sang the alto part, fighting a smile as little Ava squawked out the few words she knew in an off-key soprano. Marty had no doubt the child would eventually learn to sing as well as every other child in the congregation. She'd never encountered a Mennonite who couldn't carry a tune—a skill that traced back for generations.

They reached the second verse, and the final lines stabbed like a knife.

Hast thou not seen
How thy desires all have been
Granted in what He ordaineth?

Marty's voice faltered. She'd not seen her deepest desire granted. Could her empty arms be not a result of an illness but perpetrated by the

One she'd chosen to trust when she was a child of eleven? Had God Himself ordained her childless state? Had He seen her longing and deliberately—cruelly!—denied her? The thoughts lodged in her brain and refused to leave. Oh, so much worse than thinking He'd said no only to preventing Anthony from contracting mumps.

She couldn't sing another note. Nor did she want to. She was sick. Sick to her stomach. Sick at heart. She leaned toward Dawna, intending to whisper her need to leave, but her gaze fell on the taut fabric stretched across her sister-in-law's chest. Evidence of her ability to nourish the baby who only now began to stir to wakefulness. Marty's chest ached with the desire to nurse a baby at her breast.

Choking back a sob, she covered her mouth with her fist and fled.

5

Marty

*M*arty scuttled across the churchyard to her car. Guilt bowed her forward, as if it beat upon her back. Not once in her entire thirty-five years of living had she left a worship service before its completion. Until today. She paused and sent an accusing look skyward. "It's because of You. You did this to me. You—You failed me."

She gasped. Had she really blasphemed the Lord God Almighty? Inside the chapel, her fellowship members continued to sing, their voices drifting through the open windows and stinging her with the words.

"Praise to the Lord! Oh, let all that is in me adore Him!"

How could she adore Him, when He'd left her empty and scarred? She closed herself inside the stuffy vehicle and drove home. Quickly. Recklessly. Sending clouds of dust billowing behind her. She turned into her driveway and aimed the car for the garage stall, but midway up the gravel drive she slammed on the brakes. The car skidded slightly, the wheels crunching against the patch of rough stones.

Why go inside? Anthony wasn't there. No children were there. The empty house too closely mimicked her empty soul. She checked the gas gauge. She'd filled her tank in Lafayette, and it was still more than half full. More than enough fuel to take her to Noblesville. She started to back out. She jammed her foot onto the brake pedal again. What good would it do to drive to Noblesville? Anthony wouldn't comfort her. He might preach at her, quoting Scripture that only lashed her tender conscience. Or he might clamp his lips and glare, silently displaying his impatience and aggravation. Either way, it wouldn't help, because he couldn't fix anything even if he wanted to.

She gripped the hot steering wheel and stared straight ahead, unseeing. Did he want to? If he at least wanted to, she'd have a small measure of comfort. But not once since they left the doctor's office with the sad words *"You cannot father children, Mr. Hirschler"* ringing in their ears had he ever said he wished it could be different. After a few days of holding her and murmuring "I'm sorry" in her ear when she cried, he accepted it and went on as if being childless didn't matter. In a community where raising a family in the way of the Lord was honored and applauded, being childless was a curse. And to him, it didn't matter.

All that mattered now was his business. Building his business. Giving extra money to the church to send to those serving on the mission field. The first time they'd met, he'd told her he intended to donate a goodly portion of his income to mission work, and her heart had warmed at his benevolent spirit. He could accomplish his dream. But hers was gone forever.

She let the car roll forward until it sat in its place in the garage. Then she trudged into the house. Brooke's letter lay on top of the sealed envelope in the middle of the kitchen table, where she'd left it in the hope that Anthony would change his mind and come home. She gazed down at the neatly written pages. One line stood out, almost accusatory—*"I think you'll do yourself a disservice if you don't let some of that maternal loving come out somewhere."*

Images of Rex and Dawna's children, as well as the faces of neighborhood children, tiptoed through her mind. Her chest constricted, and she gripped the bodice of her dress. She hated herself for staying aloof, but at the same time she couldn't risk loving them. They weren't hers. They would always go home to their mothers. At the end of the day, loving them would only make her more aware of her empty arms.

With a groan Marty moved away from the letter. She entered her bedroom and yanked open the closet door. She chose a dress, changed, and slapped the pale blue dress on its hanger back in the closet. She whacked the door into place and took a step toward the doorway, but she caught her reflection in the dresser mirror, and the stark agony etched on her face drew her to a halt.

She stared at herself, at the crow's feet at the outer corners of her eyes, the pair of furrows carved between her eyebrows, the lines beside her lips pulling her mouth into a constant frown. Not even a hint of gray appeared in the hair smoothed away from her forehead, but somehow she looked . . . old. Who was this haggard, sad-looking woman? Where had the girl, the newlywed, the contented young wife gone? She looked into her own eyes and searched for a glimpse of the person she'd been.

Without conscious thought she let her hands slide to her flat stomach, which had never had the chance to grow round. Oh, she'd nestled a babe in her womb. For seven weeks a tiny life had grown inside her. She heard Anthony's tender voice in her memory.

"I hope the baby has your eyes."

Although flattered, she'd argued, *"No, it should have your eyes— yours are deeper blue."* So he'd compromised and said a girl should have hers and a boy should have his, and they'd sealed the decision with a lengthy kiss. Only two weeks later she awakened with horrible cramps and bleeding, and the fellowship's midwife stayed with her until she'd miscarried. The older woman had tried to comfort Marty by saying it was nature's way of taking a child who wouldn't have been healthy on earth— *"But its little soul is well and happy with the Creator in heaven."* Marty hadn't cared about its health then, and she didn't care now. She would have loved it and nurtured it no matter its challenges. Three months later she'd nursed Anthony through a painful, lengthy bout with the malady that affected him more severely than it would have if he'd contracted it in childhood, and never again had her womb cradled a growing baby.

Tears distorted the mirror's reflection. If she'd carried their baby to term, would it have been a son or a daughter? Would its eyes have been pale blue or deep blue? Would it have had Anthony's straight dark brown hair or her wavy chestnut hair? And why was she standing here in front of her mirror like a vain person, trying to imagine something that could never be?

Using the back of her hand, she swiped the moisture from her eyes and headed for the living room. The morning loomed long and lonely before her. How should she fill the time? What would be the greatest distraction? As she'd done many times before when she needed to drown out the voices in her head, she clattered down the basement steps to the area Anthony had sectioned off for her sewing room. She had bins of scraps from previous projects. She'd start a new quilt for the sale that benefited missionaries and relief workers. Her small contribution to Anthony's dream. The hum of the machine always lulled her to a place of, if not contentedness, at least mindlessness.

Kansas City
Brooke

Brooke frowned at her neatly folded stack of clothes on the plastic chair next to the door of the small treatment room. She yanked again at the scratchy neckline of the hospital gown. Dr. Bothwell, her chiropractor, had always allowed her to stay in her street clothes for adjustments. Now that her x-rays were done, she could go ahead and change, even though the technician hadn't expressly instructed her to do so.

She pushed off the padded adjustment table and took two steps toward the chair. The door opened, and she automatically gripped the back of the gown, holding it closed. Dr. Bothwell entered the room. He carried a large shadowy square of film and wore a stern expression.

Brooke smirked. "I take it from your scowl that I did a real number on my back. Good thing you could work me in so quickly." She had no idea skipping the gym and spending extra hours at her desk could create so much damage. She wouldn't make that mistake again. But then, she wouldn't have to once this project was completed. She could trade her desk for a lounge chair.

He didn't smile. He gestured to the table, and she climbed back on, taking care to overlap the gown flaps and tuck them under her bottom. He secured the top edge of the film in a clamp on the light box hanging on the wall at eye level but didn't turn on the box. Folding his arms over his chest, he fixed his gaze on hers. She began to fidget. Where was her normally lighthearted, lame-pun-making doctor?

"Brooke, did you empty your bladder before going back for the x-ray?"

She coughed out a self-conscious laugh. "What?"

"Did you urinate before—"

She waved her hand. "I know what you meant. And yes, I did." What a weird topic. "Why are you asking?"

He flipped the switch on the light box, and his finger trailed the definition of her lower spine, tailbone, pelvis, and upper femurs. "Your vertebrae show no indication of displacement, and your hips are perfectly aligned."

She frowned at the milky skeleton. If her bones were where they were supposed to be, why did pain stab her back?

His finger drifted away from the spine to an area near her left hip bone. "Do you see this dark area?"

Brooke leaned slightly toward the image, keeping her hand on the edge of the table so she wouldn't slip off. Dr. Bothwell pointed to a large, barely discernible murky blob. "Yes, I see it."

"I wanted to make sure we weren't seeing your enlarged bladder. If you emptied it prior to the x-ray, then I can probably rule that out."

Gooseflesh broke out over her body. An acidic taste filled her mouth.

She wished she had access to her purse and the package of antacids. "So what do you think it is?"

He flipped off the light and leaned against the short storage unit tucked beneath the light box. "I'm not at liberty to make a diagnosis. X-rays aren't the best means of viewing tissue inside the body. But I'd like to send a recommendation to your general practitioner to order an ultra-sound or CT scan to take a better look. The mass—"

"Mass!" Brooke wrapped her arms across her middle, but it didn't stop the trembling that attacked her body. "Do you think I've got a tumor?"

Dr. Bothwell bolted upright and closed the distance between them. He cupped his hands over her quivering knees. "I think we need to take a closer look. What appears to be a mass on the x-ray could still be an en-larged bladder. Maybe a large ovarian cyst or a section of bowel that's looped. Even a pocket of infection. There's no sense in jumping to conclu-sions and stressing yourself."

Stressing herself didn't come close to describing the visceral reaction. Her chest burned and her throat stung. She pointed to her purse. "Could you hand me that, please? I need an antacid."

He gave her the purse and frowned while she extracted the roll of white tablets and popped two of them. "Have you been experiencing a lot of heartburn lately?"

She nodded, chewing. She swallowed the chalky glob. "I've spent the last month finalizing a very large acquisition. Lots of late hours, lots of phone calls and meetings. My stress level's been pretty high." The dark blob on the x-ray wasn't doing much to bring it down, either. She cradled her purse in her lap, clutching the half-empty roll in her fist.

He glanced at the folder lying open on top of the storage unit. "Has that affected your appetite? According to your records, you've lost six pounds since you were here two months ago."

No wonder her summer suits felt so loose. She'd thought the dry cleaner had stretched them somehow. She shrugged. "No, I can't say I've been eating less than I normally do."

"How's your sleep been—normal?"

She grimaced. "Not really. I've been more tired than usual. But I haven't made it to the gym regularly, either, so I'm probably getting lazy. Like a cat." She watched his face for signs of change. He had six cats, all with biblical names—Delilah, Moses, Isaiah, Levi, and Susanna—except for a black-and-white fur ball named Sully, and he loved telling stories about their escapades. When he only nodded and didn't launch into an anecdote about a recent feline adventure, her concern rose several more notches.

She placed her hand over his. "Dr. Bothwell, what do you think you're seeing in the x-ray?"

He stepped away from her and returned to the storage unit. He slid one of the doors open and removed a pad of paper and a pen. "Do you still use Dr. Susan Classen as your GP?"

"Yes. But you didn't answer my question."

He scribbled something on the pad, tore the page loose, and tucked it in the breast pocket of his scrub jacket. He pinched the edge of the x-ray and seemed to freeze for a few moments. His breath emerged in a heavy sigh. "Brooke, I'm not going to answer your question because there's no sense in creating a false alarm." He jerked the film loose and turned to face her. "With your permission, I'd like to fax over my notes and send this image to Dr. Classen's office. I imagine her receptionist will call you in a day or two to set up an appointment, but if you haven't heard anything by the end of the week, give her office a call. Will you do that?"

Brooke wasn't a crier. She'd never been a crier. Not since she was six years old had she allowed herself to shed tears. Why bother? Tears didn't change anything. It was better to be tough. But the most intense fear she'd ever experienced—and as a child raised by a woman who wasn't choosy about who she brought into the house and as a single woman living alone in a big city, she'd faced countless fearful situations—attacked her and brought with it the desire to break down.

She cleared her throat and drew on false bravado. "Sure. When my schedule clears."

His frown deepened. "Brooke, nothing on your schedule is more important than your health. If you don't promise to make the call, I'll do it for you, with or without a release."

She bristled. She was the owner and CEO of a major corporation with a reputation for professionalism that stretched across the central United States. How dare he speak to her as if she were an irresponsible child? "I said I'd make an appointment."

He stared at her in silence for several seconds, his gaze boring into hers. She battled the urge to squirm beneath his scrutiny, certain he could see beneath the surface of her skin and past all the defensive walls built around her soul. Finally he nodded. "All right. I doubt you'll need to call, because Dr. Classen is very conscientious. You'll hear from her soon." He delivered a light pat on her knee and then moved to the door. "Since you don't need an adjustment, I'll leave you to get dressed. Please stop by the desk on your way out and sign the release for me to forward the x-ray to your GP."

His kindly face lost its stern countenance, and something Brooke recognized as sympathy glimmered in his hazel eyes. "Now, I don't want you to worry. It's as likely to be nothing as it is to be something. Don't borrow trouble, all right?" His lips twitched into the semblance of a smile.

She gave a stiff nod. "Sure. All right."

"Enjoy the rest of your day, Brooke." He left, closing the door with a gentle click.

She hopped down from the table. At the sudden movement, pain jabbed across her lower spine. Mild expletives formed on her tongue, but she held them in. The same way she held in the tears that pressed for release. Only babies cried, and Brooke Janay Spalding was no baby. She tossed the hospital gown aside and donned her gray-and-pink-striped jogging capris and baby-pink T-shirt, her motions clumsy, and then snatched up her purse. Her chest burned, but she refused to chew another tablet. The burn distracted her from the fear.

She marched up the hallway to the reception area, scrawled her signature on a release form, then slammed out the door. When she got home, she'd do some searching on the internet. Dr. Bothwell had questioned her about weight loss, heartburn, sleep, and lower-back pain. She'd explore the symptoms. He might not be willing to tell her what he suspected, but the computer wouldn't hold back. She'd get to the truth one way or another.

Brooke

*B*rooke closed her laptop and shoved it onto the sofa cushion beside her. Sliding her feet from the ottoman, she propped her elbows on her knees and rested her forehead on her palms. Seriously? Over a hundred different conditions matched the symptoms—lower-back pain, tiredness, heartburn, weight loss—she'd plugged into the search engine. After reading through the first dozen, she'd seen enough. Had scared herself enough.

The diagnoses flashed behind her closed eyelids. Depression, hyperthyroidism, multiple sclerosis, emphysema, diabetes, lung cancer, stomach cancer, rectal cancer . . .

The familiar burn built in her chest, and acid filled the back of her mouth. Grunting in annoyance, she lurched upright and stomped to the kitchen. Her bare feet left the living room's plush carpet and met cool slate tiles. A shiver shook her frame, and she double-stepped to the open shelves next to the sink, grabbed a glass, and filled it at the refrigerator's built-in water dispenser. She downed the entire glass, then poured a second, this time with ice. The burn in her chest remained.

She dumped the ice in the sink, set the glass upside down in the dish drainer, and returned to the living room. An afghan lay draped across the end of the sofa. She snatched it up and wrapped it around her the way a bird folded its wings around its body. With a little hop, she flopped onto the sofa, pulled up her feet, and sat as still as a sculpture, staring across the professionally decorated, quiet-as-a-tomb room.

She'd always loved silence. Too much of her childhood had been taken up with people yelling, items being thrown against walls or floors, the television blaring at full volume to cover the sound of other unpleasant noises. Which was probably the reason she'd attached herself to bashful Marty Krieger in first grade. Unlike every other child in the class, Marty didn't run screeching all over the playground during recess. She was content to share a teeter-totter, push Brooke on a swing, or sit and draw pictures in the dirt with a stick. Marty, with her quiet, calm demeanor, had been Brooke's eye in the storm of life. In many ways, she still was. Her letters with stories of the Mennonites' simplified lifestyle, so different from the corporate world in which Brooke lived, painted a calm that Brooke often needed.

For the first time since she could recall, Brooke found silence cloying. Maybe she should go to bed. The wall clock showed a little past ten—late enough to go to bed without feeling like an old-as-dirt lady. But she was as snug as a caterpillar in a cocoon and didn't want to get up. She laid her cheek on her upraised knee and tried to relax, but the quiet seemed to roar in her ears, as if she'd pressed a conch shell against her skull.

Grunting with the effort, she wriggled one arm free of the afghan and grabbed the stereo system's remote from the little basket on the side table. CDs with music from the 1980s and '90s—what the radio classified as light rock—filled each of the six slots. She pressed the play button with her thumb, tucked her arm back under the afghan, and nestled her head on the sofa's high, overstuffed headrest.

While Whitney Houston crooned "I Will Always Love You," Brooke closed her eyes and willed the music to ease the tension headache throbbing at the base of her skull, to help her forget the ugly illnesses she'd encountered on the computer screen, to bring her an element of peace. The Houston CD ended, and Hall & Oates began. She skipped past one of the songs midway through the album because its beat was too intense for her mood, but she listened to the remaining ballads. By the end of the second

CD, her tension hadn't eased. One more, and if the music hadn't calmed the savage beast within her, she'd search out the sleeping aid at the back of her medicine cabinet and make use of it.

Michael Bolton's voice flowed through the surround-sound speakers. She closed her eyes, humming along with the tune, occasionally singing a few lines in a rasping whisper. Caught up in the music, she abandoned the whisper and sang, " 'How am I supposed to carry on when all that I've been livin' for is gone?' "

The query brought her up short. Her heart began to pound. Sweat broke out over her body, and she wrestled herself free of the afghan. The CD continued, but the single line reverberated in her brain. For the past dozen years, she'd poured herself into Dreams Realized. The business consumed the places a husband, children, and even pets would fill—and she'd never regretted the decision. She'd lived for the next acquisition, the next restructure, the next distribution of property, always with the goal of early retirement dangling like a carrot in front of her.

At the completion of this latest project, her dream would fall neatly into place and she would be able to grasp the carrot with both hands. But what if— She shook her head hard. She wouldn't allow herself to go there. Dr. Bothwell had said it was as likely to be nothing as something. That meant a fifty-fifty chance. So shouldn't she hold on to hope? If there was a God—and Marty had done her best to convince her He existed—He wouldn't be cruel enough to give her a major illness right at the cusp of her seeing her personal dream realized. Would He?

Noblesville
Anthony

Anthony cut the straps on another pallet of two-by-fours and sent a look skyward. Clouds had been rolling in from the east since midmorning, and now in early afternoon, they looked dark and heavy. If he didn't miss his guess, his crew was going to get soaked if they stayed on-site. Not that any of them would melt in the rain. They'd worked in summer rains before. As long as there wasn't any lightning, a little rain didn't hurt anything. But none of them were keen on working in a downpour. Ladders and tools got slick when they were wet.

Could You hold it off until evening, Lord? It'd help me out a lot.

He cringed. He'd offered up another selfish prayer. But selfish prayers were pretty much the only kind that left his heart these days. Pleas for God to help Marty smile again because he couldn't hardly stand to look at her sorrowful face across the table. Pleas for God to let his business prosper so he could be on the road, busy, useful, successful. Pleas . . . Always pleading. God was probably weary of listening to him.

He dropped his pocketknife into the pouch on his tool apron and slid four boards from the stack. Balancing them against his hip, he turned toward the sawhorses set up on an even patch of ground on the south side of the structure. He'd kept his promise to work sunup to sundown, and now into their third day, the framework was complete and sheets of plywood covered most of the long back wall. The two-story building with its framed gambrel roof and trio of shed dormers was taking shape.

Hammers clanged against nails, electric drills whirred, saws buzzed, and the team's voices and bursts of laughter all combined to create the unique sound of a building site. Even though he'd listened to it numerous times before, he never tired of construction noise—the sound of hard work, sweat, and accomplishment. His ears rang with the noise as he headed across the smashed grass and patches of dirt.

Steve Kanagy intercepted him halfway to the sawhorses and took hold of one end of the stack. "I've been watching the clouds." He glanced up, his eyebrows rising. "Looks like we're gonna get wet."

Unless God answered Anthony's selfish prayer. Anthony wouldn't blame Him if He didn't. "Probably will. If we stay."

Steve laid his end of the load on a sawhorse and shot Anthony a puzzled look. "If?"

Anthony settled the other end on the second sawhorse and brushed his palms together. "We worked late Monday and Tuesday, all the way past suppertime. If we need to quit a little early today, we'll be all right." To his relief, all the materials delivered to the site had been quality, which meant he could focus on assembling the structure. The garage with a loft apartment was going up in good time.

"I don't suppose anyone would complain if we took an early night." Steve bent over and picked up the handsaw from under the sawhorse. "If we were on a job back home, we'd shut down a little early and get cleaned up for Bible study. How about we do our own in the hotel this evening? It'd be good for all of us, 'specially after working the longer days."

Anthony couldn't argue with Steve. Bible study was always a good idea, and if they were in Pine Hill, they'd all attend gatherings in various houses of fellowship members. But . . . He yanked off his ball cap, slapped his leg twice, then settled it back over his sweaty hair. "Who should lead it?"

"I figured you would. You're the boss."

Anthony cringed. True, he was the owner of Hirschler Construction. He drew the blueprints, coordinated the subcontractors, and hired the men to work at the sites. He was in charge. On the job. But in their fellowship, the deacons hosted Bible studies. He wasn't a deacon. Those positions were filled by family men. Like Porter Mullet or Steve, the two men on the team who were closest to Anthony's age.

He shifted his gaze to the dark clouds. They didn't show any signs of leaving. He couldn't see it, but he knew the sun was behind the thick bank somewhere, because heat radiated through them and caused perspiration to break out under his arms. Or was fear of looking like a fool in front of his men making him sweat? He hadn't led anyone in Bible reading—not even Marty—in more than a year. He read on his own. Every day. He couldn't bring himself to set aside the decades-long habit. But what verses would he read? What would he say to this group of men who worked together like a well-oiled machine?

Steve cleared his throat. "I need to get these two-by-fours measured and cut for door and window casings. Let me know if you decide to quit early. It'll take a while to get all the tools locked up in the trailer and tarps tied down over the materials. Might wanna give us a half hour or so's notice."

"Sure." Anthony strode away from the sawhorses and stepped through the wide opening meant to hold a garage door. He could have entered the building between studs. The sixteen-inch clearance left enough room if he turned sideways. But he always used the framed openings even before the sheathing went up. Another habit. But not nearly as important as daily Bible reading.

He stopped in the middle of the concrete floor and looked up. He examined the joists above his head where the second-story floor would be laid, and then his gaze shifted to the roof joists. The crisscrossing always reminded him of a giant spiderweb. Above the web of joists, the gray clouds were starting to form little scoops along the bottom. Those clouds would surely send down raindrops. Anthony lowered his scowl to the smooth floor. He'd be foolish to make his team work through a storm. Better shut things down for the day.

He cupped his hands beside his mouth. "Men! You, men!" It took almost a full minute for everyone to stop using their tools and shift their attention to Anthony. "Let's get everything put away before the rain starts. We'll have some supper and turn in early. If we're lucky, the rain'll leave before morning and we can get started first thing, same as we've been doing."

Todd Bender descended his ladder as quick as a fireman sliding down a pole. Pat Gingerich and Nate Schrock pocketed their hammers and began climbing down from the roof joists. Myron Mast started winding the cord for the drill, and Porter Mullet hopped off the scaffolding. The men merged into cleanup with the same practiced ease they applied when putting up buildings. They didn't need any more instruction, so Anthony snagged a tarp and a half-dozen bungee cords from the tool trailer and headed for the pallets of two-by-fours.

The first rumble of thunder reached his ears. Or maybe it'd already been thundering and the noise of construction had covered it up. Either way, Anthony was glad he'd made the decision to take an early night. While he fastened the tarp into place, his thoughts moved on to the evening hours stretching ahead. Steve would probably repeat the idea of doing a Bible study before the men went to their rooms for sleep.

Anthony chose another selfish prayer. *God, gimme something to say to them that won't let 'em know how unworthy I am to share Your Word.*

God had ignored the one about rain. Anthony sure hoped He wouldn't ignore this one.

7

Pine Hill
Marty

> But now thus saith the LORD that created thee, O Jacob, and he
> that formed thee, O Israel, Fear not: for I have redeemed thee, I
> have called thee by thy name; thou art mine.
> When thou passest through the waters, I will be with thee;
> and through the rivers, they shall not overflow thee: when thou
> walkest through the fire, thou shalt not be burned; neither shall
> the flame kindle upon thee.
> For I am the LORD thy God, the Holy One of Israel, thy
> Saviour.

Marty followed along in her Bible, which was draped open on her lap,
while the leader read aloud from the forty-third chapter of Isaiah. She'd
heard the passage before, had clung to its promises in past times of hardship.
But this evening the scripture seemed to taunt her. She was weary of battling
the ever-crashing waves. Even if He walked alongside her—and she suspected He'd abandoned her long ago—she wanted out of the searing flames.

She scanned the faces of the others seated in chairs forming a circle in
the Bontragers' living room. If one of them—just one—showed a sign of
uncertainty or derision, she would feel so much better. They all appeared
attentive, focused, certain. Defeat slumped her shoulders. She no longer
had anything in common with these fellowship members.

"'Remember ye not the former things, neither consider the things of
old. Behold, I will do a new thing; now it shall spring forth; shall ye not

know it? I will even make a way in the wilderness, and rivers in the desert.'"
Deacon Bontrager lifted his gaze from his Bible and sent a smile around the
circle. "The children of Israel must've been encouraged by these words.
They'd had a long, hard journey. They were ready for something new."

So was Marty. But what was available to her? Leave the fellowship?
Anthony would never choose to do so. Leave her husband? Heat filled her
face. She ducked her chin and waved her hand to stir the air. She shouldn't
even consider it. He was a hardworking, God-fearing, well-respected man.
Deep down she still loved him, even if resentment had nearly drowned the
emotion. Besides, divorce was unheard of within the fellowship. Her parents and brothers would be too ashamed to take her in, and there wasn't
anywhere else for her to go. Even if she found someplace to settle, she could
never live with the guilt of such a decision. She was stuck here in her raging
river. Somehow she must reconcile herself to it.

While the men in her Bible study group discussed the scriptures and
how they applied to today's challenges, she listened but didn't participate.
Even though they sat intermingled, unlike the separation of genders in
chapel, none of the women spoke in front of the men, just as they never
spoke during worship service. It didn't matter. What Marty longed to say
would only shock and dismay her fellowship members.

Deacon Bontrager offered a prayer at the end of the discussion time,
and the women rose as one and went to the kitchen. Edith Bontrager always prepared a snack, and the women always served it. Marty went, too,
out of habit. The others chatted as they chose a task. Marty didn't join the
conversations, but she held dessert plates close to the cake pan while Edith
transferred squares of moist pineapple upside-down cake from the pan to
the plates. Sally Lehman and Twyla Troyer took turns adding a fork to
each plate and then delivering the treats to the men, their exits and en-
trances through the narrow kitchen doorway perfectly timed. Lucinda
Wengerdt and Judy Eicher poured coffee and filled a tray with the cups, a
sugar bowl, and a cream pitcher.

The deep male voices drifted through the opening, adding a low rumble to the women's higher-pitched chatter. Although the sounds were far from intrusive, Marty found herself wishing her hands were free so she could cover her ears. The mix of voices reminded her too much of family gatherings around the table on Sundays or at holidays. Something she and Anthony would never host because they didn't have a family.

"That's the last one." Edith stepped past Marty, put the spatula in the sink, and washed her hands. When she turned around, Marty held the plate to her. Edith put up both hands. "No, that's yours." The older woman's eyes crinkled at the corners with her smile. She put her hand on Marty's back and urged her toward the doorway. "Chet and I each had a piece when the cake came out of the oven. He said it smelled so good he couldn't wait, and of course I couldn't let him eat alone." Her merry laughter pierced Marty to the core. "We'll be fine with coffee now, so you enjoy that piece, Marty."

She wasn't really hungry, but she carried the plate to her chair and sat. Lucinda offered her a cup from the tray, and Marty took it, giving the woman a tight smile. As soon as they were done eating, the deacon would pray again, and then she could go home. To her empty house. She'd spent the past week and a half bemoaning her loneliness, so why did she want to escape the company of the study group? Maybe she was losing her mind, the way some women on the prairie had more than a century ago, driven mad by the endlessly howling wind and the isolation. When she'd read about prairie madness in a book, she'd scoffed at the notion, but now it didn't seem so farfetched. Loneliness did strange things to a person.

"Marty, what do you hear from Anthony?" Deacon Bontrager pinned her with a serious look. "Are things going smoothly for him now?"

Marty swallowed the tiny bite of cake she'd carried to her mouth and forced a smile. "I haven't talked to him since Saturday evening, but at that time he said things were ready for the men. I'm sure he and the team are making good progress."

"Give us ten days, Marty, and then I oughta be home," he'd told her

at the end of the call. She had vacillated between eagerness to see their separation end and a strange desire to let it go longer.

The deacon nodded, his expression solemn. "That's good to hear. Edith and I prayed he wouldn't have any other delays with the project. I know it's hard on him to be away for so many days at a time."

Marty wouldn't have guessed that based on how many projects he chose to take on outside Pine Hill. Of course, as he often reminded her, if he limited himself to Pine Hill, he'd quickly run out of things to do. He needed the jobs in other communities.

Edith reached across the little gap between their side-by-side chairs and gave Marty a soft pat on the knee. "I tell you what, when it gets too lonely at your house, you come over here. With school out, I've been helping my daughters-in-law by taking a grandchild every day of the week. By noon I'm pooped. You could entertain while I take a nap." Laughter rolled around the circle, women's heads nodding in understanding.

Marty managed a halfhearted chuckle. "Thank you for the offer, but I'm keeping myself busy working on a quilt. For next year's relief sale."

"Oh, Marty . . ." Twyla sighed, longing glowing in her blue eyes. "I wish I had time to sew on quilts. My sewing machine is always making shirts and britches. The twins are growing so fast I can't hardly keep up."

What would Twyla say if Marty admitted she would cheerfully give up her entire day to sew for one child, let alone two?

"What pattern are you making?" Lucinda spoke around a bite of cake. Her round face and figure gave evidence of her penchant for sweets. "The trip-around-the-world quilt you made last year was so pretty. Are you doing another one?"

Marty shook her head. "Flying geese this time, using solid colors of muslin. I have enough sky blue for the sashing and background on the blocks, but every 'goose' will be a different color." She closed her eyes for a moment, envisioning the finished product. She moved her hand as if it rode in a roller-coaster car. "Reds to oranges to yellows to greens to blues to purples."

Edith released a little gasp. "I can't hardly wait to see it. It will probably look like a rainbow."

A rainbow baby . . . Pain sliced through Marty's chest. She set her half-finished cake and the barely touched coffee on the end table behind her. Her hands trembling and tears burning the corners of her eyes, she retrieved her Bible and stood. "Thank you for the cake and . . . and everything, but I'm not feeling very good. I think I better go."

Edith stood, too. "Would you like Chet to drive you?"

"It's only three blocks. I can walk."

"Then let one of us walk with you."

The woman only meant to be kind, but Marty didn't want kindness. She wanted to be left alone. She shook her head and wriggled between chairs. She nearly stumbled, but she caught her balance and took the final two steps to the front door. As her hand closed on the doorknob, someone touched her arm. She angled her head and found herself looking into Deacon Bontrager's concerned eyes.

"Before you go, let's pray together."

A hysterical laugh built in the back of Marty's throat. Pray? Why? Who was listening? The others were rising, moving close. They would join hands and form a united circle, as they always did at the end of Bible study. Marty couldn't join them. Wouldn't join them. It would be hypocritical, given the thoughts parading through her mind.

She wrenched the knob and flung the door open. "Please pray without me. I have to . . ." She fled.

Noblesville
Anthony

"Amen." Anthony's breath wheezed out behind the word. He'd done it. He'd read Scripture and prayed with his team of men. Not a selfish prayer,

either. One incorporating elements of gratitude, adoration, and even confession, releasing the anger he felt toward Mr. Packer. And it had felt
good. So good. Conviction filled him. When he was home again, he
would read aloud from God's Word and pray with Marty every day, the
way they used to. They needed it.

He set his Bible on the bed and stood, and the men rose from their
various places around the small motel room. "If you want to take some
pizza to your room with you, feel free." Each of the three boxes they'd had
delivered from a nearby pizzeria still held at least a piece or two. This motel
didn't have small refrigerators in each room. The pizza wouldn't last long
without refrigeration, and Anthony hated to waste money.

Nate slid the last slice of pepperoni from the box and wrapped it in a
napkin. "This'll make a good breakfast. Thanks, Anthony."

Myron closed the box on the cheese pizza and picked it up. "Me and
Todd can share this. Late-night snack." The youngest of the team grinned.

Steve nudged Myron with his elbow. "But not too late. Early start
again tomorrow, right, Anthony?"

"Leave here by six thirty, like usual," Anthony said.

Nate shifted from foot to foot, his hand on the doorknob. "Even if it's
raining?"

The rain that had begun shortly after they left the jobsite continued to
patter on the motel's flat tin roof. During their study time, Anthony had
prayed it would let up by morning. He shrugged. "Unless it's downpouring
or there's lightning, we can probably work. I always carry hooded slickers
in the tool trailer. Since we got a late start with this project, I'd like to not
let anything else slow us now."

Porter Mullet scratched his graying temple. "What's on the calendar
when we get back to Pine Hill?"

Anthony inwardly cringed. The next several projects were piddly
ones—painting a house, building a couple of deer blinds, tearing down a
dilapidated shed and hauling away the rubble. The bricked garage for Mr.

Packer in Kokomo had been the only major job scheduled after this one in Noblesville, and now someone else was tackling it. But he didn't want to pass his financial worries on to his team of workers.

He gave Porter a light slap on the shoulder. "I'll write out a schedule for each of you when we finish this job. But you can all plan to take a day or two of rest to recover from the long days we've put in here."

The men nodded, murmuring approval or thanks, and they headed out on the concrete balcony leading to their rooms. A tin overhang protected them from the falling raindrops, and they ambled rather than jogged to the rooms on either side of Anthony's. Anthony stayed in his doorway, breathing in the moist air, until each of the other three motel doors closed. Then he sealed himself inside the room and crossed to the bed.

He perched on the edge of the firm mattress, where he'd sat for Bible reading and prayer, and ran his thumb over the red-tinted edges of his Bible's pages. The soft *thwip thwip* mimicked the sound of the raindrops dripping from the overhang onto the balcony's iron railing. Was it raining in Pine Hill, too? Marty should be home from Bible study by now. They attended Deacon Bontrager's group, which met at the Bontrager house only a few blocks over from their bungalow, and they always walked unless the weather was foul. Maybe Marty hadn't gone, with him away. He hoped she'd gone. She'd sounded so lonely when he called on Saturday.

Longing to talk to her again washed through him. The motel room seemed too quiet, too empty, with only the lingering smell of pizza reminding him he'd had company a few minutes earlier. He stared at the cell phone lying on the stand next to the bed. *Thwip thwip.* His thumb stilled on the Bible. Even though he hadn't intended to call home again, he wanted to talk to her, to tell her he was sorry for giving up their Bible-reading and prayer time, to find out if she had missed it, too.

He grabbed up his cell phone, flipped it open, and scrolled to their home number. He punched the button and lifted it to his ear. He listened to the rings—one, two, three, four . . . After five, it would go to the answering machine. His heart pounded, and eagerness to hear his wife's voice writhed through his middle.

"Hello, you've reached Anthony and Martha Hirschler of Hirschler Construction." Marty's sweet voice came through the speaker. "I'm sorry we missed your call. Please—"

He snapped the phone closed rather than listening to the full message. Marty must still be at the Bontragers' place. Disappointment niggled, but he told himself it was good she wasn't home yet. She needed to be with others. Between him traveling and her hiding in the basement, she'd nearly forgotten how to be part of a group. He plugged the phone into its charger and then headed to the bathroom to brush his teeth and change for bed. Tomorrow would be another full day.

Pine Hill
Marty

Marty waited, holding her breath, but the phone didn't ring a second time. She puffed her cheeks and blew out the held air. If it had been something important—such as an emergency within the community or someone wanting to hire Anthony for a job—the person would call a second time or leave a message. Neither happened, so it had probably been one of the Bible study group members checking to see if she'd made it home all right. She bit her lip. Maybe she should have answered instead of letting it go to the machine. Would whoever had called come over since she hadn't answered the telephone? She hoped not. She was already in her nightgown, her hair released from its bun and falling down her back in a thick, wavy curtain. She shouldn't let anyone but Anthony see her this way.

Just in case, she scurried to her bedroom, quickly twisted her hair into a braid, and slung on her bathrobe. She returned to the living room and flipped on the porch light. Dusk sent long shadows across the yard and the porch. The light would help guide someone. If someone came. She peeked between the curtains, which she'd drawn across the front picture window, and searched up and down the street.

On the opposite side of the street, barefoot children chased lightning bugs while their mother watched from the porch, her smile brighter than the bugs' flashes. Two doors over, the husband and wife sat in lawn chairs under the maple tree at the edge of their yard, holding hands and sipping what looked like lemonade from tall glasses. Other neighbors were also outside, enjoying the mild summer evening, but no one appeared to be heading toward her porch. Apparently it wasn't a concerned fellowship member who'd called. They must not care after all.

"*Tsk-tsk . . .*" Great-Grandma Lois gently scolded from the recesses of Marty's memory. "*Don't judge folks, Martha Grace. That's the Good Lord Almighty's job, and it's best left to Him.*"

With a sigh, Marty trudged to the front door and turned off the light. What was wrong with her? She wanted to be alone, but she wanted someone to check on her. She wanted someone to check on her, but she didn't answer the telephone when it rang. She needed to be with people, but every time she joined a group or met someone on the street, something reminded her of her heartache and sent her scuttling for cover to lick her wounds.

"I need out of this place." The sound of her own voice startled her. Her statement stunned her. Had she really said her thought out loud? She'd spoken the truth, and her stomach lost a bit of its ache with the confession. So she said it again. "I need out of this place. I need *out* of this place." She aimed her gaze to the ceiling and pointed her finger. "Do You hear me? I . . . *need* . . . out."

8

Kansas City
Brooke

Leapin' lizards, I want out of here . . .
Brooke lay on a narrow length of hard plastic with her hands linked on her stomach. She battled a shiver. How she hated hospital gowns. Thinner than a bedsheet—no warmth at all. Always scratchy. And ugly. This one was faded army green with dingy white squiggles dancing erratically all over it, and it stunk like bleach. She tried to breathe shallowly to avoid sucking in the foul aroma, but fear pumped her lungs like a bellows, inviting repeated assaults to her nostrils.

A youngish technician in gray scrubs slipped a small pillow under her head. She surreptitiously eyed him. He was a lot cuter than the paunchy man who'd given her the gown and instructed her in a monotone to remove everything from head to toe, put on the gown, and wait for the MRI tech. This guy's clean-cut, all-American appearance was a nice distraction in otherwise unappealing surroundings, but he smelled bad, too. Like antiseptic soap. When she got home, she'd stick her nose over the coffee canister and sniff to her heart's content. She'd also bundle up in her afghan. They could keep meat from spoiling it was so cold in here.

"All right, Ms. Spalding, you'll need to hold very still for the duration of the scan."

Brooke bobbed her chin toward the giant tube waiting beyond her bare feet like the open mouth of a whale. "How long will I be in that thing?"

"About half an hour."

She shuddered. "I tend to get claustrophobic." Probably a residual effect of cowering in her closet when she was eight. Mom's boyfriend that year had been the biggest jerk of a whole host of jerks.

He patted her shoulder, his hand warm compared to the temperature of the room. "I'm only taking you in as far as your rib cage since we need images of your pelvic region."

She averted her gaze. She'd never discussed her pelvic region with a stranger. Especially one who was built like a star on a college track team.

"Most people close their eyes during the test. It helps them relax. Besides"—he chuckled softly—"there's not much to see in here."

Apparently he underestimated his appearance. And why was she drooling over a man—a kid, really—at least a decade younger than she was? Obviously she'd spent too much time of late in the company of overweight, over-the-hill bankers and businessmen. "Close my eyes. Yes. I can do that." Perfect way to block out the world.

"The machine is noisy, so if you'd like, I can put headphones on you and pipe in some music."

She wrinkled her nose. "What kind of music?" In the lobby of the hospital's MRI center, they'd been playing some sort of instrumental stuff that made her think of funerals. She didn't need that piped into her head while a giant tin can discovered what kind of weird something was growing low in her belly.

He smiled. "Whatever you like. Classical, rock-and-roll, inspirational, country-western . . ."

"Do you have oldies?"

"Sure." He produced a pair of headphones similar to the ones the technician had used in the hearing-check mobile unit when Brooke was a kid. "I'll just put these in place and—" The rest of his words were muffled by the thick foam-cushioned cups over her ears.

In her peripheral vision, she followed his retreat to a glass-enclosed booth to the left of the machine. His gaze lowered to some sort of panel in front of him. Static crackled in her ears, and then a Beach Boys number filtered into the headphones. Maybe she shouldn't have used the term *oldies*. She hadn't wanted music from her mother's generation. He met her gaze through the glass and held his thumb in the air, smiling.

She sighed and looked at the ceiling tiles. Too late now. *I get around . . . from town to town . . .* While the perky words sang through the headphones, the platform jerked, and it slowly slid her feetfirst into the huge tube. She automatically closed her eyes as the tube seemed to swallow her legs. Her mouth went dry, and she wished she had a peppermint. Or even an antacid. Anything to mask the bitter taste of fear on her tongue. The platform gave another little jerk and stopped. Moments later, a rumble vibrated her plastic bed—the machine coming to life.

Eyes tightly closed and her heart pounding like the surf the Beach Boys probably performed next to during their heyday, she ignored the muted *whir* and rhythmic *thump*s outside the headphones and tried not to think about why she was in this machine. But no matter how hard she tried, she couldn't erase Dr. Classen's compassionate yet concerned expression when she told Brooke they needed to schedule an MRI as quickly as possible.

"Now, let's not leap into worry," the woman had said, sounding like Dr. Bothwell. But Brooke had already made the leap. When doctors moved fast, they did it because they believed something was seriously wrong. No amount of shoulder patting or too-cheerful platitudes would convince her otherwise.

I'm pickin' up good vibrations . . .

She gritted her teeth. If only.

Pine Hill
Anthony

Anthony slowly backed up the driveway, using the pickup's side mirror to watch the trailer's progression toward the garage. He'd accidentally backed into the corner of the old garage about five years ago, and he'd made a vow never to repeat the mistake. He'd built a new garage a year later, but the trailer still carried an indention that made closing the left-side door a challenge.

The crunch of tires on gravel carried through the open truck window, and something—probably a brake pad—gave a high-pitched squeal. He better take the truck to Dan Penner at the auto-repair station tomorrow and have him give the pads a look-over. He didn't need the brakes giving out when he was pulling the trailer. That would be a disaster, in more ways than one. Maybe it was good he'd decided to give the team a weekend break from the project instead of staying and working Saturday. Dan wasn't open on Sundays.

The trailer eased alongside the garage with a good two feet of clearance—perfect. He put the truck in park and shut off the engine. Not until he opened the door and started to hop out did he notice Marty standing on the top step of the back-porch stairs, holding the screen door open with her shoulder.

His heart leaped at the sight of her. His lips wobbled into a hesitant grin as he set his feet on the ground. "Surprise."

She came down the stairs, letting the door whap into its frame, and crossed the grass on bare feet. "I hope soup is all right for supper. I didn't expect you, so I didn't fix anything special."

He slammed the truck door and took one step in her direction, regret slowing his progress. She used to run across the grass to meet him when he returned from a job. Even when he'd been gone for hours instead of days.

"Soup's fine. It'll be good to eat something home cooked. I'm pretty tired of restaurant food."

"It's from a can. Chicken noodle."

He grimaced. He'd never cared for those soggy noodles and thin broth.

"I know it's not much. I can fix you a sandwich to go with it."

"That'll be fine. Thanks."

She stopped a couple of feet away from him and tilted her head. One black ribbon from her cap crunched on her right shoulder, an ugly mar on her yellow floral dress. "Is everything okay at the jobsite? I thought you planned to work Saturdays, too."

He searched her face for signs of either disappointment or elation. Nothing. Just . . . nothing. Didn't she *feel* anymore? He swallowed a knot of mingled sadness and frustration and reached into the truck's bed for his suitcase instead of reaching for her. "Things are fine there." He swung the suitcase out and swiveled to face her again. "Been workin' the guys so hard I decided to give us all a day to catch up at home, have some family time."

As soon as the words left his mouth, he knew he'd made a mistake. Her face went white, and she clutched her stomach as though someone had kicked her hard in the gut. She started to turn away, but he dropped his suitcase and caught her arm. He gathered the courage he needed to tell her what he'd wanted to say for days. Weeks. Months.

"Marty, just because we don't have kids doesn't mean we're not a family. You—you're my family. And I'm yours."

She lowered her head. Her chin wobbled, but she didn't cry. He wished she would. Maybe it'd do her some good. She stood there clutching her stomach, all wrapped up like a ball of twine. Frustration roared through him. When would she accept the truth and move on?

He let go of her and scuffed the grass with the toe of his boot. He spoke through clenched teeth. "This must be how Elkanah felt."

She slowly lifted her head and frowned at him. "What?"

He frowned, too. "You're like Hannah, always mourning for something you don't have instead of appreciating what you do. Don't I matter to you at all?" Now, why had he said that? He'd come home to surprise her, spend time with her, pray together and maybe take the first step toward healing together. Right away he'd said something that would only lead to a fight.

He sighed and shook his head, stretching his hand toward her. "I'm sorry, Marty." Was he sorry? Even though the timing was all wrong, the tone too harsh, he'd meant everything he said.

Fury blazed in her blue eyes, and she backed up a step, out of his reach. "How can you compare us to Elkanah and Hannah? They're nothing like us. They eventually had a baby together—Samuel. And probably many more after him. You and I will never have that joy. I wish we could be like Elkanah and Hannah. At least then I'd have hope that God would bless us, too." She spun on her heel and darted for the house.

Anthony grabbed his suitcase and tromped after her. He left the suitcase on the back porch beside the wringer washer and entered the kitchen, popping off his ball cap as he crossed the threshold. He tossed the cap on the table and moved to the stove, where she stood stirring the soup in stiff little sweeps of a wooden spoon.

He wanted to slip his arms around her middle from behind, press his cheek to her scratchy linen cap the way he used to. But if she bolted, she could burn herself on the stove. So he eased up to the counter beside the stove and leaned his hip against it, fixing his gaze on her stern face.

"I bet if you asked Linda Wiens, she'd say you've been blessed more than her. She's what now? Forty? She doesn't even have a husband."

She sucked in her lips and kept stirring, eyes downcast.

He'd said this much. Maybe he should say everything that had rolled through his mind but never came out of his mouth. "We could . . . adopt."

She shot him a brief look and lowered her gaze again. "No, we can't. It's too expensive."

So she'd thought about it, too. And never said a word. "How do you know?"

"I asked the Yoders. Mrs. Yoder's youngest sister and her husband adopted two little kids from Haiti, and it cost more than twenty thousand dollars."

She was right. He didn't have that kind of money. Not even close. He fiddled with a loose button on his shirt. "Well, then couldn't we be—what do they call it when you take in kids because their parents can't take care of them?"

Her eyebrows descended. "Foster parents?"

He nodded. "Yeah, that. Doesn't the state pay the foster parents? That wouldn't cost us anything."

"You don't get to keep those kids, Anthony." Her tone made him feel foolish. "Eventually they go back to their parents or another relative. I don't think I could do that—take them in, grow to love them, and then give them back." She turned off the gas under the soup pan, opened the cupboard, and brought out two bowls.

He watched her ladle steaming soup into the bowls. What else could he offer? Nothing came to mind. He opened the silverware drawer and picked out two spoons. He gently clacked them together. "If I could give you kids, I would. But I can't. So . . . can you let me be enough? Can you let me matter?"

She stood for several seconds, gazing directly into his eyes. She didn't smile. She didn't move. She didn't tear up. She didn't even breathe. Then air whooshed from her parted lips. "Let's eat. After we're done, I have something to show you."

9

Marty

*M*arty carried their empty soup bowls, spoons, and cups to the sink. She returned with a rag and gave the table a quick scrubbing even though neither of them had dripped broth. Not once. With such intense focus on carrying their spoons to their mouths, no wonder. They hadn't even exchanged a glance after Anthony prayed.

Her stomach whirled, and it wasn't because of the soup. Stupid emotions, anyway. She'd been counting down the hours until she could open Brooke's envelope with Anthony, and now that he was here—earlier than expected—anxiety seized her. *Get me out of here.* The thought or prayer or command, whatever it was, blasted through her mind again as she picked up the sealed envelope from a little basket at the edge of the counter.

She carried it to the table, two handed, pressing it against the modesty cape of her dress. She slid into her chair and then laid the envelope flat on the table. With trembling fingers, she pushed it slightly toward Anthony.

His blue-eyed gaze drifted to the envelope, and a puzzled scowl instantly formed on his face. "What's this?"

"How should I know?" She winced at her sharp tone. She drew in a calming breath and forced herself to speak evenly. "It came in Brooke's last letter to me. I didn't open it because . . ." She pointed at the message written on the outside. "But now you're here, so . . ." Using her fingertips, she pushed it a scant half inch closer to him.

He hitched up on one hip, straightening his leg, and slid his hand into his trouser pocket. He pulled out his pocketknife, opened it, and picked up the envelope. He shot her a questioning look. "Do you want to . . ."

Could neither of them finish a sentence? She crossed her ankles, slipped her hands beneath her knees, and curled her fingers over the edge of the wooden chair seat. "No. Go ahead."

With one smooth motion, he used the slim blade to slit the top of the envelope. He took several seconds closing the knife and returning it to his pocket. Marty fidgeted, battling the urge to grab the envelope and empty the contents across the table. But as much as her hands were shaking, she'd probably end up scattering them all over the kitchen. So she waited for him to lift it again and tip it. One gentle tap, and several pages of what appeared to be typing paper plopped out onto the table. Brooke's neat handwriting filled the top sheet.

"Looks like it's a really long letter." Anthony set the envelope aside and pulled the stack of paper close. He looked at her again. The uncertainty in his expression probably matched hers. "Do you want to read it, or should I?"

"Go ahead."

"All right." He cleared his throat, as if preparing to deliver a speech. " 'Dear Marty and Anthony, you're probably wondering why I am writing to both of you. Please be patient and you'll understand by the time you reach the end of this letter. As Marty knows, I started a business called Dreams Realized shortly after I graduated from college. At first, I purchased run-down houses and flipped them. When I'd gained enough capital and a reputation to go bigger, I began purchasing run-down business properties, rebuilding them, and selling them. Each sale netted me a greater profit. I've been very successful.' "

His eyebrows rose, and he whistled through his teeth. "She's pretty ambitious, isn't she?"

Marty nodded. "She didn't have much when she was growing up. She was always hungry for . . . something more."

"Sounds like she got it."

Material things, yes. But sometimes Marty didn't believe Brooke was really happy. Not underneath, where it mattered. Something the two of them had in common. She bobbed her chin toward the letter. "Keep going."

He smoothed the paper with his hand, then leaned close to the page. "'While I built my company, I harbored my personal dream—to retire by age forty, take my hard-won earnings to a beach, and spend the rest of my life enjoying the spoils of my efforts.'" Anthony aimed a disapproving frown in Marty's direction. "She intends to go from industrious to lazy?"

Defensiveness stirred in Marty's chest. He didn't know what kind of childhood Brooke suffered. "What does it say in Matthew? 'Judge not, that ye be not judged. For with what judgment ye judge, ye shall be judged: and with what measure ye mete, it shall be measured to you again.'" Odd how easily the words left her tongue when her heart felt so numb to God and His Word.

Contrition flooded his features. "You're right."

"Besides, she isn't going there out of laziness. She wants peace. She said the sound of the surf is the prettiest sound on earth." Melancholy struck. The prettiest sound to Marty would be her own baby's first cry. She hoped at least Brooke could one day enjoy her prettiest sound. She pointed at the letter. "Keep reading, please."

He bent over the page again. "'Now my latest acquisition offers me the chance to see my dreams realized. I recently purchased a sixteen-acre plot of land in northeast Kansas, less than an hour's drive from the center of Kansas City. In the 1800s and early 1900s, a bustling town resided there thanks to paddleboat traffic and the mining industry. Thousands of pounds of limestone were carved from the ground and sent to various places to be fashioned into headstones, fence posts, or blocks. Of course, some limestone was kept and utilized in the community. Several buildings still stand in the now-abandoned town—a tribute to the ingenuity of early construction workers.'"

Awe bloomed on Anthony's face. He tapped the page. "This is

interesting. Can you imagine building something that still stands more than a hundred years later? The structures my company puts up . . . they're well built, with the best materials I can find. But the wood will rot a lot faster than these buildings made of limestone blocks will crumble." He sighed. "What a legacy those builders left behind. I wouldn't mind seeing the buildings she's talking about, examining them and trying to figure out how the long-ago builders put the structures together without the use of modern equipment and power tools."

Marty stared at Anthony, her heart stuttering. She couldn't recall the last time he'd been so open with her. She'd been given a peek at his soul, and it softened her toward him. Bonded her to him. She unlocked her hands from their grip on the chair and brought them up. She grazed his sleeve with her fingertips. "Maybe you'll get to someday."

He offered her a quick, sheepish grin. "Maybe."

She linked her hands on the tabletop. "What else does she write?"

He turned his attention back to the letter. " 'Sadly, the Civil War and World War I took a toll on the town, and its population of three thousand dwindled to five hundred. By the early 1940s, the town once known as Eagle Creek was, effectively, a ghost town. The last resident died in 1963, and the town has sat empty, subject to vandals and weather, for several decades. I intend to bring it back to life. A dozen investors have joined with me in seeing my vision for Spalding—yes, I intend to give it a new name—realized.' "

Anthony flipped the page over, eagerness lighting his features. Marty found herself watching his face while he continued to read.

" 'Its location, nestled near a paved roadway, the Missouri River, and Brush Creek, is an ideal getaway spot. Enclosed you'll find maps, blueprints, black-and-white photos, and detailed plans—' " He lifted the letter and fanned the other pages across the tabletop. He scanned them briefly, his eyes aglow, then jerked his gaze back to the letter. " '—for breathing life into the soulless community. I've already arranged for the wells to be unplugged and electrical and gas lines repaired. I've hired a landscaping crew from Kansas City to clean up the overgrown trees and shrubs, and a fence builder to enclose the area with a six-foot-tall ornate iron fence complete with a coded gate to prevent future vandalism. So restoration has begun, but the most important part of turning this former ghost town into a beautiful resort area lies in securing a construction team. Anthony, I would like to hire you as the contractor to restore Eagle Creek to its former glory.'"

Marty gasped. Brooke couldn't— She wouldn't— Her thoughts were too scattered to complete. She clamped her hand on Anthony's wrist and stared helplessly at his stunned face.

Anthony

Anthony gulped. His muscles went weak, and he dropped the letter. Marty's grip on his wrist was so tight it almost hurt, but he welcomed the reminder of her presence. It kept him from blurting his thought—this friend of hers was a troublemaker, trying to peel him away from his community and everything he held dear. Yet somehow the prospect of restoring buildings that had stood for more than a century, putting his hands to something that would likely stand for another century, intrigued him.

He pressed the page flat against the table and licked his dry lips. His voice sounded like sandpaper on steel as he read the next paragraph. "'I would like to have a team assembled by mid-July at the latest, with a goal of completing the project within eighteen months. This would allow for a New Year's grand opening. Please examine the enclosed documents. Call me if you have questions. Let me know as soon as possible if you aren't able to come, because I'll need to search for a suitable replacement. But'"—he paused to let his galloping pulse settle down—"'I want you. I trust you. You'll find a proposed compensation document in the packet. If the amount isn't suitable, let's negotiate.'"

Marty let go of his wrist and shuffled through the pages. Her sharp intake of breath signaled when she found the document. She held up the single sheet of paper. Anthony looked at the amount stamped in bold print, and his mouth fell open. Brooke was obviously very successful if she could offer him such a large sum. He'd have to divide it up by eighteen months, figure in salaries for his team and living expenses for his time away, but he suspected his company would receive a more than adequate profit. His concerns about replacing the quarterly tax payment fled, but he chewed the inside of his lip as a new worry struck. Should he leave Marty for such a long time?

A single paragraph on the letter remained unread. He peeled his gaze from the proposed compensation and focused on Brooke's closing words. "'One more thing, you two—come together.'" He jolted and glanced over his shoulder, half expecting to find Brooke there, reading his mind. He zipped his gaze back to the letter. "'If I might be straightforward with you, being apart for that length of time won't do your marriage any good.'"

Anthony grimaced. The short separations hadn't done them any good. But how did Brooke know that? Maybe he should have asked to read the letters Marty sent over the years. He grunted under his breath before continuing. "'You'll need someone to cook for you and your construction team. It makes more sense to have Marty prepare your meals than to cater in food three times a day or hire a cook.'" He couldn't argue against her reasoning. "'If you haven't wadded this up and tossed it aside already, thanks.'"

Marty laughed softly and shook her head. "I can hear her saying that." The fondness glimmering in her eyes both pleased and pierced him. She was *feeling*. But not for him.

He lowered his gaze to the letter. "'Peruse the project plans. Talk it over. Pray about it, if you want to—seems like that's something you would do. Then let me know. But I hope you'll say yes. I want you both to play a role in seeing these dreams realized.'" She'd signed it "Love, Brooke," making the entire thing sound more like a friendly request than a prospective business deal.

Marty was staring straight ahead, lost in thought, so Anthony remained quiet and let his thoughts roll free. The money was tempting. Instantly, 1 Timothy 6:10 blared through his mind—*"For the love of money is the root of all evil: which while some coveted after, they have erred from the faith, and pierced themselves through with many sorrows."* He shook his head, sending the reminder away. He didn't love money. Of course he didn't. But having it when he needed it, like when he had to make quarterly tax payments, helped a lot. He liked the idea of having extra he could add to the basket when they did their special offering for missionaries. And what if—

He snatched up the compensation proposal, his pulse doubling its tempo. If they kept their expenses to a minimum, could they save enough to apply for adoption? Could this be God's way of opening the door to Marty and him bringing a child into their home? But a year and a half away from their community, from their house? What about his men? The ones who had families wouldn't want to be away from their wives and children for so many months, and taking the entire families along would add to their expenses.

Anthony slowly paged through the documents, maps, blueprints, and images Brooke had sent. The photos of the dilapidated buildings and drawings of an artist's idea of how the town's main street could look captured his attention even more than the payment proposal. To be able to bring these buildings back to beauty and purpose. This was an opportunity that would likely never come again. But he needed his team. He couldn't do it on his own. Not in only a year and a half.

As much as he wanted to be part of Brooke's project, as much as the money appealed to him, he couldn't say yes. There were too many things in the way. He turned to Marty and started to share his thoughts with her, but she spoke first.

"We have to go."

He gave a start. "What did you say?"

Slowly she angled her face until she looked directly into his eyes. Moisture brightened her pale blue irises, making them look like dew-touched periwinkle petals. "It's the first prayer He's answered in . . . so long."

Anthony frowned. She wasn't making any sense.

She slid her hand across the distance between them and linked fingers with him, something she hadn't done in more months than he could remember. "Yesterday I prayed. I haven't prayed in—" She ducked her head for a moment, biting her lip, then met his gaze again. "I gave up praying because it seemed like God wasn't listening. But yesterday I prayed, a selfish prayer but a prayer all the same."

He nodded. He understood selfish prayers. "What did you ask for?"

"To get away from here."

His heart lurched. He tightened his fingers on hers. "Away from me?" The question grated past his suddenly dry throat.

She shook her head hard. "From here. This town. The constant reminder that I'm different from every other woman in our fellowship."

He sighed. "Marty, I—"

"It hurts so much, Anthony, to see mothers with children, with babies. To encounter women with blossoming bellies."

He already knew that without her telling him, but at least she was talking. Sharing. Opening up. It was more than she'd done in a long time. So he let her talk.

"So I asked—no, I told God. I told Him I needed out of here." She gestured to the papers spread over the kitchen table. "And here's the answer." The tears swimming in her eyes spilled over and ran in two trails down her flushed cheeks. "Let's go, Anthony. Let's go . . . heal."

10

Marty

*W*hat a foolish notion. If she hadn't healed in her community, surrounded by the people with whom she worshipped and fellowshipped and worked side by side, how could healing come far away from everything familiar? Yet deep down, the place once known as Eagle Creek tugged at her. Marty swallowed the knot of longing filling her throat and squeezed Anthony's hand. "Please . . ."

Anthony grimaced, as if a pain gripped him. "I don't know, Marty. I'll admit it sounds like an interesting project." He ran his fingers over the line drawing of tall, stately buildings with decorative crowns and ornate door and window casings the way she'd seen Dawna caress baby Audrey's cheek. "But would my men want to be away from their homes for so long? And what about our house here in Pine Hill—who would take care of it?"

Marty gazed at the name Eagle Creek written in Brooke's neat handwriting. A verse tiptoed through the back of her mind. She couldn't grasp all of it, but she thought it included words spoken by God to the children of Israel. She lurched for her Bible, which still lay at the opposite side of the table where she'd left it Wednesday evening. She flipped to the concordance and searched for a specific word. She released a little gasp when she found what she wanted, and she paged eagerly to the beginning of the Bible. When she located the passage, she turned the Bible to face Anthony.

"Look. Read this." She pointed to Exodus 19:4.

He frowned, but he leaned forward and read aloud. " 'Ye have seen what I did unto the Egyptians, and how I bare you on eagles' wings, and brought you unto myself.'" He lifted his puzzled gaze and met hers. "So?"

Marty huffed. "Eagles' wings. Eagle Creek. Don't you see? It's our place of deliverance." She couldn't find the words she needed to explain the feelings coursing through her, but somehow she knew—she just knew—she was meant to go to Brooke's abandoned ghost town. Something of importance waited for her there. Why else would God have chosen to open a door in response to her plea for escape?

Anthony slowly straightened and dropped one arm over the top rung of the chair back. For long minutes he sat motionless, silent, his brows pulled low. Then, without a word, he jerked his face toward the clock hanging on the soffit above the sink. "Seven twenty . . . Is the time the same in Kansas?"

Marty stacked her hands on her bodice. Her heart pounded so hard she felt the beat against her palm. "No, it's an hour behind us. Why?"

He shifted her Bible aside and began leafing through the papers Brooke had sent.

"Anthony, what are you doing?"

He barely glanced up. "Looking for her phone number. She said to call if I had questions. I have lots of them. I need to talk to her before I can make a decision."

Marty sucked in a short, hopeful breath. "So you're considering it?"

He finally fixed his full attention on her. His expression turned tender—a sweet look she'd yearned to see for months but thought was gone forever. "I want to find out the details. I need to think through whether I—we—could be away from here for that long. There's a lot to consider, Marty, but . . . yes, I want to explore the possibility."

A giggle escaped her throat. She pawed through the papers until she located Brooke's business card clipped to the top of some sort of materials list. "Here it is. Call. And put your phone on speaker, okay?"

He grinned at her. A grin so reminiscent of the grins he used to give her in their early years of marriage that tears stung her eyes. He pulled his cell phone from his shirt pocket, tapped in Brooke's number, then punched the speaker button. He placed the black phone on the table between them, and Marty listened for the buzzes that meant Brooke's phone was ringing. After only two buzzes, there was a click, and then a voice Marty hadn't heard since she was a young teenager came through the little speaker.

"Well, hello, Anthony Hirschler. Marty must have given you my letter."

Anthony drew back, his brows high. "How did you know it was me?"

Brooke's throaty chuckle rumbled, deeper now than it had been when she was a girl but just as recognizable. "I searched out your information online and put your number in my contacts about a month ago when I knew this project had the financial backing it needed and would take place. I've come close to calling you a time or two, but I held off. I wanted you and Marty to discuss the Spalding Resort before I launched the idea at you. By the way, is Marty close by? I'd love to say hi to her."

Marty's breath came in little spurts. She hadn't realized how much she missed her friend until she heard Brooke's voice. "I'm here, Brooke. How are you? Feeling better?"

Another chuckle rolled, but it didn't sound as carefree as the first one. "Oh, you know me, Marty. I'm like a cat. I always land on my feet." Something clinked—ice in a glass, maybe? "But let's save our catching up for when we're face to face, huh? I'm assuming, since you called, you're interested in the project and there's the possibility we'll all be face to face before long. Am I assuming correctly?"

Anthony cleared his throat and rubbed the end of his nose with his knuckle. "Your letter said if I had questions, I should call. Well, I have questions."

"Then shoot them at me. I'm ready with answers."

Marty couldn't hold back a grin. Brooke's confidence carried across the miles. At times she'd suspected her friend's boldness was a mask to hide insecurity, but she heard no hint of uncertainty in her tone this evening. Apparently her successful years in the corporate real estate business had chased the childhood insecurities far away.

While Anthony quizzed Brooke about housing issues, access to materials, the size of his crew, and other things pertaining to business, Marty boiled tea bags with a scoop of sugar in a pint of water to make a pitcher of sweet tea. By the time the tea was ready to pour over ice, she'd learned even more about her friend's organizational and business skills. Four trailer houses were already on-site for temporary housing, and the list of materials she'd sent in the packet were ordered and would be delivered as soon as the workers took up residence on the property. She requested a crew of six workers, and she suggested they use the summer and fall months to stabilize the buildings' foundations and exteriors so the winter months could be spent remodeling the interiors.

Marty placed a full sweaty glass in front of Anthony and slipped into her chair. She sipped the sweet, strong tea while Brooke continued.

"I don't expect your crew to do the interior designing. No offense, but given your spartan lifestyle, I doubt you have the ability to create what I envision." She laughed lightly, taking the edge off what could have been construed as an insult. "But creating the floor plans indicated on the blueprints I sent, putting primer on the walls, and framing out the windows and doors will get the buildings ready for the final touches. Now . . . what else?"

Anthony took a long draw of his tea, swiped his mouth, and bent over the phone again. "This isn't a question. It's more of a concern."

"What's that?" Although she sounded interested, she also sounded tired. Marty glanced at the clock. It wasn't even seven o'clock in Kansas. Brooke might not be feeling well. Marty hoped they weren't overtaxing her.

"The thing is, if I agree to rebuild your ghost town, I'll be away from here for a pretty long time. I'm a little worried about my business." He flicked a scowl in Marty's direction. "That people will get used to using other construction companies and forget all about me. Besides that, I'm not sure my whole crew of men would want to pack up and leave Pine Hill for more than a year. Their homes and families are here."

"Okay, I understand your concerns. Now, let me ask some questions."

Anthony raised one eyebrow and aimed a smirk at Marty. He mouthed, *She's very take charge.* Marty nodded, grinning. He said, "Go ahead."

"How many men do you have on your crew?"

"Six."

"Are all of them married, like you?"

"Four of them are, two of them aren't. Three of the ones who are married have kids, too." He glanced at Marty, his brow creasing as if in silent apology. "So I don't think they'd want to be away for so long, and I doubt they'd want to uproot their whole families."

Marty lifted her glass and took a drink, attempting to wash away the warm flush of envy his words inspired. It didn't help. She focused on Brooke's voice as a distraction.

"Assuming the four who are married would want to stay behind, could they operate your business in your absence?"

Anthony cupped the tea glass between his palms and frowned at the phone. "Well . . ."

"Do you trust them?"

"Sure I do." His tone reflected defensiveness. "They've been with me for years and are dependable, hard workers. But I've always done the subcontracting—you know, hiring outside workers to take care of the things I couldn't."

"I know what subcontracting means." A hint of humor colored her tone. "I suspect if you left a list of reputable businesses with your crew members, they would be able to make the contacts. If there's one man who stands out—who's been with you the longest or has the strongest leadership abilities—you could name him as foreman and give him the responsibility."

Anthony pinched his chin, his forehead puckering. "That would be Steve Kanagy. He's what I guess you'd call my unofficial foreman."

"There you go. So that solves the issue of your company crumbling while you're away. I might also add with two separate crews operating, you stand to bring in even more revenue than you are now with one crew."

Marty examined her husband's face. He'd never expressed a hunger for riches—not the way Brooke had when she and Marty discussed the future—but something flickered in his eyes that made her wonder if he harbored a secret desire. "Yeah . . ." He drawled out the word. "Yeah, I could see how that might happen."

"As for your remaining two, do you suppose they'd object to being gone for more than a year?"

"I won't speak for them. I don't know."

Marty closed her eyes for a moment, picturing the men in Anthony's crew. Would they be willing to leave Pine Hill for such a long time? She'd left her small Kansas hometown when she was eighteen and had gone back only for brief visits. Maybe the single men would find wives and choose to stay in Kansas. Anything was possible.

"If you prefer, I could easily hire local construction workers and put them under your leadership," Brooke was saying, her tone crisp. "There are always men looking for work. I've spoken with several businessmen here in KC, and they agree a team of six to seven men will be needed to complete the reconstruction, which would be your focus. No need to worry about wiring or plumbing. I've established relationships with electricians and plumbers from previous projects, and I'll subcontract those services."

Anthony blew out a soft sigh. "That's good. I'm not certified for electrical or plumbing."

"Talk to your crew, find out for sure if they're interested or not. If they're not, maybe you could hire some new workers, men you already know and trust. Whatever transpires—whether you decide to bring a whole team, a partial team, come on your own, or not come at all—let me know as quickly as possible. It's already close to the end of June. I need to finalize the details if this project is to proceed on the timeline I've set."

Marty tipped her mouth near the phone. "I'll invite Anthony's crew to our house tomorrow evening for a snack, and Anthony can talk to them all at once. Then he can let you know on Sunday what they want to do."

Anthony gawked at her as if she'd sprouted green feathers from the top of her head, but she didn't care. Brooke didn't want delays, and Marty needed time away. If hosting a gathering—something she hadn't done in years—would speed up the process, she'd swallow her misgivings and call them all herself.

Anthony cleared his throat. "I will more likely call you on Monday. The men will need a little time to think about their answers, and I don't do business on Sunday. It's the Lord's day." A hint of rebuke showed in his narrowed gaze. "But I promise we'll talk and not let you wait too long for an answer."

"Please don't. As I said, the clock is ticking. I don't have months to spare."

Although nothing changed in Brooke's tone, Marty experienced a chill. Before she could explore its source, Anthony picked up the phone and held it under his chin.

"We'll say goodbye for now, Miss Spalding. Thank you for the opportunity."

"You're welcome for the opportunity, but if you call me Miss Spalding, we aren't going to get along very well." The familiar chuckle rolled. "In this particular case, I don't mind mixing business with friendship, so

Brooke is fine. I'll be waiting for your call, Anthony. Bye now, Marty. I hope to talk in person soon." The connection ended.

Anthony closed the phone and dropped it into his shirt pocket. He gave Marty a look that somehow reflected both eagerness and nervousness. "Are you sure you're ready for this?"

Marty nodded hard. "I'm ready. I'd pack and leave tomorrow if you were ready."

"I've gotta gather a team first. I guess we'll know if I have one after I talk to my crew tomorrow evening. That is, if you're still wanting to host—"

"I am." She gestured to the wall phone. "Do you want me to call each of them, or do you want to?"

"I'll do it. They're my men."

"All right. Tell them seven o'clock. The wives and I will"—she gulped, gathering courage—"keep the children entertained while you men talk." She put her hand on Anthony's taut arm. "Then I'll pack the day after and be ready to go whenever you say the word."

He sighed, and his gaze drifted somewhere beyond her shoulder. "The day after tomorrow's Sunday. No packing then. Besides, no matter what my team says, I gotta talk to the deacons after worship service—get their opinion about what we should do."

Marty chewed her lip. "What if they advise against it?"

He didn't answer right away. He didn't look at her, either. Finally he sighed. "I don't know, Marty. We'll have to wait and see."

11

Anthony

*A*nthony sat forward on a hard metal folding chair with his elbows on his knees, hands linked to hide their tremble, while he explained everything Miss Spalding—Brooke—had told him about the project in Kansas. He'd given his employees the comfortable seats in the living room. Even though they could lounge on the soft sofa, love seat, and chair, they perched on the edges of the cushions like sparrows on a wire, their attentive gazes pinned on his face.

He reached the end of the information and sat up straight, holding his hands wide. "So . . . that's what I know. What do you think?"

Steve Kanagy blew out a breath and whisked a glance left and right at the others. "It's sure different from anything we've done before. Sounds like it'd be a good business decision for Hirschler Construction with the expected high profit margin."

The others murmured and nodded at each other.

"But . . ."

Bursts of laughter carried through the open windows—the kids having a water balloon fight in the backyard. Marty's idea. Anthony hoped she was having fun, too, but he expected she'd end up quiet and sad for the next few days, the way she usually did after an extended time with children. He pushed aside the gloomy thought and bobbed his head at Steve. "But what? Tell me what you're thinking."

"It's pretty far away. I know we sometimes are gone for a week on a job, but over a year? I couldn't leave my family for that long."

Myron, the youngest of the group, wriggled in place. "Take 'em along."

Steve made a face. "For a year and a half? I can't see me packing up my wife and kids and hauling them to Kansas with me. I mean, Julie could teach the kids so they wouldn't miss out on lessons, but they're eight, ten, and thirteen already. Too big for all of us to live in a little trailer. Not for that long."

Pat Gingerich sent an apologetic grimace to Anthony. "I'm with Steve. Michelle's whole family lives here. She's all wrapped up in the women's quilting group and Bible study and . . . well, everything you can think of in the fellowship. She wouldn't want to leave for so long. And I'm wondering about the jobs you've committed to around here. If we all head off to Kansas, what happens to the people who've hired us? Do we not honor our word?"

Anthony held up both palms as if under arrest. "Let's stop for a minute. Steve and Pat are out, but what about the rest of you? Nate, Myron, Todd, Porter . . . are any of you interested in going?" If his whole team resisted, he'd have to say no to Brooke. Even if she could hire men to work under his instruction, he couldn't break in a whole new crew and get the town rebuilt in a year and a half. He held his breath, waiting for each of the men to speak.

Todd shrugged. "I don't have a family or anything holding me back. Sounds like a good adventure to me. I'll go, if you end up going."

Myron grinned. "I've never been away from Pine Hill my whole life. I'd like to see the ghost town, have a hand in bringing it to life again. Count me in."

Two in and two out. Anthony let his breath release slowly through his parted lips and turned to Porter and Nate, who shared the love seat. "What about you two?"

The pair exchanged a look. Porter hung his head. "I think I'm gonna have to say no, Anthony, for the same reasons as Steve and Pat. I don't wanna haul my wife and kids away from their home."

That meant three of his men unwilling to go. Anthony waited in silence for Nate's answer. Nate was still young, just a little older than Myron and Todd, but he had a new wife. They'd all attended Nate and Charlotte's wedding last February. Anthony braced himself for another no. Newlyweds wouldn't want to leave the little house they'd settled into only a few months ago.

Nate pulled in a big breath and planted his hands on his knees. "Lemme talk to Charlotte. We don't have kids yet, so maybe this'd be a chance for us to do something interesting—just the two of us—before we have a family tying us down."

Myron punched the air. "So you mean you wanna go?"

A sheepish grin crept across the young man's face. "Yeah. I kinda do. But I can't say yes unless Charlotte's okay with it."

So maybe three. Anthony rose and folded his arms over his chest. "All right. I'll talk to the deacons tomorrow after service, see if they are opposed to us going. If they are, then we'll stay here and keep working as usual." Although he didn't know how he'd keep the whole team busy the entire summer unless some bigger projects came his way. "If they give their blessing, I'll need to talk to you three"—he nodded toward Steve, Porter, and Pat—"about keeping Hirschler Construction operating while I'm in Kansas."

Pat scratched his chin. "Anthony, I just thought ... My nephews Lucas and Justin—you know, my sister Evelyn's twins—helped us at the Wengerdts' place. They did real good, and Lucas especially liked the work. The boys are eighteen and don't have jobs other than helping at their granddad's dairy and their dad's farm. Maybe Lucas would want to go. That is, if the deacons say yes and if you'd want to hire him."

Anthony's heart gave a little jump. If he could take four reliable workers with him, he'd have a better chance of finishing up even with one or two unknown men hired by Brooke. He nodded. "I like the idea, Pat. Would you check with Lucas and his folks—see if they'd okay it if he's interested? Remind him we'll be heading out pretty quick if the deacons say yes."

"I'll call his folks tonight."

The men stood around for a few more minutes, talking about the possible changes, and then Steve silenced them with a gruff "Fellas?" His expression turned serious. "Before we gather our families and go home, I think we should pray together. We want to be sure this job in Kansas is God's will for Hirschler Construction and for all of us."

"That's a good idea, Steve." Anthony gestured, drawing the team into a circle around the coffee table. They joined hands and bowed their heads.

Steve offered a prayer for guidance and discernment, for God to speak clearly to each of them, and for Him to bless the work of their hands whether they labored in Indiana or in the Kansas ghost town. "We will follow You where You lead, our dear Lord and Savior."

Anthony's chest tightened. *Let Marty accept Your will, whatever it might be.*

Steve's solemn voice rumbled, "Amen."

Anthony echoed, "Amen." *So be it.*

"They didn't even hesitate." Anthony still marveled at the deacons' response to his taking half the Hirschler Construction team to Kansas City, Kansas. He tapped a potato chip on the edge of his plate and gazed at Marty's smiling face across the table. She hadn't stopped smiling since they sat down together, and she hadn't eaten a bite. Of course, neither had he. His stomach was too busy jumping to accept any food. "Deacon Troyer spoke first—said it sounded like the chance for me to be a missionary and I should do everything I could to make the trip."

Marty laughed softly. "A missionary? To Kansas? It's not exactly the Congo."

He laughed, too, and shrugged, a little sheepish. "Oh, I know. They know it, too. But they said I'll likely encounter lots of people who don't know the Lord. It will give me a chance to witness to them while I work alongside them." He sighed, closing his eyes. "It might be the closest I get to serving on a mission field."

Fingers touched his arm, and he opened his eyes to find Marty's eyes swimming with tears. He took her hand and frowned. "What's wrong?"

She shook her head, and one of the tears rolled past her eyelashes and down her cheek. "Nothing. I know it's always been a dream of yours. I'm glad you're getting to see it fulfilled."

He chuckled and released her hand. "Well, as you said, Kansas isn't the Congo—not even close to what real missionaries get to do—but I'll share the gospel if God opens the door." He jolted. "Marty, the money Brooke is paying me . . . Maybe we could . . ." Worry descended. Should he mention his thought about using some of the money to adopt? Having a child was her dream. What if he didn't end up with enough left over to pay for adoption fees? He'd only disappoint her.

She tipped her head. "Maybe we could what?"

He shouldn't say anything. Not yet. No sense in getting her hopes up and then crushing them. He smiled and waved his hand. "Never mind. I'll need to wait and see how much profit the company makes." He picked up his sandwich and took a small bite. "The deacons had a suggestion for our house while we're gone. Remember the Hiltons—James and Beverly?"

She scowled for a moment, then brightened. "Oh, you're talking about the couple who visited our church two or three years ago to share about their work in China."

"Yes, them." He plopped the sandwich on his plate. "Deacon Lehman has stayed in touch with them through his nephew, who also works on a ministry team in China. They adopted a baby girl from an orphanage over there. The baby has several medical issues, things that require surgery, so they're coming back to the Unites States for a year or so. A doctor at one of

the hospitals in Lafayette has volunteered to do the surgeries. They're looking for someplace close to Lafayette to stay, and they really can't pay a lot,
so that's caused problems for them. Deacon Lehman wondered if we'd let
them use our house if they pay for the utilities."

Marty's mouth dropped open. "It's . . . They . . ." She paused, laughed,
and shook her head. "It's like God is sending us to Kansas."

He grinned. Most of the apprehension he'd held on to had flown out
the window when he realized he could serve a missionary family in such a
personal way. If God needed to use their house, then He probably needed
to use them in Kansas. Even though it still made him a little nervous to go
so far away from the fellowship for a long period of time, his eagerness now
outweighed his fear. "They're due to arrive in the United States the first
week of July, so I'll leave our keys with Deacon Lehman. If for some reason
they decide not to stay here, the Lehmans will keep an eye on the house,
keep the yard mowed and so forth while we're gone."

"I can't believe how fast everything is falling into place." Marty pushed
her plate aside and laughed. "I'm too worked up to eat. I want to pack.
Would it be a sin for me to start packing?"

Anthony's first impulse was to say yes—they shouldn't labor on the
Lord's day. But the joy shining in her eyes had been absent for so long. He
didn't want to erase it. Besides, they didn't have a lot of time to get things
ready to go.

He rose, picking up his plate. "I'll put this in the fridge to eat later, and
I'll help pack."

12

Marty

*E*arly Monday morning Marty walked Anthony to his truck. The grass wore a light covering of dew, and it dampened the soles of her bare feet, but she didn't mind. The ground would warm quickly, and she loved the way the sun sparkled on the tiny droplets, turning them into a carpet of diamonds.

He paused at the driver's door to lean in for a kiss, and this time she met his lips with her own. Only a peck—the neighbors might be watching—but her heart rolled over. She didn't realize how much she'd missed his affection until he offered it again.

She wove her fingers together and looked into his face, shaded by the brim of his ball cap. "Call me tonight?"

He grinned as he pulled the truck door open. "Even though I'll probably be back on Wednesday? That's not hardly long enough for you to miss me."

"Yes, it is."

He climbed behind the steering wheel and closed the door.

She curled her hands over the window opening. "Do you want me to call you if I hear from Drew or Evelyn about Lucas?"

"Yeah. I probably won't answer, but you can leave a message on the cell." He shook his head, making a *whew* sound with an expelled breath. "I sure hope he says yes. Brooke's got enough to do without hiring construction workers, too."

"I'm sure she can handle it."

"Probably." He checked his wristwatch and grimaced. "I gotta go. The men'll all be at the site by eight. I should get there first."

She took a backward step. "Bye, then. I'll talk to you tonight?"

"Tonight." He sent another grin in her direction before starting the engine. He stuck his hand out the window and waved as he pulled from their driveway onto the street.

She waved back, then hurried inside to start the kitchen cleanup. She washed and dried their breakfast dishes and gave the floor a good mopping. As she was putting the damp mop on its hook on the back porch, the telephone rang. She hurried to the wall phone. "Hello, Hirschler Construction, Mrs. Hirschler speaking. How may I help you?"

"Hello, Marty, this is Evelyn Mast."

Marty's heart skipped a beat. "Good morning, Evelyn."

"I hope I'm not calling too early."

"Oh no, this is fine. I saw Anthony off to the jobsite in Noblesville almost an hour ago, so I've been up for a while." She would have risen early even if she hadn't wanted to send him off with a good breakfast. She had much to do to prepare for their temporary move to Kansas. "Are you"— *please, please*—"calling about Lucas?"

Laughter rang. "I sure am. He wanted us to call last night already, but we wouldn't let him bother you on a Sunday. He went with his dad and brothers this morning to help with the wheat harvest. As long as he's still here, he might as well be working."

Marty double-gripped the telephone receiver. "So you told him . . ."

"We've given him permission to go, but we told him he has to be in service on Sunday mornings. I'm sure you and Anthony will make sure of that."

Marty nodded even though Evelyn couldn't see her. "We will. We've already committed to finding a Mennonite church in the area and taking the whole team to services every week." If there wasn't a Mennonite chapel within driving distance, they'd attend another evangelical church. The deacons had approved several denominations.

"Good, good. I'll pack plenty of work shirts and trousers along with his church clothes and necessities. Is there anything in particular he needs to bring with him other than his Bible, clothes, and toiletries?"

She and Anthony had talked until late last night, discussing things to bring, and she repeated everything to Lucas's mother. The trailers were furnished, and each had a compact equipped kitchen even though the men wouldn't do much cooking—she would take care of all the meals. So they'd only need bedding, towels, games or books to entertain themselves in the evenings, a few favorite snacks to last until they located a grocery store, and tools.

"Lucas doesn't have any tools of his own." Uncertainty came through in her tone.

"Anthony has plenty of tools in his work trailer, so don't worry about that. Just see to his personal needs."

"All right. When do you think you'll set out?"

Excitement quivered through her frame. "Unless Anthony gets stuck at the site in Noblesville longer than he expects, the end of the week. Friday morning is our plan. It's a full day's drive to Kansas City, and Anthony wants to have Saturday to get settled in and Sunday to rest before starting work the first Monday in July."

"So you'll want to leave pretty early, won't you?"

"Yes. If you could have Lucas to our house by seven, we'd appreciate it."

"I can." Silence fell for a few seconds, followed by a heavy sigh. "That boy of ours is as eager as a spring colt ready to break out of the corral, but I confess it'll be hard for me to see him leave for so long. He and Justin are our oldest, you know, so this is a new experience for us."

Marty couldn't imagine what Evelyn was feeling. She wanted to know, though. She wanted to feel every joy and pain of motherhood for herself. She closed her eyes, battling a sudden rush of tears.

"At first I wanted to say no because I couldn't imagine not having him here. I thought it'd be too hard on Justin, too. Being twins, he and Lucas are so close. But Drew told me maybe it'll be good for them to be apart for a while, to figure out they can get along all right without the other one. And he reminded me that our children aren't really ours anyway. They belong to God. We have them for one season of life, but then they have to move into their own season."

Marty tried to think of something to say that would comfort Evelyn, but no words formed. She bit her lower lip and stood in silence.

"Well . . ." Evelyn sighed again. "I better let you off the phone. You have lots to do, I suppose, to get ready. If you end up needing some help, please call me. I think I'm gonna need to stay busy this week so I don't spend too much time crying about letting Lucas go."

Marty cleared the lump in her throat and forced herself to speak. "Thank you for the offer. I'll let you know, but I should be all right. Goodbye." She hung up, then leaned against the wall and lowered her head. All the bright joy of the morning had been overshadowed. But soon she'd be away from references to children and motherhood. She'd be gone for more than a full year, which would give her time to come to terms with her childless state. Of course it would.

She pushed off from the wall and headed for the back porch to start a load of laundry, but halfway across the kitchen floor she changed direction and returned to the phone. Brooke needed to know how many men Anthony would bring on the work crew. Hadn't Brooke said the sooner she knew, the better?

Marty located Brooke's business card. A long-distance call from the home telephone was expensive, but she wouldn't talk long. Just long enough to give Brooke the good news. She positioned her finger to punch in the first number, but then she remembered the time difference. Not much past seven in Kansas. Brooke might still be asleep. She'd better wait.

With a sigh, she returned the card to the stack of papers on the table and trudged to the porch. She'd do what Evelyn had said—stay busy. Then she'd call Brooke around lunchtime. A talk with her friend should restore her positive outlook.

13

Kansas City
Brooke

*B*rooke's phone had rung at two minutes past eight. Thirty minutes ahead of her alarm. She'd grumbled at the intrusion until
she saw the name on the cell phone screen. *Dr. Susan Classen*. Nothing
like a call from a doctor first thing in the morning to bring someone to
complete wakefulness.

The receptionist's too-chipper request for Brooke to come in at her
earliest convenience that morning—*"Dr. Classen will carve out an hour
for you when you get here"*—had instantly raised a wave of heartburn.
Although the call was already two hours past, acid still burned in her
throat as she sought an empty spot in the clinic's parking garage.

She located a slot between an SUV and a car that looked like something from a 1930s mafia movie. Both vehicles were silver, the same color
as her Lexus. For reasons beyond understanding, she found comfort in
leaving her car nestled between its like-colored partners. The moment she
stepped from the air-conditioned interior of her Lexus onto the concrete
parking pad, perspiration broke out over her flesh. She flapped the neckline of her fuchsia silk tank as she strode to the elevator, the leather soles of
her gladiator sandals slapping softly against the hard surface. Ridiculous
summer heat. Or maybe it was fear sweat.

She'd battled outbreaks of perspiration while she dressed, applied
makeup, and styled her hair in its simple fluffed pixie. Not even the lightweight tank and knee-length white denim skirt—generally a combination
that kept her comfortable on the hottest day—seemed to help. By the time

she reached Dr. Classen's reception area, she'd wiped her brow so many times she was sure not a touch of powder remained, and her hair felt sticky.

Several people were already seated in chairs that lined the walls of the small waiting area. As if in sync with one another, they glanced at her upon her entrance, then shifted their attention to the big-screen television mounted between two magazine racks. The racks looked full. Didn't anybody read anymore?

Giving her forehead one more swipe, she moved to the first of two window openings in the glass wall separating the receptionists' desk from the waiting patients and cleared her throat. The young woman glanced up from her computer screen. "Good morning. Name, please?"

"Brooke Spalding. I was told—"

The woman abruptly rose, sending her wheeled chair backward a couple of feet. "Yes, I'll let the doctor know you've arrived. Please wait right here." She hurried off. The remaining receptionist sent Brooke a tight smile and then appeared to busy herself sorting through a stack of folders next to her computer. Another outbreak of perspiration attacked.

Brooke blocked out her surroundings and played music in her head, a Carpenters song. *Sing, sing a song, let the world sing along* . . . As the verse began its repeat with a choir of children's voices, the door to the right of the reception wall opened. A middle-aged woman wearing pale blue scrubs and holding a clipboard pushed the door against the wall with her well-padded bottom.

"Brooke Spalding?"

Brooke ended the song midphrase and forced her feet forward. "That's me."

Those in the chairs scowled or nudged each other and murmured, clearly irritated about her preferential treatment. She didn't blame them. Ordinarily she would wait her turn—she'd never been pushy about being first and tried to follow the rules of fair play—but today she wouldn't offer to trade places with any of them. If a doctor called first thing in the morning and carved out an hour that same morning, then she deserved the preferential treatment.

The woman gestured Brooke into the long hallway, where examination room doors stood at staggered intervals on both sides. "Step up here on the scale, please."

Brooke complied, comforted a bit by the standard routine. The large weight was set on one hundred and the small one at zero. The nurse—her name tag identified her as Trista—slid the small weight to thirty. The right side of the bar went down. Trista used her finger to bounce the little black weight backward. When it landed on twenty-three, the bar balanced.

Brooke gaped at the number. She'd been 135, give or take a pound or two, for the past ten years. If she subtracted the usual two pounds for her clothes, the weight was even more alarming.

Trista scratched something on the clipboard's pad and then held her hand toward a door on the right. "Let's get your vitals now."

An exam table took up most of the floor space in the room. Brooke automatically headed for it. Trista pointed to the chair next to a small table. "It's okay, honey. You can sit over here."

Brooke had never liked being called *honey,* finding the term demeaning. But at that moment it seemed warm and kind. She sank onto the chair's seat, grimacing when her bare legs squeaked on the blue vinyl. Trista perched on a round, wheeled stool she pulled from beneath the table and took Brooke's blood pressure. Then she pinched Brooke's wrist, frowning at her watch.

She released Brooke and picked up her pen. She shook her head as she recorded something on the pad. "The number of pounds you lost turned up on your blood pressure. You must be nervous." She grinned, giving Brooke's forearm a quick squeeze. "But don't worry. Dr. Classen doesn't bite. At least, not very hard."

Brooke tried to laugh in response, but she couldn't find even a hint of humor in the situation. Fear gnawed at her, and her throat stung from acid. She pawed in her little cross-body bag for a new roll of antacids. Hadn't she put them in her purse? She turned the leather pouch upside down and emptied its contents into her lap.

Trista crossed to the door, taking the clipboard with her. "Dr. Classen will be in real soon." She glanced at the few random items in Brooke's lap and frowned. "Did you lose something, honey?"

Brooke choked back a half sob, half laugh. "I must have forgotten my antacids. Do you have any?"

Sympathy creased the woman's round face. "I'll see what I can find. Now, you try to relax, all right?" She stepped out and shut the door behind her.

Brooke closed her eyes and leaned her head against the wall. *Sing, sing a song . . .* She played the song in her head until the panic that had risen in her chest abated. She tucked her wallet, cell phone, keys, hair pick, and fingernail file back into her purse and snapped it closed. Then she hugged the pouch against her stomach and watched the second hand move smoothly around the clock's dial.

On the fourth round, her phone vibrated—a call coming in. Whoever it was could leave a message. She wasn't in the mood to talk. She watched the second hand make two more circles. Midway through the third circle, the door opened and Dr. Classen breezed in. The scent of oranges came with her—an aroma much more pleasant than the antiseptic smell lingering in the sterile room. The doctor stuck out her hand, and Brooke took hold of it.

"Thanks for coming in so quickly, Brooke."

Brooke forced a dry chuckle, pulled her hand free of the doctor's cool grip, and drew on the false bravado that had carried her through her tumultuous childhood. "How could I resist such an intriguing invitation? I don't think I've ever been so privileged." She lifted her chin and forced the corners of her stiff lips to curve upward. "Is this when you ask if I want the good news or the bad news first?"

Dr. Classen placed a large folder on the desk and dug in the pocket of her white jacket. She withdrew a sample pack of antacids. "Here. Chew these."

Brooke's hands shook so badly she had trouble tearing the pack open. She tipped the little packet and poured the two tablets into her open mouth. Fruit flavored. Orange, matching Dr. Classen's perfume. "Thank you."

"You're welcome." The doctor sat on the round stool and crossed her legs. She hooked her chin-length bob of blond curls behind her ears, folded her hands on her knee, and looked directly into Brooke's face. "You asked about bad news or good news. I suspect that your gut reaction will be to take what I'm about to disclose as all bad news, but I want you to try to overcome that. Your attitude from this point forward will play a major role in successfully beating this disease."

"A disease . . ." The various conditions she'd encountered in her internet search paraded through Brooke's mind. She swallowed. "Is it curable?"

"There's a seventy percent survival rate, and those are good odds."

Survival rate? Did that mean— Panic swooped in hard and fast. Brooke began to tremble from head to toe. Her stomach whirled. She clamped her hands over the chair's armrests to prevent herself from vibrating out of the seat and commanded herself not to throw up. She glared at her doctor. "I have cancer."

Dr. Classen didn't respond verbally. Nor did she offer a gesture of assent or denial. But her eyes . . . Her brown eyes that had always reminded Brooke of chocolate drops glimmered with such compassion that Brooke didn't need to hear an answer. She knew.

The doctor put her hand on Brooke's knee. "I'm sorry. I know it's a word no one wants to hear."

Brooke choked back a bitter laugh. "Ya think?"

Dr. Classen's fingers tightened. "You have ovarian cancer. We believe it's at stage two. That in itself is good news. Many women aren't diagnosed until it's stage four, and by then there's less than a twenty percent survival rate. We're fortunate your chiropractor recognized the symptoms and acted quickly."

Brooke didn't feel fortunate. She was too scared to feel fortunate. Tears threatened, but she stubbornly set her jaw and blinked them away. "So what happens now?"

"I refer you to an oncologist."

Brooke shook her head. She didn't want to see an oncologist. She didn't want to need to see an oncologist.

Dr. Classen rolled the stool a few inches closer and cupped her hands over Brooke's white knuckles. Despite the doctor's calming presence, Brooke continued to quiver, as if an earthquake rumbled beneath her chair. "I recommend Dr. Scott Dickerson. He's the best at the KU Cancer Center. I've already sent over copies of your test results, and as soon as I receive a confirmation, I will schedule your first visit with him myself."

"When . . . might that be?"

"Soon. Later this week, in all likelihood."

A buzz filled Brooke's head, as if her brain sizzled. This was happening too fast. Her throat was so tight she wondered if her tonsils had tripled in size. Questions flooded her, but she couldn't bring herself to ask them. She didn't want to hear the answers.

"Would you like me to give you an idea of what to expect?" Dr. Classen spoke softly, kindly, like someone trying to calm a crying baby.

Brooke shook her head, but she rasped, "Yes. Please."

The doctor's hands slid from Brooke's hands. She leaned sideways and picked up the folder from the desk, then flopped it open across her lap. A black sheet of paper with what looked like a series of white inkblots lay on top of the stack. Dr. Classen pointed to various shadows on the blots as she spoke. "The cancer is in both ovaries and fallopian tubes and the uterus, and it has affected your bladder. The standard treatment is a surgical cytoreduction."

Brooke frowned. "A what?"

"Surgery to reduce the number of cancer cells. In other words, the surgeon will remove your ovaries, fallopian tubes, and uterus—a radical hysterectomy." Her chocolate-drop eyes took on the sympathetic glow again. "I'm sorry, Brooke. This means you'll never bear children."

Brooke had never considered bearing children. But with the possibility ripped away, she experienced a sense of loss that took her by surprise. "I . . . I see."

"Before they perform surgery, however, the oncologist will most likely order a full-body CT scan. He'll want to make sure no cancer cells exist outside your pelvic region, because that will change the plan for treatment."

Brooke processed what she'd heard so far. "You said my bladder was affected. Will they take that out, too?"

Dr. Classen shook her head. "They'll probably use chemotherapy to eradicate those cancer cells. Depending on what the CT scan shows, you might also have radiation therapy."

This was too much to absorb all at once. Brooke slumped forward and pressed her fingertips to her forehead, where a headache was beginning to pound. Her bangs brushed her fingers and she gasped. Would she go bald? She jerked her hands down and stared at Dr. Classen. "What if I don't want chemotherapy? Do I have to have it?"

The doctor's expression didn't change. "Ultimately it's your choice whether to undergo any of the standard treatments. No one will force anything on you—whether surgery or chemo or radiation—that you don't approve. But you need to understand that the cancer has spread beyond your ovaries."

"You can take those out." Pain stabbed Brooke's chest with the statement. She'd heard how women who lost their breasts to breast cancer felt less like women afterward, but she had never quite understood why. Now she understood too clearly. But the cancer needed to be removed from her body. "The . . . tumors . . ." Could these ugly words be coming out of her mouth? "Take all of them out. Then the cancer will be gone, right?"

"Not necessarily." Dr. Classen closed the file and set it aside. "Often women with ovarian cancer will have cancer cells elsewhere that are too small to be detected with any of the currently available tests. We refer to these cells as micrometastases. The small cells cause cancer recurrence following surgical treatment alone. So to cleanse the body of micrometastases and improve your duration of survival and potential for cure, chemotherapy is the best course of action we can provide."

Brooke stood, forcing Dr. Classen to roll her chair backward. "I've heard enough. I . . . I need some time to think, to come to grips with—" Would she ever come to grips with this unwelcome invasion in her body? How unfair that she, who had lived a cleaner life than her mother, should be stricken with something as ugly as cancer.

Dr. Classen rose and put her hand on Brooke's shoulder. "Is there someone you can call to come get you? You've received a mighty blow, and it might not be wise for you to drive."

Brooke jerked away from the doctor's touch. "I'll be fine. Let me know when you've set up the appointment with . . ." She searched her memory. What was the oncologist's name? She couldn't recall, and she didn't care. "The doctor at the KU center. Thank you for—" Would she really express appreciation for having been dealt such an ugly blow? She darted out of the room, up the hallway, and into the reception area.

Eyes straight ahead, she charged for the door and then half walked, half jogged through the maze of hallways leading to the parking garage. She wove around other people, lips pressed so tight her jaw ached, not caring if she bumped into them and forced them to step aside. She needed to talk to someone. To rail at someone. To receive comfort from someone. But who could she call? Her mother? Laughable. Mom couldn't pull her face out of a bottle long enough to put a coherent sentence together. Her friends? What friends? She had none. Not real ones. Only casual business acquaintances who were wrapped up in their own lives and families. She was on her own.

By the time she reached the section of the garage where she'd left her car, her entire body was drenched with sweat. Her silk tank stuck to her skin like a sheet of plastic wrap. Eager to put the AC on high and blast herself with cold air, she hurried the final distance. The SUV remained in its place to the right of her vehicle, but the mafia car had gone and an older-model green Plymouth sat in its place. The change unnerved her, and she aimed her finger for the keypad. Before she connected with it, her gaze fell on a dent and green scrape about four inches below the keypad. The Plymouth's door had assaulted hers. She released a stronger oath than *leapin' lizards* and pressed her thumb against the spot. A magnet wouldn't fix this one. It went too deep, and the silver paint was scratched all the way to the metal underneath. Her Lexus had been permanently impacted. And so had she. Tears pricked.

She unlocked the car, slid into the driver's seat, and started the engine. But instead of putting the car into gear, she slumped forward until her forehead met the steering wheel. Pain stabbed through her lower spine, and she bit down on another curse. The throb seemed to chant, *Cancer, cancer, cancer . . .*

With a growl, she sat up and slammed her palms on the hard plastic wheel. Why? Why her? She started to whack the steering wheel again, but her hands paused midstrike and she gasped as another question roared through her mind. Why not her? What made her so special that she should be immune from a malady that affected thousands of people every year? Oh, some of those people brought it on themselves with unwise lifestyle choices, but others were like her—stricken for seemingly no reason.

A soft buzz came from her purse—another call. She closed her eyes, considering ignoring it. But maybe taking the call, focusing on business, would help. She snatched the phone from her purse. *Hirschler Construction* flashed on the screen. Her heart gave a leap. She tapped the accept button and pressed the phone to her ear. "Hello?"

"Hello, Brooke."

At Marty's warm voice, the tears Brooke had valiantly held at bay broke through the dam and flowed down her cheeks. "Oh, Marty, I'm so glad you called."

14

Pine Hill

Marty

*M*arty's pulse automatically increased its tempo. Although she hadn't communicated with Brooke except through letters, she heard something in her friend's tone that seemed out of place. A sadness. A helplessness. A brokenness. She forced a hesitant question. "What's wrong?"

For several seconds, not a sound came through the phone. Marty pressed the receiver even tighter against her ear. Had the line dropped? Just as she was ready to hang up and call again, Brooke chuckled.

"Oh, you know how it is. Sometimes you just need to hear a friendly voice. I hope you're calling to tell me"—a discernible swallow, almost a gulp—"Anthony decided to take on my project."

Something wasn't right, but if Brooke didn't want to discuss it, Marty should respect her wishes. "Yes. Our plan is to leave for Kansas on Friday, so his first workday at the town will be the first Monday in July. Is that soon enough?"

Another odd strangling noise preceded a throaty chuckle. "That's perfect. Exactly what I wanted. Is he bringing his whole team?"

"No. Three of the men are staying here to handle local jobs, like you suggested. The other three are coming with us, and a new man hired on, too, so you'll only need to find one additional worker to make a team of six."

"Good. Good." Brooke's words were clipped, as if fired from a slingshot. "There are four mobile homes hooked up to water and electricity, each with two bedrooms. You and Anthony will have your own—the one with the biggest kitchen, since you'll be doing the cooking. The men can double up with whomever they prefer for a roommate, and the man I hire can take the remaining trailer."

Marty cringed. "Well, one of our men is a newlywed, so he's bringing his wife, and of course I'm coming with Anthony. So that means one of our men will need to bunk with whoever you hire. Unless we can put three men in one trailer."

"That wouldn't give much personal space for any of them. I'll see what I can do about getting an additional trailer on-site if your Mennonite worker doesn't want to room with a non-Mennonite. I . . ."

Marty waited, but Brooke didn't finish her sentence. Concern for her friend's well-being chased away worry about invading her privacy. "Brooke, are you all right? You sound kind of unsettled."

A harsh laugh blasted in Marty's ear. "I'm sitting in my car, Marty, instead of behind my desk. It's harder for me to concentrate in here."

Marty didn't believe her. From Brooke's letters, she'd learned how often the businesswoman used her car as a second office. Brooke's unwillingness to talk felt like a rebuff. "I'm sorry I caught you at a bad time. I should probably let you go anyway. I have lots to do to get ready for our move. But I wanted to let you know you don't need to search for another contractor."

"I appreciate that, and I don't want to delay your leave-taking. I'm very eager to—"

Marty frowned, straining to hear. Had Brooke's voice broken on a sob? But Brooke didn't cry. At least, not to Marty's knowledge. "Brooke?"

"We both have much to get accomplished in the next few days, so let's end our conversation now and talk more in depth when you get here. All right?" Her brisk, professional, almost unemotional tone had returned.

Marty chewed her lip, wrestling with herself. Should she press Brooke—obviously something was troubling her—or let it go? Although their friendship was decades long, the number of years without face-to-face contact left Marty floundering about what to say or do. "Um . . ."

"Now, obviously, if you or Anthony have questions or concerns, feel free to call. If it goes to voice mail, leave a message and I'll get back to you as quickly as I can. I am very pleased you will be coming. I know Anthony and I will forge a great working relationship, and you and I have so much to catch up on. Can't wait to do that. But for now, I better run. Bye, Marty." The line went dead.

Kansas City
Brooke

Brooke tossed the cell phone onto the passenger's seat and pressed her fist to her lips. It had taken every bit of self-control she possessed not to break down and share her diagnosis with Marty. She needed the release. But two things stopped her. Marty had enough to do to get ready for a move across several states, and Brooke wasn't ready to speak the awful C-word out loud. Not saying it didn't change anything, but if she didn't talk about it, she could pretend—at least for a little while—that there wasn't something awful growing inside her.

She'd left the engine idling for too long. At least four cars had rolled past while she sat talking to Marty. She should leave the parking space, let someone else have it. But she didn't put the car in gear. She closed her eyes and let her head sag against the headrest, welcoming the flow of cold air from the AC vents against her neck and chest. Soon she'd have the chance to talk to Marty in person. By the time the Hirschlers arrived, her appointment with the oncologist—another ugly word—would be behind her and she'd have a better idea of what she was facing.

And Marty would be here to be her safe harbor, just as she'd so often been when they were children. If Brooke didn't know better, she'd suspect divine intervention. But she did know better. If there was a God, He wouldn't subject children to drunken mothers and their abusive boyfriends or women to diagnoses like cancer and infertility. Believing in God made some people feel better, and that was fine. But adopt it for herself? Not a chance.

Without prompting, part of another Carpenters song began to play. *And solitaire's the only game in town . . .*

Another car inched past. She'd taken up space here long enough. Time to go home. She had work to do. If she was lucky, it would occupy her well enough to chase away the awful C-word reverberating through her mind.

Noblesville

Anthony

Anthony accepted the windowed envelope with a check peeking through and shook Robert Butler's hand. "Thank you for trusting Hirschler Construction with your project, sir."

The older man released Anthony's hand and aimed his gaze at the two-story structure that resembled an 1800s carriage house. A grin crinkled his eyes. "I had no doubt you Amish men would do a bang-up job. Seems like you're all born with a good work ethic."

People often mixed up the Amish and the Mennonites, and it only confused folks more when he corrected them. So Anthony folded the envelope in half and slipped it into his shirt pocket. "If you decide to have my team do the finish work on the apartment, call Steve Kanagy. His number is on the invoice."

Mr. Butler frowned. "Why wouldn't I call you? Aren't you the one in charge?"

Anthony nodded. "Yes, sir, but I'll be working out of state for a year or so. Steve'll be in charge of the company while I'm gone." It still seemed a little strange to state his plans out loud, but over the past few days he'd had time to adjust to the idea. At least the details were all falling into place nice and neat. An indication that God's hand was in it, for sure.

"I see. Well, thanks, but I want to do the finish work myself. Now that I'm retired, I have the time to spare, and my wife'll be happy to send me out of the house for a few hours every day." He chuckled and clapped Anthony on the shoulder. "I'll give Steve a call if I discover I need some help, though. Thanks again. You fellows drive safe, now." He glanced at the evening sky. "Looks like we're gearing up for another summer storm. I don't mind rain, but I sure don't want tornadoes."

Anthony couldn't argue with him. Tornadoes were never welcome. A hot, humid wind coming from the south hit the back of his neck, proof that the weather was changing. They'd better head for home quickly.

He jogged to the tool trailer, where his team was gathered. "Everything loaded?"

"And strapped down." Steve Kanagy sent a slow look from the carriage house's peak to the concrete footing. "Seems a little weird that this is the last building we'll all work on together for a while."

Myron scuffed his toe against the ground. "It probably sounds funny since I was one of the first ones to say I wanted to go, but now that we're done here, it makes me a little sad to split up the team."

The men murmured, glancing at each other out of the corners of their eyes.

Anthony slung his arm across Myron's shoulders. "Do you want to offer the blessing?"

Myron's eyebrows rose. "Me? Really?"

At the close of every project, Anthony or one of his team gave a prayer of blessing for the building and those who would use it. Generally one of the older members volunteered to pray, but it was time for these younger ones to do more than listen. Especially since they'd be leaving the oldest employees of Hirschler Construction behind on Friday.

Anthony grinned. "Sure."

Myron sent a quick, nervous look around the circle of men, but then he squared his shoulders and nodded. "All right. Let's pray."

They all bowed their heads, and Anthony closed his eyes. Myron might've acted nervous, but when he started speaking to God, his voice came out strong and sure. He thanked God for the safety they'd enjoyed while they worked, asked Him to bless the building for good use and keep His hand of protection and blessing on every person who entered it, and closed with a request for safe travel back to Pine Hill. Then he paused and cleared his throat several times. Finally he spoke again.

"Please be with us, our loving God and Father, as we part ways and serve You from different places. Continue to bless the work of our hands. I ask these things in the name of our Savior and Lord. Amen."

"Amen," the men echoed, and Anthony lifted his head to discover that several of the men's eyes were sheeny with moisture. He swallowed the knot that formed in his throat. He'd have a hard time telling these hardworking, dependable men goodbye. Just as saying goodbye to his brother, Rex, would be hard. But he'd go. The potential profit was too good to ignore, and he couldn't yank away the only thing that had put joy in Marty's eyes again. Yes, it would be hard to part ways, as Myron had put it. At least the separation would be temporary.

He edged toward the truck's cab. "We're done here. Let's go."

15

Kansas City
Brooke

*H*ave you ever had an allergic reaction to an IV contrast?" The woman in pink scrubs that clashed horribly with her frizzy red ponytail waited, pencil hovering over the clipboard.

Brooke stifled a sigh. Here she was, once again wearing a scratchy, uncomfortable hospital gown—this one in mustard yellow with grayish-blue piping. For the past half an hour, she'd sat on the end of a hip-high, paper-covered exam table and answered the seemingly endless list of questions. No, she wasn't asthmatic, diabetic, a smoker, a drinker, suffering from kidney or heart disease . . . She was exceedingly healthy. Oh, except for this cancer that had invaded her body.

When would the physician's assistant cease with the inquisition and take her to get this test done? Marty, Anthony, and his team of workers were on the road, and she wanted to inspect the trailers before they arrived to make sure the person she'd hired to stock the fridges, put toilet paper in the bathrooms, and turn on the AC had done things according to her instructions. This would be Marty's home—she wanted it to feel welcoming from the moment her friend stepped over the threshold.

"Ms. Spalding?"

Brooke gave a jolt. "What?"

"Are you allergic to IV contrast dye?"

"No."

The PA checked a little square.

"But then, I've never had an IV contrast until today, so who knows what will happen."

The woman flipped the pencil around, applied the eraser, and then placed a check in a different box. She didn't say anything, but her expression gave away mild irritation. Not that Brooke could blame her. She was being snarky. Deliberately so. A defense mechanism she'd drawn on in the past to keep herself from dissolving into wails of fear, anguish, or fury. The pressure building in her chest had to be expelled somehow, and being snarky seemed safer than running up and down the halls in this gaping gown, screeching like a banshee.

What was a banshee, anyway?

The PA, who'd introduced herself as Sandy—or was it Cindy?—set aside the clipboard and opened a drawer in the metal built-in station across from the table. She began removing various plastic-wrapped items and arranging them on a silver tray. "All right, Ms. Spalding, please lie back and make yourself comfortable."

Did they intend to wheel in a recliner and a plush robe? Because otherwise, comfort was an impossibility. Brooke stifled the snide remark and used her hands to scoot herself backward. The gown caught under her rear and pulled on the neckline, nearly strangling her. With a grunt, she lifted her bottom, treating herself to a stab of lower-back pain. Gritting her teeth, she released the gown and inched back until the split between the table's square cushions met her tailbone. The halfway point. She flopped against the crisp cover on the pillow, grimacing at the crinkling noise it made. Nowhere except in a doctor's office did a pillow make sounds like someone crumpling up a sheet of paper.

She linked her hands on her belly and stared at the ceiling tiles. Muffled voices from the hallway drifted through the walls, and more unique-to-doctors'-offices sounds—plastic packages being torn open, latex gloves snapping into place, tools softly clinking on a metal tray—came from the station less than ten feet away. An acidic taste flooded her mouth, and she fought the urge to gag. She picked through the songs in her internal jukebox.

As she chose Elton John's "Goodbye Yellow Brick Road," the PA turned and carried the tray to the table. When she set the tray next to Brooke's hip, the stethoscope hanging around her neck like a snake charmer's pet shifted, and Brooke got a glimpse of her name tag. *Cyndi.* Brooke set the song aside and repeated the name in her head as a distraction from the items on the tray.

Cyndi smiled down at Brooke. "Now, I know you're uptight." An understatement. "But try to relax. I'm going to insert an IV line in the back of your hand, and it will hurt a lot less if you aren't tensing up."

Brooke nodded, raising another round of crinkling from the pillow.

The PA tied a rubber strip around Brooke's upper arm and then lightly patted the back of her hand, her red brows pulled into a V of concentration. The scent of alcohol reached Brooke's nose, and something cool brushed across the back of her hand. In her peripheral vision, Brooke saw the woman pick up a needle the size of a drinking straw. She whisked her gaze to the ceiling tiles. *So goodbye, yellow brick road, where the dogs of society howl . . .* The lyrics rolled while Brooke waited, staring at the ceiling tiles and anticipating the jab.

"All done."

Brooke blinked in surprise. "Done? I didn't even feel it."

Cyndi laughed softly. "We try to make things as painless as we can." She gripped Brooke's elbow and helped her sit up.

Brooke stared at the thin plastic tube with a stopper-like cap taped to her hand. The woman removed the rubber strip, and tingles went down Brooke's arm, as if a thousand ants raced for a finish line. She rubbed her arm, careful not to bump the thin tube. "I hope that's true of everything you do here."

Her smile intact, Cyndi gave Brooke's shoulder a quick squeeze. "A lab tech will be here soon to wheel you to imaging. You can either lie back and relax or wait in a chair."

Brooke preferred the chair. At least it wasn't covered in paper. She slid off the table, holding the gown closed in the back with her tube-free hand, and settled herself in the standard doctor's office vinyl chair.

Cyndi dumped the contents of the tray into various small plastic bins and handed Brooke the bag holding her clothes, shoes, and purse. "You'll want to take this with you since you'll leave after the CT scan. You'd probably rather not go home in the hospital gown."

She got that right.

"You came alone today, didn't you?"

Brooke blinked twice, surprised by the question. "Yes, I did."

The PA's expression turned serious. "That's fine, but from here on out, you'll need to have someone else with you."

"For what reason?"

"To drive you home." Cyndi grimaced slightly, and sympathy glimmered in her eyes. "It's never wise to drive right after surgery, and the treatments that will follow when you've recovered from surgery could leave you weak and overly tired. Until you know for sure how the treatment will affect you, it's best to have someone available to drive for you."

Probably, but Brooke didn't have anyone to call. Except Marty. Although she'd rather face a herd of spiders than battle cancer, the timing of the Hirschlers' arrival suddenly seemed fortuitous. Her heart gave an unexpected flutter. "All right."

"Is there anything I can do for you before I go?"

Tell me this is all a nightmare. Brooke swallowed the pointless comment. "Actually, if there are socks around somewhere, my feet are freezing."

Cyndi nodded. "I'll be right back."

"Thanks."

In only a few minutes, Cyndi returned with a pair of purple fuzzy socks that clashed horribly with Brooke's mustard gown. Apparently no one in this place knew how to coordinate colors. "Here we are." Brooke expected the woman to drop the socks in her lap and leave, but Cyndi knelt in front of Brooke and reached for her feet. Brooke stared at the woman's hands sliding the socks into place, the process efficient yet gentle.

Once Brooke's feet were covered, Cyndi gave them a light squeeze and looked up with a smile. "Better?"

Brooke couldn't recall the last time someone had done something so kind for her. She battled a rush of tears she didn't understand. "Yes. Thank you."

"No problem." Cyndi rose and headed for the door again. "Now, remember . . . relax. The test will be over soon."

Brooke cradled the bag in her lap. She wanted the test over. She wanted the treatment over. She wanted everything over. Except her life. She did not want this to be the beginning of the end of her life.

Near Eagle Creek, Kansas
Marty

A jolt bounced Marty's head against a hard surface, jarring her from sleep. She straightened, blinking, and rubbed the tight muscles in her neck. A peek out the truck's window gave her a view of four lanes of traffic divided by a grassy median and lined by thick trees. She frowned. Where had the gently rolling, grass-covered land with sporadic clumps of scraggly trees gone? She must have slept longer than she'd intended.

She turned to Anthony, who stared straight ahead at the highway, one hand on the steering wheel and the other draped over the fold-down armrest between the seats. "Where are we?"

He glanced at her, a half grin creasing his cheek. "On I-35."

"In Kansas or Missouri?"

"Kansas. We crossed the Missouri River a few miles back. I'm sorry I didn't wake you."

She yawned and waved her hand. "It's all right. I saw the Wabash and the Illinois. The Missouri couldn't look much different." She shifted in the seat, grimacing. Although their little caravan made up of Anthony's pickup, Myron Mast's pickup, and Nate Schrock's Buick had stopped at a fast-food restaurant, two gas stations, and a rest area along the way, her hips ached from the hours spent in the truck's cab. She was ready for this trip to end. "How much farther?"

Anthony sent a grin in her direction. "Not much. The exit for Lansing is just ahead, and according to the directions Brooke sent, it's only sixteen miles to Lansing once we hit the exit. Eagle Creek is only three miles north of Lansing."

"Lansing . . ." Marty pressed her memory. "Is that the town where Brooke said we'd shop for groceries?"

"It's also where we'll attend church." Anthony glanced in the rearview mirror, then aimed his gaze out the front window. "Depending on traffic, and if no one needs to stop for gas or use a restroom, we should pull into Eagle Creek in half an hour."

Marty squinted at her wristwatch. "So . . . around four thirty."

"Four thirty Indiana time. Remember, Kansas is different."

"That's right." She pulled the crown and twisted, winding the minute hand backward a full rotation. Anticipation quivered through her frame. "Three thirty, then. I wonder if Brooke will be there to greet us."

Anthony slid his hand from the armrest to her wrist and gave it a light squeeze. "Stop worrying. She'll be there."

Marty hoped so. She'd received a telephone call from Brooke yesterday afternoon, and although she sounded more like herself than she had on Monday, she mentioned a Friday doctor's appointment that might run late. But she hadn't answered Marty's query about what kind of appointment. Brooke had never wanted to talk much about her personal life. Apparently that hadn't changed.

She tried to imagine what Brooke would look like now. In her mind's eye she envisioned the teenage Brooke—a tall, slender girl with thick, straight, waist-length brown hair. Hair that was usually tousled as if she'd forgotten to brush it. Marty always envied Brooke's green eyes with their flecks of gold. Those eyes always seemed wary, and her full pink lips rarely smiled. Unless the two of them were alone. Somehow Marty always managed to coax a smile and sometimes a genuine laugh from her friend.

Such an unusual pair they'd made, Marty in her prim dresses and simple braids, Brooke in her T-shirts and overalls and uncombed hair. Their outsides hadn't mattered to them. They had a heart connection Marty still couldn't explain. She only knew it was there and had somehow remained strong despite time and distance. Mother had been apprehensive when Marty and Brooke formed a friendship, but later—much later, after Marty was finished with her education—Mother referred to Brooke as Marty's soul sister. The title fit. Marty could hardly wait to see Brooke in person, to pick up where they'd left off over twenty years ago, to laugh and talk late into the night, the way soul sisters should.

She placed her hands on the dash and peered ahead, eagerness making her insides dance. "Can we hurry, please?"

He chuckled. "Marty, I'm driving as fast as I can. Any faster and the trailer fishtails too much."

She sagged against the seat. "I'm sorry for being impatient. I guess I'm not a very good traveler."

"I think you're just excited about seeing your friend again after so many years."

She gawked at him, her mouth falling open. Maybe her husband knew her better than she'd given him credit for.

He grinned. "Not much longer now. Maybe twenty minutes. Can you wait that long?"

She grinned back. "If I have to."

He laughed.

She turned her gaze to the window and willed the miles to pass quickly.

They drove straight through the town of Lansing and continued north on a curving two-lane highway lined by thick trees. After only a few miles, Anthony reduced his speed and searched the right-hand side of the road. "Watch for a sign or a break in the trees. The turnoff should be close."

Marty sat on the edge of the seat and scanned the area. Despite her careful attention, they drove past the turnoff before she realized it was there.

Anthony rolled to a stop alongside the road, put the truck in park, and hopped out. Nate's car and Myron's truck stopped, too, and the drivers joined Anthony on the grassy shoulder. Marty turned sideways in the seat and watched the men engage in what her father would have called a powwow—gesturing hands, serious expressions, and a bit of pacing. Anthony pointed to the dirt road they'd passed, Myron nodded, and the three separated and returned to their vehicles.

She faced forward again as Anthony climbed in behind the wheel. "Is it the right spot?"

"There's no sign, but it's the right distance from Lansing. Myron's gonna drive in a ways, make sure it's where we're supposed to go before I take the trailer in. There might not be a place to turn around if it proves to be wrong."

Marty chewed her thumbnail and watched the opening in the trees. Several minutes crept by before Myron's truck reappeared. He drove up beside Anthony, and Myron's passenger, Lucas, rolled down his window. Anthony did the same.

"This's gotta be it." Lucas's tone and expression held the same excitement Marty felt. "A mile in, there's a huge iron gate standing open and a row of trailer houses inside to the left and a street of old rock buildings about a hundred yards beyond the gate."

Anthony nodded. "That sounds right."

"A fancy silver car's parked between a couple of the trailers." The young man's eyes glimmered. "You figure Miss Spalding left it for us to use?"

"I doubt it. It's probably her car."

Lucas's face fell. "Aw."

Myron punched him on the arm. "Your dad would have your hide if he found out you were driving a fancy car like that."

The younger man shrugged, grinning sheepishly.

Anthony shot a smile at Marty. "So she beat us here. You'll have your reunion soon."

16

Eagle Creek, Kansas
Marty

*M*arty sat on the edge of the seat, her hands braced on the dash, while Anthony drove slowly up the dirt road leading to Eagle Creek. Ahead, two halves of a massive black iron gate stood open, as if inviting them to enter. As Lucas had said, inside the gate a flat, grassy area that appeared to have been recently mowed stretched to the left, and four trailers—one significantly longer than the other three—formed a neat row.

Anthony pulled the truck and trailer to the edge of the road and parked on a narrow slice of grass across from the trailers. Before he shut off the ignition, Marty was opening her door and sliding out. Hot, humid air brought an immediate outbreak of perspiration. For a moment she stood beside the thick growth of bushes, willing her stiff limbs to move. When her legs were ready to cooperate, she rounded the front of the pickup. Across the street, the door to the largest trailer opened, and a reed-thin woman with short white-blond hair stepped out on the metal platform serving as a porch. Marty's pulse gave a leap—Brooke!

Marty started to cross the street, but Myron's and Nate's vehicles rolled past, blocking her passage. She waved away the dust that filled the air, coughing, and waited until the men parked in front of Anthony's truck. Then she darted through the lingering dust cloud to the grass on the opposite side. Brooke descended the platform and met her halfway. Both women broke into laughter and embraced. They pulled back, smiled for several seconds into each other's face, then laughed and hugged again.

Brooke pulled loose and caught Marty's hands. She swung them slightly and looked Marty up and down. "Look at you, still so proper and ladylike."

Marty gave Brooke's white-and-pink-plaid blouse and white denim skirt an examination. "Where are your overalls?"

Brooke laughed. She ran her fingers through her hair, shaping the streaky bangs into a soft poof above her arched eyebrows. "Oh, I got rid of those awful things years ago." As Brooke lowered her hand, Marty noticed a small purplish bruise on its back. Apprehension immediately pricked.

"Brooke, what—"

Anthony, the other men, and Nate's young wife ambled up. Anthony extended his hand to Brooke. "Miss Spalding, it's nice to meet you."

Brooke put her hands on her hips and tipped her head. "What did you call me?"

Anthony chuckled, ducking his chin for a moment. "Excuse me. Brooke."

She grinned. "That's better." She shook Anthony's hand. "It's great to meet Marty's husband. And please introduce me to your crew."

Anthony introduced each of the workers, and Brooke shook their hands in turn. She took Charlotte Schrock's hand last and cradled it between her palms. "I'm especially glad you were able to come. Marty will appreciate some help keeping these fellows fed, and I'd hate to be responsible for splitting up a pair of newlyweds."

Charlotte blushed. "Thank you. It's nice to meet you." When Brooke released her hand, Charlotte pressed close to Nate, the way Marty had always pressed close to Anthony in the early months of their marriage. Would they rediscover that closeness, now that they were away from Pine Hill?

Brooke swiped her hand across her brow. "I'm sure you have things to unpack, but how about taking a few minutes to relax in the trailers after your long drive? The AC is running in each of them, and I imagine it'll feel good, considering the temperature out here today."

The men looked expectantly at Anthony. He grimaced. "If it's all right with you, after sitting so long, I'd rather walk around a little bit. How about we take a tour of the buildings and get an idea of what kind of work needs to be done? There'll still be plenty of daylight left to unpack and get settled."

"That's fine for you," Brooke said, slipping her arm around Marty's waist, "but I've seen the buildings and I'd rather have time with this friend of mine. So you all go ahead. Marty and I will be inside if you need us." Then she gave a jolt and shifted her gaze to Charlotte. "Do you want to come in with us, too?"

Charlotte hunched her shoulders, making the black ribbons from her cap scrunch up. "I think I'd rather go explore."

Nate frowned down at her. "Are you sure? It's awful hot and dusty."

She nodded. "I've been sitting for a long time, so I'd rather walk around. Besides"—her grin turned bashful—"I think Marty and Brooke would like to talk alone."

Such a kind, unselfish thing to say. Marty warmed to the younger woman.

"All right, then." Did relief underscore Brooke's tone? "You all have fun exploring. Marty, let me show you your home away from home." She looped her arm through Marty's elbow and guided her to the trailer while the others set off up the street toward the old rock buildings. "Did you know you can buy fully furnished trailers? Sure makes it easy. I did upgrade the mattresses on all the beds—who wants to sleep on a slab of foam?—and bought a bigger table for your kitchen. I figured you'd like to get everyone around the table at once."

Inside the trailer, Brooke hugged Marty again. "It's so good to see you. I can't believe how little you've changed. Except for these. They used to be white, as I recall." She lightly tugged one of the black ribbons trailing from Marty's cap.

Marty smoothed the ribbon across her bodice. "Black is for married ladies." She shook her head, taking in Brooke's short hair, impeccable makeup, and casual yet somehow classy outfit. "You've sure changed. A lot."

"For the better, I hope."

Marty met Brooke's gaze. "You're beautiful."

"Aw, thanks." Brooke finger-combed her bangs again and shrugged. "I guess I don't mind that I've changed. I was always such a ragamuffin, you know? I've worked really hard to be a lady and remove every trace of the trailer-trash kid I was." She laughed and held her arms wide. "And here I am, sticking you in a trailer house for the next year and a half."

Marty sent a quick glance around the space. The mobile home was much smaller than her house, but everything from the light fixtures to the appliances to the furniture looked shiny, clean, and new. "There's nothing trashy about this. Thanks for providing such a nice place for us."

"You're welcome. It's the least I could do." Brooke crossed to the counter peninsula that separated the kitchen from the living room and leaned against it. Her eyes shimmered with unshed tears. "Marty, thanks for coming. It . . . it's really good to see you again." Her voice broke.

Marty closed the distance between them and caught hold of Brooke's hand. She turned it palm down and brushed her finger across the bruise and the nearly invisible scab in its center. "Does your happiness to see me have anything to do with this?"

Brooke pulled her hand free and folded her arms across her chest. "We don't have to talk about that right now."

Marty touched Brooke's arm. "I'd like to. You said you had a doctor's appointment this morning. That spot's probably from a needle. An IV needle?"

Brooke turned her face aside, but she nodded.

"What are they testing for?"

For several seconds Brooke didn't answer. Her lips quivered and she blinked rapidly. Then she jerked her head and met Marty's gaze. She lifted her chin and shrugged. "Most of the testing's already been done. They've confirmed I have cancer."

Her final word struck Marty like a blow from a fist. She staggered sideways two steps and collided with a tall barstool tucked under the peninsula. She gripped its black metal backrest and gaped at Brooke, speechless.

Regret flooded Brooke's features. "I shouldn't have blurted it out that way. Come here." She took hold of Marty's elbow and guided her to the overstuffed tan love seat on the opposite side of the trailer. They sank down side by side, and Brooke loosely gripped Marty's hands. "Before I say anything else, I need you to promise you won't cry. Because if you do, I'll probably join you—out of sympathy for you, you know—and wash off my makeup. I don't want black rivulets of mascara running down my cheeks. Not at all attractive. So promise, no tears."

Marty bit the inside of her lower lip and forced a nod.

A wobbly smile formed on Brooke's face. "Remember I told you in my last letter that I'd been feeling kind of under the weather? Tired and achy?"

Marty swallowed and nodded.

"Well, it turns out I have ovarian cancer. Stage two, the doctor told me, which means it's moved to places beyond my ovaries. This morning I saw the oncologist and had a full-body CT scan." She coughed a harsh laugh. "Ever been sent by inches through a giant doughnut? It's quite an experience."

Brooke's flippant tone pierced Marty more deeply than wails would have. She was trying so hard to be brave, but inside she had to be frightened half to death. The way Marty was.

"They want to make sure the cancer's only here"—she ran her hand across her abdomen—"and not up here, too." She touched her chest. Her fingers were trembling. She linked her hands as if in prayer and pressed them into her lap. "Once they know for sure, I'll have the privilege of my very first surgery." She made a horrible face. "It'll probably leave a scar. No more bikinis for me."

Marty swallowed, licked her dry lips, and forced herself to speak evenly. "And after the surgery you'll be . . . all right?"

Brooke splayed her hands in front of her and seemed to admire her bold pink nail polish. "My doctor said I'll need chemo. Maybe radiation, too. She said my chances for survival depend on frying every little cancer cell in my body." She dropped her hands to her lap and rolled her eyes. "I think the worst part will be losing my hair. I'm pretty fond of my hair. I don't think I could rock the bald look like Demi Moore or Sigourney Weaver." She angled her head and squinted at Marty. "So . . . do you want to go wig shopping with me?"

Marty recognized the ploy. Even when they were children, Brooke had chosen lighthearted topics to steer attention away from the serious issues in her life. But they weren't children anymore, and Marty wouldn't pretend a lackadaisical attitude she didn't feel.

She grabbed her friend's hands. "It's okay to say you're scared. I won't think any less of you."

Brooke went motionless. Her eyes bored into Marty's with intensity. She sat so still and unmoving it seemed she'd turned to stone. Then her cinnamon-scented breath whooshed past Marty's cheek, and her hands curled into fists within Marty's grasp. "I've never been so frightened in my life." Her tone was flat, unemotional, but the fear in her wide-eyed gaze raised a wave of sympathy that roared through Marty's chest.

Marty wrapped her arms around Brooke. She didn't reciprocate, but she rested her cheek on Marty's shoulder and accepted the embrace. Marty rubbed Brooke's taut back. "I'll do everything I can to help. Stay with you in the hospital. Take you to appointments. Take you wig shopping."

A half sob, half laugh briefly shuddered Brooke's frame.

Marty tightened her grip. "Whatever you need, I'll do it. I'm here for you."

Brooke sniffed, her head still nestled on Marty's shoulder. "I wanted you to be here for Anthony. To rebuild the happy marriage you once had.

I didn't want—" She sat up abruptly, dislodging Marty's arms. "I'll take your help because, quite frankly, I don't know anyone else who would care enough to help. Sad, isn't it? I've lived in the Kansas City area since I graduated from college. I have countless contacts—loan officers, contracting specialists, laborers—but I can't name one single solitary person who would care enough to offer what you just did."

Marty worried she might regret asking, but she had to know. "Have you told your mother?" No matter how self-centered Jeralyn Spalding had been during Brooke's growing-up years, surely she'd want to help her daughter navigate such difficult waters.

Brooke waved her hand. "Why bother? I haven't seen her in over four years. I went back to Newton for Christmas to surprise her, took her a commissioned stained-glass piece—a butterfly hovering next to a delphinium. Did you know the meaning of a delphinium is remembrance?"

Marty shook her head.

"Well, it is. I specifically chose that flower to let her know I'd been thinking about her. I hoped it might mean something to her." Brooke snorted. Her expression turned cold. "She gave me something to remember. She threw the gift at me, accused me of thinking myself too good for her, said I only came back so I could show off. She told me to leave and never bother coming home again. I was more than happy to accommodate her. I have no intention of letting her know about this. The only thing she'd care about is if she's listed as the beneficiary on my million-dollar life insurance policy." She raised one eyebrow. "For the record, she is not."

Marty wanted to encourage Brooke to reconsider letting her mother know, but the fury in Brooke's eyes told her now wasn't the time. She swallowed and took Brooke's hand again. It felt icy. She gently rubbed it between her palms. "When will you know if the cancer has spread to . . ." She glanced at Brooke's chest.

"Early next week. Once they have that information, the oncologist will schedule surgery." A weak smile lifted the corners of Brooke's pink-stained lips. "I'm glad I have a reliable team of workers on board. I probably won't be in any condition to crack the whip over them. I'll leave that to your Anthony."

Your Anthony . . . Why did the phrase make Marty want to cry? Maybe because there wasn't anyone Brooke could call hers. "He's very reliable, and he'll do everything he can to help you in your battle."

"I know he will, but I still—" Brooke clamped her lips tight.

Marty gave her hand a squeeze. "I still . . . what?"

Brooke sighed, wafting the scent of cinnamon again. "I wish I didn't have to depend on him to take charge. I've always been in the midst of every project, you know? I've had great help. No way I could revitalize the buildings all by myself. But I'm always very involved, arranging deliveries of materials and organizing the schedules. More than once I've even plopped on a hard hat and grabbed a hammer or paintbrush."

Marty tried to envision Brooke in a hard hat. The image wouldn't jell.

"If he takes all my responsibilities, he won't be as available to you. I'm sorry about that. It isn't what I intended."

"I know. But you know what?" Marty chose her words carefully, aware of Brooke's fragile emotional state despite the strength she was exhibiting. "Anthony would say the cancer didn't take God by surprise. That our being here right now serves a purpose other than rebuilding the town." She heard herself, heard the certainty in her tone, but underneath she wondered if she was feeding her friend a lie. She hoped Brooke didn't suspect her doubt. "Anthony always says we make our plans but God directs our steps and when we follow where He leads, things fall into place." She held her breath for a moment, struggling to believe. "So don't worry about Anthony and me. Think about getting well. All right?"

17

Anthony

$\mathcal{N}$ate nudged Anthony on the arm. "The trucks and trailer still need to be unloaded. Should we carry stuff in now?"

Anthony barely glanced at the younger man. Each of the old buildings on Eagle Creek's main street had a certain charm, but the decorative stone headers above the arched windows on the second story of the limestone building that had once served as Eagle Creek's bank and community center intrigued him the most. The rosettes and raised swirls weren't from a poured concrete form but were hand-carved into the slabs of limestone. How had the carver made them all identical?

The others waited, shifting in place. Nate cleared his throat. "Anthony?"

Anthony nodded, not taking his gaze from the rosettes. "Yeah. Yeah, we should."

"You coming, too?"

"I'll be there in a minute or so. I'm trying to . . ." He squinted against the sun, wishing he could climb the wall and examine the decorations more closely.

Nate waved his arm. "C'mon, gang. Let's start unpacking." Charlotte, Todd, Myron, and Lucas ambled off with Nate, arguing good-naturedly about which mobile home they'd claim—a silly argument since the three set aside for the team were exactly the same in size and appearance.

Alone now, Anthony shuffled backward until he reached the middle of the wide street. From this angle, he counted a dozen places where the carvings were chipped and crumbling. A result of time and erosion? Maybe from vandals throwing stones at the windows. The windows were all new, probably done at Brooke's instruction, but even with shiny glass panes, the misshapen carvings made the building look scruffy. It deserved to look majestic. The way it'd looked in 1872, when artisans finished applying their chisels and hammers.

Hands on his hips, he contemplated his choices. He could either carefully chisel away the remaining parts of the carvings, giving the window casings a smooth front, or he could fill in the missing pieces and restore them to their original appearance. He preferred to restore rather than remove. He'd repaired chipped plaster moldings in the past, but he'd never worked with stone. Before he went to bed, he'd do some research on the computer—if Brooke had established an internet connection out here—and find out what kind of materials were needed for stone repair.

Not for the first time, he sent up a prayer of gratitude that the fellowship elders had given business owners permission to use computers and telephones for work-related purposes. He could compete with secular companies because he had access to the same resources they did. He pulled out the small pad of paper and pencil he always carried in his pocket and jotted down topics for research. Looking at the list, he grimaced. Before he got too far ahead of himself, he should ask Brooke what she preferred. She was the boss of this project, not him. That'd be hard to remember. He'd been in charge for lots of years, and he hadn't been as excited about putting his hands to a project since the very early days of his construction company.

He jammed the pad into his pocket, then glanced at his watch and gave a start. Almost five thirty already? Where had the last hour gone? He better get the trailer unloaded. Full dark didn't come until after nine, but the tall trees surrounding the little town would block the setting sun, making it get dark a lot earlier than on the open prairie. He broke into a jog and closed the distance between the main-street buildings and the temporary housing area inside the fence.

Someone had closed the gate, and Brooke's fancy car was gone. The back of Myron's truck was almost empty, and the doors to Anthony's trailer gaped open, proving the others had been industrious. The sound of voices, scuffs, and bumps drifted from inside the trio of matching trailers—getting-settled noises. He glanced into the back of his truck. It didn't look like Marty'd taken anything in. Since Brooke had left, he wouldn't feel guilty about asking Marty to help him.

He climbed the steps of the black metal landing that served as a porch to their temporary home and pushed the door open. He stuck his head in. "Marty?" He searched left, right, and left again, then released a short, self-conscious laugh. She sat slouched low in an oversized chair near the front door, staring out the window. He'd looked at her and missed seeing her.

"Marty, wanna come give me a hand?"

She jerked and peered at him around the chair's winged back. "What?"

He grinned. She must've dozed off. "Come help me carry in the groceries and kitchen things we brought. You probably ought to set out some supper. It's closing in on six."

She stared at him but didn't get up. Didn't change expression. Didn't even act like she understood what he'd said.

With a frown, he went in and stood in front of her. "Are you all right?" She pointed to the matching chair on the other side of a round table. Even though he didn't have time to sit, he settled on the edge of the cushioned seat, keeping his gaze fixed on her somber face. "Okay. What's going on?"

"I know we'd talked about using the second bedroom for your office and my sewing space, but I want to let it be a bedroom."

He shook his head and pretended to ream his ear with one finger. They had to discuss this now? "Why?"

"For Brooke."

He knew Marty was excited to see her childhood friend again. She'd written letters to her every week for their entire marriage. Sure, she'd want time with Brooke now that they were only an hour apart, but how would he and Marty have any privacy at all if Brooke moved in with them? He sighed and propped his elbows on his knees. "If Brooke wants to be out here while we work, why not ask her to get her own trailer? Seems like that'd be better for . . . everyone."

"She didn't ask. I'm asking."

He held his hands wide. "But why?"

She made a terrible face, the kind of face he'd make if he drank spoiled milk. "The doctor appointment she had this morning . . . is because she has cancer."

Anthony couldn't have been more surprised if she'd shot him in the face with a rubber band. He flopped back into the chair, and his ears began to ring. He'd known only two other people who'd been diagnosed with cancer—a great-uncle and the cousin of one of their fellowship members. One had it in his bones, the other in his brain. In both cases, they'd faced lengthy battles and eventually lost. "Is . . . is it bad?"

"She said if it hasn't spread beyond her abdomen, then there's a seventy percent chance she'll beat it. For at least five years."

Anthony sat up again and reached for Marty's hand. "I'm sorry." She kept her hands tightly clamped together and didn't reach back.

"She doesn't know yet if it's spread. She should know by the end of next week. No matter if it's spread or not, she knows for sure they'll do surgery to take out all the parts of her that would let her be a mother."

He looked aside, heat filling his face. He shouldn't know something so intimate about a woman who wasn't family. He also didn't want to see the pain in Marty's eyes. She had the parts she needed to have a baby. He'd never get over the guilt of not being able to plant the seed in her womb. He swallowed and repeated, "I'm sorry." Ridiculous words. They didn't help anyone. Not Brooke, and not Marty.

"She'll need care, Anthony, and she doesn't have anybody to help her. I could stay at her town house. She has extra bedrooms. But then I wouldn't be here to cook for everybody and . . . and . . ."

. . . *fix their marriage.* He finished the sentence in his head, but he didn't say it out loud, either. He rubbed his jaw with his knuckles and looked at her again. "If you want to stay with Brooke, Charlotte could probably cook for all of us."

Marty shook her head so hard the ribbons on her cap flopped across her shoulders. "Even more than she's scared of the cancer, she's scared I'll spend more time with her than with you. She'd never agree to me moving in with her. She'll let me take her to her appointments—she said she would because there isn't anyone else she can depend on—but she'll stay alone before she'll let me stay with her. But she shouldn't be left alone. Not after the surgery, and not while she's getting chemotherapy. She'll be weak and sick."

Anthony grimaced. "I don't know, Marty . . ."

"It wouldn't be right away. They haven't scheduled her surgery yet. And she isn't sure what will happen after the surgery, if she'll have radiation or chemotherapy or both, or how long she'll have to go in for treatments. She said she'll know more after the oncologist calls." Her light blue eyes flooded with tears. "I know it'd be inconvenient to have her with us."

Inconvenient didn't come close to the way he saw it.

"But please say yes. She needs me. She needs us."

Anthony tried to ignore the begging in her eyes. He'd seen the expression before. In their bedroom, when the midwife said their baby was gone. In the doctor's office, when they'd been told there was no hope of them conceiving another child. From across the table, when he knew she was thinking about what they'd been denied and was wishing things were different. He couldn't bring back their lost baby. He couldn't change the damage the mumps had caused. He couldn't take away Brooke's cancer. But if agreeing to have Brooke stay with them would satisfy at least one of Marty's wishes, he could set aside his discomfort.

He nodded. "All right. We'll find someplace else for my desk and your sewing machine."

With a little sob, she lunged out of her chair and fell against him. She buried her face in the curve of his neck. He wrapped his arms around her and drew her onto his lap.

"Thank you."

He barely heard her with her voice muffled against his collar. He pressed his lips against her hair, didn't answer, and just held her. He wished it hadn't taken Brooke's cancer and need for help to bring Marty so close again.

Brooke

Midmorning on the Fourth of July, Brooke drove out to Spalding. She hadn't intended to visit until she'd heard from the oncologist about surgery. The Mennonites needed to settle in, and she'd only distract Marty. But restlessness and, admittedly, selfishness pushed her out the door. She needed a distraction.

She pulled up to the keypad outside the gate and lowered her window. Dust filtered in, and she tried to hold her breath while she poked the code into the pad. The winged halves folded inward on well-oiled hinges, and she closed her window, releasing her held breath. She scowled at the fine coating of dust now on the dash and her clothes. She needed to hurry the surfacing contractor out here to pave these roads or at least put gravel down until he had time in his schedule to pour and stamp the tinted concrete streets that would mimic brick streets from long ago. There were so many things vying for her attention. How would she keep up when chemotherapy made her sick and tired and weak?

Gritting her teeth, she bit back a huff. Hadn't she decided to take one day and not think about cancer? She slammed the door on worry and drove through the opening. As she rolled to a stop on the grassy area opposite the trailers, a man wearing blue jeans, a blue shirt, and a dark blue ball cap climbed down a ladder that was leaning against the porch roof of the row of buildings on the east side of the street and ran behind one of the limestone structures on the west side, stirring dust with his boots.

She shut off the ignition and got out, her gaze fixed on the spot where the man had slipped from sight. Who was prowling around the buildings? And what was that sound? She'd expect the pops and booms of fireworks. After all, it was Independence Day. Which was why she'd brought hot dogs, burgers, and all the accompaniments to share with Marty, Anthony, and the team of workers. But if she wasn't mistaken, the ringing taps came from hammers on nails and not firecrackers. Were the men working on a national holiday?

"Hello, Miss Spalding!"

The cheerful female voice came from Brooke's left. She turned and spotted Charlotte, the young wife of one of Anthony's team members, in the patch of grass between the first two trailers. Someone had strung lines from trailer to trailer, and shirts similar to the one she'd seen on the man running across the street flapped in the morning wind. As Brooke crossed the road, the woman removed another shirt from a basket near her feet and gave it several flicks that made the fabric snap. The fresh scent of soap met Brooke's nose. A pleasant aroma that never emanated from her dry-cleaned suits.

Brooke stopped next to the line and watched Charlotte pin the shirt next to the others. "Is your dryer not working?" Granted, she hadn't paid for top-of-the-line machines. She'd assumed even low-budget ones would last the length of time they'd be needed. If the dryer was already out of commission, she'd have plenty to say to the salesman.

Charlotte smiled. "Oh, I'm sure it's fine. I didn't try to use it. The sun and wind dry things quickly, and clothes smell so good when they come in." The breeze tossed the black ribbons from her cap across her cheek, and she tucked them into the neckline of her mint-green-and-white-checkered dress. "I hope it's okay that we hung up the lines. Anthony and Nate had to screw eyebolts through the siding into the studs so the lines would hold. Nate put some caulking around the bolts, and he'll be sure and fill the holes and paint over them when we're done so no moisture gets in and ruins the siding."

These people were nothing if not conscientious. "It's fine. If I'd known you preferred the, er, wind-and-sun method for drying clothes, I would've had a clothesline set up out here." Did somebody still manufacture clotheslines? "But I told you to make yourselves at home. I trust you not to tear things up."

Charlotte beamed. "Thank you."

More banging drifted from the main-street buildings. Brooke frowned. "Are the men working?"

"Yes, ma'am. Anthony said they needed to repair the roofs first so the buildings would be protected from the weather."

Sound thinking, but Brooke still didn't understand something. "Why are they working on the Fourth? It's a federal holiday."

Charlotte scooped up the empty basket and balanced it against her stomach. "Our fellowship doesn't celebrate holidays that relate to war."

Ah. She should've known. "Hmm. Would you folks consider a cookout a holiday celebration or just a picnic?"

Charlotte shrugged. "I don't know, but you could ask Marty. She's inside the trailer."

Brooke thanked Charlotte, then ducked under the damp clothes and crossed across the grass to the trailer's back door. A set of wooden risers marched upward, and her back twinged as she climbed them. Pressing one hand to her lower back, she knocked on the siding with the other. Within seconds the door popped open and Marty greeted her with a worried frown.

"Brooke . . . Have you heard from the oncologist?"

Brooke stepped onto the linoleum kitchen floor and closed the door behind her. "No, not yet. I came out to—" She gave a start. The windows were open, and a fan whirred from the middle of the living room floor. The

AC must be on the fritz, because no one in their right mind would choose a fan over AC in July in Kansas. "Do I need to get an air-conditioning repairman out here?"

Marty guided her to the chair at the head of the long dining table. "No, it works fine, but I really don't need it until noon or so. The shade trees keep things cool enough until the sun's directly overhead." She wrinkled her nose. "Anthony and I talked it over, and since you're paying the utility bill, we want to keep the cost as reasonable as possible. So even though we love the convenience of air conditioning, we promise not to overuse it."

Brooke shook her head, smiling. "Marty, I appreciate your attempt to be frugal, but it's actually harder on the unit to repeatedly cool a hot house than to maintain an even temperature. It'd cost less to keep it running twenty-four hours a day."

Her eyes widened. "It would?"

Brooke nodded.

Marty stared at Brooke, unmoving, as if trying to decide if she was being honest.

Brooke put up her hand, Scout style. "I kid you not." She shrugged. "But if you're really concerned about it and want to save a few pennies, you can close the vents in the second bedroom and bathroom and only cool the parts of the house you're using."

Marty scrunched her lips, as if holding back a mighty sneeze.

"Of course, that's assuming you aren't making use of the second bedroom." Brooke searched her friend's expression for a hint of what she was thinking. She hoped Marty and Anthony hadn't laid claim to separate bedrooms. How could they work out their differences if they kept themselves on opposite sides of the house?

Marty sighed. "I'll tell Anthony what you said." She rose. "Can I get you some tea? Lemonade? Ice water? Then you can tell me what brought you out."

"Lemonade, please. And I came out to treat you all to a cookout. The trunk of my car is packed with a cooler full of picnic foods, two charcoal grills that need to be put together—I presume you have the necessary tools—and bags of charcoal briquettes. Does a cookout sound good?"

Marty carried two sweaty glasses to the table and sat again. "It does. Thank you."

"You're welcome." Brooke took a sip. "I figure before long I won't much feel like picnics, so I better grab the chance while I can, right?"

Marty had lifted the glass to her lips, but she lowered it to the table without taking a drink. "Speaking of you not feeling well, there's something I want to talk to you about. And I might as well tell you straight out, I won't take no for an answer."

18

Marty

*N*o. And that's final."

Marty hadn't expected Brooke to agree. In fact, she'd anticipated more of a fight from Brooke than she had from Anthony. She folded
her arms over her chest and gathered every bit of stubbornness she possessed. "Then I'll pack a bag and move into your town house with you."

Brooke's mouth dropped open.

Marty maintained a stern expression while her insides churned in
uncertainty. Should she state a condition she knew she wouldn't carry
through? Did God view it the same as lying? But how else would she convince Brooke to stay with them? She gave a firm nod. "Yes, you heard me.
You move here, or I move there. But you won't be left unattended. And
that, my friend, is final."

Brooke sat for a few more seconds with a look of surprise rounding her
eyes, and then her chin began to quiver. She stretched her hands toward
Marty, and Marty took hold and squeezed, the gesture meant to plead and
insist at the same time.

"Marty, what you said means a lot." The tears moistening Brooke's
green eyes proved how much she'd been touched. Marty blinked back
tears, too. "Please don't think I'm not appreciative, but it wouldn't be fair
to you or Anthony for me to move in here."

Marty started to speak, but Brooke broke loose and put her hand in
the air.

"And before you give your ultimatum again, I will not allow you to
leave him to take care of me. So that's out." She picked up her glass and

took a long, slow draw of the lemonade with her eyes closed. When she set the glass down, a mix of resolve and resignation played on her expression.

"I actually considered hiring a private nurse to stay with me during the months of treatment because everything I've read indicates I'm going to need someone close at hand." Brooke used her fingernail and made a pattern of overlapping circles in the condensation on her glass. "But honestly, the thought of getting so close and personal with a stranger doesn't appeal to me. I'd rather have someone I know and trust." Her gaze met Marty's for a brief second and then returned to the circles. "I guess that's you."

Marty's heart gave a leap. "Then you'll accept? You'll move into the spare bedroom?"

Brooke set the glass aside. "No. You and Anthony need your privacy. Frankly, I need mine, too. There's no sense in us intruding on each other's space 24/7. But"—her fine eyebrows came down—"what if I had another trailer brought in and set up next to yours? Then you'd be close by if I needed something, but I wouldn't be underfoot."

Anthony had suggested the same thing, which made Marty wonder if God was nudging them in that direction. "Are you sure you want the expense of another trailer? You've already bought four of them."

Brooke waved her hand as if shooing away Marty's concerns. "After four, one more isn't a big deal. The manufacturer gave me a package price on these. I suspect he'll offer the same discount on a fifth. Even if he doesn't, they'll get plenty of use after the resort opens. I always intended to leave them here and rent them out to vacationers, so I'll get a return on my investment."

Her forehead pinched, and she drummed her fingers on the table. "If I use the trailer as an office, it'll be a tax write-off. Of course, I'd need to get someone out here pretty quickly to lay the foundation and secure tie-downs, add another water line, and get power hooked up. But since I've already got a team coming to pour a patio behind the trailers, it wouldn't be a stretch to have them ready the ground for another mobile home.

Especially if it's one of the smaller models, maybe fourteen-by-forty-five feet."

Marty got the impression Brooke had forgotten anyone else was in the room. She gazed at her friend, awed by the ease with which she planned her next moves, as if she didn't need to consciously think but only let the ideas emerge.

"Being on-site would allow me to oversee the project . . . answer questions as they come up and so forth." Brooke turned a speculative look on Marty. "Plus, it would make things easier for you to get me to and from appointments if you didn't have to come all the way into the city and pick me up at the town house. So having a base here on the property makes sense from both a business and personal viewpoint."

Marty shook her head.

"Are you saying it doesn't make sense?"

"No, I'm trying to figure out . . . How did you do that?"

Brooke frowned. "Do what?"

"Think that all out. Put all the details in place."

Brooke laughed. "Well, I hope you wrote it all down, because if chemo makes my brain as foggy as the articles I've been reading warn it will, I might not remember the plans when they're needed."

Marty put her hand over Brooke's. "I'll help you remember if it's necessary. But I'm glad we found a compromise. I feel a lot better knowing I'll be able to give you whatever help you need."

Brooke pointed at Marty. "As long as you don't get so focused on helping me that you forget to help yourself. This is supposed to be a bonding time for you and Anthony. So I'm not going to put up with you hanging out at my place all the time. I'll accept your help, but not your hovering." She stuck out her hand. "Deal?"

Marty chewed the inside of her cheek. If she gave her word, she'd want to keep it.

"C'mon, Marty." Brooke bobbed her hand.

"Define *hovering*."

Brooke rolled her eyes. "You aren't stupid. You know what I mean."

Yes, she did. Marty sighed. "All right. No hovering." She gave Brooke a solid handshake.

Brooke rose. "Good. It's settled. Now, let's get my trunk emptied. We'll put the grills together and—"

"We?" Marty raised her eyebrows and pointed at herself and then Brooke. "You mean . . . us?"

Brooke gave her a puzzled look. "Yes. What's the problem?"

Marty held her hands outward. "Anthony always puts everything together." To her surprise, Brooke burst out laughing. Marty scowled. "What's so funny?"

Brooke's laughter died, but her eyes continued to sparkle. "I wish you could've seen the look on your face. It was the same face you made when I asked you to go skinny-dipping in the Arkansas River. The summer between fifth and sixth grades, remember?"

Heat filled Marty's cheeks. Brooke had dog-paddled in the shallow river, her white rump shining in the sun, while Marty sat on the bank and dipped her feet, the only thing she'd bare in front of someone else.

Marty carried their glasses to the sink. "I remember you getting sunburned in places most people don't. But that doesn't explain why you laughed."

Brooke crossed to the sink and touched Marty's arm. "Half the things we buy these days come unassembled. Have you really never put a desk or a table or a bicycle or . . . or anything together?"

"No, because Anthony takes care of it. He has the tools and the know-how and . . . and . . . and it's something the man does." Defensiveness sharpened her tone. Defensiveness brought on by embarrassment. But why did it embarrass her to acknowledge she left such tasks to her husband? She'd never been ashamed of it before.

Brooke shook her head slowly, and all humor faded from her

expression. "Well, I've never had a husband, so I've become self-sufficient. There've been a few times over the years when I wanted someone's help with something, but I can't honestly say I ever needed it." She sighed. "Until now." She put her hand on Marty's shoulder. "I'm pretty sure I'm not going to be the easiest person in the world to take care of. If you want to back out, now's your chance. I won't hold it against you."

Marty wrapped Brooke in an impulsive hug. "I won't back out. I want to help you. Even if you get ornery." An odd thought swooped through her mind. Would she be available to care for Brooke if she had the responsibility of children?

Brooke laughed again and stepped from Marty's embrace. "Betcha before this is over I'll get you to say 'leapin' lizards' in aggravation at least once."

Marty forced a weak laugh, still a little rattled by where her mind had drifted.

Brooke headed for the back door and aimed an impish grin over her shoulder. "Help me with the grills, huh? Let's surprise your husband with our ability to take care of something on our own."

Brooke

By utilizing the hex keys and ridiculously tiny wrench that came with the grills, Brooke and Marty managed to put both of them together in a little more than an hour. Brooke probably could have done it in half the time if Marty hadn't kept getting her fingers in the way, but the proud expression of accomplishment on her friend's face made it worth the sweat-matted hair and the throb in her lower back from kneeling so long out under the summer sun.

Brooke decided to set the grills side by side close to Marty's back door, where the grass had been flattened somewhat by the couple's coming and going. The grills wobbled a bit on their trio of flimsy legs, but they'd last for a few uses. At least until the outdoor fireplaces were built.

She gestured to indicate the stretch of ground behind the three shorter mobile homes. "By the end of the month, there'll be a stamped concrete patio out here with stone fireplaces at both ends, a fire pit in the middle, and a pair of pergolas with lattice tops to provide a little bit of shade." She grinned. "It'll mean less mowing, because this patio is going to eat up a good section of the yard here."

The acidic taste she'd come to abhor flooded her mouth again, and queasiness rolled through her stomach. She guided Marty to the back steps and continued talking, using her own voice to distract her from the nausea. "Next summer I'll have the same company come out and build a second one on the other side of the business district. Then the people staying in the resort buildings will have a patio for their use, too."

Marty opened the door, and cool air eased out. Glad she'd insisted Marty turn on the AC, Brooke hurried inside and stood over the closest floor vent. She breathed a sigh of relief as the air dried her sweat-damp skin. "If you have any lemonade left, I wouldn't mind another glass."

"I'll make a fresh pitcher. We'll need it when the men come back to the house for lunch in half an hour."

Brooke settled at one end of the love seat and pulled her cell phone from her pocket. She waved the smartphone like a fan. "Do you need my help with lunch, or can I conduct a little business?"

Marty shrugged. "Charlotte will be over in a few minutes to help, so I don't really need you, but will anybody be open? Don't businesses usually close for the Fourth?"

Brooke groaned. She'd completely forgotten about the holiday. She probably wouldn't be able to reach the electrician, the plumber, or the concrete contractor until tomorrow. Her heart seemed to flutter, and more acid stung her throat—what she'd come to think of as an anxiety attack. Something she'd never experienced before the word *cancer* came into her life. Which was pretty ironic when she considered the turmoil of her childhood.

"I might as well give you a hand, then. What can I do?" She pushed off the sofa with a bounce, grimacing when pain shot through her lower back and a new wave of nausea attacked.

Marty skewered her in place with a serious look. "Nothing. As I said, Charlotte helps me prepare the meals, and this kitchen isn't big enough for more than two of us. Why don't you stretch out there on the sofa and rest?"

Brooke affected a scowl. "What do you think I am, some old lady who needs naps?"

"No, I think you're a young woman with a disease that's stealing her energy and causing her pain."

Brooke swallowed again. She wished she could dispute Marty's words, but she couldn't. Not unless she lied. Marty didn't fib to her, so she shouldn't fib to Marty. But there was no way she'd stretch out in the living room, where Marty's husband and his entire crew would see her when they came in for lunch.

Hating herself for conceding defeat, she poked her thumb in the direction of the front bedroom. The one Marty had offered to her. "Is the bed the mobile-home company provided still . . . in there?"

Sympathy flooded Marty's features. She nodded. "It's all made up, too. I wanted it to be ready for you, just in case. So get settled. I'll bring you a glass of lemonade. And you can rest."

If someone had told her a year ago she'd willingly lie down in the middle of the day, she would have laughed him out of the room. But now? Stupid cancer. Wasn't it enough that it took, as Marty said, her energy? Why did it also have to steal her pride?

She sighed. "Thanks, Marty." And she turned her back before she glimpsed pity in her friend's eyes.

19

Brooke

*B*rooke awakened and cracked her eyes open. She found herself in an unfamiliar room. Confusion struck, making her pulse leap, and then realization dawned. The bedroom in Marty and Anthony's trailer. She yawned and rolled over, grimacing as familiar pain stabbed her lower spine. She swallowed the ever-present taste of acid and lifted her cell phone to check the time. She gasped and sat up, causing another, fiercer stab. She gritted her teeth and stood, sliding her feet into the sequined flip-flops she'd left next to the bed when she lay down three hours ago. Three hours! Why had she slept so long?

She plodded up the short hallway and across the living room, pulled by the sound of women's chatter and soft laughter. When she entered the kitchen, Marty and Charlotte turned from whatever they were doing at the sink and smiled at her.

"Did you have a good nap?" Charlotte's perky tone matched her bright smile.

"Apparently so." Brooke shook her head, still shocked and more than a little embarrassed about sleeping so long. "I didn't intend to spend the whole day in bed."

Marty shrugged, her grin intact. "You must've needed it. You slept through lunch, but I saved a sandwich for you. It's in the fridge."

Brooke wasn't hungry. She couldn't honestly say she'd been hungry for weeks. But if Marty saved the sandwich for her, she'd at least make an effort to eat it. She crossed the linoleum floor, her flip-flops slapping against her heels. She opened the refrigerator and glanced at the women's backs. "What are you two doing over there? Can I help?"

Charlotte giggled. "I'd let you cut up the onions." She blinked rapidly and used her wrist to rub her nose. "They're making me cry."

Brooke carried the plate containing a sandwich under plastic wrap to the table. "Um, I think I'll pass on that."

Both of the Mennonite women laughed. Marty gave Charlotte a teasing grin. "Why do you think I assigned you the onions? Of course, you're standing so close, the fumes are getting to me, too." She sniffled, wrinkling her nose, and aimed her grin at Brooke. "When the men came in for lunch, I told them about the cookout. Anthony said to thank you for treating us."

Brooke lifted the top piece of bread and peeked at the sandwich filling. Chicken salad with walnuts, grapes, and chopped apples. Obviously homemade. "You all deserve to be treated, traveling so far to help me out. But the cookout's only half the reason I came. I hope I don't sleep through supper, because I need to discuss a few things with him."

She took a small bite. According to her research, chemotherapy could affect the taste of food. She hadn't even started chemo and already her taste buds seemed to be in mutiny. The frequent acid in the back of her throat probably didn't help.

Marty arranged sliced tomatoes on a plate already holding a pile of lettuce leaves in the center. "Then we'll call it a business cookout. Charlotte and I can get everything ready for supper. I found a notepad and pencil while you were sleeping. Why don't you write down all the things you talked about this morning so you don't forget them?"

Brooke usually put reminders in her digital notebook, which was in the hobo bag she'd brought with her, but if Marty had been kind enough to dig up a notepad from one of the boxes lining the wall in front of the electric fireplace, Brooke would use it. "Thanks."

While Marty and Charlotte chopped boiled eggs and potatoes for a big batch of potato salad, Brooke ate the entire sandwich—she didn't want to hurt her friend's feelings, and she didn't want to lose any more weight—and recorded everything she needed to accomplish in order to set up a temporary home out here. The more she thought about it, the more she liked the idea. Being around the noise and activity would provide a great diversion from the cancer treatments, and witnessing the buildings' improvements would enable her to keep an eye on things and chart the progress against her calendar.

She hadn't mentioned it to Anthony yet, not wanting to put undue pressure on him even before he started, but her investors expected the project to proceed on a strict schedule and with excellence. If they weren't satisfied with the pace or the quality of the workmanship, they had the option to pull their money at any time during the reconstruction process. She needed things to stay on schedule, too, to allow ample time to apply for licenses. The estimated—no, the obligatory—completion dates marched through her brain. Much depended on Anthony and the other contractors honoring their responsibilities.

By the time she finished writing down all it would take to ready her town house for a lengthy absence, set up another trailer, and have all her mail forwarded to this location, she'd filled three pages of the six-by-eight-inch notepad and she had a headache. Such a long list, and all leaning toward the personal, so she couldn't delegate any of it to a contractor or accountant, her usual hired assistants. Handling things on her own was the bane of being a one-woman show. She flipped through the pages, grimacing at the acid still burning in her throat. Was she taking on too much? She could throw away the entire list if she stayed in her town house. Already she felt, as her mother used to say after a night of drinking, like a wrung-out mop. Why push herself, especially knowing she'd probably feel worse after surgery and when she started chemo?

She nibbled the pencil eraser and examined the list again, searching for any task that wasn't absolutely necessary. She didn't find a thing.

Sighing, she closed her eyes. She couldn't do this. She couldn't pack up
and move out here even if it would be convenient. She didn't have the
energy, she didn't have the time, and—in complete opposition to her
normal behavior—she didn't have the motivation. Stupid cancer was
stealing all the important parts of her. And there wasn't anything she
could do to stop it.

Brooke gaped at the platter that only forty-five minutes ago had held fifteen charred patties and a dozen scorched hot dogs. Now only grease,
charcoal smudges, and two patties remained. Good thing she'd bought
five pounds of ground chuck instead of three, as she'd originally planned.
In addition to the burgers and hot dogs, they'd eaten every bit of the potato
salad, devoured two family-sized bags of chips, and nearly emptied the
platter of lettuce leaves, sliced tomatoes, and raw onion rings.

She shook her head in wonder. "Leapin' lizards, you all must've been
starving."

Lucas, the only one of the men still young enough to suffer from acne,
tipped his chair back on two legs and patted his stomach. "We worked real
hard today, Miss Spalding. I coulda ate more except my pants are too
tight."

Todd clapped Lucas on the back of the head with his open palm,
sending the youth's baseball cap sliding over his face and down his chest.
Everyone laughed, including Lucas. He righted the chair, settled the cap
back in place over his sandy-blond hair, and grinned at Todd.

Todd pushed up the bill of his cap, scratched his head, and sent a shy
smile across the table to Brooke. "It was real nice of you to bring out the
picnic foods. Thank you." Everyone around the table added their
thank-yous.

Brooke waved both hands, the way speakers quieted a crowd. "You're welcome, but before we do this again, I need to get some real picnic tables out here. I doubt Marty will want us dragging her dining room table and chairs outside every time we want to eat under the sky's canopy."

She crunched her brows together. Had she already ordered picnic tables? She recalled choosing a pergola design and contracting for two of them, but she couldn't recall if she'd added tables to the work order. This forgetfulness was shredding her already frayed nerves.

Anthony rose from his spot at the head of the table. "We'll get started again at seven tomorrow morning, before it gets so hot. Breakfast at six thirty. Set your alarms. There's a long time between breakfast and lunch. You can't give a full day's work on an empty stomach, so make sure you don't sleep through breakfast." He turned a pointed look toward Lucas.

The young man's face flooded pink, making his pimples glow.

Anthony bounced a tired smile around the circle of faces. "Enjoy the rest of your evening, everyone."

Lucas bounded off with the exuberance of a puppy, and the others sauntered toward their trailers, talking quietly with one another. Brooke was a little surprised to see Charlotte leave with her husband. She'd spent most of the day helping Marty. Wouldn't she help with supper cleanup, too?

Anthony headed for his trailer with a chair tucked under each arm, and Marty inched around the table, stacking the plates and silverware. Brooke automatically followed Marty and collected the glasses. "Doesn't Charlotte help you with dishes and so forth?"

Marty glanced over her shoulder. "Oh, sure. She's helped cook all the meals and helped with the breakfast and lunch dishes. She's been a great help. But I don't mind doing the supper dishes by myself. The automatic dishwasher does most of the work."

Anthony strode across the grass and snagged two more chairs, excusing himself when his elbow bumped Brooke. He headed for the trailer again.

Marty watched him from the corners of her eyes and then grinned at Brooke. "Anthony didn't want me using the dishwasher at first. Our sect hasn't approved worldly conveniences like automatic dishwashers, and I think he was afraid I'd get used to it and have a hard time adjusting to doing things by hand again. But then he said I had a lot more people than usual to clean up after so I should do whatever would help me the most."

With her hands full, Marty scuffed toward the trailer. Brooke pinched four glasses between the fingers of each hand, the way she'd learned to do when she worked as a waitress during college, and followed her friend. Anthony opened the door when they reached the steps, and he shifted out of their way, holding it open for them. As Brooke passed him, he said, "As soon as I have the table and chairs inside, we can sit in the living room and talk. Marty said you had things to discuss with me."

"I do." Brooke placed the glasses on the counter. "If you're too tired from working, though, I can drive out at noon tomorrow and we could have a lunch meeting."

He shook his head. "No, tonight is better. You probably shouldn't be driving back and forth so much with your—" His neck and face blotched red. "Well, with you not feeling good."

Unexpectedly, Brooke warmed toward the man. For the most part, the men in her world treated her as an equal, one of the gang, but Anthony had demonstrated a touch of chivalry. Misplaced chivalry, because the cancer didn't interfere with her ability to operate a vehicle, but it was kind anyway. She touched the rolled sleeve of his shirt. "Thank you for your concern, but it really isn't an inconvenience. I won't want to put it off too long, though, since it involves hiring the extra man for your crew."

He fiddled with his cap's bill and finally nodded. "All right." He marched out the door.

Marty started after him, but Brooke put out her arm and stopped her. "Go ahead and load the dishwasher. I'll get the platters." Marty opened her mouth, but before she could voice an argument, Brooke moved to the door and spread her arms to block it. "No arguing. You worked while I slept. I need to earn my keep around here."

Marty shook her head, but she smiled and returned to the sink.

Brooke opened the door and found Anthony with his foot on the lowest riser and two more chairs under his arms. She smiled and held the door wide. "Good timing, huh?"

He lobbed a quick grin at her, and she scuttled outside, swallowing a chortle. Solicitous one minute and bashful the next. As her mother always said, men were impossible to understand. Locusts began their night songs from the thick row of maples north of the trailers. Brooke paused for a moment to enjoy their chorus, but all at once the rhythmic buzz ended. She looked around. What had startled the locusts into silence? She didn't see anything out of the ordinary, but wariness sent tingles across her scalp.

As abruptly as they'd stopped, the locusts wheezed into song again. Shaking her head, she reached for the platters. "Dumb insects, anyway. And dumb me for letting them scare me." Then she jolted to a stop and choked out a laugh. The platter with the last two hamburger patties was now as empty as the potato salad bowl.

Anthony crossed the yard to the table, and Brooke couldn't resist teasing him. "You must have scarfed those things to have them gone in such a short amount of time."

He pulled back slightly and lowered his brows. "What?"

She picked up the charcoal-smeared platter and showed it to him. "The burgers. Did you think we wouldn't notice?"

He stared at the platter as if he feared it would rise up and bite him. "I didn't eat them."

She stared at him. "You didn't? Then who . . ." The uneasy prickle tiptoed from her forehead to the nape of her neck again, and she shivered despite the balmy evening. "Do you suppose one of the men came out and took them?"

Anthony shrugged, the motion so slow it appeared his joints had grown rusty. "I doubt it. They know to ask before they take something that doesn't belong to them."

Brooke searched for another explanation. "Then maybe an animal." But even she could see no evidence of tracks or left-behind bits of grass that would indicate a four-footed intruder had climbed onto the table. Besides, would an animal be able to snatch both burgers at the same time?

He whisked a glance left and right, then curled his hand around her elbow. "You go on in, Brooke. I'll get Nate to help me with this table. And when we're done talking, I'll walk you to your car."

Brooke wasn't in the habit of taking orders, but she followed his instructions without a moment of hesitation.

Anthony

*A*nthony tapped the hammer against the chisel's anvil. Hard enough to penetrate the layer of plaster covering the interior wall of the old bank building but gentle enough to keep from piercing the lath underneath. He'd hoped to salvage the plaster. It would save money now—no need to purchase drywall. It'd save money later, too, in heating and cooling costs since plaster was better insulation than drywall. But the walls were too cracked. Some had already begun to crumble on their own. He wouldn't risk having the walls collapse on guests.

Fine white dust coated his clothes and hung in the air like fog over a pond. The dust could get sucked inside a man's nose and end up in his lungs if he wasn't careful. Nearly every building on the street had plaster walls, so they'd be breathing a lot of dust. The next time he went to town, he'd buy a big box of painters' masks. But for now, his bandanna served as a shield.

He glanced over his shoulder to make sure Lucas had a handkerchief tied over his mouth and nose, the way Anthony had instructed. The boy had laughed and said they'd look like bandits. Anthony had no idea where he'd learned such a thing, but he'd been quick to let him know the bandanna was necessary for his health, so he'd be wise to keep it in place. Lucas must have believed him, because the triangle of cloth was stretched across his cheeks with the point bobbing above the V-necked opening of his shirt.

Satisfied Lucas was fine, Anthony turned his attention to his part of the room. He'd planned to take a minute during breakfast to question his men about last night's missing hamburger patties. Not to accuse, just to ask. But he'd changed his mind. Why bother? He knew his workers. They'd have asked, the way they always asked if they could take the leftovers. If he questioned them, they might think he didn't trust them, and that wasn't a good way to build a strong team. But where had the patties gone? As Marty said when he told her they disappeared, they hadn't sprouted legs and run away.

He wondered where they'd gone, but he had more pressing things to think about, so he pushed the curiosity to the corner of his mind and continued working. He needed to watch the clock, because at ten thirty a trio of men who'd answered Brooke's ad for long-term, on-site workers were due to arrive. He'd need to swat the dust off his clothes before he met with them.

He had expected Brooke to hire somebody and send him out, but she said she wanted him to do the final interviews and choose the man he thought would best fit in with his team. A wise decision, in his opinion. He planned to let Todd sit in on the interviews since whoever they hired would share Todd's trailer. It should probably make him uneasy, bringing a worldly man into their midst—working beside them, eating with them, living with them—but it didn't.

Of the three unmarried men on his team, Todd was the oldest and the most solid in his faith. Anthony didn't worry about Todd adopting worldly habits, and he liked being given the chance to witness to this non-Mennonite worker, the way the deacons had said. Not the same as being a missionary. Not even close to being a missionary. But every soul had great value, equal to the life of God's Son, and if he could impact one soul for eternity, he'd feel successful.

Another large section of plaster peeled from the wall and broke into chunks against the wood floor. Dust rose, and even with the bandanna in place, a few particles reached his nose. He sneezed, the force bending him forward. His eyes watered and his nose tickled, and he took in several short huffs that drew the cloth against his mouth while another sneeze built. The second one was even stronger than the first. He put his hands on his knees and waited for a third. But that seemed to be it.

He straightened and found Lucas grinning at him. Well, he couldn't see the boy's mouth to know for sure, but his eyes looked like he was grinning behind his bandanna. "You okay?"

Anthony nodded.

"Gesundheit."

At the familiar German blessing, Anthony nodded again. "Thank you." He stepped over the pile of broken plaster and set the chisel blade against another patch on the wall. Before he could apply the hammer, though, Marty called his name. Lucas dropped his hammer and darted out of the building. Anthony stepped over and around chunks of plaster, checking his watch as he went. Yep, ten. Snack time. And time for him and Todd to get cleaned up.

Marty stood in the shade of a tin awning, holding a tray of brownies and halved bananas. The men gathered around, helping themselves. She caught his eye as he reached for a brownie. "You've got visitors."

Anthony yanked the bandanna from his face. "Already?"

She nodded. "All three of them came in a couple minutes ago, one right after the other. I told them to wait on the porch."

So he had no time to clean up. He glanced down his length. They'd see what kind of mess they'd be getting themselves into. He crossed to his team, who'd clustered in the shade to eat their snacks.

"Todd, let's go do the interviews."

Todd had been scooping up broken shingles from around the foundations of the three wood-sided businesses. His face was sweaty and his clothes were dirt smeared, but he looked a lot more presentable than Anthony. Todd jammed the last of his brownie into his mouth, wiped his hands on his thighs, and jogged over. "Okay, I'm ready."

Anthony untied the bandanna from his neck, shook it, and then used it to mop his face while he, Marty, and Todd headed for the trailers. Todd pointed to two newer-looking cars and a rusty pickup truck lined up on the road across from the trailers. They reached the yard, and Marty went inside through the back door. Anthony and Todd rounded the front of the trailer. Two men wearing sunglasses, jeans, and T-shirts with the tails hanging out sat on the second step. A third man stood next to the porch with his elbow on the railing. He also wore jeans and a T-shirt, but he had a Royals cap instead of sunglasses and he'd tucked in his shirt. All three looked to be in their early twenties.

The two on the steps stood, and the third dropped his elbow from the rail when Anthony and Todd approached. Todd stayed off to the side, and Anthony stuck out his hand to the dark-haired, stocky man on the left.

"Hello. I'm Anthony Hirschler."

The man gave him a firm handshake. "Mitch Price."

The next one slipped his glasses into the patch pocket of his shirt as he returned Anthony's handshake. "Austin Brady. Glad to meet you."

Anthony offered his hand to the one on the right, the one who'd been standing. This young man was an inch taller than either of the other two but thinner. His shoulders were broad, though, and the sleeves on his plain green T-shirt fit tight around the thick muscles of his upper arms. He yanked the cap from his head and gripped Anthony's hand without shaking it, his gaze darting everywhere except to Anthony's face. "Elliott Kane." He plopped the cap back on and seemed to examine the toes of his worn boots.

Anthony invited Todd to join them. "This is Todd Bender. Whoever hires on will share a trailer with him, so I wanted him with us so he could meet you and you could meet him." Todd shook the men's hands and they exchanged hellos.

Anthony gestured to his dust-covered clothes. "I'd take you inside the trailer to talk, but my wife wouldn't want me in her clean house." Todd, Mitch, and Austin chuckled. Elliott's expression didn't change. Anthony held out his hand in the direction of the town. "How about we walk to the street front so you can see what we're doing here. We can talk about your work experience and get to know each other a little bit."

The four of them fell into step with Anthony, Todd on his right and the three new men on his left, with Elliott Kane at the far end. Mitch talked the whole distance from the trailers to the town, and by the time they reached the first of the rock buildings, Anthony was ready to put his hand over the younger man's mouth. Apparently Mitch hadn't been instructed to memorize Proverbs 14:23—*"In all labour there is profit: but the talk of the lips tendeth only to penury"*—when he was a boy, the way the Old Order youth of Anthony's sect had.

Brooke had already told them they'd be expected to help rebuild or remodel the existing structures, so Anthony showed them every building and discussed the repairs they would make. Each of the men shared— well, Mitch bragged more than shared—where he'd worked before, what kind of construction he'd done, and which tools he knew how to use. If they were all telling the truth, their skills and experience were almost identical. Which meant the choice came down to which one Anthony and the team would want to live with for the next year and a half. Anthony had already chosen Austin in his mind. The man seemed to listen more than talk, unlike Mitch, and he was friendly instead of standoffish, unlike Elliott.

Anthony stopped on the boardwalk at the west edge of town, put his hands in his pockets, and turned to face the three applicants. "Now you've seen it all and know what kind of work we're doing. So let me tell the rest. Because there's so much to get done, most weeks we'll work Monday through Saturday. We start at seven, take short breaks midmorning and midafternoon and of course a longer lunch break, and we work right up to suppertime, which is about six thirty. The days'll be long. It's a pretty big commitment. So lemme ask, are you sure you want to join the crew?"

Mitch grinned. "Sure, I'm in. It'll be kind of like living in the Old

West. Guess I'll need to pack a six-shooter." He made a pistol with his hand and fired off several shots, using his lips to make the sound effects. He pretended to holster the gun and nudged Austin, still grinning.

Anthony stifled a sigh and looked at Austin. "What about you?"

The young man slid a frown across the row of buildings. "I don't know. It sounded really interesting in the ad—different, you know? And I like construction work. But . . ." He faced Anthony and shrugged. "I think I'm gonna pass. I like having my whole weekends free, and I think I'd miss the city too much. Thanks for the tour, though, and good luck with the project." He ambled off.

Anthony turned to the remaining man, who stared across the street with his eyes squinted. "Elliott, how about you?" The young man hadn't cracked something even close to a smile the entire hour they'd been together. He didn't put one on now, either. Anthony didn't know why he'd bothered to ask. Clearly Elliott Kane would rather be anywhere except in the abandoned town.

"Yes," Elliott said.

Anthony gave a start. "Yes, you're still interested?"

Elliott still didn't look at Anthony, but he nodded.

"All right. Then let me talk with Todd for a bit, and we'll give you an answer." Anthony put his arm around Todd's shoulders and led him several feet from the pair of contenders. He kept his voice low, just between him and Todd. "I'll be honest. Either one would probably be able to do the work. So you decide. Which one do you think it'd be easier for you to live with?"

Anthony wasn't sure he'd offered Todd a fair choice. Mitch's constant talk had already grated on his nerves. Mitch was talking now even though it didn't seem like Elliott was paying much attention. But as much as Mitch's endless chatter chafed, Elliott's quietness and unwillingness to look anybody in the eyes made Anthony uneasy. He sent up a silent prayer for Todd to choose wisely. They'd all have to live with the consequences of his choice.

Todd sent a long, thoughtful look over his shoulder. He hung his head for a moment, rubbing his jaw with his thumb. "Actually, I think I'd like you to hire the one who'd probably be harder to live with."

Anthony raised his eyebrows. "You would? Why?"

"Dunno exactly. Just feels like it's what I'm supposed to do."

If the Holy Spirit had nudged Todd, Anthony would honor the choice. "Which one, then?"

A sheepish grin grew on Todd's tanned face. "Elliott."

Anthony put his hand on Todd's shoulder. "You're sure?"

Todd nodded. "Yeah. I think he needs to fit in somewhere."

A feeling Anthony couldn't describe swept through him, making his chest tight and his pulse increase. Todd was right. Elliott did seem out of place. Anthony recognized the source of the tightness in his chest—sympathy. How many times had he felt out of place in his lifetime, being looked at differently because of his Mennonite faith? But if his men included Elliott and made him feel welcome the way he knew they would, then—best of all—they'd have the chance to expose him to their Savior.

He gave Todd a clap on the shoulder and turned toward the waiting men. "Let's go tell him."

21

Kansas City
Brooke

*W*hat would they tell her? Brooke tucked her thumbs inside her fists to keep herself from chewing on her nails—she'd already ruined her manicure—and tried to relax in the stiff vinyl chair. Another vinyl chair in yet another doctor's office. At least no institutional blue or stark white glared at her from the walls. Imitation Monet paintings in soft pastels hung on the dove-gray background. Soothing colors. A vast improvement. But she still couldn't bring her racing pulse under control. How she hated this fear. Hated it as much, maybe even more, than the thing causing it.

Wouldn't it be wonderful if last night's dream came true? She tipped her head back and replayed the snippet behind her closed eyelids. *The doctor comes in smiling sheepishly, tosses a folder in a gigantic dumpster in the corner, and says, "There's been a mistake, Ms. Spalding. You don't have cancer at all. Go on your way and be happy." And she turns cartwheels all the way up the hall to the sunshine- and rainbow-laden outdoors.*

Sighing, she opened her eyes and returned to reality. Best-case scenario was surgery only. But she'd given up hope on that. Not if she really wanted to beat this thing. And she did. She wanted this stuff out of her body for good, so whatever they recommended medicinally, she would do. Whatever she found online nutritionally, she would do. She would meditate and do yoga and even shake beads in a gourd. She would fight as hard as she'd fought to break free of her deplorable childhood, to get through college without a lick of help from her mother, to build a successful career in a male-dominated field. Brooke Spalding was a fighter, and she would pummel this vile monster into the dust. As soon as her heart stopped pounding and she could get a good breath.

A light tap sounded, and then the door eased open. The oncologist, Dr. Dickerson, stepped in. She searched his face, hoping for a glimpse of the expression of "Whoops" she'd seen in her dream. Of course, it wasn't there.

"Good afternoon, Brooke." He dropped a fat manila envelope on the desk inside the door and held out his hand. She unfolded her fist to take it. They exchanged a brief handshake, and then he slipped his hand into one of the white lab coat's patch pockets. The coat hung open, revealing his peach shirt and silk peach, cream, and aqua tie—more soothing colors. "Do you mind if an oncology resident sits in on our meeting? It's your choice, but it's a helpful part of their training."

If bringing the entire staff into the room would make this go away, she'd let them all crowd in. She shrugged. "I don't mind."

He opened the door a little wider and quirked his finger, and a smiling young woman bounced into the room. Brooke recoiled from the woman's teal, hot pink, and lemon-yellow Betty Boop scrubs. Her comical scrubs, too-cheerful smile, and perfect white teeth seemed an affront, given the circumstances.

The woman took Brooke's hand in both of hers. "Thank you so much, Ms. Spalding. I'm Raquel McNichol, but you don't need to worry about remembering my name. I'll just sit over there in the corner and be as quiet as a mouse. Pay no attention to me at all."

Then she'd have to change clothes and stop smiling, because the glare off her obnoxious scrubs and movie-star teeth was impossible to ignore. Brooke forced a smile. "That's fine." Raquel McNichol slid a wheeled stool to the corner and perched on it, as attentive as a hawk on a fence post. Brooke shifted her focus to the envelope Dr. Dickerson had carried in.

"Is that my battle strategy?"

A giggle came from the corner. Brooke fixed her gaze on the doctor and held it there.

"That's a perfect way to put it." His warm smile crinkled the corners of his hazel eyes and gave him the appearance of a kindly uncle. "It is a battle, but you aren't facing it alone. You have an entire army of well-trained soldiers fighting with you. Remember that."

Brooke swallowed acid and nodded. "So what's the game plan?"

He sat on the second vinyl chair and linked his hands in his lap. For the next fifteen minutes, Brooke listened to him outline the treatment plan the oncology team had tailored specifically to her situation. Although the doctor's words could be construed as clinical and cold, his tone was professional and kind. Even so, Brooke fought the urge to screech at the top of her lungs the entire time he spoke. Would this fear be her companion every minute of the next several months?

When he finished, he slid the envelope from the desk. "I've given you a lot to absorb, and later you'll probably scramble to remember it all."

Apparently every patient who'd sat in this chair suffered anxiety-induced memory loss.

"Everything I've talked about is in this packet, along with instructions on how to prepare for the surgery and several pages of Q and A addressing the most common queries people have about the hospital stay, the treatments, and what to expect during and after." He handed her the envelope. "If you have other questions or need clarification on something, feel free to call here during regular office hours. There's also a number that will link you to a twenty-four-hour hotline if something pressing comes up and you need to talk to someone after hours."

Brooke hugged the packet to her chest. Knowing someone was only a phone call away should ease her worries, but her heart still pounded like a child's fist on a toy drum. "Thank you."

"You're welcome." He stood, and she rose on quaking legs. He cupped her upper arm. "We'll see you back bright and early on the twelfth for your surgery."

Her mouth went dry. Only four days away. She'd have to be as industrious as the Mennonite workers to finalize all the arrangements for her move to Spalding. She nodded. "All right."

Raquel "Betty Boop" McNichol bounded from the corner and captured Brooke's hand. "Thank you again, Ms. Spalding, for letting me be here. Good luck on your surgery and treatment. But you won't need luck, because you've got the best team in the whole state of Kansas."

Brooke withdrew her hand. "Will you assist with the operation?"

The woman shook her head, making her blond-streaked ponytail swing. "No. I can't yet. But I'll be in the observation deck, watching the procedure. And I'll cheer for you the whole time."

Brooke imagined Raquel hopping around, waving pink and yellow pom-poms. Thank goodness for anesthesia. She'd be blissfully unaware of the cheering squad's antics.

"One last thing . . ." Dr. Dickerson's tone held an edge of apprehension. "I noticed in your file that you left the next-of-kin lines blank."

"That's right." Brooke forced a blitheness she didn't feel. "I'm not married, I've never met my father, I have no siblings, and I'm estranged from my mother."

Raquel affected a pouty face and patted Brooke's shoulder.

Brooke gritted her teeth and resisted shrugging the hand away.

The doctor frowned. "Is there someone we could contact in case you're unable to speak or respond to questions?"

At least he hadn't said "in case you die on the table." Acid stung her throat, and she swallowed twice. "I have a friend who has agreed to bring me to appointments and so forth. I could give you her name."

"Please share the information with the receptionist on your way out." He opened the door and gave her another wise-uncle smile. "Goodbye, Brooke."

Miss Betty Boop chirped, "Have a good day!"

Brooke headed out the door, commending herself for holding back a sarcastic, *Yeah, right.*

Eagle Creek

Marty

Marty turned the hot-water spigot and glanced out the window above the kitchen sink. She gave a start. After a week at the ghost town, she'd finally adjusted to seeing a tall iron fence with a row of bushes and thick trees behind it instead of her Pine Hill backyard, but now the scenery had changed again. The newest trailer, which had been delivered that morning and set up on cinder blocks rather than on a poured foundation, obstructed her previous view. Too many changes in such a short amount of time. But the changes she was facing were minimal compared to all that Brooke was enduring.

While Marty rinsed pans, utensils, and plates and stacked them in the dishwasher, the entire team of men plus Brooke and Charlotte sat at the dining room table, visiting and enjoying the chocolate cake Charlotte had baked for dessert. As soon as they finished the cake and coffee and Marty had all the cups and dessert plates loaded, she and Brooke would return to Brooke's trailer. After tomorrow's surgery, Brooke wouldn't feel like arranging furniture or organizing cupboards and closets, so even if it meant staying up late into the night, they intended to find a place for all the belongings delivered today by the moving company Brooke had hired.

Marty still marveled at everything Brooke had accomplished in the past few days. Her drooping shoulders and the dark circles under her eyes told a story of exhaustion, but not once had Brooke complained or lashed out or shed a single tear. Marty thought it would benefit Brooke to have a good meltdown and had even told her so, but Brooke brushed off Marty's suggestion with a flip of her hand and an equally flippant "It'd be a waste of time, and I don't have time to waste." Marty hoped Brooke was referring to the limited hours remaining until tomorrow's surgery instead of limited days remaining in her life.

She placed the last dish in the tray, and Charlotte eased past her and picked up the percolator staying warm on a stove burner. Charlotte leaned close to Marty, her eyes wide. "Did you hear what Elliott just said?"

Marty hadn't been paying attention to the conversation, but it pleased her that Elliott had said something worth repeating. The new man on the team had said little more than "thank you" since his arrival. She shook her head.

"When him and Todd went to their trailer to clean up for supper, the package of peanut butter crackers he'd left on his nightstand for snacking was gone. Then they looked around, and their bread, cheese, and baloney weren't in the fridge anymore."

Marty's heart skipped a beat. She hurried over to Anthony. "Someone broke into Todd and Elliott's trailer?"

Anthony slid his arm around her waist. "We can't call it breaking in because the door wasn't locked, but yes, someone apparently went in and helped himself to some food." His tone was light, but his creased brow let Marty know the situation worried him.

Brooke folded her arms over her chest. "So much for my ten-thousand-dollar fence keeping out riffraff."

Marty gasped, and Charlotte froze with the percolator held above Nate's coffee cup. The younger woman's blue eyes widened. "You paid ten thousand dollars for a fence?"

"And a coded electric gate. Don't forget the coded electric gate." Brooke's expression seemed especially grim with the purplish circles under her eyes. "Yes, I did, because I wanted the area secure." Brooke turned a disgusted look on Anthony. "How could someone scale that thing? There are only two horizontal bars, one six inches from the ground and one six inches from the top. That means a five-foot reach in between them. The iron pickets are three-quarters of an inch in diameter. Nobody could bend those things. I had the pickets set five inches apart, which is too narrow for even a child to slip between, and I paid extra for a high-gloss coating to make them slick—no traction. Even if someone did manage to reach the top, they'd have to deal with the pointed finials in order to get over it."

Anthony's fingers tightened on Marty's waist. "You chose everything right. I wouldn't try to climb it."

Marty envisioned the arrow-shaped finials and shuddered. "Neither would I."

Brooke snorted. "The salesman assured me the spikes would discourage trespassers. I'm going to give him a call and let him know he misled me."

"I wouldn't do that yet." Nate took the percolator from his wife and poured himself a cup of coffee. "I'm not so sure someone climbed the fence. I think . . ." He looked at Myron as if asking permission, and Myron gave a quick nod. Nate sighed. "Maybe when you built the fence, you closed somebody in. Myron and me did some exploring yesterday after church, and we found a pile of old blankets, a bunch of tin cans, and what looked like the remains of a small fire in one of the houses farthest away from the main street."

Lucas sat forward. "You did? I wish I'd gone with you instead of staying behind and playing checkers with Todd."

Anthony released Marty and frowned across the table. "Why didn't you say something then?"

Nate shrugged. "I didn't really think much about it until Elliott started talking about somebody going into their trailer and taking food. Then it made me wonder if there could be a homeless person camping on the property."

Brooke huffed. "If they've claimed one of the old houses, they aren't homeless anymore."

Nate took a sip from his cup, grimaced, and reached for the sugar bowl. "The person would be able to leave and get food someplace else if the fence wasn't up. But now that it is and we're all here, they're kind of . . . trapped."

Todd snapped his fingers. "Do you think it's the same person who took those hamburger patties last week?"

A chill rattled Marty's frame. "Then he was right outside our door." Did someone hide in the bushes and watch her when she hung clothes on the line or carried snacks to the men? She reached for Anthony. "This frightens me."

He caught hold of her hand and squeezed. "No sense in getting scared yet. We don't know for sure someone's living on the property."

"But we don't know they aren't, either." Brooke's comment did little to reassure Marty. "Anthony, when you go to town next, use the credit card I gave you and buy security bars, padlocks, and several sheets of plywood. I'll hire some men to come out and board up the windows and put locks on the doors of the remaining houses. The last thing we need is for Spalding to become a squatters' village."

Anthony ran his thumb back and forth on Marty's hand. She sensed it was a nervous gesture, but she took comfort from his touch anyway. "Just to be safe, I think we'd better lock the trailers when we're away from them. And you ladies"—he glanced from Marty to Charlotte to Brooke— "keep the door locked behind you when you're by yourselves. The men and I will start coming back here for our morning and afternoon snacks instead of having you bring the treats to the worksite. At least until we're satisfied there isn't a stranger lurking around." He stood, still holding Marty's hand. "I'll go over to Brooke's trailer with you. It'll likely be dark before you're done helping her get settled, and I don't want you walking back here by yourself."

She'd walked from one edge of Pine Hill to the other—more than a mile one way—by herself without a moment's hesitation. Only fifteen feet separated the two trailers. She should tell him she and Brooke would be fine, that he didn't need to treat them like helpless children. But in that moment, she couldn't find the courage to travel to Brooke's front door without Anthony's protection.

She clung to his hand. "Thanks."

22

Kansas City

Marty

"Why are you nervous?"

Marty shot a startled look at Charlotte. The two of them had chosen a pair of chairs in a small waiting room set aside for family members of patients undergoing surgery. They had the room to themselves, which Marty appreciated. She also appreciated Charlotte's company so she didn't have to wait alone during the two to three hours Brooke would be in an operating room. But she didn't appreciate the question that held a note of admonition.

"It's pretty hard not to be. Brooke looked so helpless . . ." Marty closed her eyes, remembering the lines trailing from Brooke's hand, the paper cap covering her hair, the paleness of her skin. And the fear that seemed to pulsate from her friend. She opened her eyes and glared at the younger woman. "There are all kinds of risks when someone has surgery. And think about why she's having it. She has cancer. That in itself is enough to make me nervous."

Charlotte's expression remained puzzled. "But we all prayed before we came. We put Brooke in God's hands. We shouldn't worry, because what better place is there for her to be?"

"Worry's a waste of time." Without warning, Great-Grandma Lois's gentle admonition tiptoed through Marty's memory. One of the farm dogs—Pepper or Jack?—had run off during the night, and Marty feared he wouldn't return. She'd sobbed out her concern to Great-Grandma, expecting consolation. Great-Grandma had tenderly stroked Marty's hair,

an act of sympathy, but she hadn't minced words. *"It don't solve anything. Just gives you indigestion. So don't make worry a habit. If you're gonna have a habit, let it be trusting the Lord, do you hear me, Martha Grace?"*

Marty rose and paced to the opposite side of the room, a feeble attempt to escape her great-grandmother's instruction. She prepared a cup of coffee—two sugars, powdered creamer, a sprinkle of cinnamon. She had no intention of drinking it, but it gave her something to do.

"We put Brooke in God's hands." Charlotte's statement stung because Marty wasn't part of the "we." Not since her demand for God to take her away from Pine Hill had she sent up another prayer. She held Anthony's hand when he prayed every morning and at bedtime. She bowed her head at the table when one of the men blessed the food. She sat reverently in the church pew when the minister or one of the leaders from the Southern Baptist church they attended in Lansing prayed out loud. But she hadn't added her prayers early this morning when the entire team formed a circle and prayed for Brooke before the women set out for Kansas City. Great-Grandma Lois would be so disappointed that Marty hadn't put Brooke in God's hands, but she'd put her desire for motherhood in God's hands and He'd crumbled it to dust. Why would she trust Him with her friend?

She reached for a stir stick, and someone touched her elbow. She jumped, knocking over the little cup of paper-wrapped stirrers. She turned a frown on her intruder—Charlotte, whose blue eyes glowed with such assurance Marty could hardly bear to look at her.

"She'll be all right."

Marty sighed. "How old are you, Charlotte?"

Charlotte's blond eyebrows pinched together. "Twenty-one. Why?"

At twenty-one, Marty had been just as naive, as starry eyed, as certain of God's loving presence as Charlotte was now. If someone had told her then she would someday question God's care, she would have laughed. She wasn't laughing now. She wouldn't say anything to rattle Charlotte's faith, but neither would she blithely accept that Brooke would be all right. Sometimes people got better. Sometimes they didn't. If God was really there, then He knew whether or not Brooke would conquer cancer, but Marty refused to ask Him. Or trust Him.

"I just wondered." She gestured to the cup of milky-looking coffee. "Do you want this?" Charlotte nodded. Marty handed her the cup and poured a second one. She left it black.

A television hung on the wall, its volume off but with what seemed to be some sort of game show playing on the screen. A stack of magazines waited on an end table. Marty sipped the strong coffee and searched through the magazines for one that didn't have a scantily clad woman on its cover. She found one about gardening, and she flopped it open on her lap. She began reading about preparing the soil for spring planting—a subject that didn't require her to think hard.

"Marty?"

Marty barely glanced up. "Hmm?"

"Is Brooke going to let them give her chemotherapy?"

Brooke had showed Marty her "battle strategy," as she called it, and according to the papers the doctor had given her, she would do a chemo treatment every three weeks for up to eight months. Marty nodded. "Yes."

Charlotte made a face. "I don't think I'd do it. Those drugs are really like poison. Why would she want to put poison in her body? Nate said when one of his relatives had breast cancer, she went on a really strict diet and took vitamins. He didn't remember what kind. But that was three years ago and her cancer hasn't come back. Maybe Nate should tell Brooke about his cousin's wife."

Marty set the magazine aside. "No, Nate should not tell Brooke about his cousin's wife."

"But why? She—"

"For one thing, every cancer is different. What worked for Nate's relative might not work for Brooke."

"But chemotherapy . . . isn't it dangerous?"

Fear for her friend as well as the desire to protect her welled in Marty's chest. She shifted slightly to look full in Charlotte's face. "Listen, I know you mean well, but the last thing Brooke needs to hear right now is that she's doing the wrong thing." Marty didn't want to hear it, either. "She's a smart woman. She researched ovarian cancer, and she researched the different ways to treat it." Marty'd seen pages and pages of information printed from various websites when she'd organized the desk in Brooke's trailer. "Based on everything she read, she decided to do chemotherapy as well as change some things in her diet. It's her choice. What she needs from us is support, not advice."

Charlotte bit her lower lip and stared at Marty for several seconds. Then she sighed. "All right. I'll tell Nate not to tell her about it. Unless she asks." She leaned back and yawned. "I think I'll take a little nap while we wait. I'm not used to getting up at four in the morning."

Neither was Marty, but she was too tense to sleep. She wouldn't be able to rest until the surgeon came in and let her know Brooke had come through the surgery all right. While Charlotte dozed, Marty read several magazine articles and retained nothing from any of them, drank three cups of coffee, visited the bathroom twice, and checked the clock so many times she lost count.

A little after ten, Brooke's cell phone, somewhere in the bag one of the nurses had given Marty for safekeeping, sang and roused Charlotte. Marty dug in the bag and pulled out the phone. The screen showed a number with the title *Park's Plumbing* underneath. Should she answer it? She could take a message to share with Brooke. Her finger aimed for the connect button, but before it descended, the ringing stopped. She sighed. Just as well. They would leave a message in Brooke's voice mailbox. In Marty's troubled state, she probably wouldn't remember anything the plumber told her anyway.

Charlotte rose and stretched, then invited Marty to walk up and down the halls with her, but Marty stayed in the little room. She didn't want to miss the surgeon. Charlotte returned half an hour later and settled in a chair with a magazine. Marty prowled the room, chewed her thumbnail to the quick, and watched the clock.

Finally, three and a half hours past the eight o'clock surgery time, Dr. Dickerson entered the waiting room. The room suddenly felt half its size with the tall, stately man standing in the middle of the floor. He pulled the paper hat from his graying hair, folded his arms over his blue scrubs, and flicked his gaze from Charlotte to Marty. "Mrs. Hirschler?"

"Yes." Marty crossed to him, amazed her quaking legs held her up. "Are you done? Did you get it all?"

"Brooke underwent a radical hysterectomy, and we removed several tumors from her bladder and omentum."

Charlotte sat forward. "What's an omentum?"

He smiled at Charlotte. "It's the layer of fatty tissue that supports the intestines and organs in the lower abdomen." He turned his attention back to Marty, the smile fading. "We'd spotted tumors on her bladder in the CT scan but hadn't realized they were also in the omentum. All very small, less than half a centimeter, but their presence makes a difference in the kind of chemotherapy we'll use. I'll talk with Brooke about it when she's awake and cognizant."

"When will that be?" Marty wrung her hands. She wanted to see Brooke, to assure herself her friend had come through the surgery, to be there as a support when the doctor gave her the unexpected news.

"She'll be in recovery for an hour or so. When we move her to a room, a nurse's aide will come get you and you'll be able to sit with her for as long as you want to. There's even a chair that folds out into a bed if one of you would like to spend the night." He slipped his hands into the pockets of his loose scrub pants. "Do you have any other questions?"

Is she going to die? hovered on the tip of Marty's tongue, but she held the query inside. She didn't want to hear the honest answer. "Not right now. Thank you, Doctor."

"You're welcome. The cafeteria is in the lowest level of the hospital. I suggest you go down, get a little something to eat. If the aide comes in and you aren't here, she'll page you." He shook Marty's and Charlotte's hands and left.

Charlotte picked up her purse and started for the door. "Well, let's go find the cafeteria."

Marty sat. "You go ahead."

Charlotte stopped. "You don't want anything to eat?"

"Not until I've seen Brooke." Her stomach would probably give back anything she tried to put in it. She shouldn't have had so many cups of coffee. She glanced at the clock again. The men were probably gathered in her trailer, eating the sandwiches and fruit salad she'd left in the fridge for them. "I've got the prepaid phone Anthony got for me. I'll call and let him know the surgery is done. You can go if you want to."

Charlotte worried her lower lip between her teeth. "I don't like to eat by myself. But maybe . . ."

Marty waited, but she didn't finish her sentence.

Charlotte waved her hand, stirring her cap's black ribbons into a gentle dance. "Go ahead and call Anthony. I'll be back in a little bit." She stepped into the hallway, looked both ways, and then disappeared to the right.

Anthony answered on the first ring, and Marty told him everything the surgeon had said. Her voice quavered when she mentioned the tumors found in the fatty tissue, but she commended herself for not breaking down. Brooke was tough. Marty could be tough for her.

"Will you be back before suppertime?"

Marty stifled a sigh. She hadn't left enough prepared food to carry the men through supper. Could they fend for themselves for one meal? "If it's okay with you, I'd like to stay with Brooke. The doctor said there's a fold-out bed in her room and I could even sleep there if I wanted to."

"All night?" She didn't need to see his face to know he was frowning. "What about Charlotte? She'd have to drive back here all by herself."

Marty hadn't wanted to drive Brooke's fancy car, and three adults didn't fit well in Anthony's pickup, so Charlotte had used Nate's car and driven her and Brooke to the hospital. If she'd made it to the hospital all right, Marty didn't see any reason why she couldn't make it back to the worksite without trouble.

A second masculine voice muttered something, and Anthony said, "Just a minute, Marty. Nate wants something." He must have covered the speaker, because she couldn't hear a thing they were saying.

"Marty?" Anthony's voice crackled through the phone's speaker again. "Kansas City is a big city. Lots bigger than Pine Hill. Nate doesn't want her driving through it all by herself."

"Then maybe she can stay here, too." Marty blinked back tears. "The doctor is going to give Brooke some bad news, Anthony, and she's going to need me."

She heard a click, the sound of a door latch, and then a sigh. "Marty . . ." She pictured him sitting on the edge of their bed, his head in his hand, the way he sat when he was upset or needed to think something through. "You're there for her now. You'll be there for her when she gets out of the hospital. You'll be taking her to her appointments and helping her for the next several months. Do you really have to stay overnight?"

How many times had he left her overnight because of his business? Even when she'd begged him to come home for nights, he'd found reasons why he couldn't. "No, I don't have to, but I want to. It's one night. You can't make it one night without me? Heaven knows I survived lots of nights without you." The resentment she'd managed to hold at bay came out in the sharpness of her tone.

Silence fell on the other end. Marty's heart thudded hard. Had she really spoken so harshly to her husband? She cringed, yet she didn't regret the words. He needed to understand how it had felt for her to be left alone.

After what felt like an eternity, Anthony finally spoke. "All right. Stay. I'll let Nate quit early and borrow my pickup to drive in to get Charlotte. You can stay at the hospital and use the Schrocks' car to get back again when you're ready."

He'd conceded. Shouldn't she feel more victorious? She swallowed. "Are you sure?"

"No, but I don't want to argue with you. I need to get back to work. Call me when you're leaving Kansas City so I know when to expect you. Bye, Martha."

She dropped her phone into her purse and hung her head.

"Ta-da!"

Marty jolted. Charlotte stood framed in the doorway. In one hand she held a bright red ribbon tied to a floating Mylar balloon emblazoned with Get Well, and she cradled a good-sized fuzzy teddy bear against her rib cage. Her smile was as bright as the yellow letters on the balloon.

"I got these for Brooke. To brighten up her room."

Marty crossed the floor and fingered one of the teddy bear's soft ears. She blinked back tears. "That's really nice of you, Charlotte."

Charlotte shrugged, blushing. "I wanted to do something to help her—and you—feel better."

Such a kind gesture. Marty forced a smile. "I'm sure these will lift Brooke's spirits." But it would take more than a balloon and a furry stuffed bear to make Marty feel better.

23

Eagle Creek
Brooke

*B*rooke eased back, supported by Marty's arm, until her spine and head nestled against the stack of pillows on her own bed. She released a long, contentment-filled sigh. So soft. So comfortable. And so much better smelling than the disinfectant-scented hospital room, thanks to the candle burning on the corner of the dresser.

She turned a lazy smile on Marty, who remained beside the bed, the teddy bear Charlotte had bought in her arms. "Now I'll be able to regain my strength. How can anyone rest in a hospital with all the people coming and going twenty-four hours a day?" Brooke's conscience pricked when she looked at the dark circles under Marty's eyes and the tiredness etched into her friend's features. Staying two nights on the stiff makeshift recliner bed in the corner of the hospital room had taken its toll. "Now that we're out of there, you deserve a long soak in a tub and about twelve hours of uninterrupted sleep."

Marty smiled and laid the bear next to Brooke. "I'm fine."

"Well, you look like you've been run over by a truck." Brooke touched the tender incision on her abdomen. Shouldn't her stomach be concave? After all, the doctor had taken out several of her original parts. Since she'd emerged fully from under the anesthesia, she'd had an uneasy feeling of emptiness, yet there seemed to be no outward change. The lack of evidence stirred an anger she couldn't explain. "Seriously, Marty, the pain pill I took before we left the hospital is kicking in. I won't stay awake much longer."

Sleep was a good escape. She'd come to appreciate hours of blissful uncon-
sciousness compliments of a Percocet. "Go to your trailer and rest, too."

Marty ran her hands down the front of her rumpled dress. The same
one she'd worn Tuesday morning for the drive to the hospital. Since she'd
come unprepared for an overnight stay, a hospital rep had loaned her a set
of scrubs and given her a bag of basic hygiene items. Brooke wished she'd
taken some pics on her cell phone of Marty in those faded, too-big blue
scrubs, but Marty had kept the phone under house arrest, insistent that
Brooke not think about work. So she'd have to rely on her memory to hold
the image of Marty's white cap and trailing black ribbons paired, so very
incompatibly, with the baggy scrubs. The hospital laundry had put her
dress through the wash for her, but obviously they hadn't ironed it. Brooke
had never seen Marty so disheveled.

"I'll wait until you fall asleep." Marty covered a yawn with her hand.
"Then I'll change clothes, let Anthony know we're here, and be right back."

Brooke battled her own yawn, thanks to Marty's example. Why were
those things so contagious? "What did I tell you about hovering? Nothing's going to happen to me while I'm asleep. Go. Get out of here." She
forced a crabbiness she didn't really feel. "Let me rest in peace." Marty's
face went white, and Brooke recognized her poor choice of words. She
winced. "Sorry. Didn't mean it that way. But really, I won't rest well if
you're prowling around in here. Please just . . . leave me alone for a while?"

She hoped Marty would concede defeat and go. She hadn't had a
minute to herself to process the surgeon finding additional tumors and
changing the chemo protocol—the same number of treatments but using
a more powerful combination that would likely be harder on her system
than the one originally planned. Not to mention trying to adjust to constant company after living alone for so many years. She appreciated Marty's concern. Of course she did. But she needed some space. To think. To
accept. To grieve.

Marty sighed and hung her head. "All right. I'll blow out the candle.

I don't feel good about it burning when you're sleeping and no one else is around. I'll put your cell phone where you can reach it and go put mine on its charger. Call if you need me."

Fuzziness crept through Brooke's brain—the pill was definitely taking effect. "Yeah, recharge that thing. And the next time you leave home for more than a day, take your charger with you." What was the sense of carrying a cell phone with a dead battery? She yawned again and weakly waved her hand. "Go."

Brooke's eyelids slid until she viewed the room through mere slits. Marty's frame seemed to float to the dresser. A poof of breath extinguished the flame, and a hint of smoke smell reached Brooke's nose. Marty straightened and then stood still, her pale face aimed in Brooke's direction.

Brooke whispered, "Go." Her eyelids drooped shut before she witnessed Marty leave the room.

Anthony

"Hey, look who's back."

Anthony kept hold of the piece of drywall Nate was securing to the furring strips with screws and glanced over his shoulder. His pulse gave a little hop when he spotted Marty standing in the doorway of the old bank building. He waited until Nate applied the power drill to the last screw, then ambled toward his wife, brushing the dust from his clothes as he went.

Part of him wanted to rush over, grab her up in a hug. But his men were looking on, and underneath he was still a little aggravated with her for staying at the hospital so long. His lips quirked, caught between a welcome-home smile and an it's-about-time scowl. He got close enough to reach her, but his hands were so dirty. He jammed them in his pockets instead.

"Hi. When did you get back?" Behind him, the power drill *rat-a-tat-tatted* a screw into place. He cringed and gestured to the porch. They stepped outside, and he pulled the door closed behind him. The noise was muffled enough for them to hear each other. He repeated the question.

"About an hour ago."

Her voice and face reflected weariness, and Anthony wanted to be sympathetic. But she'd been back for an hour and was only now letting him know? It took some effort, but he held the accusatory question inside. No sense in starting a fight. "How's Brooke?"

"Sore. Tired. Overwhelmed. The cancer spread further than they realized. She's got a tough battle ahead." Marty sighed, and her gaze drifted to the road leading to the trailers. "She's sleeping right now. I'm going to take a bath, change my clothes—"

For the first time he noticed she was wearing the same dress she'd put on Tuesday morning. Had she really worn it for three days?

"—and then go over and wait for her to wake up. The doctor said she shouldn't try to pull herself out of bed without help for another couple days. To give the incision a chance to heal."

Anthony zeroed in on *another couple days.* "Does that mean you'll stay with her day and night?"

She jerked her gaze to meet his. Her lips formed a stubborn line. "Yes, I plan to. At least until Saturday." She folded her arms over her chest. "But I'll be right next door if you need me."

He caught the barb. The *I missed you and really want you with me* hovering on his lips went unsaid. "Will you at least help Charlotte with cooking for all of us? She's had a hard time doing it all herself while you were gone."

Something flickered in Marty's eyes. Hurt or resentment? He couldn't be sure. Both emotions rolled through him. Sure, he felt bad for Brooke. Cancer was scary and he wouldn't wish it on an enemy, let alone someone his wife counted as a friend. But Marty was his wife. Supposed to be his helpmeet. Why couldn't she understand the heavy burden he carried bringing this old town to life, being the spiritual leader for his work team, and worrying about the unknown person who'd apparently slept in the bank building last night? Yes, Brooke needed Marty, but so did he. Shouldn't he come first?

He sent a quick look in both directions to be sure no one was watching. Then he pulled his hand free of his pocket and reached for her. "Marty, I—"

"If Brooke is up to walking to our trailer later this afternoon, then I'll be able to help Charlotte. But I want Brooke where I can keep an eye on her to make sure she doesn't try to do too much. It's really important that she gets plenty of rest before the chemo treatments start five weeks from now. But don't worry. I'll make sure you and the men are taken care of, too." She turned her back and sighed. "I'm tired, and I don't have a lot of time before Brooke's pain pill wears off. I better go." She took off before he could finish his sentence.

Grinding his teeth, Anthony pushed the door open and then bent over to wedge a chunk of two-by-four under it as a doorstop. When he straightened, he found Lucas nearby, leaning on the wooden handle of a push broom.

The young man grinned. "When I saw Marty out there, I thought maybe she'd brought some cookies. Isn't it snack break yet?"

Anthony glanced at his wristwatch. "It's only a little after two. We'll go up for a snack at three thirty."

"Aw . . ." Lucas made a face. "I hope it'll be something better than crackers and peanut butter. I've missed Marty's cookies and brownies."

Anthony had missed more than his wife's cooking. He snapped, "We'll eat whatever Charlotte sets out without a word of complaint when the time comes."

Lucas drew back, both hurt and puzzlement on his face. "I wasn't complaining, Anthony, honest. I know Charlotte's doing her best. I was trying to pay Marty a compliment. She's a really good cook."

Anthony closed his eyes for a moment. He shouldn't take his frustration with Marty out on Lucas. He put his hand on the younger man's shoulder. "Thanks for saying something nice about Marty. I'm sorry I barked at you. Will you forgive me?"

The boy's face flushed, making his pimples glow. "It's okay. I know you didn't mean it. My dad sometimes barked when he was tired or worried. I figure you're probably both."

Anthony couldn't deny the statement. He hadn't slept well, partly because Marty wasn't there and partly because he hadn't gotten used to his new surroundings quite yet. And worry? The ratty blankets he'd found folded and stashed in the corner of an upstairs room made the hair on the back of his neck stand up. Who was hiding away in this little town?

He gave Lucas's shoulder a squeeze, then stepped past the broom. "Finish sweeping, and then go across the street and give Elliott and Todd some help with the porch roof, okay?"

"Sure thing, Anthony."

The afternoon passed quickly, and Anthony and the team put away their tools and closed up the buildings at six. They headed to their own trailers to clean up for supper. A good aroma—something rich and savory—floated on the breeze, making his stomach growl in anticipation. He pulled the key from his pocket as he bounded up the steps to the back door, but he didn't need it. The door was unlocked, and Marty wasn't inside. He stifled a growl and reminded himself she'd been gone for a couple of days. She was tired and stressed and had probably forgotten his instruction to keep the doors locked.

A cool shower revived him, and he set the table with eight plates. Enough for himself, his workers, Charlotte, and Marty. Charlotte and Nate carried over two tater-tot-and-hamburger casseroles and a big bowl of salad at six thirty. Marty hadn't come in, but the men were hungry, so Anthony blessed the food and they started eating. By the time they finished, Marty still hadn't come in, and she didn't show to help with the cleanup. She finally knocked on the front door a little before nine.

He let her in and gave her a reminder about keeping the doors locked. She apologized and promised to do better, then headed to their bedroom. He followed, hoping for some conversation, maybe even something more than conversation, but he caught her putting her nightgown into a bag.

He frowned. "What are you doing?"

She glanced at him, her brows low, like she didn't understand the question. "I told you earlier. I'm going to stay at Brooke's in case she needs something during the night." She passed him and entered the bathroom.

He leaned against the bathroom doorjamb and watched her put her toothbrush, her hairbrush, and a couple of other items in with her gown. "You're going right now?"

She shot him an impatient look. "Yes."

"You can't even stay here for an hour? So we can talk a little bit?" She turned toward the door, bag in hand, and he stepped aside to let her out. He followed her into the living room. "What about your supper? Charlotte left a bowl of casserole for you. Why not heat it in the microwave? I already ate." Of course he had. It was almost bedtime now. "But I'll sit with you while you eat."

"Brooke had some canned soup, so I heated that for us."

Canned soup. They'd had a supper of canned soup not so long ago. He'd hoped coming here would take them away from the cloud of tension and regret that hung over their house in Pine Hill, but apparently the cloud had come with them. "So you're going right back over there."

"Anthony, she just got out of the hospital. She's very weak and shouldn't be left alone. I—"

He held up his hand. "All right, all right, go back over. I'll be going to bed soon anyway."

She stared at him, unblinking, for several seconds and then sighed. "I'll get up in time to help Charlotte with breakfast. Okay?"

He shrugged in reply, fearful of what might come out if he opened his mouth.

After another few silent seconds, she opened the door without a word and left. But she hadn't turned the lock in the door handle. Grumbling under his breath, he stomped to the door and reached to flick the lock. As his fingers connected with the silver button, a woman's scream pierced the air.

24

Anthony

*A*nthony's blood ran cold. He threw open the door and leaped off the porch. "Marty!"

Marty fell against his sturdy frame. Her shoulders heaved and her breath puffed out, as if she'd just finished running a race. She pointed up the dirt road. "He . . . he took my bag!"

Anthony glanced over his shoulder and saw a shadowy figure disappear into the bushes. He'd deal with the thief later. He curled his arms around his shaking wife. "Are you all right? Did he hurt you?"

Tears brightened her eyes. "I'm fine. He scared me. Came at me so fast."

She shuddered and pressed her cheek to his chest. He hated her fear, but it felt good to hold her. He cupped the back of her cap-covered head, the mesh scratchy against his palm, and placed a quick kiss on her forehead. "Your scream probably scared him off."

"Well, good! He deserved to be scared! But he took my bag, Anthony. My nightgown and toothbrush . . ." She pulled loose and peered up at him. "Why would he want those things?"

Anthony rubbed her back. "He couldn't know what was in there. Probably thought it was food. What did he look like?"

Marty scrunched her face, as if struggling to remember. She shook her head and blew out a breath. "I can't really say. He wasn't very tall—no taller than me. And pretty thin, I think. But I didn't really see his face or . . . or anything else. It all happened so fast."

Nate trotted up to them. Worry marred his brow, visible even in the dusk. "We heard Marty scream. What happened?" Before Anthony could answer, the other four men pounded up, all barefoot and Elliott in baggy pajama pants and no shirt. They added their questions.

Anthony raised his hand. "Someone grabbed Marty's overnight bag. He ran toward the town. Nate, get Charlotte and have her stay with Marty and Brooke." Nate darted off. "Everybody else, get dressed, put your shoes on, and grab your flashlights. We've got to find him and get him out of here." If he was brazen enough to grab a bag right from Marty's hand, what might he do next?

"Sure thing, Anthony," Myron said. The men ran toward their trailers.

Anthony turned Marty toward Brooke's trailer. "Let's get you inside. Then I'll—"

Marty clung to his shirtfront. "No. Don't leave us by ourselves."

Her fear made her want him. He understood that. But it still felt good to be wanted. He guided her to Brooke's little porch. "You'll be all right. Just lock the door, okay?" Marty didn't release his shirt.

Brooke's door opened and light spilled across Marty and Anthony. "What's going on out here?"

Marty broke free of Anthony and bounded up the steps. "Brooke, why are you up?"

"I heard someone scream. Was it you? Did you see a snake or what?"

Marty slid her arm around Brooke's waist. "Let me get you back to bed and I'll tell you." She eased Brooke inside and shut the door.

Anthony stood for a moment, staring at the closed door. She'd done what he wanted her to do, so why was he aggravated?

Nate and Charlotte jogged up to him, holding hands. Nate kissed her on the lips and gave her a quick hug. "Go on in, honey. I'll come get you when we're done searching."

Charlotte nodded and scampered up the steps. She opened Brooke's door—which the women hadn't locked. Anthony called after her, "Lock that door behind you." She nodded. Anthony waited until he heard the dead bolt turn. Then he grabbed Nate's arm. "Let's go."

The men headed up the road in a group, their flashlight beams bobbing like a gathering of ghosts. When they reached the cluster of buildings, Anthony instructed Todd and Elliott to search the main-street buildings and Myron and Nate to explore around the old houses west of town. He chose to look around the houses on the east side of town with Lucas as his partner. "Give a shout when you find the intruder. Hold him down, and we'll all come running."

They all nodded grimly. Except Lucas. The youngest of the team couldn't stop grinning, as if they were playing some kind of cops-and-robbers game. Anthony pushed through the bushes close to where he thought he'd seen the thief disappear, and Lucas ducked in behind him. Lucas kept his flashlight beam straight ahead, but Anthony scanned his back and forth, his gaze seeking any movement.

The company Brooke had hired to clear the area of dead growth had done a good job, making it fairly easy for them to cross the ground even in the dark. They were noisy, though. Years of accumulated dead leaves and small twigs littered the ground, and their feet crunched with every step. Anthony both bemoaned and welcomed the sound. They might alert the thief to their presence, but if he took off running, they'd hear him.

Lucas came to a sudden stop. He held his flashlight steady. "What's that?"

Anthony squinted through Lucas's flashlight's bright beam. His pulse leaped. A plastic shopping bag, one identical to the one Marty had used to carry her nightgown, lay at the base of a large maple tree. So the thief had come this way. He double-stepped to the bag and picked it up. It still held Marty's overnight items. He tied the handles into a knot around his belt loop.

"Good find, Lucas. Let's keep—"

Lucas put his pointer finger to his lips.

Frowning, Anthony fell silent. He crunched across the ground to the young man. "What?" He kept his voice soft so the slight breeze rustling leaves in the trees would cover it.

Lucas didn't answer, but he slid the beam of his flashlight upward. Anthony followed its path along the tree trunk to the branches above them. Lucas moved the beam slowly back and forth, then nodded. "Yep. I was right."

About fourteen feet up, highlighted by the beam of light, someone huddled on a sturdy branch. Even though it was summer and the night was plenty warm, he wore a military-type jacket, a stocking cap, and what looked like hiking boots. The crisscrossing of smaller leaf-covered branches partially shielded him, but Anthony noted that Marty's "pretty thin" description fit.

Lucas bumped Anthony with his elbow. "Guess you could say we treed our prey, huh?"

Anthony nodded, but oddly he experienced no sense of elation. He couldn't stop staring at their intruder's pale face nearly overtaken by a pair of wide, fear-filled eyes.

Lucas kept his beam in place but turned his head and cupped his mouth. "Found 'im! Everybody, we found 'im!"

While Lucas gripped his flashlight in both hands, Anthony reached toward the intruder. "Come on down from there." The person shrank against the trunk, as if trying to hide. It was too late for that now. "I'll climb up and get you if I have to, but I'd rather you came down on your own."

The boy—because Anthony was now pretty sure this was a boy and not a man—buried his face in the bend of his elbow. Anthony sighed. He hoped he wouldn't have to climb the tree. They'd had a long day, he was tired, and all of a sudden he felt twice his age.

Myron and Nate broke through the bushes. Moments later, Elliott and Todd joined them. They all stood in a half circle under the tree and gaped at their intruder. Nate shook his head. "I expected somebody bigger. Bet he's even younger than Lucas."

Anthony put his hands on his hips. "Last chance to come down before I come up." The kid didn't move a muscle. Stubborn kid, anyway. Anthony sighed and took a step closer to the tree. "Nate, gimme a boost, would you?"

As Nate stepped forward, the boy stood on the branch. Hugging the tree, he sent a frantic look across the men on the ground. "All right, mister. I'll come down."

Anthony froze. His voice . . . Could he be a—

Nate clamped his hand on Anthony's shoulder. "That sounded like a girl." Behind them, the men muttered their agreement.

The boy—or was he really a she?—blinked down at Anthony. "But you gotta promise not to turn me in. I don't wanna go back. Please . . ." The flashlight beam glistened on twin tears sliding down the girl's grimy cheeks. "Don't make me go back."

Brooke

Marty had done her level best to coax Brooke back to bed, but she wasn't budging from the sofa until Anthony returned and she knew whether or not the men had caught the thief who'd had the audacity to accost Marty not ten feet from her front door. After a good twenty minutes of fussing, Marty had finally settled at the opposite end of the sofa, but Charlotte still paced, casting uneasy glances at the stereo with each pass.

Brooke knew she shouldn't find the young woman's angst amusing, but really, what was the harm in listening to Ronnie Milsap croon "I Wouldn't Have Missed It for the World"? Now, if she were playing one of her mother's acid rock eight-track tapes, Charlotte's consternation would be understandable. But Brooke never listened to acid rock. Occasionally classic rock. The Beatles lurked somewhere in her stash of CDs. But she used music to soothe herself, not drive herself into a frenzy. Life did that well enough on its own. Tonight's activity coupled with the message Tim Park had left on her cell phone—drat Marty for keeping the phone from her!—was proof of that.

Charlotte stopped midstride and turned her gaze to the window. "I see flashlights. Two of them. Looks like Nate and Anthony are back."

Brooke hit the mute button on the stereo remote and braced her arm against her midsection, preparing to stand.

Marty bolted over and took hold of Brooke's arm. "Stay put. You don't have to get up. Charlotte will let them in."

Brooke sagged against the cushions. As much as she wanted to argue, her muscles still ached from getting herself out of bed less than an hour ago.

Charlotte unlocked the dead bolt and swung the door open as feet clomped on the metal porch. Nate came in first, his expression unreadable. He went straight to Charlotte, and she melted against him, as if they'd been apart for weeks instead of an hour. Brooke experienced a quick, unexpected prick of jealousy. What would it be like to have someone welcome you after an absence?

Anthony entered, holding the upper arm of a scruffy-looking youth. His gaze skimmed past Marty and landed on Brooke. "Well, here's your squatter."

Brooke examined the thin, filthy teenager from his scuffed army boots to the gray floppy stocking cap drooping toward his left ear, all speckled with tiny bits of dried leaves. "I expected someone older. And bigger."

Anthony let go of the youth's arm and grabbed the stocking cap. He pulled it straight up. Long, matted red-blond hair spilled across the thief's narrow shoulders. Marty gasped. "A . . . a girl?"

For the first time, Brooke noticed a slight protrusion at the thief's chest level. She shook her head, releasing a disbelieving snort. "You've got to be kidding me."

The girl folded her arms over her chest and glared at the floor.

Brooke held out her arms. "Marty, help me up." Marty made a face that expressed her reluctance, but she caught hold and helped lift Brooke to her feet. One arm across her middle, Brooke shuffled across the floor to the girl who stood with her head down, chin jutted, body stiff. Brooke's heart rolled over. It was a belligerent pose, but she suspected, underneath, this girl was quaking with uncertainty. The same way Brooke had so many times as a teen. The way she was now, with Park's message rolling in the back of her brain.

"What's your name?" Brooke used a conversational rather than confrontational tone.

The girl didn't answer. She didn't even blink. Brooke glanced at her audience. Anthony appeared aggravated, Nate and Charlotte uncertain, and Marty flat-out worried. Marty's worry was probably because Brooke had taken a pain pill fifteen minutes ago and would soon be too woozy to stand. Brooke needed to get answers quickly, and she sensed she'd have more success if the four other people weren't standing around, watching.

She straightened as best she could and turned to Nate. "Why don't you two go on back to your trailer? You both have an early day tomorrow, so go get your rest."

Nate flicked a questioning look at Anthony.

Brooke rolled her eyes. "You don't need his permission. Go on."

Anthony gave a barely discernible nod, and Nate escorted Charlotte out the door.

Brooke shifted her attention to Anthony. "The drain in my bathroom sink burbles. I might've dropped something in it. Would you go take a look? If you have to take it apart, there's a toolbox in the cabinet above the washer."

He didn't seem happy, but he trudged off. Now to get Marty out of the way. That would be the hardest. Despite her promise not to hover, Marty had become an ever-present helicopter. Maybe if she appealed to Marty's maternal side, she could buy a few minutes of privacy with this girl.

"Marty, I imagine our young guest is hungry. Would you mind making her a sandwich? You know where to find everything."

Marty's forehead creased and she chewed her lip. But she nodded and moved into the little kitchen area on the other side of the eating bar. With everyone else occupied, Brooke pinched the girl's dirty jacket sleeve between her fingers and tugged. "Come sit down over here." To her relief, the girl didn't resist. She sat stiffly on the edge of the sofa cushion, and Brooke flopped down beside her.

"Now, let me ask you again. What's your name?"

The girl hung her head, and her hair hid her face. She seemed to hunker into herself, like a turtle in its shell. "They call me Iris."

A chill wiggled up Brooke's spine. "So is that what you want me to call you?"

She shook her head, making her hair sway.

"Then please tell me your name."

She raised her hand slowly and pushed the thick fall of hair behind her ear. Head still down, she licked her lips. "It's Ronnie."

"Short for Veronica?"

"No. Just Ronnie."

"All right, Ronnie. How'd you happen to end up here in Spalding? I mean, you seem like a smart enough kid. The big iron fence should have told you this is private property."

Ronnie angled her head until she faced away from Brooke.

Marty approached the sofa with a sandwich wrapped in a paper towel. She offered it to Brooke.

Brooke tapped Ronnie on the shoulder. It took more effort than she wanted to admit to raise her hand that far. Her muscles were turning into rubber, and her head was going fuzzy. "Here's your sandwich."

Ronnie jerked around, grabbed the sandwich, and took a bite so big it bulged her cheek. She chomped twice, swallowed, and jammed another bite into her mouth.

Not many things made Brooke cry, but whether it was the pill kicking in or Ronnie's obvious hunger, she had to blink back tears. She looked at Marty. "Make her another one, okay?"

Marty hurried off without a moment's hesitation.

Brooke angled her gaze at the teenager. "Listen, Ronnie, I'm not mad at you for being here. I'm not even mad at you for stealing food. A person does what she needs to when she's hungry." Brooke's mouth felt dry, which made forming words a challenge. "But you can't stay here. You're what—thirteen, fourteen?"

"Sixteen," she said with her mouth full.

Brooke didn't believe her, but she let it go. "You ought to be with your family. Tell me your full name and I'll—"

Ronnie jumped up, scattering crumbs and little bits of dried leaves. "If you open the gate for me, I'll leave. I won't bother you again. I promise."

Brooke struggled to the edge of the sofa cushion. She didn't dare try to stand, not with the way her head was swimming. "It's late. It's dark. You shouldn't be out by yourself."

"I'll be fine. I can take care of myself."

Exactly what Brooke would have said at sixteen. Or fourteen. So she knew what to say now. What she wished someone had said to her. "I'm sure you can, but you shouldn't have to. You need somebody looking out for you."

Marty brought a second sandwich into the living area. She held it out, and Ronnie eyed it but didn't reach for it.

Brooke battled to keep her eyes open. "Tell me your name. Let me call your family."

Ronnie shook her head.

Brooke's strength gave out. She slumped against the couch's padded backrest. "Then I'll have to call the police."

Ronnie sprinted for the door, but Marty cut in front of her, calling, "Anthony!" He came at a run. Ronnie seemed to freeze in place, her wide-eyed gaze darting from Anthony to Brooke to Anthony again, back and forth like someone watching a tennis match. Tears welled and rolled down her face, leaving tracks on her dirt-smudged cheeks.

"Please don't let them arrest me. I don't want to go to jail."

Brooke forced herself to sit up. "I already told you I don't care that you stole food. I won't press charges. I just want the police to take you home."

"But they won't!" Her voice emerged two decibels higher than before. "They'll put me in jail. Because I'm—" She clamped her mouth closed and breathed so heavily her nostrils flared.

Brooke pulled herself to the edge of the couch again, inwardly cursing her uncooperative body. "Because you're what?"

Her panicked eyes fixed on Brooke. "I'm a prostitute." She covered her face with her hands and burst into sobs.

25

Anthony

$\mathscr{A}$nthony had a hard time swallowing the scrambled eggs and bacon Charlotte fixed for the men's breakfast the morning after finding a fourteen-year-old self-proclaimed prostitute hiding from the man who'd, as the girl had described it, pimped her out. Of course, he knew about prostitution. The practice dated back to biblical times. But he'd never looked it in the face before. He'd never imagined such a young participant in the vile industry. After seeing its evil etched into a young girl's features, he feared he'd never be the same.

The men had been affected, too. None of their usual breakfast chatter livened up the morning. Instead, they sat with sober faces. Even Lucas, the least serious of the whole bunch, was quiet, his forehead scrunched as if he had a headache. A bitter taste soured Anthony's tongue, and he reached for his coffee, hoping another swig of the strong brew would wash the unpleasantness from his mouth and his mind.

"What do you think's gonna happen to Ronnie now?" Lucas blasted the question, and every man around the table seemed to freeze in place.

Anthony lowered his cup to the table and curled both palms around it. Despite the warmth of the chunky mug, a chill exploded through him. "I don't know. The policemen who picked her up said she'd probably go to a juvenile facility until they could find a foster home placement."

Charlotte crossed behind Nate and put her hands on his shoulders. Tears glistened in the corners of her eyes. "I wish there was something better for her. After all, she ran away from a foster home. That's how she ended up with the awful man who . . . who sold her." She shuddered, and Nate caught her hands and crisscrossed her arms over his chest. She sighed. "But she was so brave to run away from the truck driver who paid to be with her, and she must be very strong to have walked all the way here from Kansas City. Someone so brave and strong will be all right eventually, don't you think?"

Anthony considered Charlotte's question and her comments about the girl named Ronnie. Last night the girl had quaked in fear, but mostly because the man who had forced her to sell something that should only be offered in love had convinced her she would be taken to jail if she tried to leave. What other lies had he told her? Probably many, yet she'd found the courage to escape. He nodded slowly. "Yes. Yes, I think . . . eventually . . . she will be all right."

A small smile lifted Charlotte's lips. She slipped free of Nate's loose grasp and started toward the kitchen.

Elliott snorted. "All right? How can she ever be all right?"

Charlotte stopped and turned back. "What do you mean?"

He pushed his empty plate aside. "She was violated again and again by strangers. Worse, she was sold by someone she trusted to take care of her. She might be away from her pimp, but where she is now—a juvenile facility—isn't much better. It's a bed and three meals. That's it. She won't find any kind of healing there."

Anthony gaped at Elliott. In their days of working together, the man hadn't said more than a few words. His outburst took Anthony by surprise, but more than that, his words struck like blows. He leaned forward and looked intently into Elliott's face. "How do you know about the facility— that it won't help her?"

Elliott's expression turned grim. "Because I've been in one, too."

All around the table, jaws dropped. Lucas drew back. "How come?"

"My folks cut me loose when I was thirteen. I lived on the streets for a month or so. Then the cops picked me up. Said I was a vagrant."

Anthony couldn't decide what bothered him more—what Elliott shared or the unemotional way he shared it.

"They put me in a juvenile detention center, said I'd be there for a week, maybe two, and then go to a foster home. I stayed there almost two years." His gaze dropped to his gripped hands, and he set his lips in a firm line for several seconds. "I never got put in a foster home. Most of 'em don't want teenage boys."

"So where'd you go? Back on the streets?" Lucas's face reflected both curiosity and revulsion. Anthony felt the same way, but he hoped it didn't show.

Elliott lifted his head and stared past Anthony's shoulder. "A youth center. Kind of like a boarding school on lockdown. That's where I learned construction and carpentry. They tried to keep us busy. If we were busy, they said, we wouldn't cause trouble. So I helped add a wing to the dormitory." He didn't move his head, but his eyes shifted until they locked on Anthony's. "Does all that make you want to fire me?"

Anthony thought back to what Todd said the day they brought Elliott on the team, that it seemed Elliott needed to fit in somewhere. Todd had been right. Anthony shook his head. "It sure doesn't. You're a good worker, a good team member. I'm proud to have you with us."

"Yeah." Todd slapped Elliott on the back. "You're a good roommate, too, even if you do beat me at checkers most of the time."

Elliott blinked several times, and his chin raised a notch. "Well, I can tell you, if Ronnie's gonna get better, she needs out of juvie hall. She needs to be with a family. Or someplace where she'll get counseling. 'Cause if she doesn't, she'll probably end up doing what she did before she came here." He shrugged. "Sometimes when you're treated bad, you think that's what you deserve. That it's the only way. If she doesn't learn different . . ." He pushed away from the table and glanced at the wall clock. "It's almost seven. We better get to work." He strode out the back door.

Charlotte returned to the table and stood next to Anthony, wringing her hands. "What he said about Ronnie going back to . . . to what she was doing. Do you think that's true?"

Anthony wanted to say no, but he couldn't. Didn't most people do what was familiar? He'd grown up in the Old Order lifestyle. Even with all his traveling to secular communities, he'd always returned to what he knew best. So it seemed to follow that whatever a person knew, whether good or bad, would become their practice. Then again, Brooke had carved a different path than her mother, who, according to Marty, had spent too much of her salary on alcohol and neglected her daughter. So maybe it depended on the person. On their resilience.

Everyone was looking at him, waiting for an answer. Waiting, probably, for wisdom. But he didn't have any to offer. He pushed back his chair and stood. "Elliott's right. We need to get to work. So let's go." The cell phone in his pocket rang. He pulled it out and waved at the men at the same time. "Go on—I'll meet you there after I take this."

A glance showed Marty's cell number on the little screen. His heart rolled over. She must have missed him last night as much as he missed her. He flipped the phone open and pressed it to his ear. "Morning, Marty."

"Morning." No tenderness, only tension, came through the phone's speaker. "Could you come by Brooke's trailer before you go to work? She needs to talk to you about something."

Anthony swallowed a knot of part disappointment, part concern. "Is something wrong?"

"She won't tell me. She'll only say she needs to talk to you and that it's important."

Then something had to be wrong. Worse than a teenage prostitute hiding out on the property? He choked back a wry snort. Not likely. "Sure. I'll be right over."

Brooke

Anthony entered the trailer, looked her way, and turned brighter red than a vine-ripened tomato. Obviously he wasn't accustomed to seeing a woman in pajamas. Other than Marty, of course. Even though her two-piece jammies hid everything except her head, hands, and feet, she grabbed the afghan from its spot on the sofa's back and covered herself with it—chin to toes—for his peace of mind. Besides, she couldn't seem to get warm. Probably the residual effects from the surgery.

Marty gave him a quick hug, then headed to Brooke's bedroom. She'd insisted on stripping the bed and washing the bedding—claimed Brooke would rest better on fresh-smelling sheets. Brooke doubted fresh sheets would make an ounce of difference in her ability to rest well. If pain from the surgery site didn't disrupt her sleep, worry would surely keep her awake.

Anthony sat in the recliner next to the sofa and plopped his cap over his knee, his gaze aimed beyond her shoulder. "What do you need?"

She wriggled one arm free of the afghan and grabbed her cell phone from the end table. "Listen to this first." She punched the voice mail button, and Tim Park's voice came through the speaker.

"Ms. Spalding, when my workers were at the site yesterday to connect the water lines for the sinks and toilets in the new bathrooms in the bank building, one of them saw dry rot in the floor joists in that corner of the building. The floor will have to come up and the joists be replaced before we can put fixtures in there. I assume that's something your general construction team can do, but if not, let me know and I'll recommend someone for you. Either way, we're at a standstill until that's done. Call me if you have questions."

Even though she'd already listened to the message several times, she still shook her head in disbelief. She dropped the phone into her lap. "Unreal that the inspector who came out didn't find this. He must not have gone into the crawl spaces, the way he's supposed to." She closed her eyes, battling weariness and self-recrimination. He was a new inspector to her, chosen by one of her investors. She should have come out with the man and supervised the inspection instead of trusting that it would be done right. She'd been in the business long enough to know dry rot was never good news. Tearing up the floor, replacing joists, and putting down new hardwood wouldn't be inexpensive, but she could deal with the added expense more easily than the delay it would cause.

She opened her eyes and frowned, a headache building in her temples. "Have you or your men noticed dry rot in any of the buildings?"

Anthony toyed with the cap's brim, his eyebrows low. "No, but none of us have been in the crawl spaces. Haven't needed to since you hired other workers to do the wiring and plumbing."

She shot him a sharp look. Was he blaming her? She searched his face and saw no sign of accusation. Only concern. She was plenty concerned, too. She sighed. "I guess the best thing to do now is get someone out here to inspect the crawl spaces of every structure on the property. If dry rot's in one building . . ."

Anthony nodded, his expression solemn. "It's likely somewhere else. I'm sure sorry."

Brooke massaged her throbbing temples with her fingertips. "Me, too." According to her schedule, the investors planned their first walk-through on the fifth of August to see how things were progressing. Only three weeks away. A certification inspector was on the calendar for mid-September to check the plumbing and electrical systems. She needed the investors' continued support, and she needed the certificate in hand before applying for licenses. "How long do you think you'll have floors torn up?"

"Hard to say." Anthony pinched his chin between his thumb and finger, his forehead puckering. "If it's only one building and only one corner, we can probably have the floor back in place in no more'n a couple weeks. But if it's in more than one building or in several places, then . . ."

He didn't need to finish his sentence. Brooke knew how to read the writing on the wall. She gritted her teeth. "Work as quick as you can, huh? There's a lot riding on this."

26

Brooke

*B*rooke climbed behind the steering wheel of her Lexus and set off for the hospital. Today she'd have her chemo port installed. According to the paperwork Dr. Dickerson had given her, getting the port was pretty simple. Especially compared to the intensive surgery he'd performed on her three weeks ago. But they'd give her mild sedation for the procedure, and it wasn't smart to get behind the wheel of a car when fighting off the effects of any kind of anesthesia, so Marty was along to drive Brooke back to Spalding afterward.

As much as she disliked the idea of having a line inserted in her vein, the procedure had given Brooke a reprieve. The investors had agreed to postpone their first visit. If she had any luck at all, Anthony and his men would have all the areas where they'd discovered dry rot torn out and new materials in place for the important visit. He'd talked her into using iron joists instead of wood. Initially she'd balked—iron cost a lot more than wood, but she'd decided the extra expense was worth it. Iron wouldn't rot. How could a person put a price on security?

She glanced at Marty, who sat in the passenger's seat with a scowl on her face and her arms folded. Brooke fought a grin. What a sourpuss. All because Marty was opposed to using Brooke's "fancy" car instead of Nate and Charlotte's older-model Buick. But Brooke wasn't going to give up the chance to drive, and she certainly wasn't going to use someone else's car when she had a perfectly good vehicle of her own. Charlotte would need the Buick to make the biweekly grocery store run, and if the Lexus sat for a year, all kinds of things could go wrong in the engine and with the tires. So Marty needed to buck up and deal.

Brooke stayed quiet and let Marty stew until they'd driven through Lansing, but the silence in the car—she left her radio off in deference to her friend—proved too unsettling to ignore any longer. She released the steering wheel long enough to deliver a light bop on Marty's arm.

"Leapin' lizards, are you going to pout the whole way to Kansas City?"

Marty aimed the scowl at Brooke. "I'm not pouting."

Brooke snorted. "Pull down the sun visor and take a look at yourself in the mirror. That's a pouty face if I ever saw one."

Marty sighed, and her face relaxed. She dropped her hands to her lap. "I'm sorry. I wasn't really pouting. I was . . . thinking."

"About how to keep from having to drive my Lexus?" Brooke grinned. "Too late. If we want to get home again, you'll have to drive."

"I know, I know."

Marty fell silent again, and the only sound filling the car was the whine of tires on the highway. Brooke waited a few minutes, but when Marty didn't say anything more, she reached for the radio knob.

"Can you believe it's been a month?"

Brooke jolted. "What?"

Marty shifted slightly in the seat. "A month. Since Anthony and me left Indiana and came to Kansas."

Brooke had flipped the calendar to August that morning. "Hmm, I guess you're right. You left on the first of July, and here we are starting August." She paused, uncertain if she wanted an honest answer, but curious. "Do you regret it?"

"Of course not." Marty's adamancy made Brooke smile. "It was meant to be. Truly. The missionaries from China have the use of our house and my car, I'm here to help take care of you, Anthony's business is flourishing in two different states, and—" She clamped her mouth closed.

Brooke's curiosity rose another notch. "And . . ." She could have sworn Marty looked guilty.

Marty fiddled with a ribbon hanging from her cap. "And God answered a prayer."

Brooke chuckled. "I didn't realize that was big news. At least not for you." When Marty didn't laugh or even smile, the curiosity whisked away on a breeze of concern. "What's going on with you, Marty?"

"Nothing important." She pasted on a too-bright smile. "So tell me what all will be available at your resort when it's done?"

Brooke wasn't fooled. Something troubled Marty, and she suspected it had to do with her being childless. Brooke was still coming to grips with her own mixed emotions concerning the hysterectomy and what it meant, and she had no desire to open that topic. She set the cruise control and adjusted the seat's angle a bit to relieve the slight catch in her incision. "Available at my resort . . . Well, of course there'll be a top-notch restaurant. Think grilled steaks and chicken, seafood, pasta—a well-rounded menu to appeal to all different tastes. The two-story rock building that was originally a saloon and later a hardware store will be perfect for the restaurant. Way back when, the upstairs was a hotel, and I want it to retain its original use. I plan to furnish each of the rooms with antiques and claw-foot tubs. Kind of a step-back-in-time setup while being comparable to a high-class B and B."

"Sounds nice."

Brooke nodded. "Oh, it will be." She shifted her focus to another limestone building. "In the former mercantile, on the front half there'll be an ice cream and sweets shop with a soda fountain. Can you believe I located a complete 1940s soda bar at an architectural salvage warehouse? It's massive, with cut glass in the cabinet doors and brass accents and four attached electric sconces. I fell in love with it and bought it on the spot. It's waiting in storage. I want maybe a dozen different, exotic ice cream flavors—like lemon lavender, coconut curry, and blackberry champagne."

Marty wrinkled her nose, and Brooke laughed. "If you don't want ice cream, then you can pick from a variety of cupcakes, brownies, and fudge, all made fresh daily. The back half will be the resort's gift shop with the requisite T-shirts, mugs, magnets. You know, touristy stuff."

Marty released a self-conscious laugh. "I don't know much about touristy stuff. Our trips have been to visit my folks or brothers near Newton. Anthony and I haven't ever taken a real vacation anywhere."

Brooke gawked at her. "You're kidding!" She shook her head. "Well, when the whole place is done and open for business, you and Anthony will have to come back as guests. All at my expense, of course."

Marty grinned. "So . . . a restaurant, a sweets shop, and what else?"

Brooke drummed her fingers on the steering wheel, eagerness buzzing through her like an electrical current. "I want to make the whole west side of the main street a row of specialty shops for local vendors to lease and peddle their own wares. Mostly high-end stuff. I envision a jewelry store, some kind of art or pottery gallery, maybe something funky like a print-your-own-T-shirt shop where visitors could get creative. A local winery has already asked to lease half a space when I'm finally open, and I hope one of the Kansas cheese makers will fill the other half. That would be such a perfect pairing. But if not cheese, then maybe locally made honey or jelly."

The car in front of her was going at least five miles under the speed limit, forcing her to slow down. Brooke checked her rearview mirror, allowed two fast-moving cars to pass her, and then eased around it. When she pulled back into the right-hand lane, she reset the cruise and flashed a smile at Marty. "The original church for Eagle Creek is still standing. Probably because it was built out of limestone. Someone stole all the stained-glass windows so the inside's a mess, but I'm going to have it restored and turn it into a wedding chapel. Great idea, huh?"

Marty tapped the air, as if counting invisible somethings. "There's still one more building on the east side of the main street. The one that has Eagle Creek Bank and Trust carved at the top. What's going in there?"

"Ah, yes." Brooke sighed. "That will be the pièce de résistance, the main reason people will flock to my resort. The old bank building will become a brand-new two-level casino." She waggled her brows. "Like that old Kevin Costner movie says, if I build it, they will come."

Dismay sagged Marty's features. "A casino? Where people will gamble?"

Brooke laughed. "Of course where people will gamble. Casinos are great moneymakers. As soon as I said the word *casino* in my planning meeting, investors were scrambling for the chance to be part of the project."

Marty continued to gaze at Brooke with sorrow.

"What's the matter? I mean, obviously you and Anthony don't gamble. I'm sure gambling's listed as a no-no in your church rule book." She hadn't intended to inject sarcasm, but it emerged anyway. She grimaced. "I didn't mean that as an insult. You're good people, and I admire you for your stance. You know that. But from a business standpoint, opening a casino is one of the smartest moves I've ever made."

Marty turned her face to the passenger's window. In the side-view mirror, Brooke glimpsed her biting her lower lip. She nudged her again.

"Tell me what you're thinking."

Very slowly, Marty angled her head until she met Brooke's gaze. "If Anthony had known you were building a gambling resort, he wouldn't have come. He wouldn't want to be part of something that cheats people out of their money."

If Marty had used an accusatory tone, Brooke would have bristled. But she only sounded sad and disappointed, which pierced Brooke. "It wasn't meant to be a big secret. I hope you know I didn't trick you into coming."

A sorry excuse for a smile tipped up the corners of Marty's lips. "I know. You come from a different world than us. It probably didn't occur to you that we would . . . object."

No, it hadn't. But it should have. She knew how strictly Marty and Anthony practiced their religion. If Anthony packed up his team and returned to Indiana, she could find another construction team to finish the work on the old buildings. It would mean yet another delay, which she'd like to avoid, but she'd find a new team. But if they left now, her friend would go right back to where she'd been for the past two years with her husband—living together physically and apart emotionally. And Brooke would face this cancer battle alone. What would she do then?

She curled her fingers around the steering wheel and squeezed. "Leapin' lizards . . ."

27

Marty

*T*he entire drive from the hospital to Eagle Creek, while Brooke dozed in the passenger's seat, Marty debated with herself about whether or not to tell Anthony about Brooke's plan to make Spalding a gambling resort. Eventually Brooke would end up saying something about slot machines or blackjack, so he would find out at some point. When that moment came, he'd immediately ask her if she'd known. She wouldn't be able to lie, and he'd be upset with her—rightfully so—for keeping it a secret. But if she told him right away, would he pack up and leave? Brooke didn't need the stress of finding a new construction team when she would start chemotherapy in only one more week.

If Great-Grandma Lois were here, she'd tell Marty to pray. Her great-grandmother had taken every care, question, and heartache to the Lord. How many times had Marty knelt beside her and listened to her quavering yet strong voice address the One she trusted? The desire to pray and seek God's guidance pulled hard at Marty's heart. The habits formed in childhood and the faith she cherished into adulthood still lay dormant inside her, and it took every bit of self-restraint she possessed to keep from turning her concern into a prayer. Her parents and especially Great-Grandma Lois would be very disappointed in her for refusing to communicate with God, but the hurt from having to give up her dream hadn't healed. Might never heal. So she had no intention of trusting God with her concerns ever again.

Marty parked Brooke's Lexus in the patch of grass next to her trailer and turned off the ignition. Brooke stirred and rolled her head lazily until her gaze met Marty's. Marty smiled. "We're back. The nurse said you should sleep, so let me help you inside and get you settled in bed."

"Sounds good. I'll be glad when I'm off these pain meds. They make me so groggy."

Marty opened Brooke's car door and cringed when her gaze fell on the bandage sticking out from the scooped neckline of Brooke's top, showing where the technicians had placed a catheter into the vein leading to her heart. She assisted Brooke from the seat and kept her arm around her waist while they crossed the expanse of grass to the trailer's small porch. They climbed up slowly, Brooke clinging to Marty and the handrail. Marty took the key from Brooke's purse and unlocked the door. Although it was only a short jaunt from the car to the trailer, the Kansas heat and humidity raised perspiration all over her frame, and the rush of cool air from the trailer felt good.

Brooke had worn a loose-fitting tank and shorts made of T-shirt material, so Marty didn't suggest she change into pajamas. Brooke sat on the edge of the bed, and Marty removed her sneakers and socks. She lifted Brooke's legs onto the mattress, and her friend sank against the pillows, releasing a sigh. Her eyes slid closed.

"Thanks, Marty."

"You're welcome." She retrieved Brooke's cell phone from her purse and laid it on the nightstand. "Your phone's right here next to the bed. Call when you wake up and I'll come help you—don't try to get out of bed by yourself."

Brooke's lips lifted in a tired smile. "Yes, Mother."

The teasing comment brought the sting of tears. Marty couldn't resist smoothing Brooke's tousled hair away from her forehead. "Rest well."

Brooke didn't answer. She was already asleep. Marty covered her with a sheet, careful not to touch the slight bulge near her collarbone from the port, and tiptoed out of the room. She didn't bother locking the trailer door behind her. With Ronnie in a youth facility somewhere, the fear of theft was gone. She pushed aside thoughts of the teenager who had sobbed out her pathetic story in Brooke's living room. Thinking about Ronnie, wondering about her, only made her sad. She entered her own trailer and found Charlotte peeling potatoes at the counter.

Charlotte gave Marty a sheepish look. She gestured to the strips of brown peel in the sink. "I hope you don't mind me working here. My trailer doesn't have a garbage disposal. I can take the potatoes to my trailer and boil them if I'm in your way."

Marty crossed to the sink and washed her hands. "No need to take the potatoes, but if you want to go rest, I'll finish up." The menu calendar showed shepherd's pie for supper. Marty could take care of it on her own.

Charlotte's blue eyes flew wide. "I can stay and help."

Marty took the peeler from Charlotte's hand. "You'll probably have to do double duty again when Brooke starts chemo next week. She'll need me close by. So go on. Take a little time for yourself."

Charlotte twirled her cap's ribbons with her fingers, uncertainty pinching her brow. "Are you sure? I really don't mind helping."

"I know you don't." Marty smiled and picked up a potato. She began whisking bits of peel into the sink. "But I'm fine. If I might be honest, I need a little time to myself, too. To . . . think."

Charlotte nodded wisely. "I understand. I have those kinds of days myself. All right." She removed her apron and draped it over her arm. "I'll go wash towels, then. Can you believe Lucas and Myron haven't washed their towels since we got here?" She made a sour face. "Lucas said why bother washing towels? They only use the towels to dry off after a shower when they're clean, so how can the towels get dirty?" Her cheeks flamed red. "Even so, the idea . . ."

Marty laughed. "I guess men look at things differently than women do. I tell you what, I'll take care of supper tonight if you'll carry a snack to the men this afternoon. There are plenty of cookies left from yesterday, and you can take some apples, too."

"All right. Enjoy your afternoon, Marty."

While Marty boiled and mashed potatoes, snapped green beans, and kneaded dough for dinner rolls, her mind bounced back and forth between keeping quiet or telling Anthony about Brooke's intentions for the resort. When her phone rang shortly after four—Brooke calling to let Marty know she was awake, steady on her feet, and in need of nothing—Marty sagged in disappointment. Taking care of Brooke would give her a break from her troubling thoughts. But music was playing in the background, which meant Brooke had made it to the living room and had her stereo going. In other words, she was fine. Marty agreed to bring a plate of food to Brooke at suppertime, and Brooke agreed to call Marty if she needed help with something.

Anthony came in at six and headed straight for the shower. Marty had everything ready when the whole team of workers arrived at six thirty. Myron offered grace, and the men passed around the shepherd's pie, fruited Jell-O, and rolls. Marty waited until they'd filled their plates before she scooped a serving of the casserole made of hamburger, green beans, mashed potatoes, and tomato sauce onto a plate for Brooke. She covered it with foil, then used a leftover margarine container to hold a spoonful of Jell-O. Items in hand, she crossed the yard between the two trailers and let herself in. Brooke was stretched out on the sofa, sleeping soundly. So she left the food on the counter, put Brooke's phone on the sofa cushion close to her hand, and left.

As had become their custom, while the men ate dessert—peach cobbler with store-bought ice cream—they talked over the day's accomplishments and Anthony assigned tasks for the next day. Marty listened in, awed by how easily Anthony handled the responsibility of leading the team. Since he'd usually worked away from home in Indiana, she hadn't witnessed him in his role as boss until now. Pride swelled through her. He was knowledgeable and professional yet also humble, and it seemed obvious to her that the men respected him. They engaged in teasing camaraderie with one another at times, but when Anthony gave them instructions, all teasing fled and they listened intently. Even Lucas.

Anthony dismissed the men for the evening, and they filed out, chatting and laughing. Anthony picked up the empty casserole dish and carried it to the sink. "The supper was real good tonight, Marty. Thank you."

She turned on the water to rinse the dish. The tomato sauce had already dried to a crust around the edges. "Did you get enough to eat? Maybe I should have made two casseroles. There's not even a bite left."

"It's all gone because it tasted so good." He flicked a look over his shoulder, as if ascertaining they were alone, then leaned down slightly. "Charlotte's a sweet girl, but she hasn't learned how to season things when she's making bigger batches. It was good to eat your cooking tonight." He straightened and shrugged. "By the time we're done with this project, though, I bet she'll have learned a lot from you."

Marty bit her lip. Charlotte wouldn't have a chance to learn from her if they returned to Kansas early. She circled the table, stacking the plates, while Anthony followed and collected the silverware. He'd never helped with cleanup before. Why was he doing it tonight? They reached the sink at the same time, and when they lowered their loads, their hands brushed. Anthony smiled at her. A bashful, somehow boyish smile that carried her back to their courtship days. Her lips twitched into an answering grin, and she turned her attention to rinsing the plates.

As she opened the door on the dishwasher, he leaned against the counter and crossed his arms. "How'd the procedure go for Brooke today?"

"Okay, I guess." She lined up plates in the bottom rack. "They said they didn't have trouble inserting the catheter, and she wasn't in a great deal of pain afterward."

"That's good."

"Yeah." She scooped up silverware and began sorting the pieces in the holding cups. "I'll take her in next Tuesday for her first chemotherapy infusion. Plan on me being gone all day. The doctor told her they're going to give her a mix of carboplatin and pac . . . pac . . ." She grimaced. "Pacli-taxel? I think I'm saying it right. They added the second one because of the tumors they found in her abdominal wall."

He frowned. "She'll probably be pretty sick."

Marty nodded, her stomach twisting. "Dr. Dickerson said she'd be the sickest a couple days after the treatment. He's scheduled nine treatments for now, three weeks apart."

"Why so far apart?"

"It gives her some recovery time in between, so she isn't sick all the time."

He nodded slowly. "So she'll be doing the treatments all the way into next year."

"The last one is scheduled for the end of January."

"But then she'll be better?"

Marty paused and met his concerned gaze. "That's what we hope."

"No, Marty, that's what we pray. Right?"

Marty's chest went tight. She finished arranging the silverware, pushed the tray in, and started placing the glasses and dessert bowls in the upper tray. "She's not just doing chemo, though. She read a book about the benefits of yoga, so she ordered a mat and a couple of DVDs. She's got a whole lineup of vitamins to take every day, and she says from now on she won't eat any red meat, dairy products, processed sugar, white potatoes, or wheat flour."

Anthony's eyebrows shot up. "What's left?"

Marty chuckled. "Quite a lot, actually. Organic fruits and vegetables, brown rice, fish, nut butters . . ." She frowned. "I forgot about her list when I made the shepherd's pie. I used fresh green beans and tomatoes from Lansing's farmers' market, but she won't want the ground beef, potatoes, and cheese." She started toward the fridge. "I better find—"

Anthony caught her arm and drew her to a stop. "Let her tell you what she'd rather have. No sense in fixing something different, only to find out she doesn't want it or isn't hungry at all."

He was right, and she should appreciate his reasonable suggestion, but she was aggravated with herself and embarrassed for not thinking before taking food Brooke wouldn't eat to her trailer. Some caretaker she was. "Can I at least look and see what I have in case she asks me to fix something?"

He let go, and she hurried to the refrigerator. If nothing else, she could slice some fresh tomatoes, steam the rest of the green beans, and broil one of the chicken breasts she'd taken from the freezer for tomorrow's chicken fettuccine. If Brooke would eat chicken. Chicken wasn't red meat, was it? She closed the door and stood, gripping the handle and biting her lip. It would take a lot more effort to fix special foods. If Brooke was sick from chemo, she wouldn't be able to shop and prepare meals for herself. Brooke needed Marty.

The same worry that had plagued her since Brooke's admission about a casino swooped in again. What was the right thing to do—tell Anthony or not?

Anthony

Anthony watched Marty's face. Clearly something was bothering her, just like Charlotte had said. Not that the young woman had tattled. When she brought the afternoon snack to the worksite, Anthony had asked if Marty and Brooke were back yet, and Charlotte smiled and said, *"Yes, Brooke is resting, and Marty asked for some thinking time. So I'm letting her be."*

Thinking time . . . About what?

He'd been doing a lot of thinking, too. More than he could understand. About Ronnie and girls like her—and boys like Elliott—who didn't have good homes and didn't have anyone to guide them. He couldn't understand being raised that way. His childhood home had always seemed safe and secure, and his parents raised him to respect God. Dad said respect for God was the best thing anybody could learn because respect for God led to good decisions in all areas of life. Was Marty thinking about Ronnie and Elliott, too? Maybe thinking about what he'd said about being foster parents? He'd meant fostering babies so Marty could have the chance to love on an infant, but Elliott's comment about how nobody wanted teenagers haunted him. Would she be interested in helping a teenager—or maybe more than one—get a better footing in life?

They couldn't do it now. Not in this trailer. And not until they'd bridged the gap between the two of them. What kind of example would they set if they were at odds with each other all the time? Since the night Ronnie snatched Marty's bag and Marty held on to him in fear, she'd been a little better about talking to him. When she wasn't with Brooke. But if they came together about fostering teenagers, wouldn't that give them more reasons to talk to each other? To grow together instead of staying apart?

"Marty."

She jumped and turned from the fridge.

"Is there something bothering you?" He pushed away from the counter and crossed the linoleum to her. He cupped his hands around her upper arms. "If there is, I'll listen. I'll do my best to understand."

She gazed up at him, her lips slightly parted and her eyes round and filled with uncertainty. Was she afraid of him?

He swallowed. "I want to help. If I can."

She seemed to search his face, as if trying to believe him. She stayed quiet for several more seconds, and he stayed quiet, too, even though it was hard. If she was thinking the same as him, it would mean they weren't as far apart as he'd feared.

Finally she nodded. A jerky nod. "There's something I should tell you. But promise you'll . . . think about everything that will be affected . . . before you answer."

His pulse pounded with hope. "All right, Marty. I promise."

28

Anthony

*T*his resort . . . Brooke plans to have a casino here."

Anthony sure hadn't expected something like that to come out of Marty's mouth. He shook his head to clear what he'd anticipated. "I thought there'd be restaurants. Hotel rooms. That sort of thing."

"Those will be here, too, and different kinds of shops. But there will also be a casino. In the old bank building."

His favorite of all the buildings still standing on Eagle Creek's main street. He was putting his hand to restoring a building that would be used to entice people to squander their money. He coughed a short laugh. "I need to sit down."

Marty trailed him to the living area and stood at the end of the love seat, chewing her thumbnail, while he sagged onto a cushion. "She told me about it today while we were driving to the doctor's. She's sorry she didn't say anything about it . . . before. She didn't realize it would matter."

Of course Brooke didn't realize. Casinos and gambling and whatever else took place in what his mother would have called a "den of iniquity" were most likely normal parts of her big-city world. Marty had never talked about Brooke being a gambler—except in her business dealings, taking chances on properties—but that didn't mean she wasn't. Maybe she just hadn't written to Marty about it.

He planted his palms on his knees and looked into his wife's worried face. "I—"

She jerked her hand away from her mouth. "Remember, you promised to think about it before you said anything."

Yes, he had. But his brain was so fuzzy he couldn't form a sensible thought.

Marty perched on the edge of the opposite cushion and pinned her gaze on him. "I know we were taught that gambling isn't a good way to make money."

"'The desire of the slothful killeth him; for his hands refuse to labour.'" Anthony automatically recited Proverbs 21:25, one of the verses he'd been required to memorize before he joined the fellowship.

She nodded. "Yes. But Brooke wasn't taken to church. Her mother didn't believe in God. So Brooke wasn't taught the things we were from the Bible. We can't hold her to the same standard as someone who was brought up in faith."

God, not Anthony Hirschler, was Brooke's judge. So he wasn't worried about Brooke's standards, other than wanting her to come to salvation, the same as he wanted for every lost person. But he needed to think about his standards, to pray about what God would have him do. Which was worse—working on a building that would someday be used as a casino or leaving Brooke without the help she needed right now?

Closing his eyes for a moment, he listened for clear direction, but no voice whispered through his heart. Dad had always told him, *"If you don't know which way God is pointing, then stand still and wait until He tells you."* Anthony knew better than to run ahead of God. So he would wait until the Lord clearly spoke to him, and while he waited he would labor with his hands, as he'd been taught was productive and honorable.

Brooke

The Monday before her first chemo treatment, Brooke styled her hair in its poof, applied makeup—heavier than she'd worn before her diagnosis, because her pallor needed it—and slipped her fuchsia summer suit jacket over a white lace tank. She checked her reflection, focusing particularly on the patch of jacket covering her port. She didn't want it to show. It didn't. She gave a satisfied nod.

She looked professional. At least from the waist up. The matching skirt for her suit still hung in the closet. She could pin the waist, but she didn't want to. Consequently, her pumps would stay in the closet, too. She'd donned blue jeans and tennis shoes instead. Practical for tramping through the old buildings. And of course, given her occasional unsteadiness, sneakers were a safer choice. Not that she would share that with the team of investors.

Entering her kitchen, she glanced at the clock on the stove. Eight forty-five—fifteen minutes before they were due to arrive for their walkthrough. Her stomach trembled, and she pressed both palms to her middle. "Steady, girl. Stay positive." Eyes closed, she spoke aloud, giving herself the pep talk she'd want to hear from a business partner if she had one. "Point out the patio and pergolas behind the trailers, the new tin roofs on the buildings, the rebuilt boardwalks, the new double-hung windows that resemble the old ones but have a point-two U-factor—top of their class for energy efficiency. Remember to smile. Keep them focused on what's been done instead of what hasn't."

She grimaced. She wished what was already done outweighed, or at least equaled, what was still undone, but if someone mentioned how much work remained, she'd remind them there were sufficient months available to finish the project and open the resort on time. She hoped they'd take her word for it and not check the progress against the written plan she'd distributed the night of the investment meeting, because if they did, they'd see how many of her intentions didn't match the actuality.

"Smile. Stay positive."

She poured herself a glass of juice, fresh squeezed from organic oranges, but took only a couple of sips. Her stomach wasn't up to juice. Or food. Or conflict. A soft *beep-beep* from the intercom alerted her to cars outside the gate. She quickly pressed the code to open the gate, drew in a slow breath, ran her hands down the front of her jacket, then stepped out the door to greet her visitors.

Apparently the investors had decided to carpool, because only three cars pulled onto the grassy parking area. They exited the vehicles, a dozen men wearing business suits and impassive expressions. They didn't fool her, though. Beneath those masks of detachment, excitement bubbled within them. They loved making money, the same way she did. Now to convince them wealth waited at the other end of the soon-to-be-paved street.

"Good morning." She made her way from man to man, greeting them by turn with handshakes and the brightest smile she could muster. "Thank you for your willingness to be flexible and work around my schedule. I know you're eager to see how things are coming together here at the Spalding Resort. So I won't delay you with chitchat. Let's go have a look." She set off for the buildings, trusting they would follow.

As she led the group up the dusty street, she listened to the sounds of power tools, men's voices, and the slap of lengths of wood dropping onto solid floors emerging from behind the walls—music to a renovator's ears. The evening before, she'd instructed the Mennonites to go about their business and pretend the investors weren't there, and she had no doubt they'd continue working without pause. She wanted the men behind her to see the team in action, approve her selection, and believe in this project as much as she did despite the unexpected dry rot found in the old bank building and in one corner of the old mercantile.

The early August sun beat down hard, heat and humidity high even so early in the morning. The men swiped their glistening foreheads with the backs of their hands or tugged at the collars of their shirts. Marty had offered to have cold drinks available, but Brooke declined. If the investors were comfortable, they'd stay longer. She wanted them to peek, approve, and depart.

While they peered through windows or stood back and surveyed the buildings, she delivered her planned spiel, surreptitiously gauging their reactions. Although several of them lowered their brows or held their lips in a downturned position, she didn't sense any major concerns. She stopped in the shade of the lap-sided building's porch roof and folded her arms over her chest.

"Well, that's it. Everything's looking good, isn't it?"

They murmured, nodding, gazes scanning the street. Relief eased through Brooke's chest. Home free.

"Aren't we going to be allowed to look inside any of the buildings?" The question came from Tucker Boyle, a banker from Lenexa, who was new to Brooke's circle of acquaintances.

Ronald Blackburn, a longtime associate, harrumphed and maneuvered his bulky frame to the front of the group. "I believe I'd enjoy taking a look inside, too."

Brooke's lips trembled with her effort to maintain a casual smile. "As I'm sure you can hear, the construction team is hard at work. I'd rather not disturb them. Especially since I don't have enough hard hats to go around." She forced a light laugh. "Construction areas aren't exactly the safest places to explore."

"But things are progressing on schedule?" Mr. Blackburn's beady eyes fixed on Brooke.

Brooke wouldn't lie. Lies had a way of finding you out and destroying trust. She'd built a reputation for honesty, and she wanted to keep it, so she chose her words carefully. "These are old structures, some dating back to the Civil War. One can encounter unexpected issues in buildings of any age, but I'm sure we're all aware that it's more likely to happen with historical buildings."

"So you've encountered . . . issues?"

She stifled a sigh. "Yes. One."

Mutters rose from the group.

Brooke wished she could lay the blame on Mr. Blackburn, who'd insisted on hiring the original inspector. They wouldn't have been blindsided by the dry rot if the man had done his job correctly. But blame casting wouldn't change anything. She held up both hands. "However, I have a qualified construction team in place, and I fully trust them to handle whatever challenges they uncover."

She linked her hands behind her back and allowed her gaze to drift across each of their faces. "It might take them a few minutes to gather up their tools and remove any barriers that could prove troublesome for your safe progress, but if you'd like me to ask the workers to ready the buildings to allow you to explore the interiors, I'll do so." She held her breath.

Mr. Blackburn shook his head. "Let them work. We'll plan a tour of the buildings' interiors when we make our second visit. November second?"

Brooke nodded, letting her breath ease out. "Yes. That's what I have on my calendar."

"Good." He stuck out his hand, and Brooke took hold. "Thank you, Ms. Spalding, for your efforts to rebirth this town into something useful. We're all looking forward to the end result."

29

Kansas City
Brooke

rooke slipped her hand through the bend of Marty's arm and ambled up the hallway toward the treatment center's front doors. The acetaminophen she'd been given an hour ago had kicked in, and she felt no discomfort from her hours in the recliner receiving her second chemotherapy infusion, but she knew from the first one she'd be sick as a dog by Thursday. And probably bald as an egg. Already she looked henpecked, with only a few thin strands of hair still clinging to her scalp. She'd slapped a pink baseball cap on this morning, but she didn't care to wear something so bland for the duration of her treatments. Before she was too sick to be out and about again, she wanted to hit the mall. If she couldn't locate a wig, then she'd grab a wardrobe of scarves and hats.

She hoped Marty wouldn't give her any arguments about a shopping expedition. Leapin' lizards, the woman babied her worse than her mother ever had. But then, comparing Marty to Jeralyn Spalding really wasn't fair. One faithful, the other faithless. One compassionate, the other self-centered. One tender, the other hard. They didn't even have love for Brooke in common because she was pretty sure her mother didn't give a rip about her.

They reached Brooke's car, and she pulled her keys from her purse. Marty held out her hand, but Brooke shifted them out of reach and grinned at Marty's surprised face. "Lemme drive, huh? At least to the mall."

Marty put her hand on her hip. "What mall?"

"The largest one in Kansas." Brooke punched in the code to unlock her door and slid behind the driver's seat. "You'll love it."

Marty remained outside the car as if her sandals had set down roots.

Brooke raised one eyebrow. "Are you coming or not? The mall's in Overland Park, which is about half an hour in the opposite direction of Spalding, so the sooner we get there, the better. That is, if you want to help with supper for the men tonight."

Finally Marty scurried around to the opposite side of the vehicle and climbed in. She frowned across the console as Brooke turned the ignition. "Are you sure you're up to this?"

Brooke looked over her shoulder and backed out of the parking spot, wincing a bit when the skin at her port pulled. "I'm sure I won't be by the end of this week, and I want something to cover my pate."

"What's a pate?"

Brooke stifled her chortle. "My head."

"Oh." Sadness flooded Marty's features. Her gaze seemed to drift slowly across Brooke's baseball cap, as if trying to envision what was underneath, and then she turned forward and was quiet and solemn the entire drive to the mall.

Brooke parked outside one of the larger department stores. She'd bypassed the section in the past, disinterested, but she'd seen a good selection of hats on shelves and spinning display racks. As she recalled, the hats were near the purses, and she led Marty to the area. A few summerish hats lay in a heap under a sign reading Clearance, and Marty began picking through them, her motions slow and halfhearted at best.

Brooke nudged her. "Come on. Cheer up. You're always wearing a cap, so why is me putting one on such a big deal?" Marty's lips remained downturned. Unexpectedly, impatience stirred in Brooke's chest. "Will you stop with the morose routine? I need some levity here. It majorly torques me off to even think about losing my hair. My hair, Marty! A woman's crowning glory—isn't that what you called it when you explained to me why Mennonite women don't cut their hair short?" She yanked off her hat and pointed at her nearly bald head. "Well, my crowning glory is going down the shower drain, and I need something to replace it. So help me."

Marty's blue eyes widened. She ducked her head for a moment, then jerked her attention to the hats. She snatched up a pink beach-type hat with a cloth band sporting flamingos and palm trees and slapped it on Brooke's head. "There."

Brooke caught her reflection in a mirror next to the display. The hat fell so low even what was left of her eyebrows was hidden, and the brim flopped toward her shoulders like a pair of puppy dog ears. She burst out laughing. Marty laughed, too, although tears twinkled in the corners of her eyes.

Brooke removed the hat, cringing at the strands of hair caught in the straw, and tossed it back on the stack. "Something a little less flamboyant—or *flamingo-ant*—if you please." They laughed again, and suddenly Brooke found herself caught in Marty's embrace. Her port got squished between them, and the pressure hurt, but she clung to her friend, needing the comfort more than she could express.

Marty pulled loose and lifted a tan straw bowler from the table. "This is cute."

Brooke agreed. She tried it on. It was a little loose, but she could tuck some paper into the inside liner and tighten it up. She nodded. "Sold."

They found three more hats Brooke liked. A saleswoman carried them to the counter, and Brooke sorted through the new fall hats. Only one appealed to her—a fuchsia felt cloche with a little fan of feathers on the side—and she added it to her stack. Then they rummaged through the scarf pegs and chose half a dozen long scarves in various patterns. The saleswoman put each hat in its own box, except the newsboy-type pink, gray, and white plaid, which she dropped into a bag. She rolled the scarves, tucked them in with the newsboy cap, and stated the total. Marty gasped, but Brooke ignored her and paid the bill.

She started to lift the stack of boxes, but then she drew back. "Ma'am, could you put these behind the counter for a while?"

The saleswoman smiled. "Sure. I'll put your name on top of the stack. Come get them whenever you're ready."

"Thanks." Brooke scrawled her name on a piece of paper, handed it to the saleswoman, and then caught hold of Marty's arm. "Come on. There's something we need to do."

Marty's puzzled expression remained intact while Brooke led her through the mall's wide corridors past various shops, two sets of escalators, and a food court. They moved so briskly that the ribbons from Marty's cap fluttered, and by the time Brooke caught the tinkling notes drifting from the mall's carousel, she was winded. She huffed as she stepped up to the ticket window and purchased two tickets for the merry-go-round.

Marty frowned at the ticket Brooke offered her. "What's this for?"

Brooke pointed to the brightly colored carousel and its circle of horses. "To take a ride."

Marty gawked first at the carousel and then at Brooke. "You're joking. We're too old for that."

A sense of urgency filled Brooke. An urgency that had overtaken her at odd times ever since she'd received her diagnosis. She gripped Marty's upper arms, bending her ticket in the process. "We aren't too old. We're never too old to do something fun and spontaneous. As long as we still draw breath, we can have fun." She blinked away hot tears. "Come on. Let's pick a horse and take a ride."

Marty's lips wobbled into a smile, and she nodded. The two of them got in line behind squirming children and their accompanying grown-ups. Brooke couldn't help but observe the adults' faces—some smiling, others seeming tired or impatient. She'd often witnessed tiredness and impatience on her mother's face. If she'd had children, would she have gloried in their exuberance or told them to chill out or else, the way Mom usually had? She hoped she would have been a better mother than the one who'd raised her.

Sadness gripped her, and she pushed the emotion aside. She was going to have fun and that was final. She and Marty chose a pair of painted steeds—Marty's snow white with purple and pink flower embellishments and Brooke's as black as the ace of spades with hot-pink and turquoise flowers—and climbed aboard. Marty sat sidesaddle since her dress wouldn't allow her to sit astride, but Brooke straddled her horse and grabbed hold of the leather loop serving as reins. She lobbed a grin at Marty. "Ready?"

Marty double-fisted the brass pole. "Ready."

The carousel's music swelled, the ride jerked into motion, and the horses glided up and down. When Marty's was up, Brooke's was down, and they giggled at each other at every pass. The ride lasted only a few minutes, but in those few minutes Brooke savored the joy of spontaneity, of friendship, of feeling good, because she knew it wouldn't last. The carousel eased to a stop, and Brooke reluctantly slid off the horse and stepped to the floor. If she were still five or six, like the little girl who'd ridden the horse in front of her, she would beg for a second ride. But a glance at her wristwatch told her they needed to head for Spalding.

School had let out, and high school and junior high kids stood in noisy groups in the corridors. Brooke and Marty wove around shoppers, teenagers, and kiosks all the way back to the department store where her hats waited. As they walked to the car, an idea struck—a spontaneous idea that brought a smile to her face. She stopped and grinned at Marty over the stack of boxes in her arms. "Let's do it."

Marty turned back. "Do what?"

"Something silly and fun at the end of each of my chemo infusions, for as long as I'm able. Let's make it our . . . tradition." Brooke knew about Marty's family traditions—big dinners with everyone around the table, summer picnics, morning and nighttime prayers, quilting bees and harvest parties and fellowship dinners to celebrate happy events. Brooke's only childhood tradition had been weekly chaos. She wanted—even more than she wanted, she needed—something she could look forward to over the next months.

The urgency struck again, harder than before. She hugged the stack of boxes to her middle. "Come on, Marty, say yes. I want to build some happy memories, like the one I have of the two of us playing on the swings and the teeter-totter and the slippery slide at the grade school playground after the blizzard when we were eighth graders. Remember?"

Marty sighed. "I remember. It's one of my favorite memories, too."

Brooke nodded hard. "Yeah. So freezing cold our breath almost turned into ice cubes, but we stayed out until we couldn't feel our toes and fingers anymore. And we laughed . . . We laughed so hard. I can't tell you how many times I've thought about that day to help myself smile when life got rough. It's pretty certain the next few months are going to be rough. I'll need more happy moments to think about, so let's make some. Okay?"

Marty sucked in her lips, and Brooke identified guilt in the pinch of her brow. "I'd like to, Brooke, but I—" Her gaze zipped to something behind Brooke, and she gasped. She pointed, her hand bobbing as if caught in a blender. "Look! Look! Someone's being kidnapped!"

30

Marty

*M*arty took off at a clumsy run. Brooke hollered at her to stop, but she kept running toward the idling car and the well-dressed middle-aged man who was forcing a young teen girl into the vehicle's back seat. She rued her sandals. If she'd worn her tennis shoes today instead, she'd be able to sprint. *Don't let them leave before I can help her, God!* The demand—because she no longer prayed—repeated itself in her head while the soles of her sandals pounded the pavement and her purse bounced against her hip.

She stopped a few feet from the pair, gasping to catch her breath. "Sir! Sir!"

He sent a scowling look over his shoulder. Then in the span of a second, his expression changed to a smile that somehow chilled her more than his scowl had. "Yes? What can I do for you?"

Now up close, Marty got a good look at the teen, who was half-in and half-out of the sleek gray car that reminded her of a shortened van. The girl's clothes—tight, the shirt low cut at the neck and so short it exposed two inches of her belly above the waistline of a skirt that seemed barely more than a band of fabric—made Marty blush. She started to withdraw, but then her gaze met the girl's. A mix of sullenness and fear warred on the teen's heavily made-up face.

She gestured to the girl. "Is she all right? It doesn't look like she wants to go with you."

The man laughed and gave the girl a final shove. She fell into the seat and he slammed the door, sealing her behind tinted windows. "No, she doesn't. I grounded her yesterday, and she disobeyed me by coming to the mall with some friends. I embarrassed her pretty badly when I pulled her away from them, but she has to learn she must abide by my rules."

He spoke so smoothly, so confidently, Marty wanted to believe him. But something raised alarm bells in the back of her mind. "You're her father?"

"That's right. And if you'll excuse me"—he brushed past Marty and rounded the front of the car—"I need to get her home for a stern talking-to." He yanked open the driver's door and slid inside. The car lurched forward with a squeal of its tires, and Marty jumped back. She stared at the license plate as the car sped away, then pulled a gas station receipt and pen from her purse and scrawled the series of letters and numbers on the back of the receipt.

Brooke huffed up beside her. "What . . . what did he say?" Her pale face dotted with perspiration and her heaving chest pierced Marty. Brooke shouldn't be running around parking lots in the heat and humidity.

Marty put her arm around Brooke's waist and aimed her for the Lexus. "He said he's her father, but I don't know if I believe him." She waved the paper. "I got the license plate number, and I'm going to give it to the police." She waited for Brooke to argue with her—to tell her she was making a big deal out of nothing.

"I think that's a good idea."

Brooke's grim tone increased Marty's concern for the girl. Sitting behind the steering wheel with the engine running and the air conditioner on high, Marty retrieved her phone from her purse and tapped in 911. She told the woman who answered what she'd seen, gave a description of the car and both of its occupants, and recited the license plate number. Suddenly her hand began to shake, uncertainty gripping her. What if the man really was a father trying to discipline his rebellious child? A false accusation could fuel the girl's defiance. "I . . . I don't want to get anybody in trouble, but it . . ." She swallowed. "It looked funny to me."

"Ma'am, you did the right thing by calling." The assurance in the woman's voice relieved a bit of Marty's angst. "It's always better to err on the side of caution when children are involved. The situation will be investigated. Thank you for giving such detailed information. This will help the officers." She requested Marty's telephone number in case an officer needed further clarification, and then they disconnected the call.

Brooke shook her head, gaping at Marty. "What happened to my timid, mild-mannered friend? You took off like a raging bull. Did you even consider that the man might have a gun or, at the very least, a terrible temper?"

"No, I didn't." Marty dropped her phone into her purse. Her hands were still shaking, and nausea rolled in her stomach.

"Leapin' lizards, Marty, you put yourself in harm's way." Brooke reached across the console and placed her hand on Marty's arm. "And even though you scared the mustard out of me, I'm proud of you. You might have saved a girl from an abusive situation."

Tears filled Marty's eyes, distorting her vision. "Do you think so?"

"You never know. I mean, the man was dressed to the nines and drove a nice car, but that doesn't mean he was on the up-and-up. After all, my mom drove the hearing-test bus from school to school and hung out with teachers and administrators. No one would have guessed how awful it was in my home based on her public persona."

A warm tear ran down Marty's cheek, and she batted it away. "I'm sorry you had such a rough childhood, Brooke. And now—"

Brooke waved her hand. "Water under the bridge. It can't be changed, so there's no sense in talking about it." She sagged into the seat. "I'm pooped. Between the long chemo session, our shopping, and then running across the parking lot, I need a rest. Glad you're driving. I hope you don't mind if I sleep all the way home." She leaned against the headrest and closed her eyes.

Marty used Brooke's GPS to find her way through Kansas City and onto the highway that led to Eagle Creek. Their stop at the mall and her call to emergency dispatch put them home past suppertime, and Anthony could have berated her for leaving Charlotte in charge again. Instead, he said he'd been worried and then listened when she explained what she'd seen. He hugged her afterward, and she clung to him, grateful for his support, concern, and understanding.

Marty carried a bowl of the casserole with ham, potatoes, and peas that Charlotte had prepared for supper to Brooke, who thanked her but said she wasn't hungry. She left Brooke stretched out on the sofa with the stereo playing softly and returned to her trailer. She wasn't terribly hungry herself, so she put the leftovers in the refrigerator and began the supper cleanup.

While she loaded the dishwasher, Anthony sat at the table and told her about his efforts to repair the plaster moldings above the windows on the old bank building. Although they hadn't discussed Brooke's plan to turn the bank into a casino since the night Marty confessed it to him, his mentioning the building stirred questions. Would they see the project through? Leave when Brooke's treatments were complete? Or did he want to leave sooner? Brooke wanted to create a do-something-fun tradition, but Marty couldn't commit to it until she knew she'd be there for each of the treatments.

After they had changed into their nightclothes and were ready for bed, she gathered the courage to ask him what he intended. He was propped up against the pillows, his open Bible on his knees. She sat on the edge of the mattress and touched his wrist. "Before you start to read, may I ask you a question?"

He nodded and gave her his full attention.

"About the old bank . . . Are—"

Marty's cell phone rang. She picked it up from its spot on her nightstand and flipped it open. "It's Brooke." She hit the connect button and pressed it to her head. "Hello?"

"Marty, you need to get over here right away. Bring Anthony, too."

Panic propelled Marty to her feet. She waved at Anthony to get up. "What's going on?"

"Just come! Quick!" The phone went dead.

Marty tossed Anthony his robe, and she jammed her arms into hers and hurried through the trailer. Anthony grabbed her hand and they ran to Brooke's front door, which was standing open in invitation. He guided her over the threshold first, then burst in behind her.

Brooke was still on the sofa but sitting up with the remote control from her television gripped in her fist. She pointed the remote at the flat-screen television hanging on the wall. The image was frozen and the volume silenced. "I rewound the broadcast so you could see this. Watch and listen, both of you."

Anthony grimaced. "Brooke, we don't—"

"—watch TV, I know." Brooke rolled her eyes. "But it's important. Listen." She punched a button, and the person on the screen, who was standing outside a residential house in what appeared to be a middle-class neighborhood, came to life.

". . . call from a concerned citizen earlier today from the mall in Overland Park led to the arrest of four men and the rescue of seven children ranging in age from twelve to seventeen who, according to the investigating officers, were allegedly victims of a sex-trafficking ring."

Marty's ears began to ring. She dropped onto the end of the couch and stared at the television. Anthony sat on the arm and draped his hands over her shoulders. She watched, rapt, while the reporter explained how neighbors had suspected something wasn't quite right because they'd seen men coming and going at odd hours and the number of young people living in the house seemed to change from week to week, but no one had contacted authorities, either out of fear or an unwillingness to stick their nose into someone else's business.

The image changed to a solid blue background with lines of text from Caller and Operator. A portion of the conversation she'd had with the woman at the other end of her 911 call came through the speakers while the lines scrolled on the screen. Marty hadn't realized her call was being recorded. She covered her mouth with both hands, uncertain how to react. Anthony massaged her shoulders, his touch comforting.

The reporter appeared again, still positioned outside the regular-looking house in the regular-looking neighborhood. "Thanks to one person's instinctive call to 911 with relevant information, these children are safe and will no longer be exploited. KKSP channel 14 will follow this story and bring you updates in the next weeks, so—"

Brooke clicked the remote, and the screen went blank. She grinned at Marty. "See what you did? You saw something questionable, you acted on it, and seven kids will sleep safe tonight."

Marty leaned against Anthony's frame, too weak to hold herself upright. "Sleep safe . . ." She looked up at Anthony. "Where do you suppose they are?"

He rubbed her shoulders. "I don't know, but wherever it is, it's got to be better than where they were until tonight."

"But remember what Elliott said?" Marty's throat went dry, and it hurt to force words past it. "How the police probably took Ronnie to a juvenile facility, where she'd be fed but wouldn't find any kind of real healing? He said foster parents don't want teenagers. The reporter said the kids were twelve to seventeen years old—not little children anymore. How can we know for sure the kids taken from that house are really in a good place right now?"

Anthony leaned down slightly and rested his chin against her temple. "I don't know. I guess we have to pray . . . and trust."

Brooke grimaced. "Well, you can pray and trust. Tomorrow I'm going to make some calls, see what I can dig up. I know a few people in the news industry, and they might talk to me off record. I'd like to know where those kids end up, too. Especially since Marty and I saw one of them."

Marty recalled the girl's obstinate yet helpless expression, her full lips stained with bright-red lipstick, her eyes lined with black, and her lashes clumped by mascara. A young face but a hard face, older than her years. The same thing she thought she'd seen when she looked into Ronnie's eyes. "I'd like that, too."

Anthony kissed her cheek. "You did real good, honey."

Her face warmed. He'd called her honey, something he hadn't done in at least two years. And he'd never been affectionate in front of an audience. "Thanks."

Anthony stood and took hold of Marty's hand. He tugged, and she rose. He wove his fingers through hers. "Brooke, do you need Marty to help you to your bed?"

She seemed to grin at their joined hands. "No, I'm fine. Chemo day's not so bad. It's the two-days-past-chemo that gets me. So don't feel like you need to come around tomorrow, either, if you have other things you'd rather do."

The heat in Marty's face increased, but she wasn't sure why. She took a step toward the door. "I'll check on you in the morning after breakfast. Good night, and thanks for sharing the news story with us."

They exited Brooke's trailer and moved down the creaky metal stairs to the ground. Her frequent trips between the two trailers had carved a path, and with a full moon shining from a cloudless sky and her hand secure in Anthony's, Marty easily followed the flattened grass. The breeze, slightly cool since night had fallen, rustled the leaves in the thick trees behind the trailers, and from somewhere far away a coyote released a mournful howl. She shivered.

Anthony's fingers tightened on hers. "You're all right."

His deep voice, sure and warm, sent another chill through her frame, but it was the good kind of chill. A chill of awareness of him as her husband that she hadn't experienced in months. She squeezed his hand and gave him a shy smile. He smiled in return, and something in his eyes sent another sweet shiver from her head to her heels.

They reached their trailer, and as Marty started to step up onto the porch, she remembered how her phone had interrupted her midsentence. Under the cover of darkness was a better time to ask the question she'd meant to ask earlier. She paused at the base of the steps and turned her face up to him.

"Anthony, have you decided how long we'll stay here?"

He tipped back his head and lifted his gaze to the sky for several seconds, as if seeking guidance from the face in the moon. When he looked at her again, his expression held a mix of bewilderment and wonder. "I've prayed about that in my private time with God every day since you told me. Every time I go into the old bank building, I think about what will take place in there, and I'll be honest, it bothers me. But so far God hasn't told me to pack up and go back to Indiana. Until He does, I'll stay here and keep working."

She licked her lips. "Do you think . . . maybe . . . God wants you to stay until Brooke's treatments are done?"

"Maybe. Or it could be for something else. Something we don't know about yet that He isn't ready to show us."

Marty liked his use of *us* even though she had distanced herself from God and didn't expect Him to communicate with her.

He released her hand and placed his palm on the small of her back. "C'mon, let's go in. It's late."

He led her up the stairs and opened the door for her. Inside, he took her hand again and they moved through the dark trailer, her shoulder brushing against his upper arm with each step. Her awareness of him growing with each step. Although they'd slept in the same bed, they hadn't been intimate since the awful day the doctor had told them they wouldn't have children of their own. After that, the act of coupling had seemed pointless. Why bother if they couldn't procreate? But now . . .

They removed their robes and laid them across the end of the bed, then inched around to opposite sides and climbed in. The bed frame squeaked, and Marty cringed. Such an intrusive sound when it seemed as if a ribbon of peace had wrapped itself around the two of them.

She rolled to her side facing Anthony and rested her cheek on her pillow. He lay on his back, and she admired the firm turn of his jaw in the pale moonlight streaming through the trio of windows above the headboard. Slowly he angled his head until his gaze found hers. A smile curved his lips. He raised up on his elbow and leaned in, closer and closer, until his warm breath grazed her cheek. Longing—an earthy desire that had been too long absent—welled inside her. Then his lips brushed against hers. Her body reacted in a sweet tremor, but before she could return the pressure, he shifted away from her.

"Good night, Marty."

Unexpectedly—unexplainably—tears pricked. She swallowed. "Good night."

He rolled over and pulled the sheet up to his chin, and soon his heavy breathing let her know he'd slipped off to sleep. But she couldn't sleep. Visions of Ronnie, of the girl from the mall, and of Anthony's tender face hovering close to hers kept her awake and restless well past midnight.

31

Brooke

*B*rooke awakened on Thursday morning with the strong need to vomit. But vomit what? Her stomach was empty.

Her fist against her clenched lips, she struggled to sit on the edge of the mattress and then rocked while wave after wave of nausea rolled through her. She broke out in a cold sweat. Panting, she pawed for the half-empty water bottle she'd left on the nightstand yesterday when she'd gone to bed. Her hand shook so badly she dribbled water down the front of her PJs, but a small amount of room-temperature water made it between her lips and slipped across her tongue. She swallowed. The liquid immediately reversed and spewed from her mouth.

She dropped the bottle next to her feet. It tipped and chugged a puddle onto the carpet. One hand cradling her stomach and the other over her mouth, she staggered to the bathroom. She bent over the toilet and heaved until she was certain her stomach was turned inside out. When the fierce bout had passed, she sank down on the edge of the tub and let her head drop back. A groan left her throat. Why hadn't she listened to Marty and taken a nausea pill before she went to bed? Brooke had never liked to take medicine until she really needed it. Mom was always popping this or that, trying to eradicate some ailment, whether real or contrived. Well, this nausea was real and she needed the relief-giving pill, but would she be able to keep it down?

When she was a child and suffered from the stomach flu, Mom had told her, *"Don't barf in your bed or on the floor, Brooke. I can't handle it."* But she'd also given her cups of chicken broth and put a trash can close by.

Maybe that was the most sympathy Mom had known how to offer. To this day, a cup of chicken broth was her favorite comfort food.

Was there still a can or two of broth in her cupboard from her last bout of post-chemo nausea? She rose shakily, pulling in slow breaths through flared nostrils and releasing them through her pursed lips—something Marty had taught her to combat dry heaves—and headed for the bathroom door. As she passed the sink, she got a glimpse of her reflection in the mirror, and the sight brought her to a halt. Dark circles under her eyes, skin that seemed to hang like the jowls on a bulldog, only a few thin tufts of bleached-blond hair still clinging to her pink scalp. She grimaced. Ugly. So very, very ugly. If the chemo wasn't already making her sick to her stomach, the image peering back at her would be enough to make anyone gag.

Turning away from the mirror, she aimed her quivery legs for the kitchen. She braced her hand on the wall and then on the counter to keep herself upright. "Broth . . . Broth . . ." She chanted the word like an incantation. One can of organic chicken broth remained on the pantry shelf. Sighing in relief, she pulled it out and carried it to the can opener.

"A cup of broth and a Zofran . . ." She swallowed repeatedly while the can opener whirred. A savory scent wafted from the can, and her stomach roiled. She bent over the kitchen sink and retched so hard she feared she'd pass out. Her stomach muscles aching, she slid down the cabinet to the cool linoleum floor and sat panting, sweating, battling tears. "It'll pass. Just like last time, it'll pass." The reminder did little to comfort her. Even though she recognized its truth, it didn't help much in the here and now.

She was still sitting there when her front door opened and Marty came in carrying a napkin-covered plate. Concern pinched Marty's face when she spotted Brooke. She plopped the plate on the counter and dropped to her knees. She rubbed Brooke's shoulder, her hand cool and firm.

"Have you taken a nausea pill?"

Brooke shook her head. The simple motion made her world spin. She gripped her stomach.

Marty rose and opened the cabinet where Brooke had stashed her bottles of prescription meds. She shook a pill from the bottle, filled a glass with 7-Up from the refrigerator, and offered them to Brooke. "Here."

Brooke held up her hand. "It'll just come up again. There's no use taking it now."

Marty's forehead scrunched. "At least try. It won't get better if you do nothing."

"It won't get better anyway!" Brooke cringed. She'd sounded so harsh and unappreciative. Like her mother. She grabbed Marty's wrist and squeezed. "I'm sorry. I'm not a very good sick person."

"It's all right. You've got good reason to be grumpy." Marty set the glass and pill on the counter and caught hold of Brooke's hands. She pulled, bringing Brooke to her feet, and escorted her to the living room.

Brooke flopped onto the middle of the sofa, rested her head on the plump backrest, and covered her eyes with her arm. She groaned. A hand touched her knee, and she lowered her arm and peeked at Marty through slitted lids. The compassion in her friend's eyes stabbed like a knife. She didn't deserve any kindness. She closed her eyes. "Leapin' lizards . . ."

"I'm sorry you feel so lousy."

"Me, too."

"I wish you'd try taking a pill."

"I know."

Silence fell, during which Brooke held her stomach, practiced the breathing technique Marty had given her, and pleaded with her stomach to behave.

The sofa cushion shifted, and Brooke opened one eye. Marty was heading for the kitchen, arms swinging, black ribbons fluttering on her shoulders. She poured the chicken broth into a saucepan and set it on the stove, then dug out the loaf of cinnamon quick bread made from almond flour and cut off a slice. She popped it in the toaster and turned to the refrigerator. Her gaze whisked across the room and met Brooke's.

A bashful smile bloomed on Marty's sympathetic face. "Do you want some music?"

The offer touched Brooke deeply. Marty could get herself in trouble with her fellowship for intentionally listening to what the leaders deemed inappropriate music. She should say no, but she needed the distraction too much to be magnanimous. She nodded.

Marty took the farmers'-market, grass-fed, five-dollars-per-half-pound butter from the refrigerator before crossing to the little basket that held the remotes for the TV and stereo. She lifted the one for the stereo and pushed the power button. Cat Stevens's voice came through the speakers as the toaster popped up the slice of bread. Marty dropped the remote into the basket and returned to the kitchen.

While Marty buttered the bread and checked the broth, Brooke listened to Cat sing a ballad about the wind, words, and not making the same mistakes again. The CD ran through its songs, diverting Brooke's attention from the awful feeling in her gut and the weakness of her body. She managed to nibble a few bites of the bread and sipped half a cup of broth, swallowing a Zofran with the liquid. Then she stretched out on the sofa with a small waste can nearby, just in case, and listened to Cat croon "Morning Has Broken," a gentle ballad that always soothed the edges of her frayed nerves.

Marty had been straightening things in the kitchen, but while "Morning Has Broken" played, she stood still and stared at the stereo. Her concentration tickled Brooke, and she couldn't resist teasing, "You're not gonna turn into a Cat Stevens fan, are you?"

Marty blinked twice and then laughed, self-conscious. "I love cats, but I don't know what you're talking about."

Brooke gave a weak wave toward the stereo. "The artist who's singing. His name is Cat Stevens."

Marty picked up the dishrag and ran it over the countertop. "Is he . . . a Christian?"

Brooke shrugged. "I have no idea. Why?"

"I've heard the poem before. Our deacon's wife read it during one of our Bible study times. But it has more stanzas than he sang."

"Oh yeah?" Brooke rolled sideways and curled into a ball. The AC was a little too much this morning.

"Yes. I'll see if I can find the whole thing and read it to you. It's really pretty."

Brooke shivered. "Okay."

Marty bustled over, yanking the afghan from the back of the chair as she came. She draped it over Brooke, then sat on the edge of the sofa and smoothed her hand on Brooke's head. She couldn't smooth her hair. There wasn't enough left to smooth. The thought put a bitter taste in Brooke's mouth.

Marty's warm fingers ran lightly from Brooke's temple to the nape of her neck. "I know you feel really bad, but sometimes when I'm blue, it helps to think happy thoughts. Like about all the successes you've had and how beautiful this place will be when it's all done. I really admire you for all you've accomplished. You're so successful, Brooke. You should be proud of yourself."

Brooke scrunched her face and shifted the afghan until it covered her chin. "I'm not successful."

"Sure you are! You've—"

Brooke snorted. "Okay, I've had a hand in rebuilding nearly a hundred properties, making them shine again. I've made money—as much or more than I dreamed of having when I was a kid living in one seedy rental after another." A lump filled her throat and she swallowed hard. "But when it comes right down to it, when I leave this earth, who's gonna remember me? Nobody. What am I taking with me that matters? Nothing."

"Brooke . . ." Marty's tone held gentle admonition.

Maybe it was the awful nausea talking, but Brooke still believed everything she'd said. "Seriously, Marty, I've worked myself silly for more than a dozen years to prove that I could be successful, and for what? All that effort . . . all the stuff I've accumulated to prove my worth . . . it's meaningless. I'm going to die, and I can't take any of my money or property or belongings with me."

Marty gripped Brooke's shoulder and gave it a little shake. "You aren't going to die." Fear shone in Marty's expression.

No matter how it affected her friend, Brooke wouldn't be less than honest. "Of course I am. Even if this cancer doesn't do me in, something will, someday. We'll all die, Marty."

Marty turned her gaze aside and wrapped her arms across her stomach. "I don't like to think about dying."

"Who does?" Brooke wriggled up onto the decorative pillows and into a half-sitting, half-lying position. "But not thinking about it doesn't change the truth. It's pretty hard for me not to think about it, given the circumstances, and even more depressing than thinking about dying is thinking about not leaving something behind that really matters. Not a husband, or children, or . . . or anything else. What mark have I made on this world, Marty, that will make an ounce of difference to somebody? Nothing. Not even one."

Marty pursed her lips and stared at Brooke, blinking rapidly.

Brooke waited, but Marty didn't speak. Of course not. What could she say? She knew Brooke was right. She was just too kind to agree.

The stereo clicked another CD into place. John Denver's distinctive voice drifted across the room. *The wind is the whisper of our mother the earth; the wind is the hand of our father the sky* . . . Another song about wind. Something else that blew in, left, and was remembered no more. Brooke huffed. "Turn off the stereo. I want to sleep."

Marty clicked the remote, and heavy silence fell.

Brooke nudged Marty's knee. "No sense in sitting there watching me sleep. Put my cell phone where I can reach it and leave me alone. I'll call if I need you."

Indecision played on Marty's face. "Are you sure? I don't mind—"

"I'm sure. Go." She pulled the afghan over her head. Maybe if she were very lucky, her dreams would be more pleasant than her reality.

32

Anthony

nthony and the team cleaned up at the wash station Marty had set up next to the water pump at the edge of the trailers. She reasoned—and he agreed—that the indoor plumbing would benefit from the drywall and other dust being disposed of outside instead of being flushed down the drains. So they beat the dust from their clothes and then scrubbed their hands and arms in the cold water. They'd have to change the routine in the winter, though. He'd want warm water for washing when the winds howled and temperatures dropped.

Presentable again, he led the men into his trailer for lunch. He crossed the threshold, then gave a jolt of surprise. Marty was at the counter, pouring dressing over a garden salad. Shouldn't she be over at Brooke's trailer? The few days following Brooke's first chemo treatment, Marty hadn't left her friend's side, and he had expected her to do the same thing for this second treatment.

He gestured for the men to take their places at the table, which Charlotte was setting, and he scuffed across the floor to his wife. He'd battled a strange shyness in her presence since Tuesday night, the night Brooke had them watch the news report including Marty's 911 call and the two of them had walked hand in hand to their bedroom. He'd come so close to making love to her, but her trembling frame beneath his kiss told him she wasn't ready yet. He was ready, though. The desire had simmered under his skin for months, and it was worse since Tuesday, when he'd forced himself to turn away from her. He didn't want to frighten her or be pushy, but how long would he have to wait to become her husband again in every way?

He stopped a good distance from her and leaned against the counter. "Why aren't you at Brooke's?"

She bobbed her head toward the cell phone on the windowsill above the sink. "She said she'd call if she needed me."

He raised his eyebrows. "And you honored that?"

A sheepish expression crossed her face. "Well, I've checked in on her a time or two. She's hardly gotten off the couch." She glanced at the men and lowered her voice. "She's really sick."

He touched her arm. "Then we'll say some extra prayers for her."

Marty blinked several times. "Please do."

She carried the salad to the table and set it between the platter of sandwiches and two open bags of potato chips. She remained next to him when he slid into his seat. He asked a blessing for the food, then added, "Please grant comfort to Brooke and bring healing as You will. Amen." She squeezed his hand before taking the empty seat at the opposite end of the table.

The men engaged in their typical banter and laughter during the noon meal, but Anthony didn't join in. He ate two ham and cheese sandwiches, a handful of chips, and a good portion of salad, filling his stomach but tasting nothing. His focus was on Marty. The two months at the old ghost town had almost erased the tension lines from between her eyebrows. Several times he'd heard her humming while she worked—evidence of contentedness. At worship services they still encountered families, but she got to sit with him at the Baptist church, and that seemed to help her cope.

He liked this relaxed Marty who reminded him of the warm, smiling woman he'd married. Was God letting them stay here because the missionary family needed their house? Was the reason He had not urged Anthony to return to Pine Hill because this was where Marty would find her full healing? Where the two of them could restore everything that had been broken between them? He wanted everything mended—emotionally, spiritually, and physically. But even if they found contentment with each other here, eventually he'd finish this project and they would go back to Indiana. What would happen when they returned to Pine Hill?

Here, they were together every day. There, he'd travel to worksites in other towns and she'd be left in their house alone again. Here, there weren't any children running and playing outside her window. At home, they'd be surrounded by families. Here, she listened when he read from the Bible and bowed her head in reverence when he prayed. Back home, they hadn't read the Word or prayed together for months. Even if she hadn't openly stated her intention to return to faith, he sensed that the walls she'd built around herself were beginning to crumble. Back in Pine Hill, would the old resentment, jealousy, and isolation come back? He didn't want to live that way again.

"Is there any dessert?" Lucas blasted the question around a mouthful of potato chips.

Anthony shook his head, but he laughed. "You and your sweet tooth . . . always wanting cake or cookies or brownies."

Lucas grinned. "I don't notice nobody else turning 'em down when they're offered." He aimed the grin at Marty. "So did ya bake something for our dessert, Mrs. Hirschler?"

"No, sorry, Lucas. I didn't do any baking this morning."

"Aw." Lucas propped his chin in his hand and slumped his shoulders.

Marty rose. "Now, cheer up. I think you'll be happy with what I have planned." She rounded the table and entered the kitchen. She returned with a half-gallon container of ice cream and a stack of bowls. "Chocolate-chocolate chip, your favorite."

"Woo-hoo!" Lucas socked the air. "Thanks, Mrs. Hirschler."

The glint of fond amusement in his wife's eyes did something to Anthony's insides. She'd be such a good mother. A patient mother. A giving mother. *God, let us stay until the town is revived.*

Yes, it was a selfish prayer, but if they stayed to the very end and received every penny Brooke had promised him, he'd have enough money for adoption fees. Marty deserved the chance to love and nurture a child. Then her healing would last no matter where they lived.

Marty

For three days Marty searched for the poem "Morning Has Broken" on Anthony's and Brooke's computers. She could only grab minutes between cooking, household chores, adding patches to her current quilt, and caring for Brooke. Most sites had only the same three stanzas the singer named Cat had sung on the album, but on Saturday evening, about an hour before bedtime, she finally located an informational article about the poet, and it contained all six stanzas.

Both relieved and delighted, she copied the entire poem and pasted it into a document, then played with the fonts to make it look pretty before printing it. She rolled it, tied it with a leftover strip of pink calico fabric, and set it aside to take to Brooke in the morning before she, Anthony, and the others left for worship service in Lansing.

Sunday morning, she bathed and dressed, then headed to the kitchen. On Sundays everyone had a cold breakfast in their own trailers, which meant an easy morning for her, but while she set out boxed cereal and milk, she experienced a touch of melancholy. She paused, seeking its source. The recognition fell like a log on her head. She missed fixing a hot breakfast for the entire group. In all the years of her marriage, she'd cooked for only two, but she'd come to enjoy making larger batches of food. Probably because it felt as though she were feeding a family.

With a grunt of irritation, she slammed the door on the thought. Lots of women didn't have big families, and they got along fine. She needed to learn to be content with what she had instead of dwelling on what she didn't. Hadn't Anthony's Bible reading last night from First Timothy admonished as much?

The scripture replayed in her heart—*"But godliness with contentment is great gain. For we brought nothing into this world, and it is certain we can carry nothing out."* They'd discussed the scripture's meaning, and she'd tearfully shared what Brooke told her about leaving nothing of value behind when she died and then admitted she, too, feared dying without the chance to leave something behind that mattered. Anthony had wrapped her in a hug so tight she felt the sweet pressure of his arms still this morning, and his tender assurance whispered in her memory.

"We know Jesus, Marty, and we live to serve Him first. So every kind act—like letting the Hiltons use our house and you making those quilts for the benefit sales and even taking such good care of Brooke—has eternal value. We are leaving something of value behind, because what we're doing touches people's souls. We're storing up treasures in heaven."

His certainty had flowed over onto her, and she clung to the statements while something deep inside herself begged for it all to be true. If she couldn't leave a motherly impact on a child, she wanted to at least have a positive impact on . . . someone.

Anthony entered the kitchen, his cheeks ruddy from shaving and his dark hair combed back from his broad forehead. His Sunday white shirt and black suit served to enhance his masculine frame, and unexpectedly Marty experienced a bolt of reaction that was purely physical. On a Sunday morning. When she shouldn't act upon such thoughts.

She swallowed and gestured to the table. "I've got everything set out for breakfast. Do you mind if I run next door and check on Brooke? The worst of the sickness has passed, but she's still weak. I want to make sure she's all right."

"Sure, honey, go ahead." He delivered a peck on her cheek on his way to the table.

She remained rooted in place, her pulse racing from his use of the endearment and the sweet, affectionate kiss, while he settled in a chair and reached for the box of cornflakes.

He glanced at her. "Are you going?" Impishness glinted in his blue eyes, and she suspected he knew how much he had affected her.

Her face flooded with heat. Part embarrassment, part something she shouldn't acknowledge when the two of them were dressed for worship. "Yes. I'll be right back." She snatched the scrolled poem from the end of the counter and darted out the door before her foolish thoughts turned into action.

On the short walk to Brooke's trailer, she took in several breaths of the humid air and brought her thundering heartbeat under control. She found Brooke's front door standing open, and Brooke was sitting on the sofa fully dressed from her scarf-wrapped head to sandal-clad feet. Marty remained on the porch, staring with her mouth hanging open.

Brooke quirked her fingers. "Come in and close the front door. I've let enough cold air escape while waiting for you to show up."

Marty entered and sealed the door behind her. Then she stood on the square of linoleum that served as a foyer and gaped at her friend. For days Brooke had worn only pajamas. Before that, she'd alternated between baggy T-shirts and shorts and athletic-type outfits. She hadn't put on a bit of makeup since her chemo day, but today she wore blush on her cheeks, a touch of smoky purple on her eyelids, and eyeliner. No mascara because she no longer had eyelashes. The makeup, along with the feminine white blouse and long, flowing skirt in varying shades of pink and lavender, made her seem like a stranger. "You . . . You look . . ."

Brooke glanced down her length, then bounced a grin at Marty. "Is this okay for church? I can't wear any of my summer suits. The skirts are all too big around the waist these days. But this skirt has elastic, so . . ." She tipped her head and frowned at Marty. "What is the matter with you? You're staring at me like I've done something immoral. Is this outfit not dressy enough for church?"

Marty found the ability to scuff forward. She stopped a few feet in front of Brooke and shook her head, wonder dawning through her. "You want to go to church?"

Brooke fingered the edge of the scarf she'd wrapped around her head like a turban. "If you don't mind me tagging along. If I'm not intruding."

Her agnostic friend had asked to go to church. A laugh built in the center of Marty's chest and tickled until she couldn't hold it in. She let it flow. The incongruity wasn't lost on her. She'd done her best for the past two years to bury God, and here was Brooke reaching out a tentative hand toward Him. Without warning the laughter turned to tears. The poem fell from her grip, and she covered her face with both hands. Sobs shook her body.

Arms wrapped around her, and something silky—Brooke's scarf— pressed against her cheek. "Marty, what is it? What's the matter?"

She was frightening Brooke. She drew in a shuddering breath that brought her crying under control. She stepped free of Brooke's embrace and wiped her eyes with her fingers. "I'm so sorry. I don't know where that came from." Such a lie. She knew. But she didn't want to admit the source. What would Brooke say if she confessed she missed the assurance of faith, missed believing God was there and cared, missed talking to Him and thinking of Him as her Friend? Marty couldn't let her know how far from God's pathway she'd strayed, but she wanted to be in right relationship again. She wanted Brooke to know its fullness, too.

"Are you better now?"

The question resonated with Marty on various levels. She couldn't say she was all the way okay. Not yet. But better? She offered a wobbly smile and nodded. "Yes. I am."

"Good." Brooke pointed to the rolled paper on the floor. "Now . . . what's that?"

Marty scooped it up. "It's the whole poem for 'Morning Has Broken.' I finally found it."

"Oh, great!" Brooke sat on the sofa and leaned against a pair of throw pillows. "Read it to me."

Marty raised one eyebrow. "Now?"

"It's only eight thirty. You all haven't been leaving for church until after nine, so there's time."

"Are you sure?" Marty made a face and waved the tube. "I'm not a very expressive reader."

Brooke laughed. "I don't care. Read. I want to hear it." She folded her arms over her chest and closed her eyes.

Tamping down her bashfulness, Marty unrolled the paper. She cleared her throat, paused, and cleared it again.

Brooke opened one eye and peeked at her. "Read."

"Okay, okay." Marty pulled in a breath of fortification. " 'Morning Has Broken,' by Eleanor Farjeon." She recited each stanza, the last lines wheezing out on a note of relief that she'd made it all the way through. " 'Praise for the sweet glimpse, caught in a moment, joy breathing deeply, dancing in flight.' "

She lifted her gaze from the paper and spotted a single tear trailing down Brooke's cheek. She dropped onto the sofa and put her hand on Brooke's knee. "What's the matter?"

Eyes still closed, Brooke licked her lips. " 'Joy breathing deeply . . .' " She opened her eyes, and more tears spilled. "Such beautiful words. In my whole life, I've never experienced joy breathing deeply."

The comment almost stung. She held several happy memories of times with Brooke. She'd thought Brooke remembered them, too. "You've never been . . . happy?"

Brooke made a face. "Sure, I've had some happy times. Lots of them with you—you know, when we did silly things as kids. Even when we rode the carousel at the mall. I was happy when I could move out of Mom's apartment into my own place. When I got my college degree. Every time I made a deal on a run-down property and then when it was all done and pretty, that brought happiness. Making a profit always made me happy. Seeing my bank account grow . . . that, too."

She took the printed page from Marty's hands and stared at it. "Buying this ghost town, planning the renovations, getting investors on board—all of that gave me a rush of what I'd define as happiness, and I get another rush when I see evidence of the progress being made. But it never lasts. It's mine, and then it's gone. Fleeting. Nowhere close to joy breathing deeply." Brooke angled a crooked grin in Marty's direction. "The closest I've come was that snowy day on the playground when I flew down the slippery slide so quickly my bottom hit the ground before I knew I'd left the landing. Remember how we laughed? Laughed so hard we couldn't breathe?"

Marty nodded. Her teeth had ached for hours afterward from the cold air they'd sucked in with their wild laughter, but it had been worth it.

"That was a sweet glimpse of joy." Brooke gazed past Marty, seeming to drift away to somewhere inside herself. "But I want it for more than a moment. I want—" Her voice broke. She set the paper aside and grasped Marty's hands with a desperation that was palpable. "Help me, Marty. Please? Help me."

33

Anthony

 $\mathcal{T}$ he uncomfortable weight of inadequacy drove Anthony from bed long before the sun came up. He braced one hand on the wall next to the calendar and stared at the bold *November* at the top of the page. Where had September and October gone? How could he have let so many weeks go by without reaching Brooke with the truth of her need for a Savior? Some missionary he'd turned out to be if he couldn't lead one seeking woman to the Sustainer of Life.

He stepped away from the calendar, crossed to the window above the kitchen sink, and looked straight across the gap between trailers into Brooke's kitchen window. The light shining from inside the smaller trailer seemed especially bright since night's heavy shadows hadn't lifted. The shadows matched his gloomy thoughts.

Marty was over there with Brooke—again. She'd spent the whole night. Anthony hadn't liked the idea, but yesterday's chemo treatment— Brooke's fifth—had been rough on her. More than likely, he'd be taking Brooke's band of investors through the buildings for their second inspection. Would they find fault with him and his team? He'd never questioned his construction abilities before, but these investors were all big-city professionals, wealthy, with high expectations. The kind of men who looked down their noses at simple men like Anthony.

Marty had told him about the doctor saying Brooke would grow progressively weaker with each treatment since chemotherapy wore down the body over time. He'd seen evidence himself at their weekly Bible studies. With every infusion, Brooke's skin seemed paler, her steps slower, her shoulders more slumped. But he never heard her complain. Where did she get her strength? It wasn't from God, that much he knew.

Frustration carried on a tide of uselessness sagged him forward. "When, God? When will she choose to believe?" If he closed his eyes, he could still see Marty's excited face when she'd dashed into their trailer and exclaimed, *"Brooke wants to go to service with us this morning. She asked me to help her find joy. You'll show her how, won't you?"* The deacons had sent him here with the hope that, like a real missionary, he would lead someone to salvation, so even though he'd wondered why Marty didn't tell Brooke how to find salvation, he'd agreed.

Every evening since that Sunday, when Brooke wasn't too sick to sit up and listen, she'd joined him and Marty for Bible reading, discussion, and prayer. They invited the whole team to join on Wednesday evenings, studying together the same way the fellowship members back in Pine Hill did. Even Elliott joined them on Wednesday evenings. And Anthony preached with as much fire and enthusiasm as any of their fellowship leaders ever had from the pulpit in their chapel in Pine Hill.

After two months of him reading, explaining, and praying, Brooke still hadn't made a profession of faith. Neither had Elliott. Little wonder God hadn't called him to a mission field. He didn't have the gift of evangelism. Should he quit? Today was Wednesday. Tonight after supper, when the sun was low and the temperature cool, everyone would gather around the brick fire pit on the large patio that the Brooke-hired team of workers had constructed last month. Lucas especially liked roasting marshmallows over the pit, and all of them enjoyed the warmth of the fire as evening fell. Maybe he should ask one of the other men to lead. Nate could do it. Or even Myron. Myron's father was a deacon, and the young man's faith was solid.

He squinted at the square of light and toyed with the idea of handing the responsibility of Bible study leadership to one of his team members. Part of him wanted to let it go, and part of him resisted. The selfish part, probably. He wanted to be the one to bring Brooke and Elliott to the Savior. Maybe one more night of reading, sharing, and praying. If he couldn't get through to them tonight, then he would pass the responsibility to either Nate or Myron. They'd been making their way through the book of Isaiah and were ready for chapter fifty-five, which contained one of his preacher's favorite verses. Anthony had heard it quoted so often he knew it by heart.

"'So shall my word be that goeth forth out of my mouth: it shall not return unto me void, but it shall accomplish that which I please, and it shall prosper in the thing whereto I sent it.'"

His voice almost echoed in the empty room. Like someone else had said the words and he only heard them. He frowned, a prickle teasing the back of his neck. "*. . . shall accomplish that which I please . . .*" Who was meant by *I*? Would the words accomplish what Isaiah pleased or what God pleased? Were the words spoken by the prophet his own, or were they words given to him from God? He pressed his forehead to his palm, groaning under his breath. Of course they were from God, just as all the words found in the Holy Bible were inspired by the holy God of Israel.

His heart seemed to bounce against his rib cage. He turned from the window and stared across the quiet kitchen. None of the words he'd shared with Brooke or Elliott seemed to make any difference. Was it because he'd been delivering his own instruction? Had he asked the Lord to speak through him? He grimaced, realization stinging like a slap. In his eagerness to win Brooke's and Elliott's souls, he'd let his pride get in the way, thinking about how he could report his success to the deacons. He'd done everything backward. The prophet had shared God's instructions. Isaiah had no power on his own to change anyone, but God's words were powerful. They accomplished exactly what God wanted them to, and His Word could prosper the soul.

Anthony dropped to his knees on the cold linoleum. "God, forgive me for losing heart and thinking about giving up. It's Your will that none should perish. Help me speak what You want me to say, words from Your Book and not from my stubborn head. It will never be my words that change someone. It's all You. Let me share and then get out of Your way so You can reach Brooke's heart and Elliott's heart." *And the hearts of many others.*

He gave a jolt, as if someone had jabbed him with a pin, and opened his eyes. Had he said the last words out loud, had they been inside him, or had someone else said them? He didn't know, but the heaviness of failure lifted. He pushed to his feet. Charlotte would be in soon to start breakfast. He needed to dress for the day. But he didn't turn for the bedroom. He looked at the spot on the floor where he'd been kneeling. Something important had happened there. He couldn't explain it, because he didn't understand it yet. He'd have to wait for the Lord to reveal His purpose.

He strode for the bedroom. "I'll be patient, Lord. I can wait."

Brooke

Brooke tossed aside the afghan and glared at Marty. "No, I wouldn't rather stay in my bed. Stop patronizing me. You know I'm not a patient person." To Brooke's further consternation, Marty snickered. Brooke narrowed her gaze. "What's funny?"

"I'm sorry." Marty's sugary tone made Brooke grit her teeth. "You're being an impatient patient. It just struck me funny."

Brooke saw absolutely nothing funny about being impatient or being sick. There wasn't enough lotion in Kansas to moisturize her perpetually dry, itchy skin. She went from sweating to shivering to sweating as if her temperature were controlled by a pendulum. The bitter taste ever present in her mouth ruined the flavor of any food she managed to force herself to eat. Her entire head contained not one single, solitary strand of hair. Worst of all, Marty had started talking to her as if she were a preschooler instead of an intelligent, mature thirty-six-year-old woman. Which tempted Brooke to throw a tantrum the likes of which no three-year-old in existence had mastered. She wanted these treatments done. Today. This minute. She wanted her independence and her vitality back.

A shiver shook her frame and she reached for the afghan.

"Do you want me to turn up the furnace?"

Brooke snapped, "No, leave the furnace alone." The hurt in Marty's eyes pierced Brooke. She turned her gaze aside. Why was she so grouchy today? More than she'd been since the cancer treatments began. She didn't want to take her irritation out on Marty—after all, she'd essentially put her life on hold for Brooke. But aggravation simmered under her skin, and it would explode soon if she wasn't careful.

She picked up the glass of ginger-ale-spiked apple juice Marty had poured for her and took another sip. She grimaced. Awful. "Turn on the television, would you? I need some noise and distraction." She didn't add, *Before I bite your head off.*

Marty wrung her hands. "Wouldn't you rather have some music?"

For the first time since she could remember, Brooke did not want music. The melodies had ceased to soothe her, and it frightened her more than she wanted to admit. Would this cancer steal even that pleasure from her? "I'm sure. Noise, Marty. A news channel. See if something catastrophic happened somewhere in the world. It'll take my mind off my troubles."

Uncertainty marred Marty's brow, but she took the TV remote from the little basket and pushed the power button. The screen came to life—a game show. Brooke waved her hand. Marty tapped buttons, and images flashed of commercials, talk shows, sitcom reruns. Brooke flicked her fingers until two men and a woman behind a desk filled the screen. Then she thrust her palm outward. "Stop. There. Turn up the volume, please."

Marty dropped the remote into the basket and hurried to the kitchen, probably to escape seeing and hearing the television. She'd have to leave the trailer to avoid the sight and sound, since the space was so compact, but if she felt better staying on the other side of the eating bar, Brooke wouldn't berate her for it.

The woman reporter, who sat between the men, was talking. "Sharing a laptop led to the arrest of thirty-four-year-old Anniston Bailey on multiple counts of sexual exploitation and molestation of a child. The woman loaned a friend her computer to play the online game *Land of King Tut*. When he logged on, a chat box opened, asking for the latest video. The friend exchanged a few messages with the individual and eventually became concerned. He took a screenshot of the entire conversation and turned it over to police, who began an investigation. Ms. Bailey confessed to taping herself and a male friend with a neighbor's children and selling the videos because, as she explained it, she needed the money and didn't want to disappoint the person who requested the tapes."

The man on the woman's left shook his head. "We tend to think of sexual exploitation as a problem in poor or developing countries, but researchers affirm it's prevalent in every country across the globe, including the United States. It's been reported in every state in America."

Brooke reached for the remote. She'd wanted distraction, but this was too depressing. Marty rounded the counter and moved slowly toward the television, her gaze glued to the image. Brooke's finger stilled on the button, and she shifted her attention to her friend.

"Yes," the second man said, his tone solemn. "Between one hundred thousand and three hundred thousand children have been forced into prostitution, child pornography, or trafficking in the past year."

Marty gasped and covered her mouth with her hand.

"And some resources give even higher numbers. Here in Kansas in the past four months, we've seen—"

Brooke clicked off the television before the woman reporter finished her sentence. Marty whirled to face her. The horror in her eyes matched the sick feeling in Brooke's gut. This time the nausea wasn't caused by chemo. She tapped the remote on her knee. "I'm sorry. I couldn't take any more of that. Let's listen to music instead. How about a little Cat Stevens? I wouldn't mind singing along to 'Morning Has Broken.'"

Marty wrapped her arms across the attached cape of her dress and gripped her elbows so tightly her knuckles glowed white. "I'll tell you what's broken. Human morality. Compassion. The Golden Rule." Tears glistened in her eyes, and her chin crumpled. "None of these deplorable practices would happen if people did what Jesus commanded. 'Thou shalt love thy neighbour as thyself.' That's what He taught. But these people"— she flapped her hand at the silent television—"only think about what they can get. They don't care a bit about who they hurt as long as they get their money."

Brooke knew it wasn't intentional, but Marty's comment stung. This resort was to be her money tree, but the money would come from the pockets of gamblers. Was she hurting others by putting a casino in easy reach? She tried to stifle the thought, but it remained, pricking like the stickers she used to pick up in her socks when she walked through the empty lot across from the grade school. No matter how much she tugged on the cockleburs, somehow she always left a few spines that poked her ankles. The uncomfortable pricks to her conscience made her tone tart. "Well, you can't change the world, Marty, so there's no sense in worrying about it."

Marty turned her frown on Brooke. "I know I can't change the world. Leapin' lizards, I can't even change my small corner of it. I can't change the fact that I'll never have Anthony's child. I can't change the fact that cancer invaded your body. I can't change the fact that sin will run rampant until Jesus brings it to an end."

Brooke wished she could tease Marty about saying "leapin' lizards," but she couldn't manufacture even a hint of humor. "So why rail about it, then? If you can't change it, you'll only make yourself nuts worrying over it. Believe me, I know about making yourself nuts over things you can't change. All the worrying and trying in the world never changed my mother. All the worrying in the world won't stop man's inhumanity to man. It's been in the world from the beginning of time, and it'll be with us until the end of time. That's just the way it is."

Tears ran in rivulets down Marty's pale cheeks. Brooke groaned. She hadn't intended to make Marty cry. She patted the sofa and waited until Marty perched next to Brooke's feet.

"Listen, instead of getting yourself all worked up, think about those two little kids who won't be filmed anymore." Brooke pointed at Marty with the remote. "For that matter, think about the prostitution ring you helped break up with your phone call. Sure, there are lots of bad people out there, but there are good ones, too. Ones like you, who want to help. Think about them."

Marty sat silently for several minutes, her lower lip between her teeth and her brow puckered. Finally she swished her fingers over her cheeks, erasing her tears, and sighed. "I understand what you're saying, and I appreciate it. I really do. But somehow, after hearing what we just heard . . ." She turned a sad look on Brooke. "I've been too sheltered, Brooke. Too unaware of the ugliness taking place in the world. But since we came here, I've had to look at it face to face, first with Ronnie and then with that girl at the mall. Now thinking about how other people help isn't enough. I want to . . . do more."

Brooke's heart rolled over. She bumped Marty's hip with her foot. "You're a good person, Marty."

Marty shook her head. "I'm a sinner saved by grace. I'm a woman who was raised by parents who loved and nurtured me instead of mistreating me or exploiting me. I'm a fortunate person. And I need to take my own advice about loving my neighbor as myself."

The grumpiness that had sealed itself to her that morning seemed to have melted in light of Marty's distress and subsequent admissions. Brooke wasn't unhappy to see it go. "Isn't that what you're already doing by taking care of me?"

Marty didn't smile. "Maybe. In part. But . . ."

Brooke allowed several seconds to tick by before she nudged Marty again. "But what?"

She pressed her palm to her chest. "I don't know yet. But there's something. I can feel it, in here. I know what's causing it, too. It's God." Tears swam in her eyes again. "It's been a long time since I felt like God was speaking to me. Maybe because I refused to listen. But I feel it now. I can't hear the words yet, but I feel Him." The corners of her lips tipped upward into a smile. "It feels good, Brooke. It feels . . . so right."

Jealousy struck Brooke, the last emotion she expected in light of Marty's tearful confession. *Joy breathing deeply* . . . She saw evidence of it in her friend's face. Would she ever experience it herself?

34

Marty

*M*arty donned a sweater and loaded the men's midmorning snack into her little rolling wagon to take to the worksite. Brooke wanted to sleep, Charlotte wanted to do some laundry, and Marty wanted a few minutes with Anthony since they'd spent the night apart. She chuckled to herself as she thought about his dismal response to her request to stay with Brooke. *"I don't like being in our bed without you,"* he'd said with his arms looped around her waist. Had he forgotten how many nights she'd spent in their bed in Pine Hill while he was away on a construction job? She'd considered reminding him, but she decided it was better left unsaid. They were inching their way back to the relationship they'd had before the doctor's verdict shattered their world. Why stir conflict if she could avoid it?

The wagon's rubber wheels crunched on the gravel at the edge of the street. Two finches burst from the bushes and winged to the trees. The foliage looked so different than it had upon their arrival in Eagle Creek. The trees' leaves, which had changed from green to glorious oranges, yellows, and reds, now mostly littered the ground instead of clinging to branches. Even the last of the wild asters and sunflowers had dried up, leaving brown stems with a few withered petals. The nip in the air promised cooler days ahead. Might they even get their first snowfall before Thanksgiving arrived? When she was growing up in Kansas, they'd had a few snowy Thanksgivings. If it snowed, would the group travel to Indiana to spend the holiday with family, as they'd planned?

Even though Anthony was looking forward to a trip to Pine Hill,

Marty wasn't sure she was ready. They wouldn't be able to stay in their own house because the Hiltons were still there. Anthony's brother had offered to host them, which was kind, considering how many people already lived under their roof. Even though Marty wanted to see Rex, Dawna, and their children, she wasn't sure how she'd handle being with them day and night for that long. Baby Audrey would be six months old by Thanksgiving, old enough to coo and play with her toes and maybe even sit up in a high chair. Her heart gave a flutter of desire followed by a pinch of sorrow. Was she ready to hold and play with her littlest niece?

Mostly, though, she didn't want to leave Brooke. When she'd said as much to Anthony, he'd suggested taking her along to Pine Hill. Marty didn't argue at the time, but she knew it wasn't a good idea. Brooke's sixth chemo infusion was scheduled for the Tuesday before Thanksgiving, which meant Thanksgiving Day would be the worst as far as nausea and weakness. Brooke wouldn't want to be among strangers while battling severe bouts of sickness. Maybe Anthony would be willing to go by himself. The idea made her lonely.

She reached the edge of the business area and came to a stop. She hadn't made a trek to the townsite for weeks, and she stared open mouthed at the transformation. The row of once-dilapidated wood-sided stores wore a fresh coat of paint—creamy white with window casings, doors, and shutters sporting a variety of colors from muted to dark that brought the unique trims into prominence. The ceiling of the porch that stretched the full length of the single-story building was pale blue, the same as the porch of her childhood farmhouse. All the broken spindles had been replaced, and decorative spandrels accented the posts where they met the porch beam. The street front was so appealing she didn't want to stop looking.

Eager to see the progress on the stately rock buildings, she angled her gaze to the opposite side of the street, and a smile pulled on her lips. Paint the same color as a piece of aged cedar highlighted the window trims. A perfect choice—dark enough to give definition without pulling attention away from the unique limestone blocks. The sturdy front doors were deepest evergreen, an eye-catching complement to the tan stone. She followed the line of the buildings to the upper windows and released a little gasp of pleasure. The crumbling plaster designs were intact again. Anthony's online searches for repairing techniques must have paid off.

While she gazed at the rosettes and swirls, a shadow slinked up behind her, and she turned to find Anthony, an easy grin on his face. He gave one of her cap's ribbons a light tug. "What're you looking at?"

She examined the plaster decorations again. "The flowers above the windows. They're all fixed. They look really nice." A sudden thought slammed through her brain. She whirled to gawk at him. "How did you get up there?"

"Scaffolding. But I'm not the one who fixed them. Elliott did it." He seemed to examine the plaster designs, too. "He's a talented young man. Says he's been reading up on stained-glass art and wants to try to make windows to replace the ones that were taken from the old chapel. The team is over there now, replacing the roof. I kind of forgot about the chapel when we were repairing roofs, and it needed to be done for the building to withstand the winter weather." He reached for the wagon's handle. "I'll take the snack to them and then bring the wagon back to the house at noon."

Marty didn't release the handle. "Before you go, can we talk for a minute?"

Concern instantly creased his brow. "Something wrong?"

"No." A lump filled her throat, and she blinked rapidly to stave off the threat of tears. "I think . . . something's right." She shared the odd feeling that had crept over her after watching the segment of the news with Brooke. "I'm not saying I've completely healed from not being able to have children. To be honest with you, I might never completely heal from the loss. But I don't want to hold myself away from God anymore. I want Him to . . . use me somehow. If I can't be a mother, then I'll have to trust Him to fill the empty spot inside me somehow."

He grabbed her in a hug so fierce it stole her breath. "He answered my prayers. Oh, thank You, dear Lord and Savior, for answering my prayers."

His emotional outburst touched her more deeply than she knew how to describe. She'd been so caught up in her own loss that she hadn't considered Anthony's losses—his chance at fatherhood and, in a very real sense, his wife. But no longer. She was here now, and she intended to stay. She wrapped her arms around his torso and clung, burying her face in the curve of his neck. She held tight until his arms finally relaxed and allowed her to slip free. But his broad hands that smelled of sweat and dust and something else—maybe turpentine—cupped her cheeks and kept her from moving away from him.

He lifted her face and leaned down. She closed her eyes in anticipation, and his lips met hers in the sweetest kiss. Sweeter than the many kisses they'd shared in the past month. She curled her fingers around his wrists and leaned more fully into him, giving more of herself to the kiss. His lips tasted salty, and she realized tears were washing down her face. She opened her eyes. His cheeks were wet, too. She whispered, "Anthony?"

He touched his forehead to hers, eyes still closed. "Yes, honey?"

"I love you."

He opened his eyes and smiled at her. "That's good to hear."

She kept hold of his wrists, enjoying the feel of his warm hands on her jaw. "And I'd like you to think about something."

"What's that?"

"Thanksgiving." She swallowed. "I don't think we should leave Brooke alone, but I also don't think she'll be able to travel. Not after just having a chemo treatment. I don't want to keep you from your family, though, so would you consider going to Pine Hill without me?"

His brow furrowed, and he stared into her eyes for several seconds. Finally he sighed, his warm breath caressing her cheek. "I don't much like the idea of leaving you two women out here by yourselves, but I'll pray about it." He gave her another quick kiss and stepped aside. "I better get this snack to the men before they think you forgot about them. The three of us'll talk after Bible study, all right?"

Marty grimaced. "The way Brooke's feeling, she might not be up to joining us tonight."

The oddest expression crossed his face, but it quickly disappeared and he nodded. "We'll get it figured out. Head on back now. I'll see you at lunch."

Anthony

Anthony stopped the wagon at the edge of the flattened brown patch of grass in front of the little rock chapel. Before he could call the men to come have their snacks, Lucas glanced over and let out a whoop.

"Break time! It's break time, everybody!" The youngest crew member trotted to the wagon, his grin wide, while the other men climbed down the ladders or ambled from behind the chapel. "Whadda we got?"

Anthony hadn't examined the contents of the wagon bed. He'd been too busy kissing his wife. His face heated. "Dunno. Whatever it is, though, it'll be good." Marty had never disappointed them yet.

The men gathered around, and Anthony lifted the cloth cover from a plate of oatmeal-raisin cookies. Nate poured tea into plastic cups and handed them out while Lucas, with a cookie clamped between his teeth, held the plate out to everyone. Anthony bit into a moist cookie, and the flavor of cinnamon tingled on his tongue. Elliott murmured, "Mmm," and Anthony nodded in agreement.

The men joked and teased while they ate, the way they always did during breaks. Anthony had worked on a crew before he started his own company, and his old boss hadn't allowed any kind of cutting up even during break times. But he'd discovered if the men let loose a bit and laughed while on break, it seemed to recharge them. So he didn't mind a little good-natured ribbing. He didn't take part, though. As the men's boss, he needed to stay more professional. To keep their respect. He couldn't resist chortling or flashing a grin now and then, though.

Elliott sidled up beside Anthony. "You done any more thinking about the windows for the chapel?"

Anthony swallowed his last bite of cookie and nodded. "I have. I mentioned your idea to Brooke, too, and she said she'd like to see what you can do with a smaller project before she turns you loose on the big windows. Does that sound fair?"

Elliott's somber expression didn't change. During their months together, the young man had relaxed enough to join most conversations, but he rarely smiled. "Figured so. I scouted out the buildings, and the big back room of the old hardware store, where the kitchen for the restaurant will be, would make a good work space for me. A couple sawhorses and a sheet of plywood'll be a good enough platform to lay out the design, and I can use the old counters for a cutting table. Won't matter if I carve 'em up some since they'll end up in a dumpster later."

A grin twitched at Anthony's lips, but he reined it in. No sense in making Elliott think he found the plans amusing. But it tickled him how the young man had reasoned everything out. "You're wanting to get started."

Elliott shrugged and shifted his gaze past Anthony's shoulder like he was too embarrassed to look him in the eyes. "Wantin' to find out if I can do it. I . . . like making things." He ducked his head and scuffed his toe against the brittle grass. "Not too manly, is it?"

"To want to make things?"

"Yeah."

"Elliott." Anthony waited until the younger man tilted his head and met Anthony's gaze out of the corners of his eyes. "There's never any shame in honest work. God gives us talents and abilities. He expects us to use them for good and not evil. Being honest with yourself and putting your hand to the work you feel called to do is what it means to be a real man."

Elliott's expression didn't change, but something in his eyes seemed to light up. He nodded and looked to the side. "Thanks."

Anthony put his hand on Elliott's shoulder. "Let's talk to Brooke after Bible study tonight. This Saturday, if she's up to it, maybe the two of you can drive to Kansas City and pick up what you need to do a small project. That oughta help you find out if this is something you want to tackle."

"Okay." Elliott eased toward the wagon. "Gonna grab another cookie before Lucas eats 'em all."

Had the man made a joke? Anthony gaped at Elliott for a few startled seconds, then let his laughter roll. His happiness increased when a genuine grin appeared on Elliott's face. Maybe he was finally getting through to the outsider. He could hardly wait to tell Marty.

35

Kansas City
Brooke

*W*hat a taciturn young man. Elliott hadn't even smiled when Brooke handed him the keys to her Lexus and asked him to drive. Neither had he argued, so maybe that was as much excitement as he could display. The entire distance to the studio in Kansas City, he sat quiet and focused behind the wheel, and when her few attempts to engage him in conversation fell flat, she turned up the radio and stayed quiet, too.

The GPS on her phone led them directly to Fleming's Stained Glass Art Studio on the edge of downtown Kansas City. There weren't any parking places in front of the store, but Elliott found a paid parking lot a block away. He dug coins out of his pocket for the privilege of leaving her Lexus in spot A3, then gave her a worried look. "You gonna be okay walking to the store? Maybe I should've dropped you off before I parked."

His solicitude took her by surprise, given his unemotional bearing. She tucked the tail of her scarf-turned-turban into place and offered a glib shrug. "Thanks, but I'll be all right. It's not that far." She questioned her confidence by the time they rounded the block where the studio was located. Leapin' lizards, would she ever have energy again? She slowed her steps on the pretense of examining the various projects hanging in the windows, but within seconds legitimate desire to thoroughly scrutinize each piece replaced any kind of subterfuge.

A large placard in the center of the display announced that enrollment was open for an all-day workshop on the art of stained glass next Saturday. She pointed at the sign. "Looks like we came at the right time. It'd probably be wise to get you enrolled, huh?"

He pushed his hands into his jacket pockets and hunched his shoulders. "We'll have to see how much it costs. I, um . . ."

"I'll pay for it."

His eyes widened. "No, ma'am."

She put her hand on her hip. "Listen, Elliott, if you're going to produce windows for the chapel on my property, then that means you're working for me. As your employer, it only stands to reason that I should pay for your training."

He shook his head, his jaw jutting at an obstinate angle. "We don't even know if I'll be able to make them yet. I ought to pay for the class to find out if I can do it or not."

She rolled her eyes. "I'm not in the mood to argue." She also needed to find a place to sit for a little while. Her legs were starting to feel rubbery. "Let's go in and get more information about the class. Then we can decide who foots the bill, all right?"

He seemed to study her through his narrowed gaze, but after a few seconds he nodded. "All right." He stuck out his elbow.

She stared at his extended arm. Such a kind gesture—a gentlemanly action sorely absent in this day and age. Yet it let her know without a doubt he saw her weakness. Weak was the one thing she'd never wanted to be. Humiliation and stubborn pride warred with appreciation and need, and eventually need won. She blinked several times and took hold. He escorted her into the building and to a long counter where a row of tall, battered industrial stools seemed to beckon to her.

The moment she slid onto a stool, a bubbly young woman wearing a bold orange cobbler's apron over jeans and a plain white T-shirt hurried across the floor and introduced herself as Melanie. The girl held out her hands in invitation. "Whatever I can do to help, name it."

While Elliott browsed the shop, Brooke peppered Melanie with questions, and the girl answered each one without hesitation. By the end of their twenty-minute exchange, Brooke was convinced they'd found the right place for Elliott to learn the art of stained-glass window making, as well as a place to purchase materials if he decided to tackle the chapel windows. She surreptitiously handed Melanie her debit card to pay for Elliott to attend the upcoming classes. If things went awry and he changed his mind about the craft, she'd let him reimburse her.

Elliott offered his arm again when they left the shop, and she slipped her hand into the bend of his elbow, even though her time resting had revived her enough for the walk to the car. He seemed introspective rather than withdrawn, so she kept quiet and let him think. They reached the car, and she used the keypad to unlock it. Then he walked her around to the passenger's side and opened the door for her.

She couldn't resist grinning at him. "Where'd you learn to be so mannerly?"

His cheeks flushed, and he shrugged. "Used to watch old movies at the youth center when I couldn't sleep."

She gave his arm a light squeeze before releasing it. "Well, keep it up, and some young lady will be very fortunate to capture you."

The pink flush deepened to red, and he closed the door without a word, but he seemed to hold his head a little higher as he rounded the car and slid into the driver's seat. He reached to turn the ignition, but before he started the engine, someone tapped on Brooke's window.

A scruffy-looking girl with tangled hair cascading from a droopy stocking cap peered in. She held up a cardboard sign scrawled with "Homeless. Hungry. Help?"

Brooke looked past the sign to the girl's face. She frowned. Where had she seen this girl before?

"Ronnie?" Elliott's simple question solved the mystery and created a new question. Hadn't the police taken her to a facility?

Brooke opened her door. "Ronnie, what are you doing here?"

Recognition bloomed on the girl's dirt-smeared face, followed by panic. She scuttled in reverse several feet. "I . . . I . . ."

Brooke swung her legs out of the car and stood. "Come here. Let's talk."

Ronnie spun on the worn heels of her army boots and took off at a sprint. Her cardboard sign flew from her hand, slid across the parking lot's asphalt surface, and hooked on a parked car's back tire. Brooke called Ronnie's name several times, but the girl rounded a corner between buildings. Elliott had left the car, too, and Brooke waved at him. "Quick! Go after her!"

He took off at a full run, and Brooke retrieved the sign. She stared at it, a sick feeling flooding her stomach. Why wasn't Ronnie at the youth center or in a foster home? She hadn't been dressed like a streetwalker, so hopefully she wasn't turning tricks, but obviously she was still without any real care.

Elliott trudged across the parking lot toward Brooke. He was alone. Brooke's heart sank. "Couldn't you catch her?"

"I don't know where she went." He leaned against the hood and shook his head. "Must have a hiding spot somewhere."

Brooke sighed. "Let's hope it's a safe spot."

He took the sign from her and scowled at it. "This is no way to survive. Trust me, I know."

Brooke shivered. "Should we call the police? Have them try to pick her up?"

"Won't do any good. She'll just run off again. Kids like her . . ." He turned his gaze to the alleyway and sighed. "If she's picked a sleeping place around here, I might see her again when I come back to take the class." One corner of his lips twitched. "Melanie said you signed me up, so I guess I'll be coming back." The amusement fled. "If I see Ronnie, I'll try to talk her into going to a shelter. Since I used to stay in one, she might listen to me."

Brooke touched his arm, and he looked down at her. Compassion glowed in his dark eyes. She blinked back tears. "You're very kind, Elliott."

He didn't answer, but he didn't need to. She witnessed appreciation in his gaze.

She grabbed her purse from the car and dug out a twenty-dollar bill—the only cash she was carrying. "For now, put this with the sign in the alley and let's hope she finds it. It'll get her a meal or two at least."

He took the bill and stared at it, then lifted his gaze and met hers. "You're kind, too."

Twenty dollars wasn't nearly enough to meet all of Ronnie's needs and Brooke knew it, but she thanked Elliott anyway. She watched him as he trotted to the alley, Ronnie's sign and the twenty in his hand. Someone else might pocket the twenty when he moved out of sight, but she trusted Elliott to leave it for Ronnie. Despite his rough upbringing, she believed he possessed an honest heart. Clearly he also possessed resilience to overcome hardship, just as her high school counselor told her she had eighteen years ago. Maybe she was resilient, but she'd also had a friend who modeled a different kind of life—something Brooke could emulate.

What about Ronnie? Did she have resilience? If she didn't have someone like Marty to show her a different way to live, what would her life be like in the future? Brooke didn't want to contemplate the answer.

Eagle Creek

Brooke leaned against the counter and frowned while Marty transferred the pork roast, potatoes, and carrots from the roasting pan to a serving platter and bowls. "This is about the most incongruous situation I've ever seen." She huffed and flapped her hand at the bowl of vegetables. "You won't go out to eat on Sundays because it's *against your religion*"—she made air quotes—"to make someone work. But here you are, laboring to put dinner on the table for eight people. And of course not a man in sight to help. Why is it okay for you to work, but nobody else can?"

Marty shrugged, the gesture so unconcerned it raised Brooke's aggravation a notch. "Cooking is my job. We have to eat on Sunday, so—"

"Hmph. Seems a little imbalanced to me."

Marty clicked her tongue on her teeth. "My, my, are we feeling hangry?"

Brooke gritted her teeth. She'd been in a foul mood since she'd returned from Kansas City yesterday, and the sermon they'd heard in church that morning about a shepherd seeking a single lost lamb hadn't improved her temper. Was anyone out there trying to save Ronnie? Or wasn't she as important as a stupid sheep?

She snorted. "Not funny. Hangry? Where'd you learn that term, anyway?"

Marty carried the platter of meat to the table and returned for the vegetables. "Lucas picked it up somewhere. Would you bring the basket of bread, please?"

Brooke scooped up the basket heaped with crusty rolls and held it away from her body the way she might hold a snake. "So it's not against your religion to let me help, huh?" She plopped the basket next to the meat platter. One roll spilled from the basket and hit the tabletop. Crumbs flew. Brooke sighed. "Leapin' lizards . . . Bring me a paper towel, would you?"

Marty snatched a paper towel from the holder and gently shifted Brooke out of the way. She put the roll in the basket and swept the crumbs into the paper towel.

Brooke folded her arms over her chest. "I could've done that, you know."

"I know." Marty dropped the wadded paper towel into the trash can. She opened the refrigerator and took out two pitchers—one of water, one of fruit-infused tea if she'd followed her usual practice. As she headed for the table again, she glanced at Brooke. "Everything's ready. Would you mind ringing the bell?"

Brooke hated the sharp clang from the old brass bell Anthony had mounted outside the trailer's back door. Loud noises always grated on her nerves. She headed for the front door. "You know, Marty, I'm really more tired than hungry. I think I'll go lie down for a while. See if I can sleep off this . . ." She didn't know what to call the feeling that held her in its grip. This melancholy? Anger? Frustration? Maybe all of them at once.

She no longer recognized the gaunt, pale face reflected in her mirror. Her clothes hung on her, making her feel as if they belonged to someone else. Her days of leading corporate meetings and securing properties seemed like a distant dream. Would she ever be Brooke again—the strong, motivated, successful powerhouse that commanded respect and admiration? Or was she doomed to be as displaced as Ronnie?

Marty hurried across the floor to her. "Are you sure? I bought the pork roast from the grass-fed section of the meat counter. The sweet potatoes and carrots came from the farmers' market, so there were no chemicals used on them. I even bought some gluten-free rolls so you could have bread with your dinner."

Brooke stifled a groan. Marty'd gone to so much trouble to accommodate her. She added guilt to her list of uncomfortable feelings.

Marty placed her hand on Brooke's arm. "Not eating won't help you build your strength."

As if food could give her the strength she needed to become herself again. She stepped free of Marty's touch. "I'll eat later. Right now I need . . ." An urge struck with such force her body began to quiver. Behind Marty, at the end of the eating bar, the Bible Marty had carried to church lay next to the bulletin from the morning's service.

She turned Marty in the direction of the back door. "Ring the bell before everything is cold. Don't worry about me. I'll be fine."

Marty appeared dubious, but she went to the back door and stepped out onto the stoop. While the obnoxious bell clanged its "come to dinner" message, Brooke picked up the Bible and bulletin, hugged them to her chest, and slipped out the front door.

36

Brooke

*B*rooke filled the stereo's six slots with instrumental CDs, adjusted the volume button to low, and hit play. Piano music—love songs from movie scores—flowed from the speakers. She made a nest of the sofa throw pillows and settled in with the afghan across her legs. Then she lifted Marty's Bible from the end table and placed it in her lap.

According to the bulletin, the minister had used the first seven verses from Luke fifteen as the basis for his sermon. The Bible's table of contents directed her to the right page, and she brought up her knees to prop the book higher. She began to read. Aloud. Because it helped her fuzzy brain stay focused.

"'What man of you, having an hundred sheep, if he lose one of them, doth not leave the ninety and nine in the wilderness, and go after that which is lost, until he find it?'" She grimaced. When the preacher read from his Bible that morning, it hadn't sounded like a Shakespearean play. She might need to read the verses more than once for them to make sense.

Drawing a deep breath, she leaned over the Bible and read the entire section about the lost sheep. The story segued into a much shorter but similar story about a woman searching for a lost coin and rejoicing when she found it. The next line promised a third story, this one about a man and two sons. Ah, the prodigal son story. She couldn't recall where, but it seemed she'd heard the story before. She decided to read it anyway, to refresh her memory.

The story—the younger son's selfishness, his wild living, and his subsequent descent into taking his meals from a hog trough—made her squirm. The pictures in her head too closely matched what she'd been envisioning for Ronnie. She pushed aside thoughts about the homeless runaway and put her full attention on the story.

She nodded in approval when the boy made the choice to go home, and her heart gave a little leap of joy at the father's plan to host a welcomeback party. Her voice dropped to a rasping whisper as she read, "'For this my son was dead, and is alive again; he was lost, and is found. And they began to be merry.'"

Brooke placed both palms on the open Bible and leaned back against the pile of pillows. She closed her eyes. She'd always had an active imagination. Slipping into daydreams had allowed her to escape the harsh realities of her childhood. As a property flipper, she'd relied on her imagination to help her envision what a dilapidated building could be. Now, behind her closed lids, she pictured the boy in filthy, threadbare clothes plodding up the hill toward his boyhood home. She saw the joy on the father's face when the son came up the path, and her lips lifted in a smile when the father went running, arms open, to receive the son home again.

Her chest ached with joy at the welcome playing in her head. How would it feel to be given such a homecoming? Despite her active imagination, she couldn't conceive of it. Her hands slid from the Bible, and her arms crossed over her chest. Eyes crunched tight, she hugged herself, seeking the emotions the boy must have felt when his father's arms closed around him. But only sorrow claimed her.

She pulled up her knees and pressed her forehead to them, folding herself into a ball and crushing Marty's Bible in the process. Rocking herself, she bit down on her lower lip to hold back sobs. The deepest longing she'd ever known tugged at her, tormented her, encircled her the way the father in the story had encircled his son with his arms. From the time she was eight years old she'd told herself she didn't need anyone. She was strong. She was capable. She was independent. She'd proved it, too, by single-handedly building her business, living on her own, and traveling all over the country without a companion. But right at that moment, she would give away every penny in her personal and business bank accounts to know how it felt to be loved the way the son in the story was loved by his father.

The sofa cushion shifted. A warm hand guided her head onto a soft shoulder, and an arm curled around her, holding her in place. A firm yet tender hand rubbed circles on her back. Brooke gasped. "F-father?"

"Shhh . . ." Marty's soft voice whisked past Brooke's ear.

So Marty's arm cradled her. Marty's hand stroked her back. How foolish to think a father would draw her into his embrace.

Brooke pulled in a shuddering breath and sat up, dislodging Marty's arms. She swiped the moisture from her face with her hands. "What are you doing here?" Her voice emerged hard and ragged, partly from her dry throat and partly from embarrassment. How long had Marty observed Brooke hugging herself and rocking like a frightened child?

Marty gestured to the plate sitting on the side table. "I brought you something to eat, but you must not have heard me come in."

No, she hadn't. Between the music and her imaginative foray, she'd been oblivious to someone else's presence. "You startled me."

"I'm sorry." Contrition showed in her eyes. As did worry. Marty rubbed Brooke's shoulder. "Do you feel sick? Should I get you a nausea pill?"

A Zofran wouldn't fix what made her stomach ache. "No, I . . ." Her gaze landed on the Bible, still open in her lap. The pages looked as though someone had wadded them in her fist. She cringed. "I ruined your Bible."

Marty picked it up and smoothed her hand over the thin pages. They flattened somewhat, but deep wrinkles remained, resembling a craggy expanse of land. "It's all right. Don't worry about it."

Brooke couldn't help but worry about it. She'd permanently scarred Marty's Bible. The way her mother's cold treatment had permanently scarred her heart. She touched the crinkled corners of the pages with her fingers. There was no fixing the pages. Was there hope to repair this hole in the center of her being? For weeks she'd sought joy. Joy like the father experienced when his son came home. Joy that made one want to dance and sing and celebrate. The desire writhed within her, reaching to grasp the elusive emotion that had been alien to her for her entire life.

She lifted her gaze from the Bible to Marty's face. "If I were lost, would you go looking for me?"

Marty's eyes widened. "Of course I would." She took Brooke's hand and squeezed. "You're my best friend. I love you, Brooke."

Tears distorted Brooke's vision. "Thank you. I love you, too. You're the sister I never had."

"And, Brooke?" Marty's tone remained quiet, kind, tender, but her fingers on Brooke's hand trembled. "I love you enough to tell you . . . you are lost. But there's a Father who's waiting for your return. A Father who's calling your name. A Father who loves you and wants you to be part of His family."

Brooke sniffed and rubbed her nose. "You're talking about God, aren't you?"

Marty nodded. "Remember when you asked me to help you find joy?"

Of course she remembered. She also remembered Anthony's intensity as he read from his Bible and spoke about God's love for man. But somehow it hadn't seemed available to her. It made sense that God would love Marty and Anthony and the other Mennonites. They were kind, giving people who had lived clean, moral lives. They were lovable. But how could God love someone with her background? The child of a promiscuous alcoholic who wasn't even sure which of the men she dated had impregnated her, a child who went to school with uncombed hair and dirty clothes and unbrushed teeth, a teenager who thumbed her nose at authority, a woman who never darkened the door of a church or gave God a thought other than to occasionally murmur His name in frustration. She didn't deserve God's love any more than the wayward boy in the story had deserved his father's love.

She gasped, then gaped at Marty. "The boy . . . and the father . . ."

Marty tipped her head. "What?"

Brooke tapped the Bible with her fingertip. "In here . . ."

Marty turned the open book so the words were right side up. She seemed to scan the page. "Oh, Jesus's parable about the prodigal son."

Brooke might not have read the story from the Bible before today, but she knew what a prodigal was—someone who defied his family. The description fit. She nodded. "Is . . . is . . ." She swallowed, gathering courage. If Marty said no, Brooke's heart might be shattered. "Is the father in the story . . . God?"

The ribbons dangling from Marty's cap danced with her enthusiastic nod. "Yes."

Brooke placed both hands over her chest. Beneath her palms, her heart beat with hope.

Then Marty made a face. "Well, he isn't God Himself—"

Brooke's hope began to plummet.

"—but a representation of God the Father."

Hope fluttered to life again. "And the boy?"

"The boy represents any sinner who's wandered far away. Jesus told the story so people would understand that God is waiting for anyone, no matter how foolish or rebellious or sinful they are, to come to Him. God the Father will welcome any repentant sinner with open arms."

Open arms . . . In the story, the father opened his arms and embraced his smelly, dirty, caked-with-sin son. He looked past the sin to his beloved child. If the father represented God, and the boy represented repentant sinners, then it stood to reason that God would be able to look past Brooke's smelliness and—her heart pounded so fiercely she marveled that it didn't leave her chest—see her as a beloved child. If she was willing to repent.

She closed her eyes and considered her life. Her successful career. Her well-padded bank accounts. Her beautiful town house in one of the most upscale neighborhoods in Kansas City. Her Lexus and other extravagant belongings. Her full yet somehow empty life. Popping her eyes open, she reached for Marty's hands. "I want God to rejoice over me, saying 'the lost has been found.' What do I do?"

A smile broke across Marty's face, and tears spilled down her cheeks. "It's very simple. 'Believe on the Lord Jesus Christ, and thou shalt be saved.' Believe that God sent Jesus to the cross to take the penalty for your sins. Ask Jesus to cleanse you of your sins and ask Him to be your Lord and Savior. And all of heaven will rejoice with God the Father that the lost has been found."

Brooke bowed her head. Her soul reached out in faith. She envisioned God the Father opening His arms, and she fell into His embrace. Love enveloped her while a sweet aroma filled her nostrils—the scent of joy. She breathed it deeply.

Anthony

Anthony closed his Bible and led the group in prayer. While the fire snapped and an owl hooted from somewhere in the trees at the edge of their little clearing, Anthony prayed for each member of his team by name, lifting up any requests they'd given him or asking a blessing over them. He prayed for Charlotte, Marty, and Brooke. His chest fluttered, gratitude about Brooke's decision to follow Christ still fresh. He might not have had the privilege of leading her to the Lord, but he would play a role in growing her in knowledge of the Scriptures. He took the responsibility seriously. The prophet's words from Isaiah fifty-five, the chapter they'd read and studied that evening, found their way into his prayer.

"Let us 'go out with joy, and be led forth with peace' as we follow Your will. Amen."

The others, including Brooke, echoed the amen. Nate, Charlotte, Myron, Lucas, and Todd rose from their places around the fire and turned toward the trailers. Todd paused and looked back at Elliott. "You coming?"

"I'll be there in a minute."

Todd reversed his direction and headed back to the fire. "Then I'll stay, too."

Earlier in the day, Elliott had requested a private chat with Brooke and Anthony. Anthony wouldn't tell Marty to go inside—his business was her business—but "private" probably meant Elliott didn't want the other workers listening in.

Anthony cleared his throat. "Would you mind going to your trailer, Todd? I need a few words with Elliott."

Curiosity flickered on the young man's face, but he nodded and waved at Elliott. "See you later, buddy."

"Yeah, thanks." Elliott stared after Todd as if he didn't quite trust him to leave. When the shadows had completely swallowed Todd, Elliott faced Anthony. He leaned forward, rested his elbows on his knees, and linked his hands. "Thanks for sticking around. I wanted to . . . I dunno how to say it . . ." He hung his head.

Anthony hoped the man didn't intend to give notice about quitting. Elliott was a good worker—dependable and uncomplaining. Besides, he suspected Elliott needed to be around folks who treated him like family. "Are you unhappy about something?"

Elliott's head rose so fast his neck popped. "No. Not unhappy at all. I . . . I like it here. It's peaceful."

Anthony nearly sagged in relief. He wouldn't ask to quit, then. "What is it?"

Elliott's gaze flicked from Anthony to Brooke and back. "Well, I wondered if I could maybe"—he fully faced Brooke—"bounce an idea off you."

Brooke hunkered farther into the blanket she'd wrapped around herself like a tortilla around fajita fixings. "What kind of idea?"

Elliott sat straight up on the edge of his chair. "I went to that class last Saturday—you know the one about making stained-glass art—and I did real good at it." His voice held more excitement than it had the day the men found a dozen bull snakes coiled together under the floorboards in the old chapel. "I only made a little project, something that a person could hang from a hook in the window. Next week's class we're gonna make something a little bigger—big enough to put in a frame. I signed up for it, and if I do good with the bigger piece, I was thinking maybe I could make a whole bunch of stained-glass pictures and, if I did, maybe you'd let me sell them in one of the shops you'll be setting up out here."

He shifted his attention to Anthony. "I'd still give you a full day's work. I could cut and solder pieces of glass in the evenings, after supper. That is"—he zipped his gaze to Brooke again—"if Miss Spalding says it's okay."

Only the top half of Brooke's head showed above the blanket. She wore a stocking cap almost the same shade of blue as the blanket, and in the glow from the fire the little band of her exposed skin looked stark white. She should go in and rest. She needed to gain strength for the next chemo treatment, the one right before Thanksgiving.

Anthony leaned forward slightly. "Elliott, how about you let Brooke give this some thought and get back to—"

"Anthony, how about you let me speak for myself?"

Marty choked on a giggle, and Anthony bit down on his lower lip to keep from laughing. The firm voice coming from inside the blanket tortilla tickled him. Brooke always seemed to prove herself stronger than he expected her to be. He cleared his throat and held his hand toward her. "I'm sorry. Go ahead."

She wiggled a little bit, bringing her mouth free of the blanket. "It's a good idea, Elliott. I have every confidence that you will master the art of stained glass, and stained-glass art pieces are exactly the kind of product I envisioned being sold in the specialty shops."

Elliott's smile grew almost as bright as the embers glowing in the bottom of the fire pit. "Thank you, ma'am."

Brooke shook her head. "Let me finish."

Elliott sank back into his chair. "Okay." The apprehension on his face matched the niggle of uncertainty in the pit of Anthony's stomach.

Brooke pushed the blanket flap down with her chin. "I still have a lot of thinking to do, and even more praying." She glanced at Marty, and the two of them exchanged a smile. "But there's a possibility the specialty shops won't ever open."

37

Brooke

rooke hadn't intended to hint at a change of plans for Spalding until she had everything settled in her mind. She'd shocked Anthony and Marty as much as she'd shocked Elliott, and she regretted it. They deserved better notice than what they'd been given. But she couldn't allow Elliott to build up a dream that might not come true. The young man had suffered enough hard knocks in life. She wouldn't deliberately deliver another. She worked her arm free of the blanket and stretched it toward him. After a moment, he reached out and let her give his hand a squeeze.

"I want you to continue taking stained-glass art classes to hone your skills. It's never a waste of time to learn something new, and you never know how God will use your abilities." She wasn't sure where God was leading her to use her business skills, but something was brewing. The tingle she'd come to recognize as a new idea coming to life had awakened her in the middle of the night twice in the past week. This time, though, she knew the Source of the tingle. She wanted to be ready for whatever door He opened. She gave Elliott's hand another squeeze. "Don't lose heart, Elliott, do you hear me?"

The young man nodded, but his woebegone expression intimated that he'd already lost heart. He pushed up from the chair and ambled to his trailer, his hands in his pockets and his head low.

She sighed and pulled her arm back under the blanket. The night air seemed especially chilly with the coals dying out. She struggled to her feet. "Thanks for another thought-provoking study, Anthony. You're a good teacher." The light beside the Hirschlers' back door sent out only a dim glow, but she still noted the flush of red staining Anthony's cheeks. She'd embarrassed him, yet she surmised she'd also pleased him.

Marty stood and gave Brooke a hug. "Let me walk you to your trailer."

Brooke shifted sideways a bit. She'd need to loosen up her wrapping before she tried to go anywhere. Or maybe she could lie down and roll. She and Marty had rolled down a hill or two in their childhood. She smiled, remembering the carefree days. "I'm fine. You two go on—have some alone time. Heaven knows you don't get much of that with everything else you have to do out here."

Anthony rose slowly and pinned Brooke with a serious look. "Will we finish out here? Rebuilding the town, I mean. Have you changed your mind about bringing it to life again?"

Brooke sighed. "I'm not entirely sure I can change my mind about that. I have a dozen investors expecting the Spalding Resort and Casino to open as planned. But . . ." The tingle worked its way up her spine and sizzled under her stocking cap. She shrugged. "I want to remain open to . . . other possibilities."

Anthony nodded. "Fair enough." He slipped his arm around Marty's waist. "Well, how about we do what Brooke said and—"

"Miss Spalding?" Elliott stepped from the shadows and into the porch light. The angular lines of his serious face seemed sharper in the dim glow. He held out a fistful of bills. "I want to pay you back for that art class. It's only right since I might not be making those windows for the chapel after all."

Brooke didn't want his money, but neither did she want to shame him. She understood keeping a grip on independence—she'd never wanted to take anything from anyone, either. She searched her mind for a compromise, and she found one she hoped he would accept. "Elliott, are you familiar with the phrase 'Pay it forward'?"

He nodded.

"Well, how about instead of you paying me back, you use that money and pay it forward instead?"

His brow crinkled, and his hand lowered. "How?"

"When you go to Kansas City on Saturday for your next class, try again to find Ronnie. Didn't you tell me she's probably hanging around in that area?"

"Yeah." He flicked a shame-faced look at Anthony and Marty. "Street kids usually pick a spot—what they consider a safe spot—so it kind of feels like they have a home."

Marty released a soft, sympathetic moan, and Anthony visibly winced.

Brooke sent up a quick prayer of gratitude that despite her unhappy home, at least she'd never had to live in an alley. "Would you look for her again? We'll all"—she tilted her head to indicate Marty and Anthony—"pray you'll be successful. See if you can talk her into letting you buy her a bus ticket to someplace safe, like a relative's house or maybe her former foster home. If she refuses, then buy her some groceries, a sleeping bag or heavy coat, things she'll need to stay warm." She hoped Ronnie wouldn't end up spending the winter on the street. "That'll pay me back. Better yet, it'll pay me forward. All right?"

He slipped the crumpled wad into his jacket pocket. "All right. I'll do my best."

"I know you will." She turned to Marty and Anthony. "Can we pray for Ronnie right now?"

"Sure." Anthony stepped closer, drawing Marty with him. He looked at Elliott. "Wanna join us?"

To Brooke's surprise, the young man strode forward without a moment's hesitation. They formed a circle and bowed their heads. While Anthony asked God to keep watch over Ronnie and to help Elliott find her, Brooke added her silent prayer for the same thing. Anthony's voice turned husky as he said, "Prepare a home for Ronnie . . . and for kids like her . . . where they'll be safe and loved."

Brooke's scalp exploded with tingles. She gasped and jerked upright, staring into Anthony's startled eyes. "Leapin' lizards, if I wasn't wrapped up in this blanket, you'd be on the receiving end of the biggest hug of your life."

Anthony touched his chest, his eyebrows high. "Me? What'd I do?"

She laughed, a joyful trickle she couldn't have controlled even if she'd wanted to. "You said it. A home. That's it!"

Marty

Thursday morning when Marty arrived to prepare Brooke a simple breakfast of steel-cut oats with fresh berries, Brooke was already in her recliner, laptop open, concentration etched on her features. Wrapped in a plush bathrobe, with fuzzy socks covering her feet and a tasseled, knitted cap in bands of purple, yellow, and green on her head, she didn't resemble a business executive, but appearance didn't seem to matter. By midmorning she'd created a list of agencies she would need to contact to turn the Spalding Resort and Casino into the Eagle Creek Shelter for teens who were homeless or rescued from human trafficking.

"Eagle Creek?" Marty handed Brooke a shake she'd mixed up using coconut milk, frozen fruit, fresh baby spinach leaves, protein powder, and ground flaxseed. Marty thought the concoction looked terrible, but Brooke had developed the habit of drinking one every day as a snack. "I thought you wanted to rename the town Spalding."

"Yeah, that." Brooke took a sip of the thick liquid through a straw, then set the glass on the side table. "Having a town named after me doesn't seem all that important anymore. Besides, Eagle Creek has a nice ring to it. Doesn't it sound like a great place to heal?" Her forehead pinched, and she idly stirred the shake with the straw. "What was that verse Anthony read a week or so ago about eagles? Something like soaring on wings?"

"Isaiah 40:31. 'But they that wait upon the LORD shall renew their strength; they shall mount up with wings as eagles; they shall run, and not be weary; and they shall walk, and not faint.'" Marty quoted the verse, blinking back tears. She'd used a verse about being borne on eagles' wings to compel Anthony to consider the move to Eagle Creek. Her heart soared knowing the town would retain its lovely name.

"Yes, that's it. Isaiah 40:31." Brooke scribbled on the notepad balanced on the armrest. "That'd be a good verse to use in brochures and other marketing materials." She met Marty's gaze, and tears glimmered in her green eyes. "Renewing their strength—that's exactly what I want this place to do for people."

It already had for Marty. She smiled. "Perfect." She paused for a moment, chewing the inside of her lip. "But will you be able to manage both the homeless and those coming out of trafficking? According to Elliott, the number of homeless teens is pretty high, and trafficking must be just as bad, based on what we've seen on the news in the short time we've been here."

Brooke huffed. "If you want to depress yourself, read the statistics. One report estimated that five thousand homeless youth die each year from assault, illness, or suicide."

Marty gasped. She sank onto the end of the sofa. "So many . . ."

"That number's a small percentage of how many are living on their own, fighting for an existence."

Marty shook her head, trying to dislodge the ugly images forming in her mind. "I don't understand how children end up on their own to begin with. Where are their parents?"

Brooke's smile looked sad. "Marty, not every family is like yours. Some homes are so awful the kids run away, figuring the street's got to be better than what goes on in their house. Sometimes they end up on the street because they've aged out of the foster care system and there's no place for them to go. There are entire families who end up homeless, and eventually they get split up—some going to this shelter, others to another—and the kids just . . . drift away."

Her expression turned grim. "According to an article I read last night, kids who end up fending for themselves are prime targets for traffickers. They get lured in with the promise of being taken care of, then end up being used. Others are forced into it, and still others enter it willingly, thinking it's better than being on the streets all alone. It's a really sad deal all the way around."

Marty crossed her arms over her churning stomach. "Makes me feel sick."

"Me, too." Brooke's eyes sparked. "I want to help kids get out of that awful industry and give them a chance to heal, but I also want to keep others from getting caught in the trafficking net. They need someplace safe to live, where they can at least receive a high school education, learn the skills they need to take care of themselves, and have somebody who truly cares about them. How else can they become strong, confident, productive members of society?"

Tears flooded Marty's eyes. She sniffed hard. "What a legacy you're building. I'm so proud of you."

Brooke's pale cheeks turned pink. "It feels good thinking that when I leave this earth, there'll be something of value left behind." Then she grimaced. "Of course, I've still got to sell the investors on it. That's why I need as much statistical and practical information as I can gather. When I meet with them, I've got to be loaded for bear." She turned her attention to the computer again, and Marty allowed her to work in peace.

At noon Marty helped Charlotte serve lunch to the workers. She shared with the group what Brooke was trying to do. Myron asked, "How can we help?" Marty thought for a moment, considering the list of must-dos she'd seen on Brooke's notepad. None of those seated around the table were familiar with organizing charities or dealing with businessmen, but there was one thing they could do.

She smiled. "We can pray. There'll be licensing and inspections, fund-raising, hiring a permanent staff, and probably a dozen other hurdles for her to leap, and she's trying to do all that while she's sick. So let's pray for Brooke's strength and for God's will to be done in bringing this shelter to completion."

Every Mennonite team member vowed to lift Brooke and the shelter in prayer. Elliott made no such promise, but his serious expression told Marty he was thinking hard about ways to help.

Marty returned to Brooke's trailer after lunch. Brooke had moved from the recliner to the built-in hutch she used as a desk, and her laptop was still open. Marty suggested Brooke eat something and then take a nap.

Brooke closed her eyes and groaned. "Marty, I'm still full from my shake, and I don't have time to nap. I have this afternoon, tomorrow, Saturday, and Monday to work. Unless I use Sunday as a workday, too, and I don't really want to do that. It is the Lord's day."

Marty's heart rolled over. Brooke was trying so hard to honor the One she now called Father. "It'll do you good to take Sunday off and rest."

Brooke nodded. "I know. But then Tuesday is my infusion day, and I'll feel too lousy to think, let alone work, for days afterward." She fixed a frown on Marty. "What did you decide to do about Thanksgiving? Are you going to Indiana with the others?"

Marty sat on a barstool close to the desk. "Anthony and I have talked about it several times. He knows you won't be up to a long car ride."

"He's got that right."

A bit of Brooke's snark came through, and Marty couldn't hold back a grin. "But he says we absolutely will not leave you here alone."

Brooke rolled her eyes. "What is he now, my keeper?"

Marty placed her hand on Brooke's wrist. "No, he's your friend and he cares about you."

Her expression softened. "I know, and I appreciate it. But I don't want to hold you back from celebrating a holiday with your family. I really think you should all go."

"And Anthony really thinks it's best not to leave you on your own right after a chemo treatment. I agree with him. Still, he is hesitant to leave the two of us out here without a man around, so—"

Brooke started laughing.

Marty frowned. "What's so funny?"

"He tickles me, that's all." She yanked the belt on her robe. "I've managed for eighteen years totally on my own. I think I could handle another few days while you all have Thanksgiving dinner in Pine Hill."

Marty folded her arms over her chest. "Anthony figured you'd say something like that. He'd like to remind you that in the past, you lived close to neighbors, and a call to the police would bring help in a hurry if you needed it. Out here is a completely different situation."

Brooke wiped her hand across her mouth, and her smirk disappeared. "You're right. Or rather, he's right. I am pretty isolated out here." She propped her elbow on the edge of the desk. "So what did Mr. Fix-It recommend?"

Marty chuckled. She couldn't wait to tell Anthony what Brooke had nicknamed him. He'd probably puff up in pride. "Initially he'd intended to take Elliott to Pine Hill with us, but that was before Elliott started the stained-glass art classes. Now Elliott wants to stay here and use the weekend to put together a work area in one of the old buildings. So he'll be our protector if we need one."

"Yes . . ." Brooke's gaze went glassy, and she stared across the room as if she'd forgotten Marty was there. "That's a good idea. A work area . . ."

Marty waited a few seconds, but Brooke remained lost in thought. Marty cleared her throat.

Brooke jumped. Her gaze jerked to Marty's and she grinned. "Would you lay out some clothes for me? I'm working on a letter template"—she flapped her hand at the computer—"that I can modify to send to different bureaus and organizations, but when I finish I want to walk over to the worksite. Even though I'm pretty comfortable, I shouldn't go in my robe."

Marty pushed off from the stool. "I'd be glad to, but if you plan on making that walk, you should take a nap beforehand."

Brooke bent over the computer and positioned her fingers on the keyboard.

Marty tapped her shoulder. "Did you hear me?"

Brooke peeked at Marty from the corners of her eyes. "Yes, Mother."

So Anthony was Mr. Fix-It and she was Mother. Marty shook her head, chuckling, and set off for Brooke's bedroom. What did Brooke have up her sleeve now? Whatever it was, it would probably be a brilliant idea. She paused and glanced back at her friend. The purple circles under Brooke's eyes seemed so much darker against her pale skin. Her collarbones stuck out, evidence of how much weight she'd lost. The cancer and chemo had weakened Brooke so much, and she still had more treatments to go.

A silent prayer winged from her heart. *Please let this plan of hers succeed, and . . . oh, dear Father, please . . . let her live to see it all fall into place.*

38

Kansas City
Brooke

*H*ere's a pink one. Size two. Would that fit?"

Brooke glanced from the circular rack she'd been browsing to Marty, who held up a two-piece suit in a dusty salmon. The style was nice—pencil skirt, single-button jacket with a feminine peplum that dipped lower in the back. But . . . She wrinkled her nose. "The size might be right, but the pink is totally off."

Marty sighed, hooked the hanger over the silver rod, and rounded the clothes rack. "Maybe you should wait until spring. You're more likely to find something closer to Easter."

Brooke didn't have the luxury of waiting until spring. She intended to have a sit-down with the investors for the Spalding Resort in early December. Asking for their benevolence during the season of peace and goodwill toward men seemed perfect timing. She wanted a suit in her signature color so she could feel like herself when she addressed them.

She sighed and turned away from the display of earth-toned separates. "I wish I'd brought one of my fuchsia suits in with me. The alteration department in the store does a good job."

Marty tipped her head and gave Brooke an "Are you kidding?" look. "I could alter a suit for you. All you need to do is ask."

Brooke groaned. Why hadn't she thought of that? Because she'd used up her brain power figuring out the details for the shelter, that's why. She looped arms with Marty and aimed them for the store's front door. "In that case, let's go back to the stained-glass gallery. Elliott's class won't be over for another hour yet, but it's a fun place to browse. We can look at the pattern books and get ideas for Elliott."

After exploring the townsite again both Thursday and Friday, Brooke had assigned new purposes for each of the stone buildings. She could picture it all in her mind's eye. The general store would still have a kitchen and dining room on the main floor, with sleeping rooms above, but instead of being used as a restaurant and hotel, it would be where the residents shared cooking duties and gathered for family-style meals. She'd designated the upstairs rooms for boys' lodging. According to her research, more girls than boys ran away from home or ended up in sex trafficking, but she wanted a spot for any boys who needed a place of sanctuary.

The idea for making the mercantile a sweets shop and gift shop had morphed into classrooms on the main floor, where the kids would study to earn a GED—something she intended to require. In order to find employment, at least a high school education was a must. The upstairs, Anthony had assured her, was large enough for four studio apartments. Girls expecting babies or who arrived with small children in tow would need a more homelike setting, and the apartments would be perfect for them. Anthony suggested partitioning off a section of the downstairs for a day care, and Brooke loved the idea.

As for the old bank building, she wanted an efficiency apartment on the main floor for hired "parents," and the rest of the building would be turned into dorm rooms to house the girls. She envisioned beds with colorful spreads in place of slot machines and blackjack tables. Not a place for people to gamble away their dollars, but a place where kids could find their way to an improved life. Such a better use for the stately old building.

How to use the row of shops where she'd planned to invite vendors to sell their goods was still a little fuzzy in her mind, but she was toying with the idea of turning them into workshops where the residents would craft items—such as stained-glass suncatchers, wooden shelves or jewelry boxes, small quilts—to sell to the public to help with expenses. They could contribute toward their stay with sweat equity. Wouldn't that help build their self-esteem? She needed to give the workshops idea more thought, but she'd already decided to leave the smaller trailers for caretaker cottages. If they needed more rooms, the newest or the neediest residents could stay in the trailers close to the shelter's managers, where they'd get extra attention.

It all painted such an ideal picture in her head, and she wanted it more than she'd ever wanted anything. Even though it wouldn't earn a penny. How much her goals had changed. The verse from one of the letters to the Corinthians—she had trouble recalling references—about becoming a new creation sure seemed accurate. Her old dream of accumulating wealth had been swept away on a fresh tide of ministry. She prayed that the investors would be willing to ride the waves with her.

Brooke parked her Lexus in the lot a block away from the stained-glass store, and she and Marty headed for the sidewalk. The weather was surprisingly mild for mid-November, with temperatures closer to typical early September, and even the Kansas wind had chosen to take a break, but Brooke shivered anyway. The slightest breeze tended to chill her these days, probably because she'd lost nearly every bit of padding she'd previously possessed. She crossed her arms, held them tight to her rib cage, and sped her steps with Marty scurrying along beside her.

They passed the alleyway between buildings, and Brooke couldn't resist peeking into the shadowed space. Dumpsters, a stack of flattened cardboard boxes, paper scraps, a puddle of murky water . . . but no sign of Ronnie. Had the girl moved on to another spot? Had the men who'd taken advantage of her before found her again? Or had she decided on her own to return to the youth center or her home? Brooke prayed for the latter. Every time she thought about Ronnie, her heart ached. She wanted that sad, lonely, abused girl to be safe.

Brooke and Marty sat down at the table and leafed through a design book together. The beginning pages showed simplistic patterns similar to the tulip design Elliott made in his first class, but the farther into the book they went, the more elaborate the designs became. Although the drawings were in black and white, Brooke was able to use her imagination and add color. Marty pointed out several favorites, but they emitted identical gasps when Brooke turned the page and exposed an elaborate design of four delphiniums growing from thick green leaves.

"I love this," they said in unison and then laughed.

The store worker, Melanie, turned from dusting displays and hurried over, curiosity lighting her face. "What did you find?"

Brooke turned the book to face her. "This one. I bet it's really pretty all done."

She grinned. "It is. Wanna see?"

Brooke gawked at her. "Someone made it?"

Melanie nodded and quirked her fingers.

Brooke set the book aside, and she and Marty followed Melanie to the corner of the store, where a set of old folding doors created a nook.

"Some artisans sell pieces on consignment here, and an older man named Ernie Wedge has several available. He's especially good at the mosaic designs. See?" Melanie held up her hand Vanna White–style to a stained-glass picture secured in a weathered frame that could have come from a fairy-tale cottage.

Brooke ran her finger along the bottom of the frame, feeling as if she were looking into a garden at a blooming delphinium bush. For some reason, her throat went tight and she battled the sting of tears. "It's lovely."

Melanie nodded. "It isn't exactly like the picture in the book. That's the nature of mosaic designs. Glass isn't going to break exactly the same each time. But Ernie has a real knack for getting the pieces fitted just right." She laughed softly. "He told me one time that these projects are like life, with some days more broken than others, but when a master designer puts the pieces all together again, something of beauty emerges."

Brooke nodded, blinking to clear her vision. "Yes, the Master De-signer has a way of making beauty out of messes."

Marty squeezed Brooke's arm. "I think we need this picture, don't you? Delphiniums . . . for remembrance. Yes?"

Brooke nodded.

Melanie unhooked the picture from the chains suspending it from the ceiling. She headed for the counter, glancing over her shoulder at Brooke and Marty. "Would you mind if I shared your names and addresses with Ernie? For some reason he likes to know where his pictures end up. I can guarantee he's harmless—he won't come pester you or anything. He's just kind of . . . I dunno . . . curious."

"I don't mind at all." Brooke pulled her wallet from her purse and handed Melanie her debit card. "Does he live in Kansas City?"

"Yes, in one of the retirement homes. I think it's called Brookview." Melanie poked keys on the computer and plugged the card into the chip reader. "He's retired from the school system. I'm pretty sure he was a counselor for one of the districts. His wife died a couple years ago, and working on the stained-glass windows keeps him occupied. He's really a nice guy with a great sense of humor. He even teaches some beginner classes here. Everyone seems to love him." She returned the card to Brooke and smiled. "I'll wrap this for safe transport. Give me a few min-utes, huh?" She tucked the picture under her arm and disappeared be-hind a curtained doorway.

Marty leaned against the counter. "Mr. Wedge sounds like the perfect grandpa, doesn't he?"

Brooke didn't know anything about grandpas. She'd never had one. But Ernie Wedge sounded like someone with a big heart. She'd have to search for him online and send him a thank-you note. He'd probably ap-preciate it. People didn't do that much these days.

Melanie returned from behind the curtain at the same time Elliott strode from the back room used for classes. He took the package and opened the door for Brooke and Marty. As Brooke passed him, his stomach growled and she laughed.

"There's a sandwich shop across the street. Should we go grab something to eat before we drive back to Eagle Creek?"

Elliott put his hand against his stomach. "I can wait."

Brooke shook her head. "Unless you've got a dragon in your stomach"—she used the explanation she and Marty used to giggle about when their stomachs growled during seventh grade math, which was their class before lunch break—"you're hungry now. So let's put the picture in the car and walk across the street."

Marty touched Brooke's elbow. "Are you sure you're up to that much walking? You've already done quite a bit of running around."

Before Brooke could answer, Elliott held out his hand. "How about you give me your keys? I'll lock your package in the trunk and catch up to you. That way you won't have so much walking to do."

Brooke came close to arguing—her old, independent habits were dying hard. But she shouldn't waste her energy. She dropped the keys into his hand. "All right. We'll wait for you in the café."

He trotted off in the direction of the parking lot, and Marty and Brooke walked to the corner. They waited for the walk signal, then crossed to the opposite side of the street and stepped up on the curb. The smell of french fries greeted them as they neared the little bistro-style café, and hunger stirred in Brooke's stomach—a welcome reaction since few things appealed to her anymore, thanks to what she'd dubbed "chemo-flavor" lingering on her tongue all the time.

A menu board hung on the wall behind the cash register. Brooke chose a round table close to the front windows, where she could watch for Elliott and—admittedly—rest a bit while Marty went to check out the sandwich and soup options. Patrons in the café followed Marty with their gazes, probably staring at her cap and homemade dress, which were so different from anyone else's attire. Marty had gotten similar looks at the women's-clothing store and the stained-glass gallery. Marty didn't seem to notice the stares. At least, she didn't react to them. Brooke had gotten some curious looks herself, thanks to her scarf-wrapped head. She didn't like it, but seeing how Marty took the gawkers in stride helped her not react negatively to people's uninvited attention.

A couple at a nearby table suddenly leaned close and whispered to each other. Brooke tensed, expecting them to glance her way, but they pointed to something outside. She turned to look. Two men in torn, dirty clothes with tangled hair and whiskered faces sank down on the bench outside the café's doors. One held a small mixed-breed dog and the other cradled a battered backpack overflowing with what was most likely his worldly belongings. An aproned man charged past her and flung the front door open.

"You two go on. No loitering." The man spoke so harshly Brooke cringed.

The men slowly rose and ambled off, their shoulders slumped and heads low. People in the café murmured and nodded. The couple who'd pointed out the pair congratulated the man as he passed their table. He smiled and said, "No problem. Can't have that kind of riffraff hanging around."

Brooke scowled. Certainly there were people who could be called riffraff. She wasn't so naive as to believe that evil people didn't exist. Such as the well-dressed man who carted away the girl at the mall. If he'd sat on the bench, no one would have sent him away, because he looked good on the outside. But Brooke knew his insides were rotten. Those two ragedy men hadn't bothered a soul, but they'd been treated abominably.

Her hunger fled. She crossed to Marty and caught hold of her arm. "Let's get out of here."

Marty raised her brows. "Why? They have a good selection. Doesn't anything appeal to you?"

Brooke sent a meaningful look across the counter at the man who'd sent the homeless pair away. "I don't want to give my money to a place whose owner lacks compassion." The man's lips curled into a snarl, and he turned his back on her. She drew Marty toward the door. "Let's go through a fast-food line on the way home."

"Okay." Marty still looked confused, but she followed Brooke to the sidewalk. "We'd better wait for Elliott, though."

Brooke started to sit on the bench, but she glanced through the window of the shop next door, which was clearly a store that sold used books, based on the rows of shelves stuffed with paperbacks of all varieties. A few people sat in a grouping of faded stuffed chairs in the corner, and most of them had sodas or sandwiches. Brooke gestured to the bench. "Stay here, Marty. I'll be right back."

She entered the bookstore, scanned the area, and spotted a snack counter along the back wall. The sandwiches were the prepackaged kind used in vending machines, but she doubted that would matter if someone was hungry enough. She picked up the last chicken salad, two ham and cheese, and one pimento-cheese spread, then added half a dozen bags of chips, two candy bars, and two bottles of water to the pile.

The older man behind the counter chuckled. "You must have a big appetite." His grin turned knowing. "Or you've got some hungry friends waiting." He told her what she owed, and she offered her debit card. After he ran it, he tossed two more candy bars and a bag of unshelled peanuts into the sack. "On the house."

She thanked him, and he replied with a wink. Outside again, Brooke bounced a grin at Marty and then took off in the direction she'd seen the two men with the dog go. She found them in a little parklike patch of dried grass on the corner, sitting together under a leafless tree. They eyed her suspiciously as she approached, but the little dog wiggled in its master's arms, whining and wagging its tail. She hoped there was something in the bag the dog could eat. Without invading their space, she set the bag on the ground close enough for the men to reach, then smiled at each of them.

Not a quick glance and smile but a lingering one. So they'd know she'd seen them. Really seen them.

Neither smiled back, but she didn't hold it against them. When a person was beaten down, it wasn't easy to find a reason to smile. She turned and headed for the sidewalk. When her foot met the concrete, a gruff voice called, "Thank you, lady. God bless you."

Brooke froze for a moment, a lump filling her throat. She sent a smile over her shoulder. "You're welcome. God bless you, too." Then she whirled and faced the men. "Do you stay here"—she gestured to the surrounding area—"all the time?"

The one who'd held the dog was already digging in the bag, and the second one answered. "Lots of the time. Why?"

She took two steps onto the brown grass. "Have you ever noticed a young girl hanging around? About fifteen, long red-brown hair, probably wearing a pair of army boots."

The two exchanged a glance, and the same man spoke again. "The fellow from the bistro called the cops on a girl about that age a couple days ago. They came and picked her up."

If the girl they'd seen was Ronnie and if police officers had picked her up, she was probably back at the juvenile detention center. Brooke thanked the men and hurried back to Marty.

Elliott had arrived in her absence, and he greeted her with a puzzled look. "What were you doing?"

"Righting a wrong." She put her hands on her hips and pretended to scowl. "What took you so long? Did you get lost on your way to the car?"

He shrugged. "You told me to look for Ronnie, so I did."

Brooke shook her head. "No need." She repeated what the two homeless men had told her.

Elliott frowned. "Let's hope she stays there this time."

Brooke took hold of his arm. "We'll do more than hope. We'll pray."

His expression didn't clear, but he nodded.

She tugged his arm. "Come on."

He looked through the café's windows. "Aren't we going in there?"

She'd rather buy vending machine sandwiches than reward the hard-hearted café owner with her business. "Nope. We're going to have pimento-cheese spread on white bread. The kind of bread that sticks to the roof of your mouth and you have to scrape it off with a potato chip." She raised the skin above her eyes in lieu of raising her eyebrows. "It's likely not organic, but right now it's exactly what I want to eat."

39

Pine Hill

Anthony

On Thanksgiving Day, Anthony woke before dawn, walked out to the barn with his brother, and helped with the morning chores. Dumping pails of smelly leftovers mixed with chopped corncobs into the pigs' trough and tossing forkfuls of hay into the cattle stalls reminded him of boyhood mornings, and he couldn't resist sending one pitchfork of loose hay over Rex's head for nostalgia's sake. Rex laughed a lot more about it than he had when they were youngsters.

When they'd finished seeing to the livestock, they ambled to the horse corral, leaned on the top rail, and watched the climbing sun change the sky from gray to pink and yellow. It'd been a long time since Anthony had seen a sunrise from start to finish. The houses around theirs in Pine Hill blocked it, and trees around the little town of Eagle Creek mostly hid it, too. He'd forgotten how much he enjoyed witnessing the sun coming to life.

"Sure wish Marty could've come with you." Rex scraped the sole of his dirty boot on the lowest rail and sent a sidelong look at Anthony. "You sure it wasn't a *wouldn't* instead of a *couldn't?*"

Anthony frowned. "Of course I'm sure. Why would you ask something like that?"

Rex dropped his foot to the ground. "It's no secret she's been unhappy since . . ." He glanced at Anthony, and his lips pulled into a grimace. "For a while now. Dawna sent at least three letters to her, and we haven't gotten one back. Kind of makes us think she's trying to forget about all of us."

"Well, that's not true." Defensiveness tightened Anthony's throat and made his voice come out harder than he'd intended. "Sure, she's been unhappy. Who could blame her? But she's been busy. We both have. There's a lot of work to be done at the ghost town."

"Then it seems like she'd want a break from it. A few days with family to relax."

Anthony huffed. "Listen, Rex, if you'd been around after one of Brooke's cancer treatments, you'd understand how bad it is. There's no way Brooke could stay alone, and she doesn't have anybody except Marty to take care of her. Marty not coming doesn't mean she doesn't care about you. She knows Brooke needs her there more than you need her here."

Rex clapped him on the shoulder. "All right, brother, I'm sorry. I wasn't criticizing. She's loving her neighbor as herself, the way we're commanded." He shifted his position, leaning a little harder on the rail. "We just miss you guys, that's all."

"We miss you, too."

"But then, maybe it's best she stayed behind."

Anthony turned sideways and fixed his gaze on his brother's profile. "Why?"

A grin climbed Rex's cheek. He adjusted the bill of his cap and turned the grin in Anthony's direction. "'Cause we have some news to share, and it's got us pretty excited, but it might be hard on Marty's heart, considering."

Anthony already knew what Rex would say, but he stayed quiet and let his brother share it.

"Dawna's expecting."

A pressure weighted Anthony's chest. A blend of joy for Rex and Dawna, and jealousy because he'd never get to make an announcement like that about Marty. He pushed the jealousy aside and curled his hand around Rex's neck. "Congratulations."

"Thanks. We're pretty excited." Rex sighed and faced the sun again. "It's a little sooner than we'd planned, but we figure God knows better than we do when another Hirschler should join the family."

Anthony swallowed the knot in his throat. Did God have some reason there shouldn't be a little Hirschler born to him and Marty? "That's great. I'm happy for you. I really am."

"Dawna says it's gonna be another girl. Says she feels the same way she did when she was carrying Ava and Audrey. She's already calling it Claire Olivia. So I guess we'll see if she's right. I'm gonna have a boy's name ready, though, just in case."

"Good thinking."

"Yeah." Rex seemed to drift off in thought. "Maybe Mason. Mason Anthony."

Anthony gave a jolt. "Anthony? After me?"

Rex angled his head and gave him a sheepish grin. "If that's okay with you. Levi's got my middle name—Bradley. And Jaxton's middle name is for Dawna's brother. If you'd rather we didn't—if you wanted to keep that name for . . . your own boy—then I'll pick something else."

Anthony shook his head. "Rex, you know Marty and me won't have a boy of our own." It still hurt to say it out loud. Even though Marty had seemed to finally accept it, it still hurt that he couldn't give her a baby. He swallowed his sadness and forced a smile. "So if you want to give your son my name, I'd be honored."

"All right, then. If it's a boy, Mason Anthony. I'll let Dawna know." He pushed off the rail. "I guess we should head in, get cleaned up for—"

Anthony gathered his courage. "Rex?"

Rex turned back. "Yeah?"

"What would you think about Marty and me being foster parents?"

His brother's face lit. "You mean taking in a baby? I think that'd—"

"Not a baby." Neither of them would be able to let a baby go even if the courts said they had to. "Teenagers."

Rex's eyebrows shot high. He yanked off his cap. "Why?"

Anthony told Rex about Elliott, about Ronnie, about Brooke's hope to make Eagle Creek a shelter for kids who needed a home, about how he couldn't stop thinking about the kids nobody seemed to want. He gripped the railing with both hands and stared at the now-full, wavering ball of sunshine until his eyes watered and he had to squint them down to slits. "It seems like God put this idea in my head, and I can't get rid of it."

"What does Marty think?"

Anthony hung his head. Little dots of light danced in front of his eyes. "We haven't really talked it all out. But after what she's seen, after what she did—"

Rex leaned in. "What'd she do?"

Anthony straightened and faced his brother. "Broke up a sex-trafficking ring."

Rex bolted upright. "She what?"

Anthony explained the situation, and the awe and admiration in his brother's face made him proud of Marty all over again. "Since then, she's talked a lot about how kids need somebody to take care of them. So I think she'd be willing."

Rex stayed as still as a fence post, quiet, frowning. Then he huffed a breath. "Wow, Anthony, I don't know. Babies are one thing. But teenagers? With all their bad worldly habits and . . . and . . ." He shook his head. "I'm not sure how the fellowship would react. We try to keep ourselves separate from the world, and you'd be bringing it right to our doorsteps."

"Yeah." Anthony bit the inside of his lip.

"Maybe you should talk to the deacons while you're here. Find out what they think."

They'd told him to reach out with Christian love to those he encountered—to be a missionary. Would they see opening his home to kids who didn't know what it meant to be loved and nurtured and taught to seek and serve God as ministering to the least of these, or would they see the kids' presence as in intrusion? "Maybe."

Rex stared off again for a few seconds. "How much longer until you'll be finished in Eagle Creek?"

"At least a year." Unless Brooke's investors all pulled out and she had to abandon the project. If Brooke couldn't pay him and his crew, they'd all have to come back early. He didn't want to come back. He wanted to finish the job. To see the shelter be successful and—he admitted to himself, even though he wasn't ready to admit it to Rex—be a part of its success in more than just bringing the buildings back to life. He wanted to have a hand in bringing those hurting, lost kids back to life.

Rex slung his arm around Anthony's shoulders. "That'll give you time to think about it. Figure out what to do. I'll pray about it with you, all right? That you'll make the right decision."

Anthony nodded and headed to the house with Rex. But he'd already made his decision. He needed to pray for Marty to want the same thing.

Eagle Creek
Marty

Marty stood outside Brooke's bathroom door and listened to the sounds of retching. Her stomach ached in sympathy for her friend, and helplessness made her want to cry. Not even Zofran was keeping the nausea at bay this round. The Thanksgiving dinner she'd so lovingly prepared for Brooke and Elliott would have to be carried out of Brooke's trailer because the smell of turkey, stuffing, sweet potatoes, and green beans had made Brooke sick. Poor Elliott would have to eat dinner all by himself. Such a dismal way to spend a holiday.

The toilet flushed, and then Marty heard the sound of water splashing against the sink—Brooke apparently washing her face and rinsing her mouth. Marty tapped gently on the door. "Do you need my help?"

"No." The word grated out on a sharp note, but Marty didn't take offense. Brooke had good reason to be grumpy.

Finally the door opened and Brooke stumbled into the hall. Her red-rimmed, watery gaze found Marty's. "There can't be anything left to come up. Please help me to bed."

Elliott glanced over from the eating bar, where the Thanksgiving food was laid out in readiness for dinner. "Need an extra hand?"

Marty put her arm around Brooke's waist. Brooke was so frail Marty feared she would snap her in half if she held her too tightly. "Thank you, but no. I've got it." She guided Brooke to her bed. Brooke sat and then fell sideways against the pillows. Marty lifted her feet onto the mattress and tucked the covers around her. "I'll get you a glass of ginger ale." The sparkling soda sometimes stayed down.

Brooke groaned. "No. Nothing. Let me sleep."

Marty feared that Brooke would get dehydrated if she didn't try to drink something, but it seemed Brooke had already fallen asleep. Eyes closed, mouth slightly open, chest rising and falling in deep, heavy breaths. Rest was good medicine, too. Marty turned off the lamp on the side table, tiptoed out of the room, and closed the door behind her.

She entered the kitchen and crossed to the bar. "I'm so sorry, Elliott. This isn't exactly the way I'd wanted your Thanksgiving to go."

The young man shrugged. "It's okay. I don't guess it's what you or Miss Spalding wanted, either." He frowned, shifting his gaze to the short hallway that led to the single bedroom. "She's really sick."

Marty nodded and slipped onto a barstool. "The second day after chemo is always the worst."

"So tomorrow will be better?"

Such hope glowed in his eyes that Marty wished she could say yes. But the effects of the chemo seemed to take longer to leave Brooke's body with every treatment. Brooke might very well be just as sick tomorrow. She sighed. "I pray so."

"Me, too."

Marty gave a start. Had Elliott committed to pray?

He fiddled with the serving fork resting on the edge of the platter of turkey and lowered his head. "Do you think she'll really be able to make this place a shelter for homeless kids? I mean, she's so sick. Yeah, she's got help—Mr. Hirschler and the rest of us—but when you're all done here, you'll leave and she'll be on her own. Will she be strong enough to handle all of it after having cancer?"

Marty rose and began covering the platters and bowls with aluminum foil. "I can't say for sure. Only God knows the future. But I can tell you this. I've known Brooke since she was a little girl. She's overcome a lot of hardship. She's a fighter. God gave her an extra dose of determination because He knew she'd need it to become the successful businesswoman she is today. She isn't going to quit trying just because she's sick. So if I had to guess, I'd say Brooke will make it happen. She won't give up."

"Then . . ." Elliott had lifted his head and gazed at Marty intently while she spoke. He continued to look her squarely in the face now. "Do you think God will let it happen? You said He's the only One who really knows."

In Elliott's eyes, she saw the same longing and hopefulness she'd seen in Brooke's eyes years ago when Brooke shared her dreams and aspirations for her life—a better life than the one her mother had demonstrated. Elliott needed assurance that his life could be better than it had been so far. Marty reached across the counter and put her hand over Elliott's clenched fists.

"Elliott, one of my favorite passages of Scripture is in the Old Testament, Jeremiah twenty-nine, verses eleven through thirteen. God speaking to the children of Israel." She closed her eyes, envisioning the words on the page of her well-used Bible. "'For I know the thoughts that I think toward you, saith the LORD, thoughts of peace, and not of evil, to give you an expected end. Then shall ye call upon me, and ye shall go and pray unto me, and I will hearken unto you. And ye shall seek me, and find me, when ye shall search for me with all your heart.'"

She opened her eyes and smiled through a sheen of tears. "God makes plans for His children that lead to good, not evil. We find those plans when we ask Him with sincerity of heart to guide us. Brooke has sought Him. She's following where He leads. I don't think this change of plans is something she came up with all on her own. I think God brought Ronnie and you into Brooke's life to awaken her to God's plan for this piece of property."

He drew back slightly, his mouth open. "God . . . used me . . . for His plans?"

She couldn't resist laughing lightly at his shock. "Is that so impossible to believe? God uses everything"—even her childless state—"to work His will for us. Because He loves us so much and wants the very best for us. He has plans for Brooke, and He has plans for you, too, Elliott. All you have to do is ask Him to reveal them to you and then go where He leads. That's where you'll find the peace Jeremiah 29:11 talks about."

He sat and stared at her for several seconds, astonishment still evident in his expression. Then he nodded and slipped his hands from beneath hers. "Thanks. I'll give that some thought."

She picked up the platter. "You do that. And I'll be praying for Him to speak to your heart."

His lips curved into a bashful smile. "Thanks, Mrs. Hirschler."

They took the entire Thanksgiving dinner to Elliott and Todd's trailer. Marty promised to stop in later, while Brooke slept, and have a plate of food with him. Then she hurried back to Brooke. As she went, she prayed the time alone would give Elliott a chance to do the seeking she'd mentioned. She was beginning to see pieces of a puzzle fall into place not only for Brooke but for Elliott, as well. She couldn't wait to find out if her suppositions proved true.

40

Pine Hill
Anthony

*T*he key-wound clock on Rex and Dawna's sideboard chimed nine before the Thanksgiving festivities came to an end. Anthony waited until the children were all in bed, the neighbors had gone home, Dawna—finally satisfied that her kitchen was clean enough—trudged upstairs, and Rex headed to the barn to give the livestock a last check. Finally he had some time to himself.

He settled into the antique rocker in the corner of the living room and used his cell phone to call Marty. She answered on the first ring, and when he heard her quiet voice, his pulse leaped into overdrive. "Hi, honey. How's it going over there?"

"Brooke's had a really rough day." Marty spoke so softly Anthony had to strain to hear her. But he wouldn't ask her to speak up. She was probably trying not to disturb Brooke. "I fixed a turkey dinner for Elliott and me, and he seemed to enjoy it. Did you have a good dinner with your family?"

"I did. It's been a good day over here." He dared to admit, "Except for missing you."

A sigh met his ear. "I miss you, too."

She couldn't have said anything that would have pleased him more. Suddenly nervous, he rocked, making the runners squeak. "Listen, honey, do you have time for a serious talk?"

"Brooke's asleep and Elliott's in his trailer. What's wrong?" Worry came through in her voice.

He wished he could hold her hand for this conversation, let her look into his eyes and see how much he wanted to do the right thing, but his tone would have to do the convincing. "Nothing's wrong. There's something I need to tell you—well, ask you, I guess is a better way of putting it. I need to know what you think before I try to meet with the deacons on Sunday after worship."

"Okay, I'm listening."

He smiled. He could picture her intent face with the pair of black ribbons falling across her shoulders. Was she wearing the light blue dress he liked so much? He closed his eyes to hold her image in his mind. "I've had the hardest time not thinking about Ronnie and kids like her. Kids who, like Elliott talked about, don't have anybody who cares about them. I don't know how they stand a chance of becoming happy adults or living good lives if nobody ever steps up to give them what they need. Brooke's shelter will give them a place to go, but that's not enough. They'll still need . . . parents." He paused and tilted his head, listening for any sign of shock or disapproval.

"I've been thinking the same thing. Elliott and I even talked about it earlier today. Well, kind of. We talked about God's plan for Brooke and for him, but it made me think about God's plan for me—for us. I've started wondering if God didn't let us have children so we'd be available to take care of the ones He brings to us."

Anthony's eyes popped open. He pushed his feet against the floor and stilled the rocking chair. "Would you do it—be willing to take care of older kids? The ones nobody else seems to want?"

"I'm praying about it, seeking, the way I told Elliott to do. I'm asking God to give me peace—complete peace—so I'll know for sure."

He smiled so big his cheeks hurt. "I'm doing the same thing. I want to talk to the deacons about us taking in older foster kids. Before we do the classes or whatever else we have to do for the state to approve us, I want to make sure the kids would be welcomed into the fellowship."

"So you mean bringing them into our home in Pine Hill?"

"Yes, in case . . ." Should he tell her everything he'd thought about? It might be too much for her to grasp with her focus on taking care of Brooke. Maybe he should wait. Something seemed to nudge him. He blurted, "If Brooke's shelter opens, I'd like to stay there. To be a dad to the kids who come. But if it doesn't, I still want to be a dad to kids who need one. And the older kids need one the most. Is that"—he gripped the phone so hard his fingers ached—"okay with you?"

A strange burbling sound trickled through the speaker and into his ear. He pulled the phone away, uncertain whether Marty was laughing or crying. He put the phone back to his mouth. "Are you laughing?"

"Yes!" He heard the amusement in her tone as clearly as if he were sitting right next to her.

"Why?"

"Because I want to be a mom to them."

His mouth fell open. "You do? Even though they won't really be ours?"

"They can be ours, Anthony. At least for a season." She spoke so soft, he had to strain to hear her. "If this shelter happens, I want to stay and help. Help Brooke, help the kids, just . . . help." A gulp sounded. "And if God closes the door on Brooke's shelter, then I still want to keep our door open to kids who need us. As I said, I'm praying for complete peace. Because . . ." Now he knew she was crying. Her voice wavered and lowered in tone. "If I do this, I want to really love them. With a mother's kind of love. I need to know for sure my heart can accept other people's kids as fiercely as it holds the baby we lost."

His throat went tight. "I miss our baby, too." If they hadn't lost their baby, they'd be the parents of a teenager now. "I'll always love it. And I know we'll meet him or her when we get to heaven. That'll be a great reunion. But right now, we both have something to give. And there are kids in need. So doesn't it seem like we would be a good match for them?"

"Yes. I—" Some muffled noises came through the line. Then Marty's voice. "Anthony, Brooke needs another nausea pill. I have to go."

"That's okay. Take care of her. I'll talk to you again tomorrow?"

"Yes. I love you."

Even though she said it in a hurry and hung up right afterward, the declaration warmed Anthony like a ball of fire in the center of his chest. It was good to hear her say she loved him, because he sure loved her.

He sat for several minutes, caught in wonderment. After their years of holding each other at arm's length, now they were coming together, drawn by a common desire. It wasn't what he'd originally wanted. The idea of adopting a baby still rolled in the back of his mind. But only God could unite him and Marty in reaching out to older kids—them, who'd never raised a child or worked with teens in the past. He might not have experience, but he had something better. He had a call on his heart. If he answered the call, he knew God would give him what he needed to meet the challenges.

Now to discover where he'd welcome the kids—into his own home or at Brooke's shelter.

Eagle Creek
Brooke

Brooke examined her reflection in the full-length mirror attached to the back of her bedroom door. Marty had done an excellent job tailoring the fuchsia suit to fit. She ran her finger down the trio of one-inch pearlescent buttons marching from the collar to the belted waist, her mind slipping backward in time to when she'd worn this suit last. In the bank meeting room, with Mr. Miller, when she'd finalized her purchase of the ghost town. What a difference six months could make.

She lifted her gaze from the buttons to her face. She grimaced. The cover-up under her eyes hid the dark circles, but she should scrub off the rouge and lipstick. The colors, the same pink tones she'd worn for years, looked garish against her pale skin. But without it, she'd have no color at all. Except for her green irises, which seemed bigger and darker now that no eyelashes or eyebrows helped balance them. She leaned closer to the mirror, squinting at herself. Maybe a little bit of eyeliner would help.

Someone tapped on the door, and Brooke opened it. Marty looked her up and down, a smile of satisfaction on her face.

"It looks good. How does it feel?"

Brooke struck a pose and fluttered her eyelids. "It feels mahvelous, dahling."

Marty laughed. "You've been watching late-night movies again." She fingered Brooke's collar, pulled a loose thread, and then lifted her gaze to Brooke's head. "Would you like me to help with a scarf? Or did you plan to wear a hat?"

Brooke moved to the dresser and put on the simple pearl teardrop earrings she'd chosen. "I'll wear a stocking cap until I get there. Gotta keep warm, you know." Only three weeks now until Christmas, and the wind made the temps feel twenty degrees colder than the thermometer showed. "But when I get to the meeting, I'm going au naturel."

Marty's eyes widened. "You mean . . . bald?"

Brooke nodded. "Yep. Gonna let them see me as I am these days. Bald as a billiard ball but"—she chuckled—"still feisty." She sat on the end of the bed and put on her ivory heels. She'd worn flat shoes for months. She hoped she hadn't forgotten how to walk in high heels.

Marty wrung her hands, her brow set in a scowl. "I wish you'd let Anthony or me go with you."

"Elliott's going. He's doing part of the presentation." Who better to express the hardships of living unattended on the streets than one who'd been there? "He's very dependable, as you well know."

"Yes, I know, but . . ."

Brooke held out both hands. Marty took hold, and Brooke pulled herself upright. She kept hold of Marty's hands until she'd caught her balance, then let go and smoothed the front of her jacket. "Listen, I know you're worried, and I love you for caring so much. But really, Mother, you have to let this baby bird fly the nest." She smiled so Marty would know she was teasing.

Marty's frown didn't fade. "But—"

"Shhh." Brooke gave Marty a quick hug and then stepped back, keeping her hands on Marty's shoulders. "I have to do this myself. Elliott being there makes sense. He's sharing his story, putting a face to the statistics I intend to throw at the investors. But you or Anthony would be there only as my crutches. It would give the silent message that I'm not capable of making decisions on my own. The investors won't be able to help but notice how different I look. I need these men to realize that the underneath part of me is just as savvy and strong as it was when we met to draw up paperwork for the gambling resort. I certainly didn't need anyone holding me up then. Do you understand?"

Marty chewed the inside of her lip and stared into Brooke's eyes for several seconds while indecision played in her expression. Finally she sighed. "All right. I understand. You directed this whole thing. You need to be the one to redirect it."

"That's exactly right. And now that I have a Navigator, I'll be pointing this project in the right direction." Brooke squeezed Marty's shoulders and let go. "If you and Anthony want to help, then pray for the men to be receptive to these new plans and to leave their funding in place. Instead of a return on their investments, they'll basically be getting a major tax write-off. That might not be enough motivation for some of them."

"What happens if they refuse?"

Brooke's stomach turned a flip. "I'll have to give them their invested money back."

"Then what will happen here?"

"Everything here will come to a halt until I can raise funding." Which would probably have to wait until she'd finished all her chemotherapy. She wouldn't have the energy to organize a fund-raising campaign until she got her strength back. But why was she worrying? This project wasn't hers anymore. It belonged to the One who'd planted the idea in her head. If it was meant to happen, it would, and on His timetable.

That morning, a radio preacher had shared a verse from the fifteenth chapter of Romans, and Brooke had underlined it in her Bible. She'd left the crisp new book lying open on the nightstand, and she crossed to it. "Marty, do you know Romans 15:13?"

Marty quoted without a moment's pause. " 'Now the God of hope fill you with all joy and peace in believing, that ye may abound in hope, through the power of the Holy Ghost.' "

Brooke smiled. "Yes. I've got peace about this, Marty. Whatever happens, I trust that it's exactly what God wants for Eagle Creek. I won't stand in front of the investors today on my own, because the Holy Spirit is with me. We've got this. Right?"

Marty's lips quivered. She nodded hard, making her black ribbons bounce.

"All right, then." Brooke moved toward the door and stuck out her elbow. "Escort me to the front room, huh? I honestly don't know how I ever walked in these crazy shoes."

41

Kansas City
Brooke

*D*uring the first half hour of the meeting, Brooke's investors partook of the catered buffet she'd ordered from a local restaurant. The array of crab-filled deviled eggs, smoked salmon on sesame crackers, goat-cheese-stuffed apricots, bacon-wrapped dates, and miniature artichoke turnovers—not to mention the choice of three different imported French wines—put the dozen men in a jolly mood suitable for the season.

When they'd sated their appetites, she asked them to join her around the meeting table. She spent another half hour showing photos on her laptop of the progress made at the ghost town. The men seemed impressed, nodding, smiling, occasionally asking for clarification. While the pictures were still clear in their minds, she laid out her new plans for each building, described the programs she wanted to implement and the staff she intended to hire, and shared the statistics gathered from governmental and social service sources about the genuine need for a safe haven where young people could be rehabilitated and educated.

The expressions of approval changed to frowns of confusion, and some of the men began to murmur. Before a full-blown argument erupted, she opened the door and invited Elliott, who'd been waiting in the hallway, to join them.

"Gentlemen, this is Elliott Kane, who is part of the work team at Eagle Creek. He has a story to share with you."

She rolled her chair to the wall and listened while Elliott told the investors about his time on the streets, then living in a detention center, and finally aging out of the youth center without a home to return to. During his talk, she surreptitiously examined the men's faces. They were listening, but were they moved by this blue-jeaned, flannel-shirt-wearing young man? Sitting there in their three-piece Armani suits, stomachs full of wine and hors d'oeuvres, smelling of hundred-dollar-an-ounce aftershave, these men had lived lives far removed from Elliott's experiences. They wouldn't be able to relate to him, but could they sympathize? Would they care?

Elliott finished his presentation, thanked the men for allowing him to talk to them, and traded places with Brooke. Except he stood against the wall and insisted she roll the chair back to the table. She appreciated his thoughtfulness. Exhaustion weighted her, and she prayed for strength as she settled in the chair and faced the circle of men again.

"I'm well aware that when you joined forces with me, it was for a different project. But you have all been in business long enough to realize not every project ends the way it was originally planned."

Mr. Blackburn, who'd been the first one to toss his money into the investment pot, snorted. "I've never been involved in one that made such a significant U-turn. How can you even begin to pass this off as the project in which we invested? You've gone from money making to money spending without even the pretense of a return."

Brooke nodded at the gray-haired man. "You're right that there won't be a monetary return, but there are greater things to gain than money."

"Such as?" He folded his arms across his chest and glared at her.

"Personal satisfaction. A legacy of benevolence." She stacked her forearms on the table and pinned the man with her gaze. "Consider living with the knowledge that you've positively impacted a human life. When you drop a pebble in a pond, countless circles grow from that small pebble. Each of those circles represents a life trajectory. If you send one person's life in a better direction, then the generations that follow will also be improved."

Mr. Blackburn pushed his chair away from the table and rose. "I'm not a pebble. Nor am I a minister or a charity. I am a businessman, and my personal goal is to increase my assets. If you don't intend to hold up your end of the bargain, then I am under no obligation to contribute. In light of the holiday season, I won't demand the interest I could have gained if my investment had remained in my stock portfolio." He marched to the coatrack near the door, yanked his overcoat from the wooden hanger, and jammed his arms into the sleeves. "I'll expect a check equal to my original investment in my mail by the end of January. Good evening, Ms. Spalding."

As he flung the door open, Brooke said, very kindly and sincerely, "Merry Christmas, Mr. Blackburn."

He froze for the length of two seconds, muttered something under his breath, and departed.

Brooke turned her attention to the remaining men. She let her gaze drift around the circle of faces, pausing to make eye contact with each of them. At least with those who would meet her gaze. When she'd looked into every unsmiling face, she stood and braced herself against the edge of the sturdy walnut table.

"Well, gentlemen, I suppose it's decision time. Mr. Blackburn has made his choice. What about the rest of you? Are you in?" She held her hand toward the door. "Or out?"

Eagle Creek
Marty

Marty set her book aside and looked up at the wall clock. Was it running fast? She checked her wristwatch and scowled. Both showed a quarter to ten. So where were Brooke and Elliott? Brooke had estimated they'd be back by nine.

Anthony peeked at her over the top of his book. She could see only the top half of his face, but she knew he was smirking.

She gave him a frown. "Stop that."

"Stop what?"

"Making fun of me."

His eyebrows rose. "I'm not making fun of you."

She huffed. "Yes, you are, but you shouldn't, because I have every reason to be concerned. They should have been back by now."

He laid his book on the end table and patted the sofa cushion beside him. "Come here, my little mother hen."

Sighing, Marty stood and crossed the short expanse of carpet. She plopped onto the cushion and leaned against him. He slipped his arms around her and guided her head to his shoulder. She nestled, toying with a loose thread on the cuff of his shirt. Secure within the circle of his arms, she managed a short chuckle at her own expense. "I guess it is a little silly to worry. After all, they're grown adults, not children. But Brooke isn't as strong physically as she pretends to be. What if the meeting was too much for her? What if the investors all started yelling at her?" Worry rose again. "I don't know how she'd hold up against their fury."

Anthony kissed her temple. "Marty, you're borrowing trouble. Elliott's there. He won't let anyone hurt her."

"I suppose."

"And didn't we pray together before they left? Haven't we been praying for the last few weeks for God to work His will concerning Brooke's hopes for Eagle Creek?"

Shamed, Marty shifted a little more firmly into his embrace. "I know. I'm sorry. But we're not only talking about Brooke's hopes. It's our hopes, too." A lump filled her throat. After longing for so many years to cradle a baby in her arms and having that longing change to a desire to nurture needy young people, she couldn't bear the thought of having another dream shattered. "If the men pull their investment money, then—"

"Then God will find another way to let the shelter open, if it's His will."

She angled her head to peer into his eyes. "And if it isn't His will?"

"Then He'll open a new door for all of us. Trust, Marty." He kissed her once, then again, and whispered against her parted lips, "Trust."

The assurance in his blue eyes, the certainty in his voice, bolstered Marty's reblossoming faith. She smiled, her lips twitching as a swell of emotion—love for her husband, love for her Maker, gratitude for the second chance they'd both willingly offered her—tightened her chest. "Yes. Thank you. We'll trust."

He tipped his head as if to deliver another kiss, but the crunch of tires on gravel and the beam from headlights passing the window brought Marty to her feet. She dashed to the front door and peeked out. Relief, anticipation, and apprehension all struck with such force that she battled an attack of dizziness. She pulled the door open and then clung to it, her heart pounding while she waited for Elliott and Brooke to share their news.

Anthony crossed behind her and waved as Brooke and Elliott mounted the porch. A cold rush of air came in with them, and Brooke moved to the middle of the floor, releasing a shudder.

Marty closed the door and hurried to Brooke. She guided her friend to a chair and gave her a gentle push onto the cushions. Then she took the opposite chair. Wringing her hands, she licked her dry lips and tried to decide what to ask first. When she opened her mouth to speak, all that came out was "Well?"

Brooke removed her stocking cap and unbuttoned her coat. "Well, Mr. Blackburn—the first and biggest contributor to the project—stomped out with a demand for me to give him his money back."

Elliott propped his hand on the back of Brooke's chair and shook his head. "By the end of January. I told her after the meeting that she should deduct the cost of the food he ate at the meeting. Twice as much as anyone else." He and Brooke chuckled.

Anthony strode to Marty and perched on the arm of her chair, sliding his arm around her shoulders. She grabbed his hand and gave Brooke an impatient look. "What did the others do?"

Brooke shrugged, running the tassel from her stocking cap between her fingers. "Mr. Young wants his money back, too, but he was willing to let me pay it out in monthly increments rather than all at once. And both men forfeited any interest that might have accrued. As for the others . . ." She glanced at Elliott, and the two of them exchanged a smile. "They are willing to let their investments be a charitable contribution to the project."

A squeal of happiness found its way from Marty's throat. She clapped twice, laughed, and squealed again.

Brooke burst out laughing. "I can't honestly say there wasn't some manipulation. I mean, how can you refuse a bald-headed, cancer-stricken woman and a formerly homeless young man during the Christmas season? If we'd asked at another time of year, when I was hale and hearty, the answer might have been different. But it's like that story in Esther. God arranged everything to align 'for such a time as this.'"

And God had prepared Marty for such a time as this, too. She swallowed salty tears and nodded. "It's perfect. It's all . . . just right."

Brooke held up one hand like a traffic cop. "There are some stipulations, though. They won't leave their funds in the project unless my application to create a nonprofit shelter is accepted by the state, I pass all the inspections, I secure all the licenses, and I'm able to put together a staff of qualified people who also pass all licensing requirements. Then they'll be able to use their investments as a write-off." She collapsed against the cushions. "There are still some major mountains to climb, but we've cleared the first hill, and I'm grateful."

Anthony's fingers clamped a little harder on Marty's shoulder. "What kind of licensing requirements are there for people on the staff?"

Brooke shrugged out of her coat. "Basically a background check. There'll be kids living here—kids who've been mistreated and used. Obviously I won't want anyone on the staff with a felony record or who's been accused of abusing a child. Any staff members will have to have updated immunizations and so forth, too, to meet health department requirements, but that's pretty standard for any kind of position working with the public."

Her brow furrowed, and she used her fingers to count off. "I'll definitely want a counselor on staff, and I'll need grounds workers, workshop teachers, house parents, and at least one cook. I intend to have the kids involved in the workshops, crafting items we can sell to the public to help with expenses out here, and I'll expect them to contribute by cleaning their own rooms, helping prepare meals, doing chores . . . all the things that ready them for living on their own." She dropped her hand to her lap and aimed a grin at Elliott. "I've already got my first staff applicant—Elliott wants to stay."

He grinned. "I can be a maintenance worker or groundskeeper, and I'd like to help organize the workshops."

Brooke bobbed her thumb in his direction. "I figure someone with his experience as a street kid will be a valuable asset in understanding the residents' mind-set. I'm thrilled to bring him on board."

Marty peeked up at Anthony, and he nodded, a gesture she recognized as permission. She turned to Brooke. "We—Anthony and me— want to apply, too. To help with maintenance and cooking, or to be house parents."

Brooke went completely still, her green eyes wide and unblinking.

Uncertain how to interpret the reaction, Marty swallowed. "That is, if you'll have us."

Brooke's eyes swam with tears. She released a shuddering breath, and the trembling tears spilled down her cheeks. "If I'll have you?" The words choked on a half laugh, half sob. "Marty, I couldn't think of anyone better." She leaned forward and grabbed Marty's hands, her gaze bouncing between Marty and Anthony. "But are you sure? These kids won't be babies. They'll be almost grown, and stinky and obstinate and . . . well, pretty much the way I was as a teenager. They'll come in every color of the rainbow, with all kinds of trust issues and bad habits. Are you sure you want to stay and deal with all that instead of going home and trying to adopt a baby?"

Certainty filled Marty, a mighty rush that brought both tears and a smile she couldn't have contained if she'd wanted to. "If God decides to give us a baby somehow, we'll accept that, too, but both of us have been called to minister to the kids you're trying to reach."

Anthony gave a solemn nod. "I talked to the deacons at our fellowship when I was in Indiana for Thanksgiving. They gave us their blessing if we decided to stay here and minister to kids coming out of human trafficking, and they said if the shelter didn't open, we'd have their support in being foster parents for teenagers in Pine Hill. So, yes, we're sure."

Marty gripped Anthony's hand and beamed at him. "We're very, very sure."

Brooke again gaped at both of them for several seconds. Then she collapsed into the chair, and a deep, contentment-laden sigh eased from her. "I don't know what to say except thank you. Thank you for coming, thank you for helping me, thank you for pointing me to my Father, thank you for opening my eyes to what could be. Just . . . thank you."

Marty leaned into Anthony's frame. "Don't thank us. Thank God for putting all the pieces together. This was His plan all along."

Elliott rested both elbows on the back of Brooke's chair. "Like it says in Jeremiah twenty-nine, right?"

Anthony's hand squeezed sweetly on Marty's shoulder. "Exactly right."

Marty closed her eyes and sent up a silent prayer of gratitude. God the Father had worked His will in His time, and she'd never been so hope filled, so joy filled, so whole. She gave Elliott a watery smile. "We're moving toward His expected end. And I know it will be"—she met Brooke's gaze—"a season of joy breathing deeply."

EPILOGUE

Two years later
Marty

*H*ere, Dorothy, take this to the table, please." Marty handed the bowl of fluffy mashed potatoes to the newest resident of Promise House. "Be careful. It's hot."

"Okay, okay. I got it."

Marty smiled as she released the bowl. "Thank you." Every staff person at the youth shelter modeled good manners. What better way to teach than by example?

The dark-faced sixteen-year-old rolled her eyes. "You're welcome." She sauntered through the doorway to the dining room, her ponytail of black spirals bobbing.

Phyllis, the sweet-faced fiftyish woman who stayed in the dormitory with the girls, chuckled. "That one's all sass and vinegar, but I can't help but love her. Her sass'll probably be a blessing in the long run."

Marty couldn't argue. Sass for these girls, as it had been for Brooke, was a sign of inner strength. Dorothy would need sass, time, and a lot of prayers to recover from the emotional wounds inflicted by the so-called uncle who'd manipulated her into selling herself.

Using pot holders, Marty removed the glass dish of green bean casserole from the oven and placed it on the stove top. She sent a quick glance around the industrial kitchen. Everything else was already on the table. As soon as she brought out the casserole, they could eat. She smiled. Their first Thanksgiving at Promise House. But she doubted it would be their last. A news reporter's visit a week earlier had resulted in a front-page feature in

Kansas City's biggest newspaper. Brooke had received a dozen calls from social service organizations and police chaplains since the article released, and she'd told Marty and Anthony to brace for a deluge. Marty couldn't imagine a better kind of flood.

She entered the dining room, Phyllis following. Three tables, each four feet wide and twelve feet long, built by Anthony from materials scavenged from the abandoned buildings around the old ghost town, filled the floor. Marty had given the seven girls residing at the shelter the task of decorating a table for their holiday meal, and they'd chosen to set the center table. Appropriate, considering how these girls had managed to weasel their way into the center of Marty's heart.

She crossed to the table, leaned across the long bench that substituted for chairs, and placed the casserole dish in an open spot. Not easy to find with everything else cluttering the top. Marty's gaze trailed along the crusty rolls, marshmallow-topped sweet potatoes, mashed potatoes, buttery corn, relish plates, stuffing, and of course the beautifully browned twenty-pound turkey waiting at Anthony's end of the table, where he could easily reach to carve it.

She tapped her finger on the centerpiece, a woven basket holding dried leaves and pine cones. Jordan, a stunning seventeen-year-old runaway who'd subsisted on panhandling for nearly two years before coming to the shelter, circled the table and placed a single pine cone beside the water glass at each plate. Marty stepped back so Jordan could put the last one on the table. She smiled at the girl. "The table looks wonderful."

Jordan tossed her head, sending her blond curls over her shoulder. "It'll do."

In the three months since Promise House opened its doors, Marty had learned that girls coming off the street or out of the trafficking industry were hardened. She'd also learned, thanks to Ernie Wedge's counseling and Elliott's experiences, that the hardness was a defense mechanism. In time, when they felt safe, they would lower their walls of protectiveness and dare to show their real emotions. She'd seen Elliott blossom, so she knew it could happen. In the meantime, she determined to be patient with their seeming disinterest.

Marty grazed Jordan's shoulder with her fingertips in lieu of the hug she longed to deliver. "It's more than all right. It's very warm and welcoming. Thank you for doing such a good job."

The girl shrugged and stepped away. "We're all about to starve. I can't believe how long it takes to make dinner around here. Can we eat now?"

"Of course. Kay?" Marty called to the petite Hispanic girl who stood in the beam of sunshine flowing through the stained-glass window Elliott had crafted with Mr. Ernie's help. The mosaic rainbow painted dots of color on Kay's face and simple blue jumper, the uniform worn by all the residents. "Would you ring the dinner bell?" Kay headed for the door, and Marty gestured to Charlene, Regina, and Ronnie, who lounged at another table. "Come on over, girls. Where are Dorothy and Susan?"

The clanging bell covered Ronnie's answer, but before Marty could ask her to repeat it, the two girls emerged from the hallway that led to the bathroom. Their hands still dripped from a recent washing.

Marty welcomed them with a smile. "Take your places. As soon as everyone gets here, we'll eat."

Kay darted to the end of the right-hand bench, the spot she'd chosen for every family-style meal since her arrival. Charlene and Regina, who'd arrived the same day and had been inseparable, took the center of the left-hand bench, and Ronnie scooted in next to them. Susan and Jordan slid in beside Kay, and Dorothy left a space between herself and Susan for Mr. Ernie, as the girls called the grandfatherly man who now lived in Myron and Lucas's former trailer. With his warmth, patience, and kindness, he would probably break through the girls' barriers before any of the other adult staff members could.

Years ago when Marty had fussed about not liking the children at the neighboring farm because they played too rough, Great-Grandma Lois had quoted part of Matthew 5:46 in gentle admonition. The sweet voice tiptoed through Marty's memory. *"For if ye love them which love you, what reward have ye?' Some people are harder to love than others, Martha Grace, but when it's hard, you love on 'em with Jesus's love. You might just get rewarded by seein' a change in 'em if you do."* Marty fully expected to see her great-grandmother's words proven true in the lives of the residents at Promise House.

Anthony, Ernie, and Elliott came in, bringing a wash of cold air and the scent of fall with them. Ernie rubbed his hands together as he bustled to the table, his trademark chortle raising grins from the girls. He climbed into his spot, and Elliott sat across from Dorothy, next to Anthony's chair.

Phyllis took the end of the bench closest to Marty's left, which was also the closest seat to the kitchen. The dear woman was prone to jumping up and retrieving different items at least a dozen times during every meal.

Anthony stepped behind his chair at the head of the table, and Marty took her position at the foot. She couldn't resist sending a slow look at each face around the table. Some young, some not so young, but each so precious. Her rainbow family, her blessing after loss. She loved them, every one of them, and she still marveled at how much her life had changed since that June day two and a half years ago when the packet arrived in the mail from Brooke.

Anthony no longer owned Hirschler Construction, but Steve Kanagy, the new owner, had kept the name since people were familiar with it and the quality work it represented. She couldn't wait to welcome Rex, Dawna, and their children for a visit this coming weekend. Anthony had built wooden trucks for the boys, and she had doll quilts ready to give to her nieces. Although the dull ache of loss continued to haunt the recesses of her heart, the pain no longer consumed her. She'd be able to cradle little Claire and shower all of Rex and Dawna's children with the love Brooke had told her needed to be expressed.

Ah, Brooke, I wish you were here, my friend. The thought could have been melancholy, but it wasn't. Now a full year into her remission, with a full head of thick white hair she called her badge of honor and refused to dye, Brooke divided her time between garnering sponsors for the shelter's residents, speaking at events to educate people about human trafficking, and flipping properties to help pay for expenses at Promise House. She'd never been busier or happier, and Marty wouldn't ask her to quit running all over the state no matter how much she missed time with her childhood friend.

Anthony glanced left and right. "Who would like to ask the blessing?"

Elliott raised his hand. "I will."

Everyone joined hands, creating a circle the way Marty had always imagined her family would do, the way they did at evening Bible study in the old chapel when Anthony closed their time together in prayer. They bowed their heads.

"Dear Lord"—Elliott's low, reverent voice echoed against the old building's rock walls—"for all You have given us, may we be truly thankful. Amen."

Marty opened her eyes and met Anthony's smiling gaze at the opposite end of the table. He gave a gentle nod, and they whispered in unison, "Amen."

Author's Note

Dear Reader,

Human trafficking is a topic that is difficult for most people to discuss, but it's one we cannot ignore. This criminal industry that exploits people and tramples souls is active in every country of the world and has even infiltrated small-town Kansas, part of America's heartland. It has now overtaken drug trafficking as the most financially lucrative illegal business. After all, a packet of drugs is sold for a single use; a human being can be sold again and again. So how to bring an end to this vile, harmful practice?

First of all, be aware. If something seems suspicious, such as what Marty observed in the mall parking lot, report it. It's better to err on the side of caution than ignore it and, in so doing, allow abuse to continue.

Second, be an advocate. There are countless agencies trying to rescue individuals from the industry. Seek out those with ties to your community and support them financially or ask what else you can do to help keep their doors open. Volunteer with programs such as Big Brothers Big Sisters or become a foster parent or grandparent. If you're a business owner, be willing to hire young people coming out of the industry and give them a chance to rebuild their lives.

Third, be active. Write to your local, state, and national leaders and inquire about what they're doing to bring trafficking to an end. Submit editorials to your local newspapers, encourage school counselors to address the issue in schools (prevention is important!), or distribute pamphlets about rescue agencies in places where trafficked individuals might find them—truck stops, rest areas, bus stations, and hotels.

Finally, and most importantly, pray. Pray that those caught in human trafficking's web will find a means of escape. Pray that the abusers will see the victims as people rather than commodities to be exploited. Pray for healing for the hurting souls who've been so horribly mistreated. Pray for God's love to penetrate hearts and bring change.

As with any morally repugnant practice, change can't happen unless good people stand up and say, "No more." Every person is so precious in God's sight. Let's do what we can to save these precious souls from lives of misery and abuse.

In His love,
Kim

Readers Guide

1. At the beginning of the story, Marty and Anthony lived together physically but apart emotionally. What created the chasm between them? Were their reactions understandable? Why or why not? Why do deep hurts sometimes drive us away from the ones we love? How can we bridge the distance between ourselves and a loved one when hurt has separated us?

2. Brooke and Marty grew up in very different households and then communicated only by letters for many years, yet their friendship endured for decades. What makes friendship survive despite differences and distance? What are the benefits of lifelong friendship? Why do you think some friendships endure and others fade away over time?

3. Marty lived in a community where family was honored. When Marty's desire for motherhood was denied her, she withdrew from others who had been blessed with children. In what ways could Marty have filled the empty spot created by her childlessness? Would these experiences have been as fulfilling as raising a child of her own? Why do you feel that way?

4. When motherhood was lost to her, Marty turned her back on God, feeling as if He had abandoned her. Have you ever felt abandoned by God? Do circumstances change who God is, or do they change our view of who He is? Explain.

5. Brooke's high school counselor told Brooke she possessed resilience. What made Brooke resilient? What's the difference between resilience and independence? Can resilience be taught, or is it something innate?

6. When Anthony and Marty decided they wanted to stay at the resort-turned-shelter, Brooke warned them, "These kids won't be babies. They'll be almost grown, and stinky and obstinate. . . . They'll come in every color of the rainbow, with all kinds of trust issues and bad habits." Why didn't the warning scare them away?

7. Brooke said she understood why God loved Marty and Anthony—because they were "good." Why did she feel as if God couldn't love her? Have you ever met anyone who held that same belief? How would you convince that person otherwise?

8. Brooke indicated she wanted to know how "joy breathing deeply" felt. How would you describe joy breathing deeply?

Acknowledgments

I am so grateful to my parents, *Ralph and Helen Vogel,* for raising me in a Christian home where I was loved, nurtured, and taught to serve Jesus. What a priceless gift.

Appreciation to *Jennifer White* of ICT SOS in Wichita, Kansas, for the information about human trafficking. You helped open my eyes, and my heart, to this issue.

Heartfelt thanks and lots of hugs to *John and Connie Stevens,* whose cancer journey allowed me to paint Brooke's and Marty's experiences as patient and caretaker with the brush of reality. You have my prayers for complete and total healing.

To my college friend *Martha (Funk) Archuleta*—thank you for the carefree hour at the snow-covered playground and the laughter that accompanied it. Such a pleasure to share one of my favorite memories with Brooke and Marty.

I am thankful for *Shannon, Charlene, and Kathy,* the wonderful team who worked with me to make this story shine. Bless you!

Finally, and most importantly, to *God,* who makes wonderful plans for His children, who equips us to perform good works meant for our good and His glory, and who walks beside us every step of our life journeys—thank You for welcoming me into Your family. May any praise and glory be reflected directly back to You.